LIVING ON THE EDGE OF
RESPECTABILITY

LIVING ON THE EDGE OF
RESPECTABILITY

Suzette D. Harrison

sepia

BET BOOKS

BET Publications, LLC
http://www.bet.com

To my grandmother, Mrs. Nedra Louise Kelley.
In your absence I remember the days of sitting at your knee,
a book in your hands, a book in mine.
You were my precious librarian who taught me to love my mind
and the world of words on paper.

LIVING ON THE EDGE OF
RESPECTABILITY

VANESSA TAYLOR

Vanessa felt like honey: sweet and sticky and absolutely lickable. She sighed as Keith's rough tongue worked over her bare toes in slow, torturous motion. When he began licking a path over her toes and upward, she rolled onto her stomach, denying him access. Her foot was one thing, but Keith Lymons was out of his natural mind if he thought he could just stroll in and get a whiff of the yum-yum.

He started begging, dishing the okey-doke apologies for his unexplained absences of late, but Vanessa wasn't buying the bull. Besides, she couldn't concentrate. There it was again, that little bell chiming in the distance. Was it a warning advising her to proceed with caution? She tried to take heed, but Mr. Loverman dropped to his knees beside the bed, whining, pleading, begging, his black, beady eyes shining brightly in the dark. Downright distracting.

The more Keith whined, the louder the bell rang. The more it rang, the louder he whined, until he finally barked right in her face, his breath foul as two-week old stew.

She screamed. He barked again, then commenced to licking her on the mouth.

"Eww, no! Bad boy, Pharaoh," Vanessa scolded her overgrown Rottweiler. Gone was the loverman of her dreams. She was left with a dog breathing hot, funky canine fumes in her face. *Girl, you were only dreaming*, she told herself, mad that she should have known it was too good to be true. Vanessa knew plenty of brothers who could beg without shame when it came to getting a bit of the yum-yum. But not one of them was willing to suck on a sister's toes after her hard day's work. That was what fantasies were for.

"Better buy a foot massager, honey," she muttered to the darkness.

The doorbell chimed again, causing Pharaoh to become increasingly excited and whine even more. Vanessa's heart raced, then slowed. No, it couldn't be him. Keith had a key. Not bothering to turn on the bedside lamp, Vanessa glanced at the dark, empty space beside her. Keith's side of the bed was as untouched as it had been over the past several weeks. He came home only in her dreams, to plague her with memories of his loving. *Ol' nasty thing.*

Sliding across her mocha-colored Egyptian cotton bedspread, Vanessa dropped soundlessly onto the floor, her knees sinking deep into the thick, off-white carpet. She felt the fingers of an old acquaintance, anger, rising in her breast as she searched beneath the bed until her hand made contact with the aluminum bat stashed there for such just-in-case moments. Vanessa snatched up the equalizer, grabbed her robe off the back of the overstuffed tan-and-cream-striped Queen Anne chaise in her room, and descended the stairs in the deep of night, an aggravated Pharaoh at her heels. Her grip tightened around the bat. No telling what kind of fool was ringing her doorbell at— Vanessa glanced at the luminous face of the grandfather clock in the entryway—one-thirty in the dark morning.

One-thirty? Vanessa had had less than an hour's sleep. The television station had held its annual benefit for a local children's charity earlier that evening. It was a lovely black-tie affair for which Vanessa had been recruited as hostess. Public relations was no joke. Schmoozing, making rounds, and constantly grinning like a Cheshire cat while tactfully begging for money was hard work. But, skillful sister that she was, Vanessa pulled it off with aplomb. She even managed not to wax ghetto and keep her anger in check while telling a local politician-slash-philanthropist who'd hemmed her up in a secluded corner that her yum-yum wasn't for sale, and that she would fry his wrinkled little pee-pee and serve it to her dog if he ever touched her behind again. He left her alone, but didn't leave the soiree without handing over a check for a quite sizable contribution, his hand noticeably trembling and not with age, thank you very much.

Cautiously, Vanessa approached the front door. She was tough, a survivor. Shuffled from foster home to foster home, she had had to be. Admittedly, Vanessa had been placed with some pretty decent families with big hearts and good intentions. But she had to face the facts. A cute little behaviorally challenged black girl who became an even prettier and problematic young woman with high breasts, big legs, and an even higher and bigger—but firm—behind did not an easy placement make.

Pharaoh rushed ahead of her, growling low in his throat. Tightening the silk sash of her robe about her trim waist, Vanessa pushed aside a momentary panic. Early on, Vanessa had learned to live without love, with anger as her constant companion. Now she welcomed its familiar winds flaring deep within, fueling her bravado as she neared the dark door. Thank goodness she'd been too tired when she arrived home to completely disrobe, and had only removed her Vera Wang knockoff and her Manolo Blahnik satin pumps that still cost an arm and two legs even at 50 percent off. If she was about to kick some booty, Vanessa didn't want to have to do it buck-naked.

Vanessa raised the bat in sweaty but sure palms. Some unsuspecting person on the opposite side of the door was in danger of a serious beat-down.

Without even bothering to peer through the peephole, Vanessa recklessly unlocked and flung wide the front door, bat raised, ready to knock any somebody out cold. Pharaoh barked and dashed forward, leaping onto the bawling bundle of woman standing on the porch, mismatched luggage sprawled about the Tweety Bird slippers on her feet. Clad in ghastly sleepwear, her mother's native Spanish spiced with her father's Jamaican patois spewing rapid-fire from her lips in between sobbing and snotting loud enough to wake the dead, stood Reina Kingsley. Not exactly the best sight for sleepy eyes.

Vanessa sighed in relief and annoyance. She was not in the mood for drama. Not tonight. She ran a weary hand across her sculpted brows, then lowered and propped the bat against the inside wall. Then reality hit. Reina? On her doorstep at this time of morning? Something was seriously afoul.

"Reina, what's wrong?" Vanessa demanded, her voice tight with anxiety.

Hands flailing, kohl-streaked tears marring her otherwise flawless copper-brown face, Reina Kingsley nudged a too-happy Pharaoh aside, rushed through the door, and fell onto Vanessa's chest, almost knocking the wind out of her. Vanessa steadied herself and wrapped her arms about Reina's five-foot-nine-inch, two-hundred-plus pounds as best she could.

Jamaican-born, multiracial Reina Kingsley had been Vanessa Taylor's best friend—best friend along with Chris McCullen—since college. Funny how Reina and Vanessa had grown up in the same city, attended at least one year in the same elementary school, but never met until their freshman journey into college. It made perfect sense to Vanessa. Shuttled from home to home as a child, Vanessa had learned not to make friends, not to become emotionally tied to any anyone or anything. But Reina, U.C. Berkeley, and later Chris, helped change all of that. No matter the less-than-loving relationship Vanessa had experienced with her final foster mother; she had to give the woman credit for helping her gain access to an outstanding education. Without the woman's help, Vanessa might have missed out on the joys of Berkeley. And Reina Kingsley.

Together, they graduated from U.C. Berkeley with baccalaureate degrees, high hopes, pending student loan bills, and each other. Nearly eight years had passed. Their lives had changed in ways they had not imagined. Reina was doing well. She had yet to realize her dream of a singing career, but at least she had a steady job as an analyst with the state agency where she'd been employed since graduation. As for Vanessa, she sought therapy in order to deal with the engulfing anger that stemmed from often being abandoned throughout a childhood that was very transient in nature. Letting go of anger was not an overnight phenomenon; rather it was progressive and ongoing and, admittedly, Vanessa still had her moments. But finally Vanessa was at a place in her life where she felt powerful and in control, and having secured her dream job as the assistant director of public relations at a local television station, Vanessa was optimistic about her future. Now, if she could only find Keith. Where, oh, where had her man gone? Where, oh, where could that Negro be?

Vanessa extricated herself from Reina's crushing embrace. She glanced at her robe and found a huge, kohl-tinted puddle where Reina's head once lay. She grimaced.

A teary-eyed Reina, streams of eyeliner on her plump cheeks, made a sound of annoyance.

"What?" Vanessa intoned.

"I'm in distress and you're worried about a dang rag," Reina accused. "Send me the bill, wench."

"Don't worry, I will, stank." Vanessa fumbled in her robe pockets until she found a tissue to dab at Reina's tearstained, puffy face.

Suddenly Vanessa had a headache. Not just any old little throbbing at the back of her skull, but an outright head-banging, butt-kicking, get-on-the-knees-and-ask-God-to-take-you-now kind of pain. She needed to down a bottle of ibuprofen, crawl into bed, and pull the covers over her head. Looking at Reina's swollen eyes, tear-streaked face, and miscellaneous array of baggage at the front door, Vanessa knew that would not happen anytime soon.

Friendship is a blessing, Vanessa silently repeated over and over while reminding herself of all the times Reina was there for her every time a what's-his-face wrecked her world back in the day, leaving the two friends to pick up the scattered pieces of Vanessa's broken heart. Reina was right there, holding her hand, plotting revenge, and eating quarts of chocolate-cherry ice cream right along with Vanessa's pitiful self. Least she could do was reciprocate some sisterlicious understanding and compassion.

"Did you have another fight with *Tía?*"

Why did Vanessa have to go there? Reina frantically searched the pockets of her hot pink velour robe, extracting a yellow asthma inhaler, which she vigorously shook before plopping it in between her bow-shaped lips. Reina started huffing and puffing, squirting and sucking on that inhaler as a fresh new wave of tears sprang up and out of her eyes, causing dark eyeliner to sprint even faster down her caramel-colored cheeks. It was the only makeup Reina ever wore, eyeliner. No lipstick, no mascara, no blush, powder, nothing. Just black, kohl, navy, or chocolate eyeliner. As if it were a sin against God to wear anything more.

What a waste of a beautiful face. If I have to sedate you and roll you to the makeup counter, so help me Jesus—

"Huh?"

Reina's streaming lament cut into Vanessa's plotting.

"What? Ree-Ree, I can't understand a dang word you're saying. Stop all that Puerto Rican and try some English!"

Vanessa's words had a silencing effect, as she had hoped they would. Reina stopped sobbing, squared her shoulders, and lifted her head, all dignity and offense.

"Spanish, darling. I speak Spanish, not Puerto Rican. You're almost thirty years old. Don't act ignorant. I am Puerto Rican, as well as African and—"

"Jamaican and Dutch. Yeah, yeah, I know this already. You're a poster child for diversity." Vanessa paused. "And, dang, stop reminding me of my age! Walking calendar." Vanessa gingerly rubbed her scalp. Her poor head was throbbing. "What I don't but would like to know is why you're ringing my doorbell at black-thirty in the morning with your hair all tied up on top of your head looking like a runaway field hand. And what's with the Raggedy Ann pajamas?"

Reina glanced down at her late-night getup. She'd been in such an awful hurry to leave her parents' house that she had not bothered to change out of her nightwear before unceremoniously stuffing her clothes into her luggage, then hopping into her brand-new ruby red VW Beetle in search of a safe haven. She had to admit a twenty-something-year-old woman in turquoise blue pajamas with little red-haired dolls all over, cartoon-character slippers, and a fuzzy fuchsia robe was quite a sight. Reina laughed. For the first time since locking horns with her parents, she laughed. Laughed so hard Reina ended up crying anew.

"Girl, get in here," Vanessa urged, pulling Reina forward by the hand, deeper into the warmth of her split-level house. Vanessa managed to steer her distraught friend toward the living room to the right of and just beyond the entrance. She adjusted the dimmer switch on the wall until the recessed ceiling lights bathed the ivory and gold room in a soft glow. A tall, intricate vase filled with a brilliant bouquet of exotic flowers provided the only riot of color in the exquisitely decorated living room.

Vanessa waited as Reina plopped down on the sofa, its buttery-soft, cream-colored Italian leather groaning beneath her girth, before turning back toward the front door. It was still wide open, and Pharaoh was nowhere to be found.

"Doggone it!" She exhaled noisily in her annoyance. "Reina, I have to chase down my crazy mutt before he tears up the neighborhood." Vanessa ran toward the door, calling over her shoulder, her voice trailing behind her like purple smoke in the wind, "Wait there. I'll fix some tea and we can talk."

Vanessa paused on the porch to quickly survey the front yard. Pharaoh was long gone—like every other male in her life. Poof-pow and nowhere to be found. "Disobedient and ungrateful beast," she mumbled, and rushed down the porch steps, tripping over a much-forgotten daily newspaper in her haste. Vanessa lost her balance and wildly grabbed at the porch beam nearest her, breaking her fall into the rosebushes *and* a fingernail in the process. A fingernail that she'd paid too much to have buffed and polished just yesterday. *Memo to me: make nail appointment with Mai Ling,* her mind recorded. "Dang manicurists making bank off sisters like me," she griped, all the while considering tacking on a pedicure just to make another trip to the shop worthwhile.

Vanessa tried to regain her footing but, wobbling a bit, she stumbled over onto the soil beneath the rosebushes. "Ouch!" she yelped, as her foot made contact with a thorny branch. Vanessa felt like cussing but she had sworn off any such outbursts as part of her anger management. Still, there was no one around, and surely one little expletive wouldn't hurt. Right? Gritting her teeth, Vanessa squelched the temptation as she examined her pained foot as best she could without benefit of the porch light. Vanessa was relieved to find neither puncture nor blood. Just a long rip in her stockings—stockings she'd been too lazy to remove before crawling into bed just to rest her eyes a spell before she got up to take the shower she had yet to take because she had fallen asleep and started dreaming about Keith doing wicked things to her body until Her Highness Queen Drama's unexpected arrival interrupted her nocturnal naughties. Just like a friend—all up in a sister's business without an appointment.

" 'Nessa, you okay out there?" Reina's weepy voice whined.

"Uh, yeah," Vanessa returned, "just lovely."

Vanessa limped down her walkway, whistling as softly as she could so as not to disturb her neighbors. The smallest infraction of the peace and the pink-haired, gray-mustached widow woman next door would be speed-dialing the police. The fussy little gnome seemed to think Sacramento's finest had nothing better to do than protect and serve her ornery self twenty-four-seven. But Vanessa had to admit Widow Woman's peevish complaints had once worked in her favor.

Pharaoh, being the naughty puppy he was before Vanessa spent $250 on obedience school from which Pharaoh barely graduated, had one day relieved himself right outside the neighbor's front door, then proceeded to chase her three-legged cat up a tree. The old lady's call to 911 brought out the finest the capital city's P.D. had to offer.

Officer Keith Lymons responded, rescued Tripod from the tree, and supervised the peace as Vanessa removed the smelly dog deposit from the doorway, then proceeded to lecture the offending pet's owner on the importance of preserving neighborly relations. Discreetly eyeballing the good officer, with his thick biceps and rather tight department-issued navy blue pants, Vanessa had a few thoughts on relations herself. She fell in lust on the spot.

It jolted right through her, making her weak in the knees and eager to please. Vanessa hadn't felt anything quite like it before. Well, she had maybe once or twice or four times. But it had been such a long time ago.

Officer Keith Lymons was special. He was courteous, thoughtful, chivalrous even. He treated her with respect, didn't try to grab a little yum-yum on their first date. He could actually carry on a conversation beyond the topic of sports, and read something other than *TV Guide.* He was sane, sober, and gainfully employed, built like a black demigod, was the "deepest" lover she ever had—well, not quite but almost . . . well, not really, but anyhow—and could quote lines from *The Color Purple* and *Daughters of the Dust.* So what if he sometimes had . . . "issues" in the bedroom. Still, Vanessa gave him credit for being there. He was a good man. Or so she thought until a few weeks ago, when he started acting strange and deviating in his ways.

Vanessa screamed as a large, dark figure hurled itself at her, catching her off guard and knocking her down on the sidewalk square on her firm behind. She'd been so absorbed with troubling thoughts of Keith that she did not see the huge dog race around the corner in answer to her call. She sat spread-eagled on the cold concrete, her robe hiked up about her muscled thighs, Pharaoh's even colder nose pressed against her face as he licked her chin. *Thank goodness I was too tired to take my panties off before I went to bed,* she mused. Not that anyone was on the street to see her business. But still.

Vanessa couldn't decide whether to chastise the canine for pushing her over or praise him for responding to her whistle. Who really cared? She certainly didn't. There were more pressing issues at hand. Like getting her undignified behind up off the sidewalk, tending to her distressed girlfriend, and getting Pharaoh back in the house before he took off on another unlawful excursion of the city. So much for $250 on obedience school. She should have saved the money and beaten his backside with a rolled-up newspaper.

Vanessa hobbled back into the house clutching Pharoah by his collar, her hosiery fit for nothing save the garbage, her derriere smarting from sudden contact with the curb, her headache creeping up a notch on the pain meter. Vanessa locked the door and engaged the alarm system, something she hadn't done since Keith started staying over. She needed that added safety now. She was alone. Again.

Vanessa entered the living room where she had left Reina, only to find it dark and empty, save for the luggage Reina had managed to tote indoors. Stepping back into the entryway, Vanessa glanced down the corridor and saw a light dance out into the hallway and across the hardwood floors.

"Should have known," she muttered, and limped toward the bright light of the kitchen.

"Don't you have anything in this house besides granola or baby carrots and broccoli?" Reina demanded, her face in the refrigerator, her considerable butt in the air. She heard Vanessa slide into a chair at the kitchen table but didn't bother to turn around. "Girl, you need to go grocery shopping."

Lawd, help a sister out!

"There's plenty of food in there," Vanessa tersely replied. Her nerves were suddenly dangling by a floss-thin thread. Add to her lack of sleep, aching head, broken nail, and throbbing foot, the fact that she'd been celibate for weeks because her man was missing in action, and clearly discussing a lack of junk food in the middle of the morning with her emotionally crazed and already too-plump friend was enough to push Vanessa to the limit. But she didn't feel like dancing with anger just then. Instead, Vanessa filled her lungs with air, then exhaled. Slowly. She closed her eyes and counted backward from ten, as she'd been taught in the meditation class she had attended as recommended by her therapist.

"Food? You can't call this food unless you're a jackrabbit or a toothless resident of a nursing home. Tofu? Soy milk?" Reina held up a small rectangular carton and shook it with obvious disgust.

Vanessa lost count at six. Reina and meditation just didn't mix.

Vanessa watched Reina's double butt jiggle with every animated movement she made.

"It's good for you," Vanessa snapped back. "It helps lower cholesterol."

"This mess will kill you before cholesterol will. Where's the cous-cous? Fried plantains? Jerk chicken? I need nourishment."

Gritting her teeth, Vanessa marched to the refrigerator and pushed the door shut.

"You need to stop wasting my electricity. And stop acting like you didn't eat before you got here. I can still smell the grease."

"Don't start with me, 'Nessa. We all handle stress differently. You exercise. I eat," Reina stated without apology, pulling the inhaler from her robe pocket and shaking it violently before taking another hit. Stress wreaked havoc on Reina's respiratory system. But not so much so that she couldn't make it to the pantry, where she scoured the shelves for some morsel more in keeping with her tastes.

Vanessa threw up her hands and conceded defeat. After downing two ibuprofens and a glass of water, she returned to sit at the kitchen table, Pharaoh lounging at her feet. Legs crossed, arms folded, Vanessa shook her head slowly from side to side in amazement as she watched Reina search the pantry shelves like an archeologist on a dig.

"There's chamomile tea on the—"

"Uh, thank you, but no. Aha!" Reina sang triumphantly, stepping from the pantry with a bag of yogurt-covered raisins lifted high. Snapping open the bag, she tossed a handful into her mouth and chewed daintily.

"You're simply amazing," Vanessa murmured as her friend plodded toward her.

Reina stuck out her tongue, tiny bits of chewed raisins clinging fast. "Whatever, soapbox," she slurred, claiming a seat at the table and stretching her plump legs beside its cherry-wood, claw-leg base.

"So what happened?" Vanessa asked, kneading her still sore foot and disgustedly eyeing the runs in her brand-new pair of sixteen-dollar panty hose.

"I had a fight with *Mami*."

Vanessa looked up, eyes wide.

"No-o-o, really?"

"Your sarcasm reeks."

Vanessa smiled despite her fatigue. She had an early day ahead. Aerobics at five. Meditation at six. Shower, dress, and be on the free-way by 7:15 in order to arrive at the office by 7:45, which would give her just enough time to log on to her computer and review her notes before spearheading a staff meeting at eight. What little sleep she'd anticipated having had been cut into by Reina's grand entry. But hey, what were friends for if not to interrupt your life and drive you up a wall without a steering wheel? Vanessa brushed her freshly manicured fingernails, including the broken one, through her thick, short-cropped espresso brown hair, à la Anita Baker—the same soulful singer she was told she favored. At least her 'do was still whipped and wonderful, no matter that the rest of her felt inches from the sharp edge of disaster.

"I'm sorry. I'm just exhausted."

"You look beat down," Reina teased lightly, popping more raisins in her mouth. Suddenly she sobered. "You haven't heard from Keith, have you?"

Vanessa's deep-set, topaz eyes darted downward to look at nothing in particular. She uncrossed then crossed her shapely, cinnamon brown legs while toying with the fringed hem on her lilac silk robe.

Vanessa wasn't quite sure what had happened. One night Keith was with her. The next, he was gone, without a word, a call, an explanation. At first she thought perhaps he was on some special undercover assignment that prevented his contacting her. But that theory fell through when she called and spoke with his partner, who assured her that was not the case.

She left messages for him at work and at home, but he never returned her calls. Just as she began to imagine the worst, Vanessa found a message on her answering machine from Keith asking her to page him. Immediately she did, only to have him call back and say he couldn't talk and that he would come by later that evening. That was more than a week ago. Vanessa had yet to lay eyes on the critter.

God created nothing wrong in me. I am lovely and lovable.

The self-affirming mantra spooled through Vanessa's mind like a fine mist. She had much to offer. She had a high-profile job, owned her own home, drove a nice car. At five feet, six inches and one hundred and thirty pounds, she kept her body tight and trim. All sweet curves and swerves. Tight butt, no gut. To borrow the phrase of one of her former loves, she was luscious. In her own modest opinion, she was attractive, educated, sophisticated, and worthy of a "most eligible bachelorette" write-up in *Ebony* magazine. There was no plausible explanation why she couldn't hold on to a man for more than a minute. Finally, in response to Reina's inquiry, Vanessa shook her head, her eyes still unable to meet her friend's dark, steady gaze.

What bad timing. She had enough problems of her own to deal with without having the wacky world of Reina to tackle. But then again, maybe it was for the best. Maybe Reina's drama would take Vanessa's mind off her own.

"So, what happened?" she asked again, still not meeting Reina's gaze.

"*Papi* threw me out of the house."

Vanessa's head shot up and her mouth fell open. Vanessa leaned forward, splaying her long fingers on the well-polished tabletop.

"No, he didn't!"

Reina nodded.

"Girl, you must have broken the Virgin Mary or something, 'cause *Tio* wouldn't put you out if God asked him to."

Diversion worked like a charm. A suddenly bright-eyed and enthralled Vanessa seemed to forget about her basket of woes as she listened to Reina unload her own. Vanessa was caught up in the madness, peppering Reina's already spicy recounting with a "no, you didn't, girl" here and an "oh, see, that's not right" there. Time flew by with barely a notice.

Egged on by her captive audience, Reina let go and fully lit into a thirty-minute diatribe describing how she—being rudely awakened at midnight by the crude and rude rap lyrics blaring from her baby brother's stereo—stomped to his bedroom, granted herself entry, and confronted the boy, who she suspected was probably still high from a vaginal visit with some miscellaneous honey. When he ignored her request to turn down the stereo volume, she turned it off her-dang-self. He had the nerve to get up in her face and threaten her with bodily harm if she ever touched his property again.

And that was how World War III began, only to end with Mr. Kingsley slapping his "loose-mouthed" daughter, his wife nearly fainting, and Reina leaving the building heading straight for Vanessa's—after driving around midtown Sacramento mindlessly devouring the supersized burger meal passed through a greasy drive-through window of some nondescript fast-food joint.

The Tale of Trip City over, the two friends sat in silence. It was so quiet Vanessa could hear the avocado-shaped clock mounted on the wall above her silver Thermador stove ticking the night away. A gift from Reina, the avocado clock. Not exactly in keeping with Vanessa's taste, but hey, what were friends for if not to wreck each other's decor?

Even with silence restored, Vanessa forgot to mention to Reina her desire to find her birth parents, her mind was reeling so.

The thought had come to her again just days ago. Over the years, Vanessa had toyed with the idea of seeking out her parents. She did not wish to intrude upon their lives, as it was obvious they had no room for her. Vanessa merely wanted to meet them, to perhaps understand their decision to relinquish her so that she became a ward of a congested foster system. She tried not to focus on the hurt caused by their abandonment, not to let anger overcome or drive her. But Vanessa admitted it was hard. Perhaps finding her parents would help her conquer the bitterness that sometimes threatened to consume her. Like now, thanks to Keith and his rejection. Once again, Vanessa had been left behind, and she felt far from good.

Vanessa broke the silence with a full-mouthed and noisy yawn.

"Dang, girl, I can see your esophagus. Why you gotta open your mouth so wide when you yawn?" Reina cracked. "At least use your claws to cover that cavern."

With a sophisticated toss of her head Vanessa replied, "Whatever, stank."

"Wench."

"Test-tube baby."

"Sheep clone."

They laughed for a moment, then grew serious.

"I'm really sorry, Ree-Ree," Vanessa said with all the sincerity she could muster while unsuccessfully trying to stifle another yawn. "Somehow all of this will work out."

Reina responded with a look that indicated she was not particularly interested in optimistic clichés.

"What?" Vanessa intoned. "You're always telling me there's a brighter side to every coin, Miss Sunshine." Reina was clearly not buying it. "Well, have you considered the fact that you finally have what you've always wanted?"

"And that is?" Reina asked, crumpling the now-empty bag that had once contained nearly a pound of yogurt-covered raisins.

"Your freedom," Vanessa answered.

Reina's hands grew still. Vanessa watched her friend. Reina watched the wall behind Vanessa's head. Then, too quickly, Reina pasted a shaky smile on her pretty lips when finding Vanessa's gaze locked on her. But her eyes sparkled with a sudden gathering of unshed tears.

"Aww, Ree-Ree, girl. Don't cry. It's going to work out," Vanessa crooned, trying to soothe her friend as best she could. Vanessa held on to her friend and Reina gripped her back while simultaneously pumping her asthma inhaler. Squirt. Suck. Squirt. *Swwwww.* Breathe.

Vanessa rubbed Reina's shoulders. "Why don't you come with me to water aerobics? Your body's cushioned by water. No jarring of your joints. It would really help your breathing." *And your body,* Vanessa thought.

"Go to bed, 'Nessa," Reina said, ignoring Vanessa's invitation to splash about in a pool full of perky aerobic bunnies with their cute little selves. "I'll be all right." Reina wiped her eyes on the sleeve of her robe, leaving faint traces of watered-down eyeliner on the fluffy pink velour. "Just give me a blanket and a pillow and I'll sleep on the sofa."

"Like I really want you slobbering all over my imported leather," Vanessa remarked, fully aware of the fact that her friend had not directly replied to her invitation. She'd let the elusive chick slide for now, but she wouldn't give up. As far as Vanessa was concerned, exercise was a cure-all for just about any- and everything. In fact, she could put on her sneakers and jog a trip around a block or three right now. Vanessa stood and stretched her cramped muscles. *Naw, maybe not.* "Come on, girl. I'll put some fresh linen on the bed in the spare room." Reina followed, dousing the kitchen light as she went.

Vanessa double-checked the front door locks, then retrieved her discarded peacemaker and propped it over her shoulder. *Memo to me: have locks changed first thing tomorrow morning.* Two weeks' time was enough for Keith to put in an appearance. He had not done so. Oh, well—if and when he did, he would find things had changed. He just could not go and come as he pleased. *Ol' stankmeister!*

"You know what?" Vanessa murmured, turning toward Reina and barely missing the side of Reina's head with the end of the bat she carried. "Oops, sorry."

"You did that on purpose," Reina accused.

"Like I really want to knock you unconscious and drag your quadra-butt up the stairs."

"Then you could have your way with me," Reina quipped, making her eyebrows dance.

Vanessa rolled her eyes.

"Anyhoo! I'm too tired to be digging through the linen closet. You can sleep with me tonight. Just don't try any funny stuff."

"As if," Reina retorted in her best imitation valley girl voice. "You just make sure you stay on your side of the bed and don't start creeping in the night. I'm not your man and I don't want your fingers on my booty."

"Lay off the pipe. Your mind is going. Come on, Pharaoh," Vanessa called to her oversize canine companion. He rushed ahead of her, bounding up the steps as Vanessa helped Reina carry her quite heavy luggage upstairs. *Dang!* How much had Reina packed? Better yet, how long did she plan to stay? *Memo to self: call* Tía *first thing tomorrow morning.* Reina was her girl and all, but Vanessa was not exactly interested in having an indefinite housemate. Unless, of course, it was Keith or some eligible, delectable brother like him. Vanessa shook her head angrily as if to rid the very painful thought of a very real truth. But it persisted. *Admit it, honey,* she told herself, *the man is gone.* She was alone, an autonomous and solitary figure. At least she had Pharaoh. And now Reina. Thank God for small favors.

It was close to 3 A.M. They were finally settled in for the morning. The house was quiet. Both women, having felt lost and alone, found solace in the closeness of their shared space, the familiar comfort and presence of each other. Vanessa was at the door of deep sleep when Reina whispered her name. Vanessa's reply was little more than an unintelligible grunt.

"Rub my booty."

Vanessa groaned and hit Reina over the head with her pillow, causing Reina to cackle a bit too loudly. Vanessa pulled the covers over her head and drew her knees up to her chest in a fetal position. She wrapped herself in the covers as best she could, considering Reina had commandeered most of the blankets for her own use. Vanessa didn't care. She was actually grateful. Reina's deep breathing at her back wasn't exactly Keith's low snores, but at least it was human contact of some sort. And that was better than nothing.

REINA KINGSLEY

Days after "the Incident," Reina yet tried to sift through the sordid details of what really happened at the house of Kingsley. Had she truly flipped the script and screamed at her mother, causing her father to put her in check with a sound slap across the mouth? She must have. How else would Reina have found herself roaming the city in the middle of the morning, just she and Ruby, her VW Bug, with no particular destination in mind?

Scenes replayed themselves in Reina's befuddled mind. She remembered peeking at the dial of the purple-and-black butterfly-shaped clock on her nightstand as the timepiece glowed brightly in the dark room, casting a distorted stream of light on the far wall. It was 12:15 A.M., according to the butterfly. *Bump. Bump. Bump dee da da da bump. Boo yow.* Raj and his rap! Wasn't it bad enough that the little monster had just eased back into the house, violating curfew and, no doubt, some unsuspecting man's infatuated, simpleminded daughter? Now, he had the nerves to blast that mess he called music.

The mess was so loud, the bass so thick her walls pulsated, causing her prized collection of stuffed animals on the wall unit in her room to shift and shake wildly. The Tasmanian Devil was doing the bump with Suzy Carmichael from *The Rugrats*. And if she wasn't mistaken it looked like Kermit the Frog was getting jiggy with one of the Powerpuff Girls.

Reina rolled onto her back and contemplated her options. She could fix her baby brother with one of *Abuela*'s curses, poison his Crunch Berry cereal in the morning, or march down the hall and ask the miscreant to please lower the volume of the "deep and profound" misogynistic lyrics blaring from a stereo that cost almost as much as a semester's study at her alma mater. Well, Reina didn't have any chicken feet or feathers, and she couldn't bear to see her mother cry, so she got out of bed.

"If my phone rings be a doll, Suzy, and take a message." Reina chortled dryly at the shaking toy before stalking out the door and down the hall.

Reina paused outside Raj's bedroom door and listened. She didn't exactly understand the appeal. A singer herself, Reina appreciated a wide range of music. But as far as she was concerned, lurid and unintelligible streams of nonsensical rhyme and rhetoric albeit accompanied by phat beats did not music make. Jazz. Opera. Gospel. R and B. Dinah Washington. Sarah Vaughan. Ella Fitzgerald. Oleta Adams. Rachelle Ferrell. Diane Reeves. Will Downing! Lord, Lord, the Willster. That bald-headed chocolate drop could croon to her any day of God's good week. Now these were music makers! Unlike Raj's little crack-nosed, forty-ounce-drinking hood rats, they sang life with the lips of real lyricists. Besides, Raj was frontin'. Playing a role. What did he know about being ghetto-fabulous? The boy was an honor roll student at a private Catholic high school and lived in the 'burbs, still mowed his *Abuela*'s lawn every Saturday morning, and kissed his *Mami* good-night like the big baby he was pretending not to be.

But Reina didn't particularly care about the boy's neurosis right then. What she wanted was a full night's uninterrupted sleep for a change.

Tap. Tap.

"Raj?"

No answer.

Tap. Tap. *Bam.*

"Raj!"

He didn't even bother to open the door, just hurled his voice through it like a freaking ventriloquist.

"What!"

"Don't 'what' me. Turn that mess down." Nothing. "I know you hear me talking to you."

Reina got louder, hollering at that door as if it had personally offended her. "If I have to come in there and turn that stereo down myself it's on like Monkey Kong."

Raj finally responded. He increased the volume on the already too-
loud system.

The patron saint on the hallway shelf bounced to the muffled beat.
Reina gently straightened the crooked statue. Even the revered saints
weren't safe. She'd had enough. Reina tossed open the bedroom
door and barged in as unwelcome as she pleased. Raj, all one hundred and fifty, half-naked pounds of him, was sprawled across the bed
snacking on corn chips. A light after-sex snack, Reina presumed as
she yanked the stereo cord from the wall socket. Raj sprang to life and
off the bed, slapping her hand away from the cord, jumping in her
chest, talking loud about what he would do to Reina if she ever
touched his property again.

Reina gave Raj the opportunity to back that thing up and out of
her face, but he didn't. Poor thing. He merely acted like Sammy
Simple and slapped her warning finger away from his impudent nose.
Two slaps too many. Reina pounced, knocking her baby brother backward onto his bed, where she preceded to sit on him and attempt to
beat the black—okay, copper-brown—off his narrow behind.

Only parental intervention saved the situation. Now wide-awake,
they came running, stumbling into the scene of chaos.

"No, Re-ee-ee-na," *Mamí* wailed, overemphasizing her daughter's
name, "you're killing your brother."

Just a quirk of Reina's, insisting that her name *not* be pronounced
as spelled. She'd preferred *Reena* ever since she was old enough to
speak it herself. And so it was. But back to the commotion at hand.

It took both her parents to pull Reina off the insolent thing. Finally
separated, the striving siblings stood, chests heaving, glaring daggers,
their parents the safety between them. *Mamí* was jabbering, her accent thick as it was prone to become whenever she was excited or
upset, running her small hands all over her precious baby to ensure
he'd suffered no life-threatening injuries. That made Reina mad
enough to piss bricks.

"*Mamí*, why? Why do you always have to baby him? You're part of
his problem."

That set *Papí* off.

"Don' speak ta ya mutta like dat!"

Reina huffed. *Dang League of Nations, Mamí* wailing in Spanish, *Papí* reverting to Jamaican patois. Too much culture could make a mad sister sick.

"*Papí*, it's not me. It's Raj. You let him get away with too friggin' much."

Papí tightened the belt of his bathrobe about his paunch of a belly. The muscles beneath his smooth ebony jaw pulsed and jerked a silent admonition.

"Ya wanna tell me how ta run mah home, piss-tail gal?" *Papí* gritted out. "Ya wanna be me, da faddah, responsible for everyt'ing in heah?"

Reina checked herself as best she could.

"It's not right, *Papí*." Reina's eyes swam with frustrated tears. "Raj is only seventeen and he comes and goes like he owns the place."

"I didn't do nothing wrong, *Papí*," Raj protested. "I was just chilling in my room."

Reina rolled her lovely dark eyes, ignoring his lie, and continued.

"Practically every night now he's in here blasting music so loud that I can't sleep—"

"Buy some earplugs, *vaca*."

"Cow? Who you calling a cow?" Reina lunged for her brother, but her father's six-foot-one-inch, two-hundred-pound frame stopped her midway.

"No! Don' come in mah home actin' like no dumb hooligan!" *Papí* shouted at them both, but Reina took it personally.

"Oh, now I'm the dumb one." Reina's laugh was as dry as a five-day-old biscuit left in the summer sun. "I'm not the one violating his curfew so I can fornicate all over town. I'm not the one sneaking in the house after dark smelling like an alley cat—"

"Reina. *Mi hija*, no," *Mamí* pleaded with her daughter while holding her baby boy.

"That's 'cause don't nobody want your fat a—"

Whack!

Papí whacked smart-mouth Raj on the back of his head, but not before Raj struck blood. His remark hurt so much it dried Reina's tears.

She knew better. But before her brain could catch up with her mouth, the words were already out. All profane, all in Reina's mother's beautifully musical native tongue. *Papí* knew enough Spanish to know when his house had been defiled. So he responded the best he knew how; with a sound slap across his grown daughter's face. And that was how Reina wound up at Vanessa's at dark-thirty in the morning, leaning on the doorbell, releasing dried-up tears she'd fought to control in her father's house.

That was three days ago, and Reina imagined she still felt the sting of her father's hand on her face. Even so, it reverberated dully beneath the tremor of her joy. For the first time in her life, other than the four years she'd spent away at college that really didn't count since her parents paid most of her expenses and she drove home practically every weekend to see the clan, Reina was free. Independent. Autonomous.

Reina could not recall ever being separated from family. Apart and alone. Her world had been shaped and formed by the constant interaction with and friction caused by life amid her vast, slightly zany, and overly intrusive kinfolk. Her very person was a product of that kinship, good or bad. But for far too long now she'd felt like a prisoner of their off-brand love. Swallowed. Suffocated and intruded upon.

Reina was far from ecstatic about the fact that she was practically pushing thirty and yet living under her parents' roof. She had never planned that it should be this way. A crazy vortex had somehow sucked her deep into its maddening middle.

Like any other fresh-faced, optimistic college graduate, Reina had big plans for her future. Graduating from high school a year early, Reina entered the University of California education system at the age of seventeen. Education was primary, her parents instilling and drilling its importance into her for as long as she could recall. Still, in her heart of hearts, Reina passionately preferred to sing, and she knew early on that she wanted to pursue a professional career in music.

She could sing before she could talk. Choruses, glee clubs, choirs, and groups. Reina experienced them all, honing her skill while developing her repertoire. So Reina struck a compromise with her parents and temporarily assuaged herself by singing with an R and B group on campus until her hopes of musical fame and fortune could be realized after graduation. Reina virtually whisked through college, excelling in her studies as she always had, eventually graduating with a baccalaureate in liberal arts, and that with highest honors. Finally, the world of music awaited. But then the world turned backward and Reina found herself faced with disillusioned dreams.

It hurt to admit it, but returning home after college had been a colossal mistake. Reina felt like a damsel in a dungeon. Someone had raised the drawbridge and parked a Jamaican dragon outside her door.

Reina merely wanted to catch a second wind after dashing through college and recuperate before moving on. But her parents were quick to remind her she could and should remain home with them until she was well on her feet. After all, *Papí* was quick to point out, she really could not afford to live on her own. Her part-time position with the state was perfect in that it afforded Reina the flexibility she needed to pursue her music after hours. She could work a half day and still make it to the Bay Area in time for band rehearsals or performances. But half a salary left a sistah with some holes here and there. She couldn't afford an apartment or a new car, so Reina made due in her old bedroom and cruised the city in her father's rusty, raggedy, *Sanford and Son*–looking truck that he had the nerve to call a classic. Even so, the situation was almost bearable until things started falling apart.

The band split up. The lead singer hooked up with the keyboardist, made a baby, and the happy parents decided to marry and give music a break. The remaining band members couldn't decide who should take the lead or agree upon a replacement pianist. They even squabbled over what costumes to wear, over whose microphone was better than whose. It was silly and it was petty, and Reina told them they could wear their grandmothers' big-butt drawers onstage for all she cared. She quit. Eventually the band dissolved. Reina tried hooking up with local bands in Sacramento, but she felt as if she were losing her groove. Something was lacking. Subsequently, without her muse to feed her, Reina stopped singing and started eating.

Little by little the weight crept up on her frame like ivy on a trellis. Reina found solace in food, and food found a friend in her as she bulked up and out. She began to feel so self-conscious about her weight gain that she literally grew afraid of stepping onstage those few occasions when an old acquaintance or music buddy called on a favor, asking her to sing. Frustration set in and Reina sat down, packing up her microphone for good.

Then the world really wobbled out from beneath her size-ten feet, plunging her deeper into the abyss of her parental home.

Reina's beloved *Abuelo* passed away suddenly, but peacefully, in his sleep. Her mother's baby brother, Uncle Butchie, was so distraught over their father's passing that he came out of his cross-dressing closet and came to the funeral in drag. Then Reina's oldest and only sister, Nita—having secretly endured all the domestic abuse she could—snapped one day and whacked her husband in the knees with the Club from her steering wheel. The man limped out, Nita moved on, hooked up with the wrong associates, and found herself in jail and her two small daughters in the care of her parents. Reina couldn't leave home. Her family needed her.

The only thing that seemed to be going her way was the fact that Reina had passed the exam for and been promoted to an analyst's position. Finally, she made enough money to move out on her own, but she didn't feel right leaving her family at a time when trouble had set in. Guilt played a trip on her until the night of the big blowout at O-Kingsley corral. Suddenly her choice was clear. Guilt or no, Reina *had* to go.

Reina rushed through her morning shower, no longer in her parents' home, she was free . . . and late! Reina was thirty minutes behind schedule. And of all days. She was supposed to fill in for her supervisor, as he had a doctor's appointment that morning. Vanessa's house was to blame. It was just too dang quiet. Made a sistah oversleep. Okay, so she had pushed the snooze button on her purple-and-black butterfly clock two times too many. But goodness, the sistah deserved a break.

The thought of freedom was delicious. Who did she have to thank for this newfound liberty? Her brother, Raj? Not! *Papí*, then? Yes and no. As far as *Papí* was concerned, Reina was his responsibility, his duty. *Papí* took his rules and his role to heart. He would teach his son how to be a decent man, but his daughters? That was an entirely different bowl of rice and peas. So what if Reina was twenty-eight, college-educated, and finally financially able to support herself? Reina was his baby girl. If it were up to *Papí*, the day Reina left his house would be the day she said, "I do." Until then he was "the only boyfriend" she needed. That was what was wrong with the world today, according to her father: young ladies leaving home too soon, getting into all kinds of deviltry. Besides, according to the Bible, he was her protective covering—God's undershepherd, so to speak—and how could he protect her if she were beyond the walls of his abode?

Reina laughed. *Papí* sure could trot out and dust off his Bible if and when it suited his purposes.

Even if he was famous for misquoting scriptures, Reina had to thank her father for the stubbornness she'd inherited. It helped fuel her resolve to leave and not look back despite the overwhelming feelings of obligation.

Ingrate. That was what he'd called her, and perhaps that was what she was.

Reina tilted her face to the streaming water and exhaled slowly. Was *Mamí* to thank? Absolutely. Defending her bratty baby boy, siding with her husband, silencing her daughter's cries for help and understanding. Days before *the Incident,* as Reina and Vanessa now referred to it, *Mamí* had promised to talk to *Papí,* to reason with him and help him see his overbearing patriarchy was a thing of the past. *Mamí* seemed to understand her daughter's need for independence, even if she herself had stayed home until marrying. *Mamí* promised to help her husband make peace with the times and his child. But obviously *Mamí* had remained silent. As always, she hid her son's indiscretions and masked her daughter's discontent. A forgotten tear mingled with the water that whisked facial cleanser from Reina's upturned face. There was only one way to describe her mother's actions: betrayal to the tenth power times two. Still, did Reina really have to call her mother a "man's slave in need of a spinal transplant" before running out of the house? It took her mother and brother to hold *Papí* back on that one.

This was not the way to start her day. *Mamí* and *Papí* and Raj could have each other. She was free and she was fine and she had better things to do than cry over them. Better things like wash her hair. *Not!* The stuff was too thick and required too much time. Reina was late enough as it was. Maybe she could make an appointment with Vanessa's hairstylist, as her best friend had suggested. Maybe it *was* time Reina stepped back up on the beauty tip. But then again, who was really paying attention? Who would notice whether or not big Reina Kingsley changed her regime or her routine? No one. That person simply did not exist. Reina turned off the water and stepped from the shower, grabbing a towel from the brass rack and winding it as far around her plus-sized body as it would fit.

Determined not to be depressed over another sore spot in her life but to remain her usual cheerful self, Reina suppressed ugly thoughts and began drying off. Lovingly, she slid baby oil all over her body, rubbed some deodorant under her arms, brushed and flossed and gargled, and hopped into her cotton underwear. No perfume. Fumes made her asthma flare, and she couldn't be bothered with a breathing treatment just now. She was late enough as it was.

Fully dressed, Reina loosened the inch-thick braid that hung nearly to the middle of her back, brushed and combed the waves in her coal-black hair, then rebraided and recoiled the rope into a bun at the nape of her neck, securing it with butterfly-decorated hair clips. Slap, slap, rub, rub, went a glob of cocoa butter cream on her clear copper complexion. Just a little bit—okay a lot—of navy eyeliner to match her denim jumper dress with Tweety Bird embroidered on the pocket and Reina was ret-ta-go.

" 'Bye, babies. Be good and I'll bring you some ice cream," Reina jokingly promised her menagerie of stuffed animals and cartoon characters, Suzy Carmichael smiling as if she already savored the flavor. Reina closed her door and hurried down the stairs toward the garage.

Ruby purred like a contented kitten some ten minutes later. They just had to wait for the automatic garage door to ascend and they'd be off. "Come on, girl, let's hit it," Reina crooned as she depressed the accelerator of her brand-new candy apple red VW Beetle. Gone were the days of cruising in her father's rusty, dusty, funky, and musty junkyard truck. *God be thanked.*

Ruby shot back and down the drive and out onto the quiet street. Even the neighborhood was sedate and serene. Just what the doctor ordered for Reina's jangled nerves. She could get used to this real quick. She had to say a prayer of thanks for Vanessa. She was reliable and always came through in crunch time. So what if the girl was too high-maintenance, ate strange foods, and did some weird chanting stuff, sounding like Angela Bassett in that Tina Turner movie. To each her own. They were sister-friends, and Vanessa had provided Reina with a safe place in a time of need. That was what friends were for.

The morning traffic report came across the radio, warning commuters that northbound Highway 99 was backed up due to an overturned big rig at the Florin Road exit. Reina made an immediate U-turn on Laguna Boulevard and raced toward northbound I-5. It was ten minutes out of the way, but the way Ruby roared, Reina would make it onto the freeway in five. She shifted gears, accelerated, and kept an eye out for five-oh. A speeding ticket was the last thing Reina needed.

The traffic report complete, soft classical music filtered from the radio to fill the automobile. It was the way Reina liked to start her day, with quiet music. It helped her to think, and think she did.

The more she thought about it, the better Reina was able to conclude that Vanessa's had been the only logical place to go. *Abuela*, her widowed maternal grandmother, had more than enough room in her Victorian house in midtown Sacramento. And being the favorite of her grandmother's twenty-three grandchildren, Reina knew she would have been more than welcome there. But if *Mamí* had informed *Abuela*, which Reina was sure she had, of the things Reina had spewed at Raj while in her parents' presence the night of *the Incident*, *Abuela* would rear back her eighty-six-year-young hand and slap Reina her-dang-self. Her aunts and uncles and other extended family who had probably caught wind of all the dastardly details by now, and were no doubt adding their own spins and twists so that the saga was barely recognizable, were out of the question as well. Staying with family was not a possibility.

Friends? Reina had more than enough acquaintances. But bonedeep friends like Vanessa were few and far in between. Well, there was Chris, of course.

"That would be like dropping pig's skin in a pan of hot grease," Reina said aloud to no one save Ruby as they raced over the roadway toward her eight-to-five. Reina was not ready for that kind of burn. Besides, her father would have two coronaries and a seizure if that ever happened. Reina smacked the steering wheel with her palm and cackled heartily.

By 8:17, Ruby was safe in her parking space as Reina hurried into the lobby of the high-rise building, hoping that the rest of her day would be different from the start. The lobby was crowded with employees rushing onto the one working elevator. The other two elevators had been down for servicing for two days now. Reina had no choice. She took the stairs.

Reina only worked on the third floor, but carting two hundred–plus pounds up three flights of stairs had her catching her breath and wiping sweat from her upper lip once, twice, five times.

At 8:25 Reina practically fell onto her chair. Dropping her patch-work denim and suede shoulder bag on the floor at her feet, Reina leaned back, closed her eyes, and tried to breathe away the pain in her chest without resorting to use of her inhaler.

"Reina?"

Reina cracked the lid of her right eye just wide enough to peek out into the real world. Phyllis, a newly hired supervisor from one of the units in Reina's division, stood in the cubicle entrance, looking nice and neat in her ice-plum pantsuit, matching plum baby-butt-smooth pumps on her cute little feet. Reina forced a smile.

"Are you okay?" Phyllis asked, a look of concern on a pretty brown face framed by some seriously thick, seriously chic, and silky-looking hair.

"Y-y-yeah. I'm fine."

"Did you take the stairs?"

No, I always arrive at work looking like I just crawled a five-k, Reina refrained from blurting.

"Yes. Stupid elevators are still down," Reina needlessly, breathlessly reported.

"You need some water?"

Phyllis was sweet, and Reina genuinely liked her, but she was about to work a sistah's nerves with the twenty questions.

Reina forced herself into an upright position, turned on her computer, and put her purse away.

"Thanks, I'm fine," Reina nearly snapped, feeling her chest tighten even more. Phyllis raised a brow before offering an apologetic smile.

"I'll come back later."

Reina felt embarrassed. It wasn't Phyllis's fault that she was late and had to run—okay, crawl—up the stairs. Reina amended her tone.

"I'm sorry, Phyl. What's up?"

"I had to drop my car off at the mechanic's this morning for repairs, and it won't be ready until tomorrow. I hate to ask you, but my husband is working late tonight and—"

"Girl, yes, I'll drop you off at home. You live out past Franklin and Elk Grove, right?"

Phyllis nodded.

"Then it's no problem. I live not too far from you."

"I thought you lived in the Greenhaven area," Phyllis stated.

"I did, but I moved a few—"

Reina's phone rang, halting her midsentence. She started to pick up the receiver but glanced at the phone number flashing on the caller ID screen just in the nick of time. *Mamí.* She was calling Reina from work. Why didn't she call Reina from home? Knowing *Papí,* he'd probably forbidden anyone with the last name of Kingsley to even look in his wayward daughter's direction. And Reina was wrong for telling *Mamí* she needed a spinal transplant? *Humph!* She didn't think so.

"Reina? Are you okay?"

Reina was lost deep in the quagmire of her own thoughts; Phyllis's voice sounded loud and strange, jolting her back to the surface of semiclarity. Reina covered her disoriented self with false laughter and quick wit. "Nothing save some drama at Little House in the Hood."

Phyllis chuckled.

"Okay, I'll leave that one alone. Meet for lunch?"

"Sure," Reina sang, a false note of cheer in her tone. "One o'clock?"

"It's a date." Phyllis turned to leave, only to pause and look back. "If you need to talk, you know where to find me." Reina nodded, slightly taken aback by the generous sincerity in her coworker's voice. Phyllis Williams left, leaving Reina to stare, puzzled and perplexed, at the still-ringing phone as if it suddenly embodied the cause of and cure for her woes.

Reina was wrong. Having checked her voice mail messages she discovered *Mamí* had, indeed, called earlier that morning. From home! Several times. Her mother's messages were frantic, filled with . . . what? Worry? Contrition? Reina liked imagining there was a little bit of both. *Mamí* ought to be worried, and she sure enough needed to ask Reina's forgiveness. There was a rift between them that wouldn't mend in a minute.

It didn't make good sense, her mother's betrayal, her siding with the testosterone toters of the family. The older Reina got the more it seemed like she and her mother were at odds, on opposite sides of the feminine fence. Reina could recall a time when things were sweet. *Mamí*, Reina, and her big sister, Nita, they could talk and laugh and whisper about anything. But now? Her sister was behind bars and Reina wouldn't trust her mother with a dog's secrets. Maybe *Abuela* was right: too much estrogen in the kitchen spoiled the soup.

She felt suddenly light-headed. Her Snoopy and Woodstock wristwatch showed 10:45. Reina had worked right through her morning break and breakfast. No wonder her mind was whirling and twirling like a ballerina on crank. She was irritable and deprived.

Reina pulled opened her bottom desk drawer, pushed aside a manila folder, and grabbed a candy bar from her personal stash. It was packed with peanuts and she needed protein.

Biting into the sweet confection, Reina let her thoughts linger on her sister, only to shift to her sister's children. Her two little nieces were beautiful, adorable girls despite whatever domestic conflict they'd witnessed in their home. Children deserved stability, something Reina lacked just then. She loved children. She hailed from a large family and was accustomed to always having somebody's baby hanging off her hip. Sometimes having a bunch of loud, squalling babies around could wreck a nerve, but for the most part Reina thought them one of God's most precious gifts, a gift she wouldn't get anytime soon. Even if she wanted a child right now—and she didn't, seeing as how she had enough non–baby fat to lose as it was—Reina lacked a necessary prerequisite: a man. With all the chaos in her cosmos, Reina knew she would not find a partner anytime soon. But what if— *Papí* forbid—she decided she *really* wanted a child despite her marriageless state? There were alternatives. A sperm bank perhaps? Reina could pay a visit to a local clinic and apply for a vial of the white stuff. She had good personal references. Her credit card balance was zero. The process shouldn't be too hard, and could prove worth a try.

Stop being ridiculous, Reina told herself, glancing about the neatly arranged cubicles filled with fellow employees. Maybe she should count her blessings rather than her wants. She had a good job with great possibilities for promotion, and decent rapport with her coworkers. Even if some folks in particular thought they should socialize around the clock while others pulled the load.

"Lenny, darling, you don't mind actually doing *some* work today, do you?" Reina called out to the man perched on the side of a coworker's desk discussing sports from A to Z. She had been entrusted with the role of acting supervisor and didn't mind flexing power a bit. Besides, Lenny needed to earn his keep for a change.

"Aw, Reina, you know I'm good for it," he replied with a wink, easing from his perch at his own leisurely pace.

"I know you're good for something, but it's not always productive."

"That's cold." He laughed as he sauntered to his desk. "But I still love you."

"Uh-huh, right, Lenny," Reina replied, holding her half-eaten candy bar aloft.

Lenny's discussing his favorite pastime sparked a thought. Maybe it was the winning ticket. If Reina could pretend to be an avid sports fan like Lenny truly was, then maybe she could delve into a brother's world and gain his much divided attention.

Reina could have her baby brother tutor her in the wide world of sports, but they were no longer on speaking terms. There was Lenny. He would probably jump at the chance to lounge on her couch eating up all her hard-earned groceries, talking out the side of his neck about a field goal in basketball and a three-point basket in baseball, he was so lazy and crazy. She would pass. Well, there was Chris. *Not!* He'd probably have Reina studying cricket and croquet and talking with a British accent with his proper self.

Reina burst out laughing—laughed so loud the nearby techs and other analysts stopped working to stare her way. She tried to stifle it, but the effort caused her to laugh even harder, so hard Reina had to pee. It didn't help matters that she'd downed three mugs of coffee already. Reina pushed back her chair and hurried down the hall to the rest room before she had an accident. Let that happen and news would travel, and the next thing Reina knew her desk would be covered with coupons for products for the incontinent.

Sitting on a cold commode, staring at the nothingness of the metal stall, Reina knew she was being fantastical. Certainly, she longed for a fulfilling relationship one day. And yes, children would be nice. But she had to admit that right then and there she was not ready. Her world had been off-center for quite some time. Living at home with her parents, suffering her grandfather's death, seeing her sister's decline, caused enough grief. Her burgeoning weight added fat to the fire. Sure, with a father who was six-foot-one and two hundred pounds, bigness was in her bones. But Reina had to be real with herself and admit she was eating enough for herself and others.

She was outgrowing her fat clothes too fast for comfort. If she didn't get a handle on things soon, her age and her size would be one and the same. Next thing Reina knew she'd be barred from Lane Bryant, a neon sign flashing in their window: KEEP STEPPING, MISS KINGSLEY! WE DON'T CARRY PLUS SIZES-TO-THE-TENTH-POWER. She'd have to move from Lane Bryant to shopping at some inconspicuous, hard-to-find specialty store that smelled like bacon and liniment and featured polyester, double-knit, floral print, pleated tent dresses with angel sleeves and satin ribbons that tied prettily beneath multiple chins.

Someone had put roots on her. That was it! Some evil, playa-hating heifer had fixed her. Someone was out to grill her goat.

Reina finished her business and flushed the toilet, humored by her own silliness. If roots were the cause of her problems she had a simple cure: *Abuela.* Reina stood at the vanity, washing her hands and smiling at her reflection. One visit to her grandmother and the fix would be undone. Reina dried her hands, tossed the paper towel in the nearest receptacle, and exited the lavatory, her smile fading a bit. If only things were so simple.

The unseasonably warm February breeze was deliciously scented with hints of jasmine and honeysuckle and the smell of fresh-cut grass. The sky was soft as Reina reclined on a blue-and-white patio chaise, a glass of syrupy, sweet iced tea and a bag of BBQ pork rinds beside her portable stereo on a small patio table within reach. Smooth jazz filled the air. Reina watched Pharaoh romp across the backyard in pursuit of one buzzing nighttime insect or another. For all his size and fierce bark, Pharaoh really was a big teddy bear. Reina enjoyed his antics, his wet kisses, and his companionship. With Vanessa working overtime preparing for some big press conference, Reina found Pharaoh relying on her more and more for his basic needs. He was there waiting, stubby tail wagging, when she arrived home each evening, ready to drag Reina out on his nightly walk.

They were thrown a bit off schedule that evening due to Reina giving her coworker a ride home. The rush-hour traffic on southbound Highway 99 had been enough to make a nun cuss. But Reina hadn't particularly cared. As usual, Phyllis had proved to be good company. The woman's humor was a bit irreverent, a lot zany. Much like her own. But there was something besides shared humor that drew Reina to Phyllis Williams, something intoxicating that Reina couldn't quite name but knew she liked.

Reina stretched every inch of her five-foot-nine-inch frame, her joints snapping and popping in protest. She settled back, her head tilted toward the deep, limitless span of sky. Such quiet. It was more than Reina had hoped for. It set her mind racing, but calmly. She sat in silent assessment, mentally comparing herself against a Technicolor vision of Phyllis Williams that suddenly loomed across the dazzling screen of her mind.

Denim versus ice-plum silk. Dry cuticles and stubby nails versus a French manicure. Kohl eyeliner and thick, braided bun next to flawlessly applied makeup and not-a-strand-out-of-place shoulder-length bob. Reina felt like the Don't side to Phyllis's Do tip in a fashion column.

Reina chuckled, her voice carrying across the quiet backyard like a weightless ribbon. Phyllis was not built to suit a fashion-model size. She was a real sister with real curves. But she carried herself with a serious sense of confidence. Surely Phyllis was beautiful enough to grace the pages of *Essence*, now that they were finally representing the truth that gorgeous black women came in all shapes and sizes. Phyllis had flair and style, walked with her head high, and appeared to genuinely enjoy the life she lived.

It hit Reina like a brick.

That was it! The difference between them was peace. The realization was brilliant, thumping Reina square between her wide, deep-set eyes. It was overwhelming, so much so that Reina felt off balance and suddenly ill.

Phyllis Williams walked in a constant aura of tranquillity. Perhaps it had much to do with Phyllis's walk with God. The woman was a born-again Christian and bold about it. But she wasn't preachy and condemning, like some overzealous Bible-toting folks tended to be. Her convictions were strong, yet gentle and loving enough to be warm and inviting.

Peace. What a novelty. What a luxury that Reina had not been able to afford. Not with everything wrong in her world, draining her substance and her soul. Even the one thing she could always call on in times of trouble seemed to be failing her now: her voice.

Her voice felt tired. Perhaps it, too, was bent beneath the strain of recent affairs. Her rich, throaty, pure silk voice—with its surprisingly wide range that was perfectly suited for jazz, with its demanding improvisations, dissonant chords, and searing melodies—was worn. Reina knew plenty of exercises meant to strength the vocal apparatus. She could put them to use. A spark of excitement shot through her; then she thought, Why bother? She wasn't sleek, sexy. What if she couldn't bring in a crowd? What if she did, but once they came and saw that her body didn't fit the bill of a svelte, sophisticated, sultry singer they up and left? It would be more than she could bear. Ruby and the shower would be her only venues for now. They couldn't protest or talk back. She could sing until her heart was content. Or at least pretend.

But wait just a cotton-picking minute. Big, voluptuous sisters were doing things for themselves, Reina silently argued. Look at Queen Latifah. Chaka. Kelly Price and Jill Scott. Reina had to give the sisters their props. They were living their dreams, challenging the music industry's preconceived notions and preferred images of itty-bitty bodies as symbols of absolute beauty. They had guts and grace, whereas Reina's waned.

So what if she sang like someone twice her age, one with true-life experiences and secret knowledge? What did it matter that her voice evoked lost memories, rekindled the flavors of long-dead passions, hurled the listener backward to the old then forward into the new? Reina admitted she just couldn't do it anymore, and that admission caused her heart to break in pieces beyond repair.

Reina increased the radio volume. She could only hum as Oleta Adams's "You Need to Be Loved" filled the airwaves. Before long Reina was humming louder, until the backyard seemed to resonate with the mournful timbre of her voice. Even Pharaoh stopped playing long enough to look up in her direction. He barked, then began to howl his empathy.

Reina sighed and turned off the stereo. It was getting late. The night sky was ribbon-bedecked with deep shades of pink and lavender quickly disappearing beneath an ever-deepening blue. She pushed herself up from the chaise and unplugged the stereo. Grabbing her now-empty glass and snack wrapper, Reina whistled for Pharaoh to come and headed indoors, wiping an unexpected tear from her cheek with the back of a shaky hand.

It was late and Vanessa was still out, either at work or aerobics, or maybe one of those yoga or New Age relaxation classes or whatever the mess was she frequented in order to "center herself." *Yeah, right.* Reina needed nothing more than this quiet house, a box of white chocolate–dipped Oreos, and a large glass of ice-cold diet Dr. Pepper to align her cosmos. But she didn't go there tonight. Instead of downing her usual dessert, Reina had a cup of pineapple chunks and cling peaches topped with whipped cream. She was trying to change her bad ways.

What if her struggle had paid off? Reina thought to herself as she stood in the solitary confinement of the upstairs bathroom preparing for bed. Hmmm . . . maybe, just maybe, Reina had made a significant enough change to make a difference. Should she or shouldn't she? She toyed with the thought, her heart pounding and filling her ears with the rush of blood. She should! Reina elected to take the plunge. After all, she could use some good news from somewhere.

Naked as the day she was born, Reina stood in the middle of Vanessa's bathroom floor and stared down at the sparkling white scale. Reina inhaled so deeply her lungs ached. Her resolve was firm. Eyes closed tight, Reina stepped onto the bathroom scale and waited for the red numbers on the digital display to tell her fortune.

Reina waited a lifetime. Her mind raced with hope and possibilities. Hadn't she been walking Pharaoh every night? Hadn't she modified her cooking a wee bit since being at Vanessa's? What if . . . ? A lost pound or two would be wonderful. But five or ten? *Awww, suki, now that would be too sweet.* With weight loss, Reina could step on the stage, recollect her lost self, and sing like she was out of her ever-loving mind.

Excited by the possibilities, Reina steeled her nerves and opened one eye just wide enough for one little peek. She glanced down at the scale. She cracked open the other eye just to make sure she saw what she saw. She couldn't believe it. Eyes round as plates filled with jerk chicken, dirty rice, and plantains, Reina screamed. Pharaoh, startled, set to howling.

"Hush, Pharaoh!" Reina commanded without sympathy. He instantly complied.

Two hundred fifty pounds!

Two hundred fifty pounds? Thirty doggone pounds! Gained, not lost! She was a hop, skip, and three Junky Monkey sundaes away from the three-zero-zero. Reina stood and stared at the digitally displayed numbers so long that her vision blurred. Something was wrong with Vanessa's scale. Reina stepped off, allowed the digits to return to zero, then stepped back on. Yep, the reading was the same, 2-5-0! Five hundred divided by two. One thousand divided by four. Ten times ten times two plus fifty. Any way you sliced her, she still came up the same.

When, where, how, and why had she gained thirty pounds in one year? A year ago, at her last gynecological exam, Reina had been shamefaced to discover she weighed over two hundred pounds. But now, two-fifty? She wished she could regurgitate every fry, every burger, every shake, white chocolate–covered Oreo, six-for-a-dollar doughnut, chimichanga, BBQ pork rind, tamale, couscous, *flauta*, hot fudge sundae, and cheesecake supreme she'd wolfed like a ravenous dog in the past three hundred and sixty-five days.

Slowly, Reina stepped from the scale and reached for her cotton nightgown with the picture of a slumbering teddy bear on the front. Almost painfully, she slipped it over her head and onto her traitorous body.

Reina doused the light in the master bathroom and stumbled through Vanessa's spacious, private sanctuary with its exquisite, expensive furniture. A heavy-looking glass frame perched atop the cherry-wood dresser held a photo of the three of them—Vanessa, Chris, and Reina—smiling and clowning for the photographer. There they were, three comrades, virtually inseparable. All black and beautiful and built, except Reina. She swelled out like a swollen thumb, hand, foot, and knee. Reina sighed and started to move on. Then she paused to stare at a teeny-tiny pair of size-eight jeans—the only garment out of place in the otherwise immaculate space—strewn across the arm of Vanessa's overstuffed tan-and-cream striped chaise. Reina could barely fit a foot through the legs of those jeans, heaven forbid a calf.

Methodically, Reina trudged down the hall to the guest room that now served as her own. The door, which Reina normally left open so Vanessa could pop in upon her arrival home so they could chat a while, she closed, locking even poor Pharaoh out of sight and mind.

Reina sat on the edge of the bed and stared at nothing in particular. A river of emotions ran through her. Hurt. Disbelief. Hopelessness. Too swift, too strong, the feelings swept over her until Reina felt like hiding from herself and the world. Then fury sprang to the forefront. Her chest tightened. Her lungs began to ache. She needed a hit.

Reina trudged to the dresser and found her purse. She snatched it open and rifled through it. Hairbrush. Wallet. Cosmetic bag containing five different shades and brands of eyeliner. Gum. Mints. A *gris-gris* charm her grandmother had made her swear to wear at all times. Reina kept the odd-shaped amulet in her purse. She might like bold colors and wild prints, but she was not about to wear a little bag filled with cat bones or graveyard dust or who knew what. Finally, at the bottom of the abyss, lay what she needed and wanted: asthma inhalers and chocolate.

Puff, puff. *Swwww*, deep inhalation. *Rip.*

With a vengeance, Reina tore open the wrapper that stood between her and the luscious hunk of chocolate and caramel. Fiercely, Reina bit into it and stood there chewing and stewing until catching sight of the crumpled wrappers that already lay discarded and forlorn at the bottom of her purse. Slowly she extracted each one, casting them into the wastebasket, until they lay there like three deflated but glaring banners of dishonor.

Suddenly, her anger was gone. Reina stared at the candy bar in her hand, knowing it, and its three slain comrades, had contributed to her downfall from grace. She hurled the partially eaten chocolate bar in the wastebasket and slouched away.

Moments later, Reina Kingsley lay in bed beneath fluffy blankets covered with comic pictures of a certain fat orange cartoon cat with his *skinny*, goofy doggie friend. She stared out the window, past her stuffed animals cheerfully arranged on the wall shelves. Car lights flashed through the open curtains and across the walls. She heard the familiar sound of the automatic garage door lifting. Vanessa was home. Pharaoh, who had been curled up outside Reina's door, forgot all about the distant and distracted woman and raced down the stairs to meet his mistress. Reina imagined their affectionate reunion, envisioned the faithful canine slobbering all over his slim and trim owner, with her tight little butt and firm arms, one chin and one stomach.

Eventually Reina heard Vanessa's knock at her door. She silently ignored the request to enter. She didn't want to be bothered. Especially by someone who didn't have an ounce of excessive fat on her frame, and couldn't possibly understand the plight of a big woman on the verge of meltdown.

Reina refused to cry. Or rather she couldn't. She'd experienced too many emotional upheavals in the past few days and she was all cried out. There was no one to call. No one to blame except herself. Reina had eaten her way into a deep pit from which no one could extract her. She was stuck. No exit. No entrance. Just motionless despair.

Reina tossed back the orange kitty covers, got out of bed, and walked back to the dresser. She rummaged through her patchwork purse, to no avail. What she wanted wasn't there. Frantically, desperately, Reina glanced about her until the wastebasket came into view. She didn't flinch or hesitate. Reina reached down and retrieved the discarded candy bar.

With her nose pressed against the cool windowpane and with only the sightless eyes of her stuffed animals bearing witness, Reina stood and gazed out at the windows and rooftops of neighboring houses, slowly savoring each and every remaining bite of the chocolate-and-caramel confection until her grief was artificially, momentarily assuaged.

CHRIS McCULLEN

My name is Chris McCullen. I'm thirty-one, single, and no baby's daddy. My teeth are real and so is my hair. No process, no partials. I consider myself an upstanding, law-abiding, gainfully employed, and more-than-a-little-bit-attractive black man. I'm not Denzel or Shemar Moore, but I ain't Wesley Snipes or Busta Rhymes, either. I'm easy on the eyes. Vanessa thinks I'm *GQ* cover-come to life with a Michael Jordan smile times two. Reina says I'm fine—correction, *foine*. I consider myself decent and a credit to my parents' genes.

Speaking of parents, I'm an orphan. Well, partially so. Not as in Vanessa's case. My mother, God rest her soul, died when I was three. I hate to admit this, but sometimes I barely remember her, and that makes me feel traitorous or disrespectful. That's why I keep a picture of her in my wallet for quick reference and reminder. One should never forget the woman who virtually sacrificed herself on a delivery room table just so his big-head self could have life.

As I was saying, my mother died too early for me. How? It's a shame to say, but I don't really know. That still remains my most painful mystery. My family never discusses the issue in front of me, as if protecting me from something I can't (at the grown age of thirty-one) handle. Of course, I know they know, and I know they talk about it, because my father's mother and his sisters, Nana and my aunties, act as if they've been appointed God's public-address system in the flesh.

They know everything and keep silent about nothing, except the true cause of my mother's demise, which leads me to believe it must have been something most brutal or at least unsavory.

I can't ask my maternal relatives, for my mother has no family of which to speak. Like myself, she was an only child, her parents are dead, and I know of no other existing kin. That leaves only my father as my source of insight.

My father never talks about it. I learned when I was young that he was a closed book on the issue. I tried weaseling the truth out of him, confronting him at what I hoped were inopportune moments for him, fortuitous ones for me. Like during family or holiday dinners, or after Sunday service when he was still high with the spirit, and even once during a Bible study Q-and-A period. (By the way, my father is a pastor and has been in the ministry in one capacity or another as long as I can recall. I'm a PK—a preacher's kid. So you know I am expected to walk the straight and narrow). I caught hell on earth for getting up and asking such an "evil-inspired" question. Shaming my father before his congregation. My father whipped my butt so good that I was, for a long while, scared to ask him anything, let alone for a glass of water before bedtime, which probably was a good thing because I stopped peeing up the mattress. I find nothing humorous in my ignorance concerning my mother's passing, but Dad and I do laugh about how he spanked the piss out of me.

Looking back, I think that was the only real whipping my father ever gave me. Don't be fooled; he was no slouch of a disciplinarian. But I was a sensitive little kid. Dad had only to give me one of his looks and I'd break down like a little punk. Like any other boy, I wanted my father's approval, but maybe more so than most. Dad was all that I had, and my child's mind told me not to displease him or he, like my mother, would go away. Such was never the case. Dad stayed.

I grew up in a man's world. Just Dad and me. No perfumes. No panties. Just boxers and briefs, balls and bats. Not to say that the feminine influence didn't grace our abode from time to time. With Dad's busy itinerary as a young pastor, sisters from the church would come by to sit with me after school until my father returned from his office. Their beige, brown, and beautiful black faces blur, their bodies blending until they represent one massive icon of makeshift motherhood for me.

I'm nobody's fool. Those baby-sitting sisters wanted to be my

mama, or better told, my father's wife. Upstanding, respected, promi-
nent widowed black preacher? Steady income, homeowner, with just
one little well-mannered boy to raise? You'd better know Pops was
more than a pillar in the community. He represented solid possibility,
a single woman's answer to prayer. He was attractive in more ways
than one.

On the physical tip? Dad is phenotypically appealing. Dad inherited Papa's wide, dark eyes and full lips, and Nana's high, chiseled
cheekbones and thick, wavy hair. Yes, we're part Native American.
Dakota Indian to be exact. Unlike most African Americans who love
making claims to such "noble" ancestry as if this somehow lessens the
sting of being just "plain" black, Nana has the official government
documents to prove it. But so what? By all historical accounts, media
reports, racial profiles, and one-drop rules I'm still Negro, colored,
black to the bone.

Dad is nearly six-foot-four, with a gracious, almost proud bearing
that's perfect for the pulpit. Dad could preach and not break a sweat,
and still the sisters would be hopping hallelujah in the aisles, falling
out in the spirit at his feet. Even the young bucks, too cool to move
and too suave to get involved, found themselves whisking away a tear
or two when my father "reared back" and let God have His way. I can
remember just sitting there, spellbound and proud, wondering if I
would ever be as impressive and captivating, powerful and respected
as the man others called pastor.

As you can tell, I admire my father. He's lived an exemplary life.
Even with all the female flesh thrown his way, I've never known him to
compromise his walk with God just to solace himself in some sister's
sweetness. He could have easily remarried after my mother's death.
Instead, Dad chose to devote himself to full-time ministry and me.
Whenever Nana and her daughters rode his back about "getting that
boy a new mama," he'd merely silence them with a quiet but stern,
"He has a parent. Me."

I was a teenager before I realized and truly appreciated the fact
that Dad *chose* not to remarry. As he would tell me when I was grown,
I was his priority. He sacrificed quite a bit just so my hard head could
have a good life. I can't say that I have always had what I wanted, but I
have never done without what I really needed.

I grew up in a home filled with Bible verses and black poets' prose.
Proverbs and The Song of Solomon. Alain Locke and Langston

Hughes. Bible stories and black folks' fiction. Samson and Delilah.
Zora Neale Hurston, Jessie Fauset, and James Baldwin. Prayers and
plays. Psalms. Lorraine Hansberry. Leroi Jones/Amiri Baraka.
Spirituals and blues. Mahalia Jackson and Billie Holiday. Somehow
Dad synchronized the often opposing worlds of the sacred and the
secular, offering me a cosmos that pulsated with a synergistic culture
both rich and full. Our dining room table might have been the site of
saints at Sunday afternoon dinners, but come Friday that same table
served as a center for political and social debate, followed by a game
of bones (a.k.a. dominoes). My world was deep.

Vanessa calls me a product of the black bourgeoisie. Reina says I'm
cultured and classy. My girls have it all wrong. Simply put, I'm blessed.

I had a good upbringing. I'm grateful for having been exposed to
good things. Yes, I drive a brand-new Lexus coupe. Yes, I've just sub-
mitted a bid to purchase a modest house located in a private, gated
community in Laguna—a growing neighborhood on the southern tip
of Sacramento. And yes, last week I interviewed for a facility coordinator position with Valley Fitness, which has a string of physical-
improvement facilities (a.k.a. gyms) throughout California. If I land
the promotion I'll be bringing home big bank. As in almost but not
quite—okay near enough—six figures. Dollar dollar bills, y'all! And
with all the various stock options and investment vehicles Valley
Fitness offers, I'll have an option to buy my own facility in maybe five
to seven years.

But as I was saying, so what if I prefer Placido Domingo to Puff
Daddy, Jessy Norman or Cassandra Wilson to Janet Jackson and Mary
J., or Brie and chardonnay to pork rinds and a forty-ounce. That does
not make me bourgeois. I am no less black, African American, Negro,
colored, whatever the preference. No less in touch socially or politically or culturally than the next brother. In fact I might argue that I'm
connected with myself and my people more soundly than the brother
blasting hard-core, genocidal rap lyrics in his hoopty, or that Black
Power militant, right fist raised, left hand holding on to Blondie at his
side. It's not just about me and mine. My father taught me better. I'm
not merely about the material. And I'm not, as my ex-girlfriend put it,
stylin' and profilin' without a conscience or a cause.

I give to the United Way. I serve in the youth ministry at Dad's
church, play assistant coach to the basketball team, and I volunteer at
the local food bank on occasion. Not to mention the various fund-

raising broadcasts I've cohosted on the local public television station. Vanessa should know. I've emceed more than one of her station's little soirees gratis. Free! All in the name of giving back to my community. I'm a civic-minded kind of brother, I thank you very much.

My family is not rich. But we ain't po' neither. My father could have easily paid my full college expenses without batting an eye. But he didn't. Tuition and materials necessary to my learning success were all he would front. Dad told me straight up he, as my father, was obligated to secure an opportunity to higher learning for me. The rest was mine to do. Of course, I didn't appreciate or understand what I thought was his downright stinginess at the time. Some folk, i.e., Nana and my never-keeping-their-humble-opinions-to-themselves aunties, thought Dad's tactics a bit high-handed and low-hearted. But I can look back and admit how much I've actually gained because of his tough approach.

I worked to pay for food and clothes and any entertainment I thought I, as a college-going brother, deserved. And the fact that I actually had documents of my Native American ancestry helped in securing a modest scholarship or two. Dad sent the occasional help in the form of monetary gifts for birthdays and holidays. But it was perfectly clear that I was expected to be a man and earn my keep. I was none the worse for it. I received my B.S. in Biology with a minor in Black Studies. I was to go on to med school, but I admit I was burned out. I couldn't stomach another lecture, or read another book with terminology and words that, when pronounced, sounded like somebody speaking in tongues. Five years earning a four-year degree was enough. Until grad school, that is. Which, by the way, I've been putting off for another day.

Honestly, I don't know that that day will ever come. I may never return to school and become Dr. Christophe McCullen. Ph.D. or M.D. I'm enjoying my life and my hard-earned rewards. Sure, I could go back and pursue a higher degree, make more money, buy more things. But like I said, it's not just about the Benjamins. Besides, if I'm appointed facility coordinator with Valley Fitness, man, I'll be straight. Cha-ching!—cash flow.

Facility coordinator is the first step. Next is the area director, who is responsible for anywhere from six to ten physical-improvement facilities in the immediate area. Then there's the regional director. Now that's what I'm talking about! HNIC (Head Negro In Charge) of all locations in northern California and parts of Washington, Nevada, and Oregon. That's over thirty sites, and the regional director receives a yearly stipend based on the increase in new membership, as well as retention of ongoing members. Grapevine has it that last year that bonus was five high figures for real. I can live with that. But that's my future. Right now I'm trying to move on up from assistant coordinator to the next rung on this corporate American ladder without losing my grip.

"Hello?"

"Whatcha know good, son?"

"Know my pops must be pretty bored to be calling me on a Friday night."

Dad chuckled. My father's laughter is deep, rich. Reminds me of a calm river.

"It's only seven o'clock. The party isn't leaping off yet."

"Uh, Dad. That's jumping off. Not leaping off."

Dad sucked his teeth, as he is prone to do whenever trivial details prove a nuisance to him.

"Takes too much effort to keep up with you young folks. All this slang and mess changes from one week to the next."

"Mess" is one of Dad's favorite tags. He adds it to just about anything he can't get with.

"If you can't hang with the big dogs then you have to stay on the porch with the puppies, Pops."

Dad grunted.

"Boy, please. I was running with big dogs before you could even wipe your tail. I can teach you a thing or three about hanging with the pack."

"No, thank you. I'm not interested in being part of your wolf clan."

We both laughed.

"So, you're not having the weekly old bones tournament tonight?" I asked. "And I refer to dominoes, not to you and your cronies."

"Hush it up." Dad paused to munch on something. Popcorn. Every Friday night before his company arrives Dad treats himself to a bowl of popcorn. Old-fashioned stovetop corn with real melted butter and salt.

"You know Deacon Freeman is in the hospital," Dad says as I swallow slowly, savoring the flavor of my raspberry-peach seltzer. I'm chilling in my living room, listening to National Public Radio while watching the basketball game on ESPN with the television volume muted.

"How is he?"

"As well as can be expected after a triple bypass. Stopped by the hospital and prayed with him and Sister Freeman today. Saw that youngest daughter of theirs, too. Aquanette. Antoinette. Good girl, she is, helping her mother help her father."

Dad knows her name. As a pastor he prides himself on his close relationships with his congregants. Just messing with a brother, as always.

"Anjanette, Dad. Her name is . . . Aw, Shaq! Come on, man, set it up," I hollered at the television screen as my boy missed yet another free throw. "That's four tonight, man. Count 'em. Four!" I reiterated, holding up the appropriate number of fingers as if Shaq could see me sitting in my living room sporting a pair of the pale blue silk boxers Vanessa gave me for Christmas.

"That's it! Anjanette. She's an attractive girl, don't you think?"

"Uh-huh," I murmured, settling down.

"Why so little enthusiasm?"

Paused to pluck a cube of ice from my glass and roll it around on my tongue to cool me down before I crunched it to pieces. Dad knows the answer as well as I do. Because.

Because I begged off romance when, four years ago, the woman I was sprung on dumped me for some clown on the sad-sack San Francisco 49ers.

Haven't watched a football game since.

Daphne had a brother's nose wide open. I was in love for the first time in my life. She was smart, had a banging body, and a face that made Lela Rochon look homely. She was sensitive and sweet and the one woman I wanted to make a lifelong commitment to. Or so I thought until our second Lamaze class.

We were pregnant. I was scared *and* ecstatic. I knew absolutely nothing about being a daddy, but I had Pops to draw from. He was there in my corner, supportive despite my being an unmarried and expectant father. But being a PK with my religious upbringing, I was ready to rectify and bring honor to the situation. I emptied my savings and bought Daphne a one-karat diamond solitaire engagement ring. I was going to propose that night after Lamaze class number two. It was a special night, the night of our one-year dating anniversary.

I took her to dinner. I had our server decorate the top of her favorite dessert, a slice of lemon meringue pie, with the engagement ring. When he delivered it to our table and I dropped to one knee the girl started bawling like someone killed her parakeet, Bubba Doo.

"I-I c-can't do you like this, Chris," she sobbed. "You've been so good to us."

I had no idea what she was talking about.

"I'm pregnant—"

Duh!

"—but not by you."

Huh?

Did I remember that preseason party she'd attended in Sausalito (a cute little resort villa on the San Francisco Bay) last August with her godsister, Trunique? Well, she'd met him there. Her football-playing sperm donor. They hooked up, got busy over the course of the weekend, planted a baby, and left me to assume the position walking around like a grinning fool, crazy spending my hard-earned money on cute little infant gear.

My heart was crushed finer than ice in a Slurpee, but all I could think of to say was, "You're six months pregnant, Daphne. Why didn't you tell me before I got all emotionally invested in this?"

She didn't want to be alone. Football Head was busy during the season. He couldn't take her shopping for cute little layettes and bibs and booties or attend Lamaze. Besides, he didn't want to claim the baby as his initially, but now hearing how wonderfully involved I was, he decided to give parenting a chance.

"Isn't that wonderful, Chris? You were his inspiration," Daphne declared before collapsing into a fresh round of fat tears.

Yeah, friggin' fantastic, I thought as I paid for *my* dinner and asked our server to box up *her* slice of pie. I left Daphne there crying salt onto her half-eaten lobster. That diamond engagement ring still had a coating of crusty egg whites on its band when I returned it to the jeweler the following morning. So pardon me, please, if I'd rather lynch Cupid before he shoots me again.

I sighed into the phone, wondering when my father would stop campaigning for a daughter-in-law, if ever.

"Come on, Dad. I know where this is going and we've already been there and back more than a few times, and with all due respect, I'd prefer not to go there again. Sir," I added for good measure. "I have no desire to be romantically involved at this time in my life. I'm fine by myself."

A moment's silence passed between us. I'm a peace-abiding citizen and son. I don't particularly care to insult or offend my only living parent. But parents have a problem relentlessly crossing the boundaries of their grown children's lives without a pass and need to be brought back to a safe place before they cause things to crash and burn. Still, I didn't care for the silence between us. It made me uncomfortable and I was about to break it when Dad did in his most customary fashion. He sucked his teeth.

"Been watching too much of that Ophir mess."

I chuckled deep, relieved. Dad may not have been happy with what I'd had to say, but he wasn't about to push the issue. At least not tonight. Tomorrow? Well, that was another day and another opportunity for Dad to canvass for a daughter-in-law, and as Nana put it, "some grandbabies to warm his old chest."

"Oprah. Dad, it's Oprah, not Ophir. Ophir is a locale mentioned in the Bible—"

"Oh, so now you're the Bible scholar and I'm the student."

Civility restored.

We did our usual. We played catch-up, filling each other in on the details of the flow of our days. Told Dad all about my job interview. Tried not to sound too excited or too worried about the outcome, but Dad heard between the lines and waxed sermonic on me, reminding me to trust the Lord in all my ways. What can a brother say to that except, "Yes, sir"? Dad. He's a living, breathing, walking pool of optimism, faith, and prayer. There is nothing I, as his beloved son, cannot achieve. No goal I cannot accomplish. He's placed all his hope in me. I could never break his heart.

We were debating and failing to agree which NBA player should be named MVP this year, whether or not the Sacramento Kings would make it to the play-offs again, or which WNBA supersister would set the courts aflame, when my phone beeped.

"Hold on, Dad."

Click.

"Speak."

"Hello to you, too, Boo."

Vanessa Taylor, my girl down through the years. Some of my buddies don't understand why Vanessa and I have never hooked up like that—you know, made a love connection. The woman is gorgeous, intelligent, genuine, and good to be with. Still, Vanessa has her preferences and I have mine.

" 'Sup, gorgeous?"

"Nothing until you get up off your lanky butt and come get me."

I chuckled. At six-two and two hundred and twenty pounds of solid-packed muscle, I'm anything but lanky.

"Pop's on the other line."

Vanessa giggled.

"Oh, well. Guess I won't see you until midnight."

"I'll make your wait worthwhile," I tossed back in what my ex called my bedroom baritone.

"Don't get yourself in too deep, Boo," Vanessa purred. "I haven't smelled a man in so long my nose is throbbing."

I laughed.

"Well, let a brother get off the phone and I'll see what I can do to relieve your olfactory senses. We can get in a quick sniff before it's time to pick up Reina."

There was a slight pause. Vanessa coughed.

"Chris, Reina didn't tell you?"

"Tell me what?"

"She's staying with me."

I forgot about continuing our harmless game of verbal seduction. "Since when?"

"Since four or five days ago," Vanessa told me, sounding a bit guilty.

"See how you do a brother?" I complained, all indignant. "What's up with that? Supposed to be my girls and you're up here keeping things on the down low—"

"Don't trip ghettolicious on me, Chris." I imagined Vanessa on the opposite end of the phone, just sitting there in one of her many silk robes examining her perfectly manicured fingernails, long brown legs crossed at the knees, one satin mule–slippered foot gently swaying as if she really couldn't be bothered with anybody's annoyance, especially mine. "Besides it's Reina's business, and if she didn't tell you, then she obviously has her reasons."

I pulled a Dad and sucked my teeth.

"Whatever."

"Just hurry up before we miss the movie. And tell Papa McCullen I said hello." Vanessa was unfazed by my irritability. "Bye, Boo," she cooed, all angelic-like. I didn't even bother replying. Instead I clicked back to Dad, who was still munching on his homemade popcorn.

Dad is going on about something. I'm not really listening because I'm thinking how whacked Reina and Vanessa are. Just plain old ill-minded, no-good scrimps. Don't ask me what it means: scrimps. One of my boys made that up in a stupid moment. The fellas and I use it whenever we're too through with some indecent, infuriating, or idiotic choice or action made by someone in our lives, a.k.a. women. *Man, she actually wanted to borrow $300 for airfare so she could visit her old boyfriend in Jersey just to make sure there wasn't any chemistry left between them before jumping solid with me. Scrimp!* It was our G-rated way of letting off steam without going off and calling women, you know, female dogs or worse. We call ourselves the true NBA brotherhood, No B——s Allowed. Meaning, we wouldn't disrespect sisters, women, with our mouths. We wouldn't call them anything we wouldn't want another man to call our own mothers or sisters. So *scrimps* it was.

Back to the scrimps at hand. Reina and Vanessa were being secretive. Now, hold up before you paint me soft. Don't misunderstand. I don't need—don't *want*—to know all the sordid details of their complex little lives. I'm not Richard Simmons and I don't carry tissue boxes around with me just so a sister can cry on my shoulder. But come on now. Reina rooming with Vanessa? That's about as major as M.J. retiring from basketball. Twice! What had really gone on at the house of Kingsley?

And furthermore, is Vanessa even aware that she calls me Boo only when she's *sans homme*, without a man? What am I, a surrogate quasi-lover without all the fringe benefits? Am I an underpaid understudy keeping some other brother's spot warm until he finally arrives to play his part? I'm really not trying to be played like that.

And you know what?

I'm tripping. Getting all worked up over nothing. I'm usually a pretty mellow fellow. Truly, I am. It must be the stress of the house hunt and the possible promotion and other things that have me getting my boxers in a bunch.

The report on National Public Radio complete, a musical interlude begins. A sultry voice pierces my getting-ready-to-flip dramatic mus-

ings and puts a chill-out on my go-off plans. Smooth, dynamic. I close
my eyes and yield to her golden-throated touch. Nancy Wilson. She's
serenading me proper.

I remember a day long ago when one of those wanting-to-be-my-
mama sister saints who happened to be our housekeeper was cleaning our kitchen one Saturday afternoon and heard Dad playing Ms.
Nancy's music. She marched uninvited into Dad's study, hands on
hips, telling him how a preacher ought to be listening to Mahalia
Jackson or Sister Rosetta Tharpe or Shirley Caesar or some upstanding gospel singer like that instead of that devilish hussy spewing some
trash about guess who she saw today in a bar with another woman?
Dad didn't say a word. Just deepened the wound by humming along.
Sister Sally Housekeeper was out of there for good, fuming about how
Reverend McCullen wasn't fit to be her husband nor father to her
four children from four different ex-husbands.

Now, that was a classy lady. Nancy Wilson, not Saint Sally. If memory serves me right, I once heard Nana say my mother put her in the
mind of Ms. Wilson. I reach for my wallet atop the coffee table as Dad
shifts topics to fill me in on his week. I pull out Mother's well-worn
picture. It's a bit yellow and the edges are truly frayed, but her beautiful face is completely intact. She does favor the incredible Ms. Nancy.
Wish I remembered her more.

"Dad?"

Something in my tone made him pause. Suddenly his undivided attention was mine.

"Son?"

"I visited Mother's grave last week." I know my mother's death remains a painful subject for my father, so I try not to cause him undue
pain. But my announcement just slipped out.

Dad sighed softly into the phone.

"Your mother would have been proud of you, son."

I gritted my teeth, frustration oozing out with the motion. Dad's
voice had become too composed, deceptively calm, as it always did
when he was avoiding the matter at hand. It was as if he were disem-
bodied, his real self floating in some high region where pain did not
exist, as he cast his voice through some hazy tunnel, back down to
earth for my benefit.

"Would she be proud of the fact that her only child is no closer to
understanding her life at the age of thirty-one than he was at the age

of three?" *Oops!* I was rolling like a two-ton boulder down a slippery slope. I really needed to slow my roll but couldn't.

"That's enough, Christophe. There is no need to go over this again." Dad's voice was normal again, all authoritative, filled with pastoral and fatherly care. "What you don't know can't hurt you."

Christophe. Use of my full, formal name was as good as a benediction. Dad was not about to tread this old ground with me. I know I was wrong. I goaded my father and practically mocked his parenting in doing what he thought was right for me as his child. I think that's part of the problem. In this regard, my father still considered me childlike, in need of his protection from whatever emotional trauma the unspoken truth regarding my mother's loss might inflict. I actually laughed out loud. Family. What a paradox. They never fail to swim all up in my business without an invitation, but the moment I need a little 411 they start doing the backstroke faster than a gold medal–winning Olympic swimmer.

Stay out of grown folks' business. I've heard that more times than I care to count. I'd like for just one person to answer me this: how grown do you have to be before you can get up in the business of others? And, furthermore, who gave them exclusive rights to knowing certain things, especially when and where I'm involved?

Whatever. That's my simple answer to sheer madness. *Whatever!*

Maybe it's time a brother worked up on a plan of his own. If you want something bad enough, you'll do whatever's necessary to get it. Do I really want to know what happened? I do, after all, have a right to know. All this secrecy and mystery is for the weak of heart. I'll have to give this more thought, maybe have a deep discussion with the fellas. As Nana herself says when trying to justify her skillfully weaseling some juicy tidbit of information out of someone who obviously didn't think she need be privy to the matter in the first place, "Secrets are made to be revealed."

Darkness is not a bad thing. It's a natural progression signaling day's end. Darkness holds the glory of night in the palms of her hands. Darkness inflates our false sense of nobility, hides our imperfections, shrouds us with subtle comfort, and endows us with a sense of confidence that light exposes as fraud.

I need the dark right now.

I'm running hard. My feet are pounding packed dirt flecked with gravel. Crunch! Crunch! Dust, white against the deepening night, puffs up to slither a gritty caress about my ankles before sliding down again to the track. My sweat is part normal physical process, part release of toxins that could otherwise poison my soul. My pace is faster than normal. I'll tire myself quickly, but I don't care. I need to exhaust my mind and my body before they exhaust me.

Strangely enough I'm all alone. It's early February, but the air is cool, not crisp. The night is blue-deep; still, the dark is without malice. Yet I'm alone. Can't say I blame fellow joggers for passing on, for not detouring to join an oversize, overangry brother racing around a fenced-in high school track like he's trying to outrun ghosts of the past. Outrun or catch up with? I'm no longer sure which. I'm either pressed back or pulled forward. Cast down or just rising. This thing has me in its grip, has me going and coming. Got a brother all confused.

Things haven't always been this way. Yes, I once pestered my father, my family, for truth, for an understanding regarding my mother's passing. But let's keep it real. It wasn't an everyday, relentless kind of craving. It came and went just like any other childlike desire or whim. Sometimes it was an insistent quest, sometimes not. There were days, months, years that passed without my caring to dig for or know the truth of the matter. I could content myself with fantasies about a loving mother who, had she lived, tucked me in at night and brushed my unruly hair with a silken palm. More often than not, that was enough. And when it wasn't I simply pulled out Mother's picture and allowed her smile to soothe my soul. Maybe it was just childish rebellion that urged me to challenge my father for a knowledge I felt entitled to.

So why do I choose now to trip so hard? What has me going there again? Probably Vanessa's recent revelation that she's decided to search for her birth parents. Root digging. Gene shopping. Pieces of missing parentage. Children have a right to know their forebears. We all want to feel connected to something.

Ouch! A cramp just shot up my right side. I'm overdoing things here. Running all hard like I got slave catchers and hound dogs on my heels. *Slow down, bruh, before you rip something.* Taking my own advice, I ease up on the pace and try to breathe deeply and ease the cramp away. I almost laugh. Dad would say God was tryna tell me something, cramping up my stride to get my attention, to slow me down before I ran into some unseen danger. Maybe it was just the opposite. Maybe evil doesn't want me to run into the truth and be made free. Take your pick.

Time to call it quits and do my cool-down stretches before leaving the track.

Reina and I are supportive of Vanessa's seeking out her parents. She has a right to know her origins, her history. Right? It might prove worthwhile. My girl could have some genetic predisposition to illness or insanity or some hereditary disorder of which she should be aware. She should have access to her origins. Then again, Vanessa might find she's kin to my ex-girlfriend and has a family full of fools and freaks, and that she's inherited a legacy of plastic-covered sofas, televisions with wire coat hangers for antennas, and relatives whose names all start with *L'-* or *Ta-* or *Sha-* and end with *-qua* or *-da*, with something sounding like coughing and sneezing and speaking in tongues in the middle.

The thought makes me laugh as I walk through the neighborhood en route home. My presence startles this forty-something nonsister pulling grocery bags from the trunk of her car. Normally I run home from the track, but I listened to the cramp and decided to stroll home at a leisurely pace. Forty-something spins around so fast that sandy blond hair whips her cheeks and a box of something falls from one of her bags and hits her driveway with a loud thud. I say, "Good evening" just to wipe that ugly look of fear from her face. She gives me a pinched little grimace that's supposed to pass for a smile. I start to step toward her and pick up the fallen box, but she inches backward up her driveway.

A scene from D.W. Griffith's 1915 film *Birth of a Nation* flashes through my mind. A fine, upstanding, Southern-bred distressed white chick is running from the affections of a newly promoted army officer, portrayed by a white man in blackface. Poor girl runs through the woods, trying to escape the dark, lecherous terror at her heels, until she comes to the edge of a dangerous precipice. There is only one clear choice in her opinion. Rather than suffer the repulsive advances of her white-man-in-blackface assailant, Fair Southern Bred jumps over the edge of the cliff and, subsequently, dies from her injuries.

I shake my head in disgust. Is this Sacramento or the South? I stand there with my big, bad black self, ready to tell forty-something to go ahead and jump. Instead, I snort disdainfully and walk on, leaving her in the dark to retrieve her little box and go indoors, where she can nuke her microwaveable meal-in-minutes in the safety of her quaint little world. *Super scrimp!*

By the time I make it home, all traces of light have completely vanished from the sky. Just diamonds called stars and a half-lidded moon to shine on my way. I can feel the soft arms of night all about me. Feels like a lover's embrace . . . I think. It's been so long since I've held anyone that I probably shouldn't be drawing such parallels or analogies.

The fact that I'm still single and solitary doesn't bother me. Much.

Now, don't get a brother wrong. I'd love to have a sweet somebody in my home, my heart, my bed. But like I told my father, I have no need to be romantically involved right now. The fellas think I'm frontin' like I'm not lonely, but for real, I'm not. I have too many things that need to be worked out.

Don't paint me stupid. My need is one thing. My wants are an entirely different bowl of ham hocks and greens.

I want that job promotion. I want my offer to be accepted on the house in Laguna. Sho' 'nuff, I want to finally have that trip to the Caribbean I've been promising myself. I want to know why Reina moved in with Vanessa, and neither one of those chickenheads told me.

I want a solid, satisfying relationship with someone I respect and who respects me in return. No, I'm not contradicting myself. I fully acknowledge that I don't *need* a relationship right now. As you can see, I have issues just like everyone else, and I prefer to deal with these things without trying to make them someone else's problems. Especially that someone whom I might want to be with me in something called love. I'd rather be up front and not clandestine with mess all up in my closet just waiting to take that special someone by surprise. I admit I'm jaded when it comes to matters of the heart. My almost-fiancée jacked me, curbsiding me for some chump pro-baller. And though it's certainly not the same situation, my first love, my mother, left me before I was ready to know pain. So I have to get my stuff straight and deal with my hurts and my head. And I will do it. One day. But not now. Still, give a brother his props, because, after all,

I'm trying to keep things real. I'm trying not to house hurts or secrets that are willing and waiting to be revealed.

I have just enough time to shower and change before picking up my girls so we can meet up with my fellas at the movies. Just enough time to consider my wants and wonder when the time for their fulfillment will come.

VANESSA

Sisters just don't live charmed lives. No such anomaly as a knight in shining armor mounted on some spectacular specimen of a steed would come galloping down the street trying to rescue a sister from an overdue phone bill and an eviction notice. Who would whisk her away from the trials of corporate life where she was constantly faced with *the others* looking at her as if her success were a mere by-product of a dying commodity called Affirmative Action? Leave it to some folks and you'd be prone to believe that her success was due to government intervention. Forget that a sister attended an Ivy League school, or was a scholastic wonder, or worked multiple jobs to support herself, an invalid parent, and five siblings all while earning an education, an honest living, or the deed to a house and a ticket out of a 'hood.

Not that all sisters live in 'hoods, mind you. Still, wasn't it fair to say that most black women have some challenge to overcome or perhaps escape? But who really validates it all? Sisters are supposed to be—expected to be—strong superwomen, amazons who move mountains. Movers and shakers in the streets, the halls of justice, the school-rooms, and the bedroom. But who would move the mountain off the sister when it collapsed on top of her? She could barely get a body to hold an elevator door open, or wash something, including the plate and fork he'd just used to shovel down her hard-earned food talking about *Dang, baby, you sure can cook. Can I get seconds?* when she didn't even offer him firsts. Charmed existence? Puhleez, that was for the birds and white girls.

Such were Vanessa's thoughts as she went about wrapping up the loose ends of her day.

Vanessa admitted it. She was in a mood. And she was being unfair. Women, people of all colors, ethnicities, nationalities, had struggles and challenges to overcome. She should not be engaged in, to quote her therapist, "an olympics of oppression," weighing and judging whose miseries were worse than whose. But yet and still, she laughed to herself, sisters had it bad sometimes, being nameless faces at the bottom of a dirty well. *We just want a little recognition from time to time,* she silently mused, expressing a little of what had her silk panties all up in a bunch in the crack of her muscled behind as she reflected on the events of her day.

Not only had last week's fund-raiser been a smashing success, garnering almost twice the pledges as it had the year before, but write-ups on the event were in the newspaper and a local lifestyle magazine, as well as honors in the column of a national magazine that circulated amid highly renowned charities and nonprofit foundations. The articles were complimentary, exuding highest praise for Sacramento's television station, KSAC, especially its director of public relations. What genius she'd displayed in including local celebrities such as athletes, musicians, politicians, and other notables in their fund-raising ad campaigns. She was savvy, practically pitting one organization against the other, leaving them to battle between themselves as to which would be the most philanthropic, who would be most charitable. Just plain brilliant in using a match-my-contribution campaign slogan. There was only one thing wrong with the write-ups: the wrong *she* was credited.

All of these things were creative storms of the brain of the assistant director of public relations, Vanessa Ann Taylor. The same Vanessa Taylor who had worked her butt off to earn a marketing degree at some overpriced university just so she could pull savvy stunts like this. Not her director. But what could Vanessa do at this point? The periodicals were already in circulation. The best she could hope for was a teeny byline in subsequent issues making corrections, giving credit to whom credit was truly due. And to think her director was partially to blame. The woman should have ensured the accuracy of the statements, properly validating Vanessa's contributions to the success of the department, the fund-raiser, and KSAC before the stories went to print.

In all fairness, her director had called her into her office and apologized to Vanessa for the shortsightedness of the reporters who'd written the columns. Still, Vanessa was unimpressed. The reporters' sight could get only as deep as KSAC's executives allowed. All of this plagiarizing and borrowing was enough to make a sister light a candle and get to chanting.

Vanessa had been tempted to call her therapist that morning, just for old times' sake. That was clue enough that she was stressed and tripping way too hard. Instead, she made herself a steaming hot cup of peppermint tea to soothe her scattered nerves. And she kept right on brewing the entire day. Vanessa had consumed enough tea to fill a swimming pool, or so her bladder screamed. And as if misquotes and racing to the bathroom every five minutes weren't bad enough, her director had made the brilliant suggestion at this morning's meeting that all company officers should sign the thank-you cards being sent to their fund-raiser contributors. Hand-sign rather than computer generate a generic closing from the company proper.

Puhleez! Didn't the woman have something better to do than wreck her life? Vanessa wasn't about to develop writer's cramp signing hundreds of cards. She pulled out her rubber signature stamp and got to stamping.

Just when she thought the day couldn't get any worse, Barbie, or Brigette, or whatever her name was—the cute little curly-haired, blue-eyed brunette intern from production—ran into Vanessa's office showing off a two-karat diamond engagement ring, squealing the news about how her Ethiopian fiancé proposed to her pale little self over dinner on a chartered yacht while cruising the Santa Barbara bay last weekend. *Ooh la la and praise da Lawd.* Vanessa was too through.

Here Bambi was squeaking about being engaged and sporting a diamond big enough to knock Mike Tyson's eye out and Vanessa couldn't even get a little return phone call from her so-called man. She hadn't heard from Keith in weeks and she refused to call him again. He'd made it perfectly clear that he didn't want to be bothered. Was that what she was to him? A bother? *Oh, brother.* Sisters just didn't live charmed lives.

Vanessa could go by his house, jump real ignorant, and pull a little

Angela in *Exhale* on him and burn his stuff or sell it all, every single stinking item, for fifty cents and a book of stamps, but she was embarrassed to admit she didn't even know where he lived. Keith had moved out of his apartment. She knew this to be true because when she drove by last week it was empty with a FOR RENT sign in the window. Her man had moved without giving her notice.

Still, Vanessa wanted to see him. Just to talk. To know what had gone wrong and why. Then maybe after they'd both had their say and just before parting ways, she would give him a little yum-yum for old times' sake, if he begged hard enough. Who was she kidding? He wouldn't even have to ask. She'd probably have her clothes off and the loving ready to roll before he could even think, *Baby, please.* Vanessa laughed at herself. "Girl, you're pitiful," she muttered in the privacy of her office after bride-to-be Barbie departed, skipping down the hallway, fiery lights flashing from her heavily studded engagement ring, only to bounce back and zap Vanessa in the face.

That was her day.

At long last it was after hours, and Vanessa wanted nothing more than to go to the gym, where she could rip off the dang-blasted silk-and-lace underwire contraption beating her breasts into submission in exchange for the comforting cotton of her sports bra before marching into Tae Bo to whip her imaginary opponent. Tonight he would have a name: Officer Keith Lymons. She'd salute him one good time before giving him the beat-down of his life. Then home she would go to soak in a hot bath spiced with fragrant sea salts and bubbling oils. Maybe she'd even place a few vanilla candles strategically about her sunken Roman tub and just lie back, her nature CDs pumping through the sound system, her eyes closed, her mind a thousand miles away. Aww, there was no place like home.

Home? Home. Reina! How in the heck could she forget a houseguest who had suddenly become a roommate? Vanessa paused in what she was doing to glance at her desk calendar. Seven days. Seven long days and long nights. Seemed more like forty, like Noah himself had kidnapped her and made her walk the plank to his ark, Reina chained to her side. She'd been so busy at work that she'd forgotten to call *Tía,* and Vanessa certainly couldn't call her from home, where Reina seemed to shadow her every move.

The spare bedroom was now Reina's domain, with her own private bathroom off the hallway. Still, it seemed as if Reina just couldn't stay out of her space. Reina was quick to lounge on Vanessa's bed when she came home from work, talking a mile a minute as Vanessa changed clothes and tried her best to unwind. Vanessa assumed Reina would respect her need for space, especially considering how she herself had desperately fought to attain a modicum of privacy while at her parents'. *Not!*

To make matters worse Reina, in her I-wanna-be-helpful-and-earn-my-keep mode, was driving Vanessa crazy with all her cooking and cleaning and reorganizing things that did not need to be cooked, cleaned, or organized in the first place. Did Reina really need to smoke a spiral ham for Sunday brunch? Vanessa did not even eat pork! Did every single box, can, bag of something need to be removed from the pantry shelves, the shelves cleaned and restocked with the edibles in alphabetical order? The *pièce de résistance* was when Reina the rambunctious maid massacred Vanessa's laundry last night.

Clothing that should have gone to the dry cleaners got tossed in the washing machine. So what if the labels did not read DRY-CLEAN ONLY and Vanessa failed to separate them out? Common sense should have told Reina that certain things just did not belong in the washing machine. But then again, common sense wasn't common. Vanessa's favorite angora sweater—the long-sleeved, dropped-back one in a delectable shade of tangerine, the one she had purchased on her one and only trip to Paris—went from a size medium to something that even a flat-chested boy would have trouble squeezing into.

Vanessa sighed. She was twenty-nine living with a twenty-eight-year-old mother. It was going to be a long winter.

Vanessa activated the speakerphone and pushed a button on her speed-dial pad with quickness.

The phone rang five times before Reina's younger brother, Raj, the rap-playing alley cat, answered. It was obvious from the soft click that hers was a call waiting. His salutation was silky-smooth seduction.

"Raj, it's Vanessa."

He immediately dropped the Barry White imitation.

" 'Sup, Vee?"

"Not too much," she responded.

"How's my boy, Pharaoh?"

"You need to come walk his wild behind like you promised."

"Yeah. I will."

"When?" Vanessa asked, closing the document she'd been working on before logging off her computer. She set about tidying her desk, arranging files, checking tomorrow's to-do list and appointments noted in the calendar section of her leather organizer.

"Aww, Vee, why you wanna sweat me? I'm a busy man."

She sucked her teeth. He chuckled lightly.

"So I heard. Is your mother home?"

"Yep, yep."

There was a pause.

"May I speak to her, please?"

"I'm on the other line with my girl. We have big things to discuss."

"What? Your ego?"

"Aw, Vee's a comedienne now." Raj laughed. "Hey, you gonna let me sport the Solara?" Raj asked, referring to the new car Vanessa had treated herself to last year.

"Ha!" Vanessa responded. "Now who's the comedian? Listen, I have to go. Will you do me a favor and tell your mother I called and that I'll try to call—"

"Naw, you can talk to the old girl. I'm through with my convo for now," Raj said. "Hold up a minute and I'll see what I can do for ya."

Vanessa shook her head. The child really was too much.

After a minute of dead air time Raj was back on the line, hollering for his mother to pick up the phone. Momentarily, she did.

"Hola, Tía," Vanessa greeted her adopted aunt.

"Hola, sweetie. How are you?" There was a too-cheerful note to the older woman's voice.

"I'm doing all right, and before you ask, yes, Reina is at my house." Despite Vanessa's urgings, Reina had refused to phone her parents with her whereabouts or to assure them that she was fine. But knowing Mr. and Mrs. Kingsley as she did, they had probably already concluded—after ensuring Reina wasn't holed up with one of her mile-long list of relatives—that she was safe and sound at Vanessa's. And knowing Mr. Kingsley, with his old stubborn self, he had most likely forbidden any- and everyone in his household from calling Vanessa to confirm the fact that his daughter was indeed there.

Reina's mother sighed with relief, the false cheer evaporating from her voice. Her tone was animated, her accent increasing along with her agitation as she meandered from English to Spanish back to

English again, going on and on about how like her father Reina was. So hotheaded and impatient. Too fast to wait for anything.

"Reina should be more logical and levelheaded like you, huh, *Tía*?"

They both laughed. Mrs. Kingsley had quite a little temper of her own, if truth be told.

"Well, maybe not. But she is so impetuous. She wants to do so much so soon."

"*Tía*, she's almost thirty years old. You can't hold on to her forever." Vanessa softened her tone respectfully, as she continued as if to soothe Mrs. Kingsley. "Still, Reina does need you, *Tía*." *And I need my house back.* "Is there anything I can do to help patch things up?" *And help Reina* pack *up?* Vanessa mused.

A long silence ensued. So long that Vanessa was afraid she'd overstepped her boundaries.

Vanessa loved the Kingsley family dearly. They'd taken her in, made a place for her in their hearts the very first time Reina brought her home to meet them on spring break during their freshman year at U.C. Berkeley. She'd been a part of the family ever since. Growing up, shuttled from foster family to foster family, Vanessa loved the steadiness of the Kingsley household. The noisy and festive holiday gatherings, family reunions, the house crowded with kinfolks fellowshipping around tables laden with Caribbean and Mexican fare were food for her soul. But Vanessa did understand Reina's point of view. It could be quite overwhelming and daunting at times. Still, Reina couldn't avoid handling her business by holing up at Vanessa's.

"You're such a sweetie. Don't worry. We'll work things out. We always do," assured *Tía*.

When? Vanessa wanted to know as Mrs. Kingsley sighed into the phone.

"You know, Vanessa, *mi hija*, my baby girl, she's the only daughter left to me, and I would do anything for her. Anything! Still, Reina must respect the rules of this house if she is to stay here."

Slipping on her designer suit jacket, Vanessa sensed reconciliation was more than a stone's throw away. Reluctantly, she resigned herself to life with Reina for a few more days. She could do it. All she needed was a couple of mantras and much Midol.

"I understand. Well, I just wanted you to know that she's with me." Lord knew Vanessa supported Reina's need for freedom from her family, but couldn't Reina get that freedom at a hotel or a mission inn somewhere? Reluctantly, Vanessa bit the bullet. "Don't worry, *Tía*, Reina's welcome to stay until things are worked out." Lord, how long would that be? Vanessa wondered, locking her desk and snapping shut her leather satchel.

"*Gracias.* She's lucky to have such a wonderful friend. See, Vanessa, that's what I try to teach my children. Be good to others and they'll be good back to you."

Vanessa felt one of *Tía's* well-intended but long-winded lectures coming on. She had to nip it in the bud if she planned to get home before dawn. Besides she had to dash to the rest room again. Peppermint tea was good on the tongue but torture on the kidneys.

"*Tía,* I'm sorry, but I have to go if I don't want to be late for Tae-Bo. Give *Tío* my love, please."

"I will, sweetie. Let us know if you need any help with the grocery bill. Reina's not a light eater."

Vanessa giggled.

"We'll be fine. Good night, *Tía.*"

"*Adiós,* sweetheart."

Her office locked, Vanessa dashed down the hall to the rest room, leather satchel bouncing against her hip, sprinting as if a gold medal awaited her in the bathroom stall. She needed relief in more ways than one.

It was after eight o'clock when Vanessa finally turned onto her street. As usual, Widow Woman next door was sitting at the window with her curtains wide open pretending to be watching television, Tripod the cat curled up on her lap. Just let something happen outdoors. That old lady would give a play-by-play description of everything and everyone involved. *Watching television, my foot,* Vanessa thought. It was more like the television was watching her.

Vanessa passed by her nosy neighbor's, pressing her automatic garage-door opener just as she noticed Chris's coupe parked at the curb. So that was why he hadn't been at the gym when she arrived. He was sitting pretty at her place.

Just great! Punching and kicking then showering at the gym had mellowed her mood until Vanessa wanted to do nothing except crawl into bed and read a bit before sleeping until the roosters crowed.

Chris was her dearest male friend, more like a brother really. He was no visitor, did not pose an imposition. But for real, though. Even Tae-Bo had kicked her butt. Vanessa was exhausted and really not in the best mood to entertain or talk to anybody, no matter how fine and dark and chocolate and well sculpted and sexy he might be. Hmmm, then again, Vanessa thought she might be able to siphon up some strength from somewhere.

She parked her car next to Reina's bright red VW and watched the garage door lower itself before unlocking the door that opened onto the laundry room and dropping her gym bag onto the floor beside the washing machine.

From the sound of their voices, Reina and Chris were in the kitchen engrossed in some animated debate regarding the pros and cons of home ownership versus rented dwellings. Chris was espousing the virtues—tax breaks, ownership, and the like—of private property, while Reina argued for the simple conveniences such as repairs and yard maintenance that a rental property afforded the single woman. Suddenly Vanessa was glad they were both there. She was en route to Washington D.C. in a few weeks for her annual National Black Broadcasters' Association convention, and while there she would follow a lead one of her sorority sisters had given her, a lead that led to Vanessa's birth parents.

With newfound excitement, Vanessa hurried through the laundry room toward the kitchen, prepared to call a greeting and share her exciting news, when it hit her head on. *Pow!* Like a fat fist to the stomach was the smell of frying fish. Vanessa just about gagged and might have vomited had she consumed anything other than tea in the past several hours.

How many times did she have to tell Reina that she did not fry food in her house? She did not eat fried food. She did not like the smell of fried food. She did not like the look of fried food. Food was not meant to be dredged in oil. Steam it, broil it, bake it, shake it. Vanessa could care less. Just don't—never, never, ever, ever—fry it. Especially not in *her* kitchen. And heaven forbid that Vanessa should find an old can of Crisco on the stovetop filled with even older recycled grease floating in it, cornmeal stuck to its ridged sides.

"Hey, gorgeous!" Chris called, looking all dark and delectable, turning around on the raised stool where he sat at the chef island in the middle of the kitchen playing tug-of-war with Pharaoh. Pharaoh barked, dropping his end of the chew toy, and rushed toward her, abruptly stopping before jumping on her, as he was prone to do. The look on Vanessa's face must have spoken a thousand words that even Pharaoh could comprehend.

"Hi, roomie. How was—" Reina turned from the stove, took one look at Vanessa's face, and swallowed her sentence. "What's wrong with you?"

Vanessa didn't—couldn't—say a word. Instead she walked slowly, purposefully toward Reina and the stove. Vanessa's apron that she'd bought while on a business trip in New Orleans—the one with a picture of a smiling crab and a seafood gumbo recipe printed on the front—strained to wrap itself about Reina's multiple waistlines until the painted crab looked as if it were crying for help. Vanessa flipped a switch on the hood above the stove. The fan whirred into action.

"Reina, I thought I asked you not to fry food in here."

"Okay," she sang. "Where do you want me to fry it? In the linen closet?"

Chris cracked up. Vanessa ignored him.

"Besides," Reina offered, "I closed the doors to all the other rooms so the smell wouldn't get in."

"Like funk can't creep," Vanessa retorted, barely missing Chris's hand as she plopped her heavy briefcase atop the center island.

"Why you wanna maim a brother, gorgeous?"

Vanessa shot him an irritated look.

"Chris, please."

"Dag, Vee, it's just a little fish," Reina interjected defensively, wiping her hands on a kitchen towel.

"And it's just my kitchen," Vanessa responded as she headed toward the refrigerator. She suddenly needed something cool to drink. "And I prefer it not smell like some greasy-spoon diner."

"Oh, I see. Well, forgive me for stepping outside the lines, Roland Kingsley," Reina tossed. "I promise not to violate any more of *your* rules in *your* house, 'cause, after all, I'm just a guest." Reina extinguished the heat beneath the nonstick skillet and pushed the skillet onto a burner at the back of the stove. Hot grease sloshed about the sizzling fillets, spilling over and onto the stovetop as Vanessa walked past, snapping the cap from her bottle of chilled Evian water.

"Doggone it, Ree-Ree, you almost burned me!" Vanessa hurled the accusation in Reina's innocent-looking face. "You did that deliberately."

"I did not!" her best friend protested.

"You did too," Vanessa insisted, her topaz eyes fiery with disbelief. "Chris, did you see that?"

Chris rubbed a hand over the smooth waves of his short-cropped hair.

"Actually, I didn't. I was too busy watching you rip the head off that water bottle."

"Fine! Just fine." Vanessa found a can of country mist-scented room deodorizer in a cabinet and shook the container violently before generously dousing the air.

The kitchen took on an aroma of flowery funk.

"Really, Vanessa, is it that serious?" Reina chuckled, sliding onto the empty bar stool next to Chris. "Why the sudden aversion? Girl, you grew up on pork chops and fatback like the rest of us."

Vanessa pivoted, aimed the aerosol in Reina's direction, and showered her at point-blank range.

Reina launched into a wheezing, coughing fit accented by her gasping and flailing of arms. Chris was off of his seat, patting Reina soundly on the back, just about ready to administer CPR if the need arose.

"I n-need my inhaler," Reina wheezed, tears in her eyes.

"Where is it?" Chris asked.

Reina pointed to a kitchen drawer. Chris retrieved the bright yellow apparatus, which Reina practically snatched and popped between her lips to administer the medication. Within seconds her heaving ceased and her breathing returned to normal.

"Are you all right?"

Reina nodded, wiping tears from her eyes. "Yes," she croaked.

"Vanessa, you're really not right," Chris admonished, looking at Vanessa as if she had a couple too many screws loose.

"Yeah, and I'm really not feeling either of you, so poof-pow!" Vanessa shot back, flashing the palm of her hand for emphasis. She let out a short whistle and Pharaoh was instantly at her side. "Come on, baby, let's go." The canine obediently followed her as Vanessa marched down into the adjoining sunken den to unlock and push open the sliding glass door. She snatched back the floor-to-ceiling blinds to allow the air to freely flow. Vanessa returned to the kitchen just long enough to pull a tiny, rose-shaped crystal pot from an over-head cabinet and plug it into the wall socket nearest the stove before filling its base with loose leaf and liquid potpourri.

"Stop funking up my kitchen, Reina."

"Yeah, all right, wench," Reina shot back, sufficiently recovered from her breathing episode. "Don't hate me 'cause you can't cook. Always grilling or steaming something, with your broiled bat– and boiled cat–eating self."

"Yeah, whatever, stank."

"It takes no skills to peel a carrot, 'Nessa. You got all this kitchen and for what? What do you need with a Thermador oven and all these fancy gadgets?" Reina demanded with a sweeping gesture of an arm. "You *ain't* no gourmet. The only thing you know how to burn is water and incense."

"Like I said, stop funking up my kitchen," Vanessa yelled over her shoulder as she floated up the staircase, hoping to somehow eradicate the smell of potpourri-scented fish from her senses.

That was nearly two hours ago. By ten o'clock that same evening, Vanessa was sitting at a table in the middle of the Set listening to some seriously smooth jazz, her disposition much improved. Thanks to Chris. With his usual debonair style, Chris had entered her bedroom ten minutes after her grand exit, sat in the overstuffed chair to play with its gold-and-black-embroidered throw pillow while listening to Vanessa uncork her vat of woes without judgment or censure. She was tired of the okey-doke at work, tired of Reina's intrusiveness, tired of wondering whatever happened to Keith's stank behind. Vanessa was just tired. Chris listened, he commiserated, but he still told Vanessa she was wrong for acting the disgruntled diva and coming in the house telling folks their food stank in so many ugly ways.

"You just made it worse, gorgeous, with that potpourri bit of yours. Now the house smells like fishy fruit."

Vanessa had to laugh. Chris had a way of making her see herself in all her foulness without causing her to feel condemned. Thank God she had found this man who wanted nothing more than friendship from her. They'd met during Vanessa's last semester in college. Ten credits away from graduation, Vanessa had moved back to Sacramento to complete an internship at KSAC while completing another class via independent study. Chris was working as a part-time courier while trying to secure a job at Valley Fitness. They would stand in the television station lobby chatting whenever Chris made a delivery, Vanessa extending her break just to shoot an extra breeze with the ultrafine brother. They'd been tight ever since, Chris showing himself a true and loyal friend.

And he was right. Vanessa had mishandled the situation. But at least, she congratulated herself, she did not turn vicious and let anger send things over the top. Nevertheless, when Reina finally made her humble way into her highness's boudoir, Vanessa apologized. Even though she *had* asked Reina not to fry food in the house, especially fish, even though Reina was in the wrong, Vanessa apologized for being less than kind. What a centering moment. Her therapist would have been so proud. Feeling loads lighter, Vanessa pulled herself from bed, freshened up, and changed into something simply sexy, glad to accept her friends' invitation to join them at the Set.

The Set was a newly established club owned by one of Chris's frat brothers who, having made some serious windfall earnings on a stock investment he'd made some years ago, decided to turn his earnings over into another potential revenue maker: a nightclub. Perhaps that was putting things too simply. The Set was a bit more than your standard hole-in-the wall velvet lounge with plastic potted plants and tin ashtrays where polyester-clad, gold-plated-medallion-dripping mack daddies went to ply their outdated rap. There was great food and a wonderful ambiance, and the Set featured some of the best contemporary jazz artists a music connoisseur could ask for.

It was obvious that the owner had put much thought and preparation into his venture. While comfortably seating close to two hundred patrons, the Set, still a relatively new and secret gem, maintained a quaint, cozy atmosphere. The Set was situated on prime riverfront property surrounded by boutiques and shops, restaurants, and the marina. Strategically situated, the Set was the only music venue within miles. There were no nearby competitors to rival its position. But even if there had been, the Set could hold its own. It had ambiance. It felt safe. Sisters could sit there and enjoy the music, the food, the company without feeling pressed by some idiot trying to find a little honey to take home at the end of the night. Unless of course that was what she was looking for, which Vanessa was not, so the Set suited her just right.

Vanessa was flowing, enjoying the silky sounds of the saxophone being blown by a seriously fine Nubian lock-sporting Rasta brother onstage as she sipped her iced herbal tea, and occasionally munched on a raw carrot stick or cauliflower from the vegetable platter she shared with Reina. As usual, Reina was defeating her own purpose, daintily drowning the vegetables in some god-awful ranch dressing she'd ordered on the side. Well, at least Reina was eating raw vegetables for a change, instead of the fried zucchini sticks, onion blossoms, and mozzarella fingers with marinara sauce Reina normally ordered as an appetizer. *Maybe my good habits are finally rubbing off,* Vanessa prematurely congratulated herself just as their waitress returned, setting a plateload of buffalo wings, BBQ riblets, seasoned fries, and a large diet Dr. Pepper at Reina's fingertips.

Reina offered her plate around the table, sharing with their crew, consisting of Chris and Vanessa, and three fellas from Chris's NBA brotherhood—one with a girlfriend who clung to her man's arm as if everyone including the waiters wanted him. Reina extended the plate in Vanessa's direction, knowing full well Vanessa would rather run barefoot over a mile of boiling-hot hog maws than eat any of the slop on that plate. Head tilted down, fingers softly drumming the tablecloth, Vanessa gave Reina her best *girl, puhleez* look and snapped a carrot stick between her pearly teeth.

"You don't know what you're missing," Reina teased, popping a sauce-drenched riblet into her mouth.

"Just pulmonary disease, hypertension, and blocked arteries," Vanessa answered, which sent Cling-a-ling—the one holding her man's arm so tight his circulation was probably cut off—into a fit of giggles that sounded like a flock of seagulls cawing at high tide. Reina and Vanessa exchanged glances. Vanessa ran an index finger along her hairline, pausing at her temple, their secret sister code for "the girl is touched." Reina cracked up, covering her mouth with her napkin so she wouldn't shower diet Dr. Pepper on everyone.

Just then the houselights went up and the audience set off a round of wild applause as the band exited the stage for intermission. The house deejay took over, pumping up some danceable beats.

"Come on, honey, let's get our groove on," Cling-a-ling sang, pulling her man from his chair and onto the dance floor surrounding the modest stage. One of the brotherhood pushed his chair back and grabbed Vanessa's hand, just about dragging her from her seat, before she could even decline his nonoffer to shake her groove thing with him. Chris was about to ask Reina to dance, but a weave-wearing, lavender contacts–having, silicone cleavage–sporting woman in a too-tight leopard-print catsuit was in his face before he could get the words out.

"Care to dance, handsome?" she purred, sounding like a second-rate Eartha Kitt on five packs of smokes a day. Chris looked to Reina, but she was too engrossed in her sample platter to care. Chris shrugged his shoulders and allowed Catwoman to lead him away.

That left Reina with one of the brotherhood. Sweat beaded on his upper lip. He looked around the room as if searching for a sign of rescue. Finding none, he finally croaked out a stuttered invitation to Reina to join him on the dance floor. She declined. He breathed a sigh of relief and excused himself to the rest room. Reina kept eating as if she hadn't noticed a thing.

Vanessa saw it all from where she moved to the groove, trying to keep her toes from being smashed by Chris's three-left-feet-having frat brother. It pained her to see her friend sitting there alone, so engrossed in food that she was missing out on the world around her. It had to hurt Reina, too.

Reina, as if sensing Vanessa's gaze, looked up, made eye contact with her best friend, smiled, and waved. Vanessa waved back, maneuvering around her dance partner, turning her back to him so that she was facing Reina directly, and mouthed an exaggerated *Help!* Reina just laughed and made shooing motions with her hands, indicating that she couldn't be bothered. Vanessa was on her own.

"Hey-y-y-y," her dance partner chimed, taking Vanessa's position toward Reina as an invitation to bump against her backside like a dog in heat. Vanessa spun around, all indignant, biting her lower lip so she wouldn't go off. Three Left Feet misinterpreted her chewing on her lip as a provocative invitation. "Girl, you truly are fine. When can I get with you?" His radar was way off. No hoochie here.

When hell freezes and the devil takes up ice-skating, Vanessa thought. Instead she merely said, "Never." And with that she turned and would have walked away except something, or someone, caught her eye.

Vanessa whirled to her right, toward the exit, and saw an all-too-familiar physique. Or so she thought. Was that really Keith climbing the stairs? Could that possibly be Keith, black leather pants gripping his thighs like an indecent lover, sauntering up the stairs, his left hand pressed against the small of some woman's back? No, that just could not, no way, be the good officer Keith Lymons whispering something in that woman's ear. Something that caused her to throw her head back, bright red ringlets spilling over her shoulders, and laugh as if the world belonged to her. Vanessa closed her eyes, counted to ten— or she would have, but she lost count at five—inhaled, exhaled deeply. *Memo to me: I am in control.* She pressed her hands, palms down, against the flat of her belly. *Anger does not rule me. I* am *in control!*

"Hey, Vanessa, are you okay?" no-dancing Mr. Brotherhood asked. Vanessa opened her eyes and looked at the man, then back at the now-empty staircase. A figment of her imagination? She wasn't sure. Perhaps she'd eaten one carrot stick, one cauliflower blossom too many. Or maybe she truly was meat deprived—in more ways than one.

An hour later, Vanessa was sure she was losing it. She should have known better than to tell Reina she'd thought she'd caught a glimpse of Keith at the club with some mystery woman. Should have known Reina would fly off the handle and work up a plan. Roots ran in Reina's blood. Just look at her crazy grandmother, with all her dried herbs and chicken feet tied with string, hanging upside down from ceiling hooks in "the Room," as Reina and Vanessa had come to call the place where *Abuela* did whatever it was she did. Scheming. Reina was good for it. Maybe that was why Vanessa told her in the first place. On a subconscious level, perhaps she did want Reina to convince her to do something completely wacky and wicked, completely confrontational or out of character. Driving around after midnight looking for an unknown residence certainly fit the bill.

Being proactive was far better than passively sitting around waiting for nothing to happen—looking all pitiful and dry in the mouth was the way Reina phrased it. It did make sense. Still, Vanessa had come too far in her anger-management therapy to turn around. Furthermore, she didn't consider herself impetuous like Reina, or audacious like Chris. What would Keith think?

Keith had always complimented Vanessa for her levelheaded maturity, stability, and having-it-together style. He had even praised her having gone to therapy to deal with her issues. And there she was, sitting in the front passenger seat of Chris's luxury coupe, slinking around the streets of Sacramento like a lioness on the prowl. She was definitely losing it.

"Vanessa, are you sure you want to do this?" Chris asked as if picking up on her uncertainty. Vanessa glanced at the play of light and shadow cast against Chris's strong, scrum-deli-icious profile. The sandalwood of his French cologne tickled her nostrils.

"Of course she's sure," Reina answered from the backseat, where she watched the street signs with bright, hawklike eyes.

"Thank you, Mother, but I can speak for myself," Vanessa interjected. Reina merely snapped her gum and commenced to humming in perfect pitch with Rachelle Ferrell's satin crooning floating from the car's audio system, never straying from her valiant watch of the street signs. "And, anyhow, how did you get his new address so fast?" Vanessa asked, turning in her seat toward Reina.

Reina's smile was bright, sly in the dark car. "I never reveal my sources."

"I'll bet you'll sing like a bird if I turn you in to the authorities," Vanessa replied.

"I'll name you as an accessory in a heartbeat."

"You probably would, too, stank."

"Wench."

Chris laughed and muttered, "You two are sick."

"Whatever," Vanessa and Reina simultaneously uttered.

"How *did* you get the good officer's address, beautiful?" Chris glanced at Reina in the rearview mirror. "One of the privileges of working for my least favorite state agency?"

"DMV has its good points," Reina responded, and laughed. "Slow down!" she suddenly shouted. "Turn around; I think we just passed our street." Reina was leaning forward in her seat, hands gesturing and pointing. "No, not that one. Go up one more block. There!" You would have thought she'd just won a year's supply of curly fries and diet Dr. Pepper, Reina was so excited.

Vanessa suddenly felt sick. Her insides were in knots. She wanted to toss open the car door, curl up like a ball, bounce to the curb, and run home screaming like a banshee. Instead, she examined the long, tree-lined residential street they'd just turned onto. *What am I doing?* she asked herself, growing increasingly uncomfortable with the situation, the majesty of the late February night mocking her cowardice.

Vanessa sobered as a two-story brick house with an upper balcony outside the master bedroom, its decorative wrought-iron railing burdened with lush ivy, came into view. The house reminded her of the home of her final foster family. The lush and luxurious house of her terror and pain. She closed her eyes and blocked out ugly memories of leering looks and hard hearts.

"That's it!" she heard Reina exclaim. Slowly Vanessa opened her eyes, afraid to look. To her relief, Reina pointed to a modest gray-and-white house across from the two-story brick terror. Tiny red lanterns outlined stone steps leading from the curb, through the immaculately kept yard to the front porch. Brass numbers ran down the outer wall to the right of the front door, boldly declaring the address even in the dark. The house was charming, cottagelike in appearance, yet large enough to accommodate a growing family. It was the house of Vanessa's childhood fantasies, her grown wanting-a-man-to-share-her-world-with womanish dreams. Keith had moved out of his apartment and gone and bought a house, and without her. How utterly sad.

The structure was dark, save for a faint glow that seemingly emanated from a room deep within its interior. As if the light were cast into her own being, Vanessa suddenly realized how absolutely ignorant the entire scheme truly was.

"Let's not do this," she said. "It's disrespectful."

"What!" Reina yelled, practically blowing out Vanessa's left eardrum. "The man owes you an explanation, 'Nessa. He walked out on you. He's the one who just stopped coming around. He's the one who showed up at the Set with some Clairol-coated skeezer on his arm. Who's disrespecting whom over here? Listen, 'Nessa, don't be a—"

"Reina." Chris's soft utterance of her name was enough to silence Reina's tirade. She flopped back in her seat, folded her plump arms as far across her burgeoning bosom as they would stretch, and fumed.

"Vanessa, the choice is yours," Chris soothed, probing deep into Vanessa's eyes. "We can turn around and go home right now. Or you could be the woman you are, get out of this car, and go talk to your man. You have nothing to be ashamed of. He's the one hiding something."

Vanessa swallowed her fear, her guilt, and her shame. Chris was right. She was the one dealing on the straight up-and-up. She had been nothing except forthright and frank with Keith. She'd shared her deep secrets and painful truths with him. Was she to be repaid with lies, avoidance, silence, and grief? Not knowing what was really going on had to be worse than the truth. Right?

Vanessa stilled her nerves, wiped a clammy palm against the soft fabric of her sarong skirt, and stepped from the vehicle.

"Wait, 'Nessa," Reina called. Vanessa turned back, anxiously hoping Reina had come to her senses and was ready to help Vanessa come to hers. Reina's plump fingers were stretched toward her, a stick of gum clasped between them.

"Here, girl, freshen your grill. Can't get in your man's face with bad breath."

Vanessa slammed the car door, barely missing Reina's fingers in the process.

The sound of frogs croaking, insects buzzing, and the soft click of the heels of Vanessa's fashionable midheeled pumps were the only sounds of the night as Vanessa walked the seemingly endless distance across the street, up the red lantern–illuminated steps, and to the front door of the home belonging to Officer Keith Lymons, one of Sacramento P.D.'s finest.

He'd really left her no choice, Vanessa rationalized while trying to stir up the strength to ring the doorbell. Her phone calls went unanswered. Then he'd had the nerve to appear in public, at the Set, with someone else. Didn't he know Vanessa frequented the Set? He obviously wanted to be caught in his indiscretion. He wanted to be dealt with.

No, wait. Perhaps Vanessa merely thought the man she saw was Keith. After all, she'd never seen his face. *Get real, girl,* she told herself. A glimpse of his face was far from necessary. Those hip-hugging leather pants told the truth and nothing but, so help her God. Keith had been at the club.

Vanessa squared her shoulders, calmed her spirit, and counted backward from ten. And then she did it: she turned and walked away back toward the waiting automobile. Well, at least two steps. Then reality struck. She had a right to be here. She had a right to the truth. She at least had a right to get played to her face, to have her man be a man and tell her straight out that it was all over, that she was last month's flavor. Resuming a defiant stance before the door, Vanessa rang the bell and waited for fate to have its perfect work. She suddenly felt like doing a little Doris Day and singing "Que Será, Será," whatever will be will be.

More than a minute passed before Vanessa heard the sound of the dead bolt turning. The door swung inward just slightly. From the back of the house, along with a soft light in the otherwise dark dwelling, came the sound of violins and other stringed instruments. Classical music. Unlike Vanessa, Keith did not like classical music. But obviously she did.

Vanessa stood there on the dark porch, face-to-face with a very attractive, very slender, thirty-something-ish woman close to her own five-foot, six-inch height. The woman stood there in the dimly lit entryway, her body wrapped in a plush navy blue robe, a towel wrapped about her head, two crystal flutes and an unopened bottle of some beverage gripped between the slim, pale fingers of her left hand that was adorned by a huge, sparkling teardrop diamond set in gold so burnished it appeared silver.

"Yes. May I help you?" she asked in a slightly raspy voice laced with a hint of something Southern, something sultry. Something that hinted at pleasures had, pleasures known, and not too long ago. She had to repeat herself before Vanessa responded.

"Oh . . . I-I'm so sorry. I have the wrong house."

The woman frowned, her brows knitting, tiny crow's-feet etching the corners of her startlingly green eyes.

"Who were you looking for? I know most of my neighbors, so I might be able to help," she offered, Southern hospitality oozing from her voice and her seemingly fearless demeanor demonstrated by her opening the door of her home to a perfect stranger in the middle of God's night.

Vanessa felt like a fool. What could she possibly hope to accomplish when she couldn't even find the right house?

"No, thank you, really. I've made a huge mistake." Vanessa backed away. "I'm really sorry to have disturbed you."

"It's okay. I've done worse," the woman said, laughing at herself. "Hope you find whomever it is you're looking for, honey. Must be a special man for you to go through all this trouble. But I understand. I'm a newlywed myself and I know love can make you crazy."

Vanessa tried to smile at the gregarious stranger, but she feared her face would crack into a thousand pieces. She turned to leave, uttering another apology as she did. She hurried down the stone steps, pausing for some inexplicable reason at the curb. Vanessa cast one final glance over her shoulder. The green-eyed woman was closing the door when suddenly she lost her grip on one of the glasses in her hands. It crashed to the floor, shattering into myriad pieces. Vanessa watched the woman gingerly place the remaining flute and bottle on a table against the entrance wall. She watched the woman stoop to pick up the broken pieces of her once lovely glass, a tendril of freshly shampooed hair escaping the towel wound about her head as she did so. Vanessa watched the woman wince as a shard nicked her finger. Watched the woman place the injured finger to her lips and whisk the wayward ringlet of auburn hair behind her ear.

Vanessa turned away, somehow feeling as if she intruded upon something private. Vanessa started back toward the car until she heard the voice.

"Who was at the door?"

"Some poor woman," Red Ringlets replied, closing the door firmly, blocking their inner sanctum from Vanessa's view.

Vanessa spun about so fast she felt dizzy. Visions rushed over her with the force of a flash flood.

Keith climbing the stairs at the club, his left hand at the small of her back.

Bright red ringlets spilling over her shoulders as she laughed as if she owned the world.

Her blood raced.

Vanessa retraced her steps, counting each one just to keep from breaking down. Some poor woman, indeed!

Eleven, she concluded. Eleven steps back to the door behind which his nasty, trifling, unfaithful behind hid with his Clairol-coated skeezer-of-the-month. Vanessa rang the doorbell, counting thirty seconds before it was opened once again.

Sure enough, there he was hunkered down on thickly muscled haunches, painstakingly sweeping glass fragments into a dust pan.

Red Ringlets—a green-eyed, creamy-skinned, picture-perfect Southern belle—stood there saying something that Vanessa failed to hear as her gaze stayed locked on the good Officer Lymons, nude save for the brief towel about his trim waist. Casting a nervous glance over her shoulder, the woman shifted her body forward as if to shield Keith's nakedness.

"Puhleez! Everything that man has I've already tasted and seen," Vanessa hurled, her hands itching to lay a stranglehold on something or someone.

He sprang up and to his feet. The dustpan fell to the ground unheeded, spewing its contents every which way.

"W-w-what are y-you doing here?" Keith hollered, his voice breaking and squeaking as if he had yet to hit puberty.

"You know her?" the suddenly wide-eyed Southern beauty asked.

"In the biblical sense of the word," Vanessa tersely supplied. "And you are?"

"His wife," the woman responded, taken aback by the vehemence of Vanessa's tone.

"*His wife?*" Vanessa was dumbfounded.

"Yes," the woman slowly repeated, "I'm Tessa Jankowski." She flashed her diamond-studded wedding band as if to confirm the fact. "Oops." She giggled. "Correction, Tessa *Lymons*. I keep doing that. We're newlyweds," the new Mrs. Lymons explained, glancing over her shoulder to cast a dreamy-eyed stare at her new husband. "Ours was a whirlwind romance."

Keith just stood there dumb as a doornail.

Vanessa covered her face with her hands. Keith married? A newlywed? He'd finally jumped the broom, and with *her*? *Good God in Zion.* Life was messing with her head.

Lord, please tell me I'm dreaming, and if I am let me pee in the bed and wake myself up. Please!

Vanessa lowered her hands, only to find they were all still there and her hind parts were yet dry.

"Well, Tessa, I'm Vanessa. Vanessa Taylor."

"Oh, *you're* Miss Taylor!" Mrs. Lymons exclaimed, pulling the collar of her bathrobe closer about her neck with one hand while reaching for Vanessa with the other. Before she could react, Tessa Lymons was gripping Vanessa's hand in what was meant to be a warm and friendly handshake. The woman's hand was incredibly cool and her grip very strong. "Oh, you poor thing. I hope everything's better for you now that your stalking incident is resolved."

Vanessa shivered and freed her hand from Tessa Lymons's overly friendly grasp.

"Stalking incident?"

Tessa Lymons was all sympathy and sugar.

"Oh, I hope you don't mind me knowing about that," she apologized before explaining, "I met Keith right when he was wrapping up that undercover sting at your house. It must have given you great peace of mind knowing you had a police officer there to protect you. I don't know what I'd do if a serial stalker came after me—"

Vanessa, her mouth wide open, didn't hear another conciliatory word Tessa Lymons had to offer. Serial stalker? She looked around as if Rod Serling would pop out of the bushes and welcome her to the Twilight Zone.

Vanessa finally understood why Keith Lymons had been missing in action for weeks on end. He was busy wooing, then wedding his wife. And his wife? Poor thing was either dim or delusional. Sure, the man had been on an undercover sting, but not the type she imagined. Vanessa could only shake her head in utter disbelief. The good officer Keith Lymons was a pathological liar, a buster, a played-out, pathetic excuse for a mortal with a too-twisted imagination.

"Stalking incident," Vanessa scoffed, glaring at Keith. "How about I just stalk up in here and beat your—"

Keith came to life. He rushed forward, pushing his wife behind him.

"Uh-h-h, Miss T-T-Taylor, it's after hours now," he informed Vanessa in his most official voice while slowly closing the door, "so anything you need can wait until—"

Thud!

The closing door made contact with the shoe Vanessa wedged in between it and the doorjamb. She kicked the door free of Keith's grasp, much to his surprise.

Vanessa stood there, refusing to be dismissed. She inhaled so deeply her lungs hurt. She was tired, and she was sleepy. And after her earlier funky-fish episode with Reina, Vanessa just didn't think she had it in her to go there and go off one more time tonight. But somehow she'd manage.

"Oh, so it's like that, huh? I'm yesterday's headline?"

"Listen, you, just leave," Keith ominously advised. "This is not the time or place for your crazy histrionics."

"Crazy? Me?" She placed a hand on her chest. "I'm not crazy." She chuckled. "I'm just a distressed stalking victim, Mr. Undercover Officer, sir."

Vanessa thought her voice remained level, cool, and collected. But several neighborhood dogs set to barking. The porch light flickered on next door. Tessa Lymons said something about calling the station before disappearing deeper into the house. And somewhere in the back of her mind Vanessa thought she heard a car door open and close, followed by the sound of footsteps on pavement. But she was unsure.

"Yeah, well, whatever you are, just raise up off of my property before I haul your stupid self to jail for trespassing," Keith snarled, glancing over his shoulder as if to make sure his wife was out of earshot.

"Say wha-huh? I better . . . before you . . . Oh, okay, I feel you now, Quasimodo," Vanessa tossed, slowly and deliberately removing her earrings and dropping them into her skirt pocket before kicking off one shoe, then the other.

"Is everything okay here?" Chris asked, his deep voice sweeping over Vanessa's shoulder.

"Oh, it's about to be," Vanessa assured him.

"Keith? Tessa? What's going on over there? Need any help?" a voice called from next door. Vanessa glanced away just long enough to make out the figure of an elderly, portly couple standing on the porch clad in matching flannel robes, the woman with a frilly sleep bonnet on her head, a fluffy white something that was supposed to pass for a dog clutched in her arms.

"Thanks, Norm. We're fine," Keith called, poking his head out the door and waving, a saccharine smile masking his angry face.

"Sure you don't want us to call the cops?" the neighbor asked before chuckling. "That's a good one. You *are* the cops."

"That's not necessary. Everything's under control. Just a little misunderstanding," Keith assured the man, easing back into the safety of his house.

"Misunderstanding?" Reina was there now. Vanessa heard her come up behind Chris. "No, he is not trying to play you like a crazy corn-fed fool, 'Nessa."

"Ladies, I think it's best that we leave before things get out of control," Chris cautioned.

Keith snickered.

"Yeah, dude, take your happy little hoochie"—he tossed his head at Vanessa—"and her hungry-looking oompah-loompah friend off my property before I really get upset."

"Oh, no, no, no. Did he call me a happy hoochie?" Vanessa looked at Reina, amazed.

Reina pushed Chris aside to plant herself firmly by Vanessa's side.

"Either that or an oompah loompah," Reina returned, "because I know he wasn't talking to me with his premature-ejaculating self. What did you call it, 'Nessa? Oh, yeah, two-second sex."

Keith came at them, bristling something fierce. Chris stepped forward, intending to situate himself as a human shield between Vanessa and the growling monster hulking toward her, not sure what Keith's intent was, but trying to make certain a physical altercation did not occur.

Pow!

He was too late. The right hook flew past Chris and landed soundly against its intended target. There was silence, then a moan of intense pain.

The three friends stood, stunned, as Officer Keith Lymons crumpled against the wall of his dimly lit entryway.

"No-o-o-o!" Her wail was louder than the sirens in the far distance. Tessa Lymons reappeared, scurrying over to her husband, who held his jaw as if experiencing incredible agony. She flipped on the light switch on the wall before grabbing her husband about the waist and helping him sink down onto the floor where he sat, moaning. "Oh, sweet precious Lamb of God," Mrs. Lymons cried. "What happened?"

Dazed, Keith could only point Vanessa's way.

"You hurt him? You hurt my pookie-wookie!" Tessa Lymons screamed, rushing toward Vanessa, the towel falling from about her head, her hands flailing wildly, crying as if someone had just crowned her Miss America.

Vanessa raised her hands to merely push the thrashing woman away, but her hand got caught on something furry. It wrapped itself about Vanessa's hands and wouldn't let go.

"Ahhh!" Vanessa screamed, breaking the furry creature's grasp, flinging it away.

It landed on Reina's shoulder.

Reina hollered and hurled the fur monster so that it landed slightly askew atop Chris's head.

Chris yanked it down and the three comrades stared. There in the palms of his hands lay long, fluffy red ringlets.

Tessa Lymons stood there peeved to no end, her scalp bald except for a few patches of dull-looking crimson curls scattered here and there.

She snatched the furry hairpiece from Chris's hands.

"I'll take that, thank you," she snapped. "Never get your hair pressed, dyed, and French-braided all in the same day," she advised in her raspy Southern drawl, plopping her hair atop her head. "At least not at Madame Ebony's."

Vanessa stood, transfixed. Keith groaned. Dogs barked and Norm-the-neighbor continued calling across the distance as the sound of sirens drew increasingly near.

"Let's go, gorgeous," Chris whispered, grabbing Vanessa by the arm. Reina was already beating a path back to the car.

"And to think I used to have an abundance of beautiful, naturally curly brown hair," Tessa Lymons chattered to herself, resituating her wig. "But no, I just had to be a California fly girl and get all that color and those braidy thingies."

"Let's move it!" Chris urged, pulling Vanessa along behind him while Tessa Lymons was too busy lamenting her long-gone locks to care what happened until her husband's whining cut through her reverie so that she rushed over to cradle him in her arms.

Chris put the coupe in motion and sped toward the end of the street.

"Wait!" Vanessa hollered.

"What?" Chris barked as they turned the corner, only to pull over so that what appeared to be a squadron of police cars heading in the opposite direction could pass.

"I left my shoes," Vanessa cried.

"You can get a new pair in jail." Reina cackled. "Did you see all those cop cars? That Looney-Tune woman probably reported an officer down."

"Well, he was, technically," Chris snapped, glancing at Vanessa. "You could have gotten us all arrested. Remind me never to go anywhere with either of you ever again."

"Oh, be quiet, Boo," Vanessa fussed, thinking about how she'd gotten up at six-thirty last Saturday morning just to be at Nordstrom when the doors opened in order to save an extra 5 percent on those shoes. She should have stayed in bed and bought a pack of Certs for what she saved. "Besides, I know Keith. He wouldn't press charges because he wouldn't want anyone knowing he'd been beaten down by a woman."

Chris chuckled.

"I have to give it to you, gorgeous, that right upper cut to the brother's jaw was sweet."

"Tae Bo, baby," Vanessa replied.

"Mrs. Lymons ought to tie a bow around that wig so it doesn't come flying off anymore," Reina cracked.

There was a moment's silence before the three burst into laughter that lasted the entire ride home. Vanessa eased into bed some thirty minutes later, gratified that the mystery of the missing Keith was finally resolved. She should have been crushed but she wasn't. The entire episode culminating in tonight's bizarre scene was too comical for Vanessa to care. She drifted off to sleep thinking, *Lord, what a day, what a day!*

REINA

I'm still hurting, I laughed so hard, Reina typed with lightning-fast fingers, then pressed Enter, sending her on-line instant message across the Internet. Reina grinned, recalling the midnight debacle that had certainly taken Vanessa's trifling tramp by complete surprise.

The boy was married. Married! And to a white woman.

Okay, so really, his wife's racial identity did not matter to Reina, especially in light of her own colors-of-the-world heritage. The woman could have been orange with green polka dots and that wouldn't change the fact that Robocop had sneaked off and tied the knot.

Chris's reply came back a minute later, the letters flashing bright yellow against the turquoise backdrop of Reina's computer screen.

LOL, Chris typed, using the cyberspace abbreviation for "laughing out loud." *I almost felt bad for the brother lying there holding his jaw and crying. And his wife? Is she crazy or what?*

Reina giggled and replied.

Certifiable! I don't care how thick and "naturally curly" your WHITE hair is, you don't sit up in a SISTER'S salon chair and ask to have your hair PRESSED and dyed and cornrowed. Marrying black don't make you black.

Chris's reply was swift.

Sister probably fixed her on purpose for stealing one of the brothers.

Shoot, I oughta steal some of Abuela's roots and fix Robo Cop. Make him impotent or sterile, or just dry it up and drop it off.

She took a sip of lukewarm mocha mint coffee and awaited Chris's reply.

Remember jail: I'm not trying to go. I thought your grandmother quit the conjure business years ago.

Reina snickered.

So she says, but I don't believe her, because I found some chicken feet rolled up in newspaper on Abuela*'s back porch last week. When I asked her why she needed them she told me she was making gumbo.*

ROFL, Chris typed, meaning "rolling on the floor laughing." *You're too much. Sorry, but I have to go. Have a few things to finish up before my next exercise victim arrives.*

Reina glanced at the neon green heart-shaped clock on her desk and was surprised to see an hour had passed since she'd begun having such illicit electronic fun with Chris. She sighed and returned her attention to the words on her screen. *Tell my girl to hang in there. And remind me never to eat any of your grandmother's gumbo. Later, beautiful.*

Later, Chris. Holler at ya—

"Hey, Reina."

"Wha-huh?" Reina's chair creaked and groaned as she spun about. "Dang, girl, you're always sneaking up on a sistah." Reina laughed upon finding Phyllis Williams standing there, a smile on her full, mahogany-painted lips. Reina exhaled in relief like a guilty person.

"You wouldn't consider it sneaking unless you had something to hide," Phyllis retorted playfully. "Matter of fact, what're you doing?" She tried to look over Reina's shoulders to get a glimpse of the computer terminal, but Reina blocked her view.

"Hey, now. Stay out of other women's business."

"You sound just like my mother," Phyllis said.

"Your mother has good sense," Reina responded, reaching inside her desk cabinet to pull a pair of shoes from a plastic bag. It was time for their daily walk.

"Yeah, well . . ." Phyllis grinned, her voice trailing off. "Are you ready, Freddy?"

"Ret-ta-go, Jo."

Their laughter was shared, mutual.

Laughter was not the only thing Reina and her coworker had in common. Several weeks before, Phyllis had somehow convinced

Reina to accompany her each day during their morning and after-noon breaks. Rather than joining their compatriots in the cafeteria or break room where the temptations of fat- and sugar-laden foods awaited, Reina and Phyllis laced up their walking shoes and hit the streets.

And that was exactly how Reina felt during her initial attempts—like hitting the streets. Literally. As in flat on her face eating a concrete and asphalt sandwich. Hold the mayo.

Who knew walking one city block would take the wind out of her sails? But she stuck with it, and by the beginning of March, Reina was walking three blocks in the time it had taken her to crawl one. She even purchased a brand-new pair of purple-and-white leather walking shoes to celebrate her success.

Miss Lady was feeling good about herself, and rightfully so. In addition to her daily walks with Phyllis, Reina even managed to choke down eight glasses of water on occasion. So what if she felt as if she were floating out to sea? Eight glasses a day kept the toxins away, or so Vanessa claimed. And she would know. The woman drank enough water to satisfy a camel in a drought.

Reina decided she might as well straighten up and fly as rightly as she could. No more burgers and fries and extra-thick shakes followed by a *light* dessert of day-olds from the Donut Den or Double Stuf cookies and a large diet Dr. Pepper for lunch. Well, not daily, that is. She started bringing a sensible meal from home with just a few treats here and there.

"So how's it feel to be in motion again?" Phyllis questioned as they made their way down the street and around the block.

"Whew!" Reina breathed, "exercise is hard work."

Phyllis patted Reina's arm.

"You're doing good, girl. Just hang in here."

"I'm trying," Reina puffed, beads of perspiration dotting her caramel-colored brow.

"So you didn't advise Vanessa to do anything like put sugar in the man's gas tank, did you?"

"No, girl," Reina protested innocently. "Grits work much better."

Phyllis cackled.

"So can you come to our dinner party Saturday?"

"I'll try to fit you in my schedule," Reina teased, drawing oxygen deep into her lungs. It was a beautiful day. Reina drank in the sight of budding cherry blossoms clinging prettily to overhead tree limbs. Their fresh fragrance delighted her senses, and she felt propelled forward by the soft glory of the early afternoon.

"By all means please do," Phyllis replied. "And if you deign to dine with us peasants, would your majesty sing a tune or two for us?"

Reina frowned.

"Girl, I told you I haven't sung in a long time."

"I know, but it's just a small group of friends. Nothing grand. And I still have yet to hear you blow."

"I'm not trying to sing in your tore-up little backyard with some beat-up little karaoke machine as my band," Reina answered.

"You're not even right." Phyllis laughed. "Why does my stuff have to be raggedy?" she queried as they paused at a corner and waited for the signal light to change in their favor.

"It doesn't have to be. It just is," Reina joked.

They laughed and crossed the street to the other side.

Mamí was out of her ever-living, ever-loving mind.

"*You* want *me* to apologize to *Papí?*" Reina's laugh was shallow. "*Papí* owes me an apology. Why in the world would I want to ask his forgiveness?"

"So you can mend things and come home," *Mamí* answered, as if it all made perfect sense to her.

Reina pulled the phone away from her ear to stare at it in utter disbelief. She sat cross-legged on the floor in her room, leaning back against the foot of the bed, her stuffed Tasmanian Devil doll at her fingertips.

She had no desire to continue playing surrogate mother to her nieces, second-class citizen to her brother, or compliant little spinster daughter to an archaic-values-having father. A shift had occurred. Reina wanted more than what the strictures of her familial ties and their demands allowed. Life had become less than fulfilling. At times she felt like a gaping hole, as if she had been assigned a less-than-gratifying role in some sad melodrama. Even family Mass on Sundays had become less and less rewarding. So much so that when Reina left her parents' house she left their religion as well. Her love for God was without question, but the rigorous, ritualistic means by which to draw nigh to Him had become insipid and grueling in her sight. Reina had tired of compulsory ceremonies and robotic movements in life that left her hollow and bored. Reina Kingsley had finally determined that enough was enough. It was time to make a change, and only she held the power to initiate a difference in her world. It was far past time to set it off.

"Why should I even want to come home?" Reina needed to know.

"Because, *mi hija*," her mother answered lamely.

"Like you always tell me, 'because' is not an answer, *Mamí*."

"Don't be flippant, *mi hija*," Mrs. Kingsley cautioned. "I want you to come back home," she continued. "It's tradition."

"Tradition?" Reina pulled on Taz's ears.

"Your big sister, Nita, stayed home until she married—"

"And look at the good that did her," Reina interrupted. Nita had been a good girl, adhering to their parents' rules and regulations without fail. And what had sweet little compliant Nita gained? Marriage to a monster.

Having sustained one bruise too many at the hands of her husband, Nita finally admitted she was a battered wife and countered with a crack upside her husband's kneecaps that sent him to an orthopedic specialist and whisked their violent marriage down the drain. Unable to cope with the pressure and stress of her topsy-turvy world, Nita found solace in a newfound pastime of smoking herb with her equally newfound motley crew of so-called friends who also gave her a crash course in Fraudulent Check Passing 101. Unfortunately, Nita must have missed a lesson or three, because the darling got caught passing bad checks with false identification while possessing a very real nickel bag of ganja. Now little Miss Nita was a guest at a women's correctional facility thirty minutes outside the city.

Reina grudgingly conceded that Nita's downfall was not her father's fault. But what if her sister had actually developed a stronger sense of self, dared to buck the system and venture out on her own to enjoy the sweet taste of freedom instead of the mildewed dictates of their parents? Perhaps Nita should have pushed the envelope, done what any well-informed, educated single young woman of their generation could have done: found a life! She might have been better able to deal with her divorce and the lack of a man as head of her life—no matter how abusive and disgusting he was—and found the courage to walk boldly into the circle of life rather than exist on the fringes with reprobate individuals. And her mother had the nerve to refer to Nita as an example of propriety? Thank you, but no. Reina would pass.

"*Mi hija,* I did not call to argue." Mrs. Kingsley sighed into the phone, a sigh that held the weight of a mother's troubled heart. "I called to tell you . . ." She paused before concluding, "That I miss you."

Reina felt her own heart soften.

"I know, *Mamí.*" Reina stroked the plush brown fur on the stuffed cartoon character in her hands. And then she quietly admitted to her mother, "I miss you too." Even so, Reina did not intend to return home. She had lived beneath the shadow of her parents long enough. In light of her sister's plight, Reina felt she understood her father's increasing need and desire to protect her, his one remaining daughter. But she was grown and fully able to care for herself, and needed to make life decisions on her own without overarching parental involvement.

Reina could hear her nieces cavorting in the background.

Her mother spoke to them in her lyrical native tongue, instructing the two little girls to turn off the television and prepare for their nighttime baths.

Reina felt a customary twinge of guilt. Many times before she had resolved to leave home, only to be confronted by the feeling that she was abandoning her family when they needed her most. Her mother was still grieving over the loss of her father. Her parents were saddled with the unexpected responsibility of raising their granddaughters in Nita's absence. Raj was growing into a wild child. Reina just couldn't add to their worries.

In the rare times that guilt failed, obligation prevailed. Had not her parents saved and sacrificed that they might pay her way through college? Wasn't Reina obliged to do as they pleased? The obligation, the guilt, the sentiments folded in on each other, erecting one insurmountable wall in her mind. But then memories of the Incident rose fresh above it all as Reina relived her father striking her for the first time in her life, and the uncertainty regarding her decision to leave quickly crumbled.

Reina's musings were interrupted by her father's strident voice bouncing through the phone.

"Who's that?" he asked his wife.

Mamí removed the phone from her ear and whispered her reply.

"Ah, hang up da phone!" *Papí* shouted. "Tell dat ungrateful lil piss-tail gal no one heah has a t'ing to say ta huh."

"Roland, go somewhere and hush!" *Mamí* retorted.

"Where is she? Holed up wid some kinky-headed man? Tell dat chile dat I da onliest man she need till she marry. She's my daughter! Gimme da phone, 'oman. I'll tell huh mahself."

"Go help the girls get ready for bed before I send you back to Jamaica in a box," *Mamí* threatened.

Reina laughed despite her annoyance.

"*Mamí*, I have to go. We can talk later, okay?"

"*Sí*, Reina," her mother reluctantly agreed, a sad note in her voice. "*Te amo, mi hija.*"

"I love you, too, *Mamí*."

Reina terminated the call and tossed the cordless phone onto her bed. She sat on the floor a while longer, reflecting on her situation and the visit she paid to her maternal grandmother en route home from work a few days earlier.

Abuela was right: each member bore responsibility to uphold the sanctity of family honor and family ties. The family unit should be preserved and remain intact at all costs. Why then, Reina had asked, was she the only one expected to pay such a high price? She refused to grovel and acquiesce. Furthermore, she had neither incentive nor need to do so. The powerful sense of self she was beginning to discover since leaving home was far better than the pitiful, guilt-ridden little beast she once was. There was simply no comparison. Reina was emancipated, independently living her own life, and enjoying every moment of it. Oddly enough, *Abuela* understood her granddaughter's needs. She simply cautioned Reina not to burn her britches while trying to build a bridge.

Reina smiled at her grandmother's homespun homily. Her britches and her butt were numb from sitting on the floor so long. Reina pushed herself up and stretched her cramped limbs. Taz lay on the floor, his mouth agape in a toothy snarl.

"You don't scare me, Roland Kingsley," she said, picking up the stuffed animal and speaking directly in its face. "Get over here on this shelf where you belong and don't move unless I give you permission."

The doll complied.

Reina shook her head and chuckled deeply.

Papí knew good and gosh darn well she was not *holed up wid some kinky-headed man.* Nope, Reina concluded glancing about. Nothing but a host of furry stuffed animals kept her company. Kinky-headed or not, Reina wondered if male companionship could bring a hint of joy into her life just then and there.

"Girl, there's no such monkey as a low-fat chitterling!" Reina emphatically stated, the cordless phone propped between her ear and her shoulder.

"You haven't seen the way I prepare them," Phyllis returned.

"Honey, plain and simple, fat meat is greasy." Reina chuckled, filling the teapot with fresh bottled water before placing it on the stove and setting the flame beneath the pot on high. Okay, so she had to admit Vanessa had been right. Herbal tea was actually pretty good. Especially the gourmet peppermint and almond flavors Vanessa purchased at some swank little trendy coffee shop downtown.

"Not necessarily. It's the method, not the meat, that matters," Phyllis answered, as if she could persuade Reina otherwise.

"Okay-y-y, girl, if you say so."

"Don't be patronizing."

"Oh, you caught that, huh?"

"I did," Phyllis confirmed.

Reina giggled.

"I'm sorry. I know you're an aspiring gourmet and all, but color me doubtful on that low-fat pig innards thing."

"Forget you, girl. Anyhow, what time will you grace us with your presence this evening?" Phyllis asked.

Reina leaned against the kitchen counter, waiting for the water to come to a boil. She popped a raisin bagel in the toaster oven, anticipating the crunchy-edged, soft-centered bread. *Mmm, good.* A far cry from her usual Saturday-morning cheese eggs with mushrooms and bell pepper, grits, *chorizo,* tortillas, hot chocolate, and pancakes topped with whipped butter, powdered sugar, and fresh mango spread courtesy of her paternal grandparents, who still resided in Jamaica. Reina peeled a banana and daintily chewed as she waited.

"Sevenish," Reina eventually replied, swallowing banana. Phyllis was expecting out-of-town relatives, and as these same relatives were considering a move to California's lovely state capital, Phyllis thought it a nice idea to introduce them to other Sacramentans to grant them a feel for the place and its people.

"You should come earlier."

"Why, so I can help cook low-fat chitterlings for your health-conscious relatives?"

"Exactly." Phyllis laughed.

"Can't think of anything I'd rather do on a Saturday than slave in a kitchen with you over a sinkful of pig guts."

"Good. I'll see you later, and don't forget to tell Vanessa she's invited."

"Okeydokey. See you tonight." Reina clicked off just as the water in the teakettle came to a boil. Moments later, Reina made her way to the table and sat down to enjoy a breakfast of fruit, a raisin bagel, and a mug of fragrant herbal tea.

A sweet March sun tossed ribbons of precious light through the open kitchen window, dashing brightness into the room and all within. Reina smiled her content. She had to admit there was something to be said for living single. No wild-haired nieces with snotty noses sitting in front of the television eating bowls of sugar-coated cereal while watching Saturday-morning cartoons for hours on end. No surly Neanderthal brother stomping into the kitchen to rummage up a breakfast only for himself, only to stomp back into his cave to eat in solitary confinement. No *Mamí* or *Papí* chattering on the phone in heavy patois or lightning-speed Spanish with local or long-distance relatives. Just blissful peace and joyous quiet.

The garage door, which opened onto the laundry room, which led into the kitchen, was flung open, and an overly stimulated, canine-funky Pharaoh rushed indoors and over to Reina, jumping up on her with his forepaws and licking her face before trying to steal a bite of bagel from the table.

"Get down, hound," Reina scolded. The dog reluctantly obeyed and ran back out past Vanessa and into the garage to play with his toys.

Vanessa bounced into the kitchen, slightly out of breath, but looking tight and toned in her running gear.

"G-o-o-o-d morning," she sang as she practically skipped to the refrigerator and fished around for a small bottle of springwater. She had to push aside liters of diet soda, bags of cookies, and chocolate bars to find it, but finally she did. Vanessa twisted off the cap and took a deep drink. "Awww! That hit the spot."

"You have to be on drugs," Reina said, shaking her head and chewing the remainder of her banana. "No one who can pass a drug test is that happy so early on a Saturday morning."

"Look who's talking," Vanessa returned, pushing herself up to sit on top of the chef island. "I'm not the one who gets up every Monday morning talking about 'oh, what a beautiful new workweek.'" She took another long swig of water. "Besides, right now I'm high on life, sweetheart."

"Pee in a cup and let me send it to a lab. We'll find out what you're really high on."

"Hand me your mug."

"Whatever, psycho," Reina replied. "Hey, what are you doing today?"

"A little of this, not too much of that. Why?"

"My friend Phyllis is having a small dinner party tonight and you're invited."

"You two have been hanging pretty tough lately."

"Jealous?" Reina teased.

"Incredibly," Vanessa replied, covering her heart as if really wounded. "Tell her thank you, but I still have a few things to take care of before I leave for D.C."

"How long is your National Black Broadcasters Association gig this year?" Reina asked, getting up to discard the banana peel and used tea bag, then rinse her dishes and place them in the dishwasher.

"One week, but I might hang out in D.C. a few days after the convention."

"For what?"

Vanessa's smile was brilliant. "To investigate that lead on my birth mother. Remember I told you about it?"

"Of course I remember. 'Nessa, that's wonderful!" Reina exclaimed, squeezing Vanessa's hand. "So your sorority sister has a hookup for you?"

Vanessa nodded happily.

"She's a C.O. for a family court judge—"

"C.O.?" Reina questioned.

"Court officer," Vanessa explained. "Anyhow, she has access to all kinds of records that can help in my search."

"Is that legal?" Reina asked, her brows furrowed.

"Oh, listen to you, with your computer-cracking self," Vanessa replied. Reina laughed. "Everything is on the up-and-up. I wouldn't ask my soror to do anything that would jeopardize her job."

"Wow, that's really exciting. I'm happy for you. Are you nervous?" Reina asked.

"Not really . . . Well, yes, but I'll be okay. I'm not expecting a miracle or anything. I'd just like to have some answers to some questions," Vanessa stated, hopping down from her perch. "I'll pass on tonight, but tell Phyllis thank-you and I'll take a rain check."

"Okay. You two haven't met yet, and Phyllis is good people."

"I know she is. She has you exercising and eating like you have good sense, which was more than I could do."

"Poof, be gone," Reina said, propping the flat palm of her hand in Vanessa's face. "Hey, what are you going to do for your birthday?"

Vanessa shrugged.

"No idea. It's still weeks away," she answered nonchalantly.

"How can you not think about your thirtieth birthday?"

"Why should I when I have you here to constantly remind me?"

"We can have a slumber party with male strippers," Reina suggested, arching her eyebrows and rubbing her palms together.

"There wouldn't be much slumbering going on," Vanessa replied.

"That's what I'm talking about."

Vanessa laughed.

"I'll think about it later. Right now I have to stretch before my limbs cramp up." Vanessa let out a shrill whistle. Pharaoh came running. "Come on, baby, let's go flex some muscle."

"You need to flex your way into the shower," Reina quipped, pinching her nostrils as if she smelled something rank.

"Comb your hair, stank," Vanessa retorted, flipping her hand through Reina's wild locks before bouncing from the kitchen and out onto the back patio.

"Soap! Try some, wench," Reina sang, and headed up the stairs to attend to her own personal hygiene, which was slightly less than daffodil fresh.

Phyllis Williams's stuff was far from raggedy. Her home was a miniature mansion. Well, almost. Two-story brick with colonial-style white pillars at the front and the rear. Large bay windows with forest green shutters. Vaulted ceilings, exquisite chandeliers in the foyer and dining rooms. Massive fireplaces in the living room and master bedroom suite with its walk-in closets that were larger than Reina's bedroom back home. Bathrooms spacious enough to house a family of four. Majestic, curving staircase that gave one the sense of flight or walking on air. And the most vast collection of African, modern, and African-American art and sculpture Reina had ever laid eyes on in one place. The sheer elegance alone was enough to create an intimidating and austere environment. Instead, the house seemed to have taken on the spirit of its owners. Like Phyllis and Bryce Williams, it was warm, welcoming, and far from pretentious.

From what Reina gathered, Phyllis had come from humble beginnings and worked her way through college. While an undergrad she met and married her husband, who was then working on a law degree before eventually switching to pursue a degree in finance. Phyllis left college after obtaining her bachelor's degree in order to help her husband start his own financial consulting firm. Although the firm never really proved to be the success they imagined, her husband's business savvy and skill helped him land a promising position with a leading brokerage house in San Francisco, which required that they relocate to California from their prior home, the new black mecca of Atlanta.

Upon her husband's promotion to portfolio manager of mergers and acquisitions, Phyllis didn't bat an eye when it required they move, once again, from San Francisco to Sacramento. Her husband had promised once they were established Phyllis would not need to work. She could do as she pleased, pursue her dream of becoming a caterer, if she wanted. Finally, they were more than established, but Phyllis chose to work just a little while longer. So her husband made her agree that her earnings were hers to do with as she pleased, and she pleased to turn a major portion of her pay over to her husband so that he could invest it on her behalf. Up from, well, not exactly poverty, Phyllis Williams was pretty much set for life.

A Norman Brown CD was playing, the sounds of his oh so sensuously mellow acoustic guitar pulsing from a stereo system that piped music throughout the entire house. Smells of savory dishes seasoned the air of a kitchen filled with voices. Reina stood at a chef island that dwarfed Vanessa's in comparison, chopping fresh vegetables and salad greens with Phyllis and two of Phyllis's friends.

It was almost seven, and Phyllis's husband had not yet returned from picking up relatives at the airport.

"Phyllis, girl, I know you're going to start that catering business one day soon," one of the women commented. "Your food is better than that served by some restaurants in this town."

"I second that," the other woman concurred.

Phyllis smiled, pleasantly surprised by the compliment.

"I will, I promise. All in God's good timing," Phyllis concluded.

Reina smiled. She liked the way Phyllis constantly deferred to God, as if He knew what was best for her life. By the looks of things—the house, Phyllis's marriage, her life—apparently He did.

"Will your husband's family be too tired to eat when they arrive?" Reina asked.

The other three women paused, the two friends looking quizzically at Reina. Phyllis coughed nervously. Quickly pulling a basket filled with linens, silverware, and napkin rings from a nearby countertop, Phyllis handed the basket to the other women, asking if they wouldn't mind helping her by setting the dining room table. Exchanging glances with one another, they washed their hands, then departed to fulfill their hostess's request.

"What was that all about?" Reina asked when they were alone.

"You look very pretty, Reina," Phyllis complimented without responding directly to Reina's query.

And she did. Reina had allowed her thick hair to air-dry after washing and vigorously brushing it that morning so that it hung in deep, coal-black waves down her back, soft, curly tendrils framing her face. She had donned a flowing pantsuit in an incredibly soft shade of pink ribboned with hair-thin bronze threads that accented her deep copper complexion. She had even touched her lips with a light application of a cocoa-colored lip gloss and dabbed a tiny hint of jasmine oil behind her ears, from which hung tiny solid-gold teardrops. She really was lovely.

"Thank you, Phyllis," Reina humbly replied, not the least bit distracted. "Girl, what's really going on?"

"Uhhh, Reina. I have a confession to make," Phyllis answered, her hands busily rinsing and rerinsing the fresh-cut vegetables in a stainless-steel colander.

"Speak, my child." Reina reached over and turned off the faucet. "You're about to wash away every ounce of vitamins if you don't stop."

Phyllis inhaled deeply, then blurted, "I'm not expecting relatives, plural. Just one relative in particular."

"Okay," Reina tentatively replied, puzzled by the embarrassed look on her friend's face.

"It'll be just us, Candace and her husband, Keturah and her fiancé," Phyllis stated, referring to the women busy with table settings and their significant others, who had accompanied her own husband on his errand, "and Jamal."

"Who's Jamal?"

"My husband's brother from Atlanta." Phyllis dumped the contents of the colander onto paper towels and patted them dry before dropping the vegetables into a beautifully cut crystal salad bowl. She finally glanced up and looked at Reina, who merely shrugged her shoulders and stated, "Oh, okay."

Phyllis sighed. "Come on. Work with me here, Reina," she implored, sounding exasperated.

"Sorry?"

"Jamal is my husband's single, intelligent, *attractive* baby brother who is visiting to see if our river city is to his liking. And if he finds what he's looking for, then he just might move here."

"Oh, that's nice. I'm sure your husband would enjoy having his brother—"

"Hello!" Phyllis chimed, reaching across the space to rap her knuckles lightly against Reina's forehead.

"Ouch! Why resort to the physical, Churchlady?"

"Because you're not feeling me!" Phyllis laughed. "Do I need to spell this out?" Phyllis asked, hands firmly planted on her shapely hips. "I want to introduce you to my brother-in-law."

The light bulb clicked on. The elevator went to the top floor. Reina finally, fully, understood her friend's intent. So, that's why Phyllis had urged her to arrive early. Not to help with nonexistent chitterlings, but for an opportunity to warn Reina of her meddling ways. Who died and crowned Phyllis as Cupid? Reina was embarrassed. She might not be the world's greatest romantic catch, still Reina did not consider herself so pathetic as to need matchmaking help from her friends. Maybe it was the brother-in-law who needed a helping hand.

Reina's eyes zoned in on Phyllis's face, seeking any sign of deceit. "What's wrong with him?" she asked, her voice wary.

"Not a thing," Phyllis cheerfully replied, glad to have sparked at least this much interest.

The girl was good, Reina concluded to herself. Her jaw didn't twitch. Her eyes never blinked. She never stuttered or stammered. Phyllis was a natural-born con, with her sanctified self.

"I'm telling the honest truth," Phyllis attested, placing her hand over her heart for emphasis. "Jamal's my age, thirty-two. He has a beautiful sense of humor. He's extremely compassionate. He's gainfully employed with no significant other, no kids, and no ex-wives that I know of."

"What do you mean that you know of?"

Phyllis giggled before saying, "I'm just kidding. He's never been married."

Reina dumped fresh-cut broccoli into the steamer basket in a large pot over the stove. Reina had to wonder why in the world Phyllis would want to introduce her brother-in-law to her. If he was all that Phyllis said he was, wouldn't he prefer a woman more like Candace or Keturah or Vanessa?

Bingo! That was it! Reina would scope out the brother, see what he was really made of. And if he proved to be all that Phyllis suggested, then maybe Reina could play Cupid herself and create a magical hookup between the brother-in-law and her best friend. Suddenly Reina couldn't wait to see who was coming to dinner.

Dinner was delicious. And so was Jamal. On a scale of one to ten, Jamal Williams was pushing twenty. He truly was all that Phyllis had implied and then some. Yes, he had impeccable manners, warm humor, and proved to be most intelligent, indeed. But Phyllis had falsified one issue in particular. He was not attractive. Jamal was make-you-wanna-rise-up-and-slap-somebody's-mama fine! Let's talk *foine*, not fine. Had he not been so very male—with his deep mocha skin, broad shoulders, slim hips, piercing eyes, and baritone voice—Reina might have considered him pretty. Beautiful, even. The man was majestic, with his solid, tall, dark, and too-handsome self. He was good enough to eat with an ice-cold diet Dr. Pepper on the side. Vanessa be danged. Reina was not tossing this brother her way.

Citronella candles in tall bamboo sconces anchored in the back-yard grass cast a soft glow across the verandah. The contented group of diners sat talking, laughing, sipping after-dinner coffee and enjoying dessert while being serenaded by the sounds of the soft night and the Joe Sample and Lalah Hathaway CD playing on the stereo.

Phyllis, true to her perfect hostess self, was weaving her way through the happy gathering, placing discarded dessert dishes on a large tray that sat on a service table, pausing here and there to refill coffee cups or pass around sugar or various flavored creamers. Her husband, Bryce, abandoned his chair to help her as she lifted a tray piled with dishes. She shooed him away.

"Sit down, honey, and enjoy your brother's company."

"He doesn't even know I exist," Bryce replied with a smile and a covert nod of his head in his brother's direction. His wife shushed him before planting a kiss on his lips and heading toward the French doors that led into the kitchen.

"Reina, would you mind helping me for a moment?" Phyllis called as she passed.

"Not at all," Reina replied, excusing herself from those around her, hurrying to help Phyllis, missing the set of beautiful brown eyes that followed her every move.

"So what do you think?" Phyllis asked once in the safety of the kitchen.

"About?" Reina replied, scraping amaretto cheesecake scraps from a plate into a stainless-steel dome-topped garbage can.

"Don't make me have to rap my knuckles on your forehead again."

"Oh, Jamal," Reina purred. "Mmm, baby boy is real nice."

"I told you so," Phyllis gloated, bumping a hip against Reina's. Phyllis looked over her shoulder to ensure that no one had come within earshot. Still, she lowered her voice as a final measure of safety. "I told you he's considering moving here, right?" Reina nodded affirmatively. "That's if he finds what he's looking for. I'm hoping it's more a *who* he's looking for."

"Phyllis, you need to quit," Reina replied, feeling just the slightest twinge of excitement somewhere deep in her bones. If Phyllis was implying what Reina thought she was, then *aww suki suki* now.

Phyllis must have picked up on the vibe because she just wouldn't leave well alone enough.

"And before you even trip let me tell you this. Jamal's much like Bryce. They both appreciate a woman with a little meat on her bones." Phyllis winked and turned to store the remaining cheesecake in the refrigerator, stopping suddenly. "Jam-m-al," she stammered. "I-I d-didn't hear you come in."

"I just came to see if I could be of help," Jamal replied, looking directly at Reina before quickly averting his gaze toward his sister-in-law but not before noting the blush warming Reina's copper cheeks.

Missing nothing, Phyllis saw Jamal's direct gaze that had been momentarily aimed at the only other woman in the kitchen. Her feather smooth eyebrows slithered up an inch. She tried, but failed to conceal a triumphant smile as she cleared her throat before speaking.

"Thanks, but we're practically finished here. Go on back outside and rest yourself."

"Actually, I was getting stiff after sitting on a plane for so long. Really, I don't mind helping if it gives me a chance to stretch," Jamal assured his sister-in-law.

"Well"—Phyllis hesitated only for a moment—"if you're sure, I'll leave you two here while I collect the remainder of the dishes. I'll be back."

Phyllis disappeared before Reina could protest. That is, if she chose to, which she did not. Current company was fine by her.

Jamal grabbed an apron from a hook on the pantry door, slipped the garment on, and got busy.

The man should have looked ridiculous decked out in Phyllis's pink-and-green getup. Instead, he was so adorable Reina couldn't help but smile.

"What's wrong?" Jamal inquired, seeing the amusement on Reina's face.

"Not a thing," she replied bashfully, busying herself with the task at hand. A brother who did not mind getting his hands dirty in the kitchen? Boo-yow, he racked up an additional five points!

Jamal watched her for a moment before shrugging slightly.

"My sister-in-law tells me you're a singer."

Reina nodded.

"She says you sing R and B and jazz," Jamal supplied.

Now, just when in God's world had Phyllis found time to fill Jamal in on her 411?

"I do. Or did," Reina amended, explaining how she gave up R and B for jazz, not mentioning it had been some time since she'd sung anything anywhere at all.

"A woman after my own heart," Jamal remarked with a dazzling smile.

"Oh, so you're a bebop man?" Reina asked, any shyness she possibly felt at Jamal's presence falling completely away.

"You'd better know it. Give me a little Miles D. or C-trane on the horn any day of the week and I'll do just fine."

"Coltrane!" Reina protested. "He makes my head hurt, he's so eclectic."

Jamal chuckled heartily.

"Oh, come on now. You mean to tell me you're a jazz enthusiast and you can't ride the Trane?"

"Sure, if I had some Valium on board," Reina responded.

Jamal paused in loading the dishwasher and just stared at her. Then he laughed, a deep-down sound that made Reina smile.

"You're missing out on some good stuff there, Miss Kingsley," Jamal insisted. "You have to be willing to suspend time and just lie back with the Trane and get into his space."

Reina wasn't having it. She shook her head in denial.

"Thank you but no."

"Come on, Reina, tell me 'A Love Supreme' is not *the* piece."

"It's nice—"

"Nice?" Jamal echoed incredulously. "All right then, who moves you?"

Reina scraped food remains into the garbage before handing dishes over to Jamal.

"I'll take a little Will Downing, Gerald Albright, Najee or George Duke anytime, anywhere."

"Aww, girl, that's contemporary stuff. You have to go old school to get the real," Jamal exclaimed.

"Oh, so the era determines the validity of the music?" Reina challenged, arms crossed.

"Sure. Time in history has something to do with the weight of the message," Jamal responded.

"Are you saying modern jazz musicians are lightweight in comparison to their predecessors?" Reina queried intently.

"I wouldn't call them lightweight, per se," Jamal amended, "I'm

merely pointing out that the socio-economic and political environment of decades past was far more treacherous than that of today, and
so was reflected in the weight of the work." He paused and noted the
captive interest on Reina's beautiful face. She was feeling him. "Take
Billie Holiday's 'Strange Fruit,' for example. It was an exposé on the
lynching of black Americans."

"Valid point," Reina conceded. "But come on, our contemporaries
write and sing about what's relevant in our lives today. Take Oleta
Adams or Rachelle Ferrell—"

"I bow down there. The ladies have pipes and purpose," Jamal
agreed. "Still, there's nothing like vibing to Ella or Sarah on a mellow
Sunday afternoon."

Reina had to laugh.

"Mr. Williams, methinks we agree," Reina admitted in a mock
British accent.

Jamal grinned.

"That was pretty good, Ms. Kingsley."

"I've had plenty of practice mastering accents." Reina laughed.

Phyllis stepped into the kitchen before Jamal could reply.

"Having fun?" she sang, not bothering or needing to wait for an answer. The warm smiles on their faces told it all. "Thank you so much
for your help, Reina, Jamal. Why don't you two go on back outside
and let me finish up in here?"

Reina glanced at the clock set within the shining metal hood of the
gourmet stove.

"Actually, Phyllis, I should be going."

"It's barely ten-thirty," Phyllis responded, sounding rather alarmed.

"I know, but I promised my grandmother I'd attend Mass with her
tomorrow morning," Reina stated, sounding slightly less than enthu-
siastic.

"Oh." Phyllis was unable to hide her disappointment. "Well, why
don't you stop by for dinner afterward," Phyllis suggested.

"That's really sweet, but I have to decline the offer," Reina answered as she washed her hands at the kitchen sink. "Besides, you and
Bryce should have some private time to enjoy your brother-in-law's
visit."

"Honey, trust me, time with Jamal cannot be deemed enjoyable,"
Phyllis teased, hugging her brother-in-law about the waist before wiping her hands on a fluffy dish towel.

"Glad I'm not sensitive," Jamal retorted, wiping imaginary tears from the corners of his deep brown eyes.

Phyllis linked arms with Reina.

"Come on, girl, I'll walk you out."

"Phyllis, let me see Reina to her car so you don't neglect your other guests," Jamal offered, causing a triumphant smile to ease up the corners of Phyllis's lips. She was only too happy to agree.

Jamal patiently waited as Reina exchanged a hug with her hostess, bade farewell to the rest of the party, then retrieved her purse and light jacket from the front closet. With an air of old-fashioned chivalry, Jamal cupped her elbow in his palm and ushered Reina safely down the porch steps and across the circular cobblestone driveway, where Ruby sat amongst the other vehicles like a crimson carriage awaiting her queen.

"How long will you be visiting, Jamal?"

"Just a few days."

"That's too bad," Reina said, unlocking her car door. "I was going to invite you to a local jazz haunt called the Set so you can hear some real music for a change."

Jamal's laughter was silky-smooth and soft.

"Who knows? I may visit your little town again, and if I do will the offer still stand?"

"It will," Reina quietly replied, a bit of shyness creeping back over her as she and Jamal stood alone in the driveway, night creatures serenading them with nocturnal noises. Reina hurried to unlock Ruby's doors with the remote. She was beginning to feel self-conscious standing there beneath Jamal's keen gaze and the light of a full moon. This enigmatic marvel was having a strange effect on her, and she was not completely at ease. It was time to go.

"It was a pleasure meeting you, Jamal, and I hope you enjoy your stay."

She extended her hand cordially.

"Actually the pleasure was truly mine," Jamal replied, reaching for and holding on to Reina's warm fingers.

Reina waved good-bye as Ruby purred down the driveway and out onto the quiet street. Was her imagination playing cruel tricks on her? Had Jamal held her hand a bit longer than necessary? Her heart was racing. Reina wanted to snatch up her cell phone, call Phyllis, and ask if she had spiked that amaretto cheesecake with a little something

something with her good little sanctified self, because surely Reina had to be tripping and slipping. A brother as handsome and debonair as Jamal—though kindhearted he might be—couldn't possibly be interested in her. Could he? Phyllis said he was inclined toward a woman with a little meat on her bones. A little meat was one thing, Reina silently argued with herself. A side of beef was another.

Reina's dry laughter filled the car's interior. Her heart rate and her reality returned to normal. It was too good to be true, Reina thought, her mind flashing back to her recent phone conversation with her mother.

Reina remained unaffected by her mother's cajoling. She was not returning home no matter how hard her mother begged or cried. *Mami*'s words fell flat on unheeding ears. It was *Papi*'s voice Reina recalled as she drove down the dark boulevard.

I da onliest man she need till she marry.

The thought was enough to make her chest tight.

CHRIS

I need to a make a trip to the county courthouse and file a petition for a legal name change, because I'm beginning to suffer from an identity crisis. In the past week, Reina has "accidentally" slipped and called me Jamal more times than I care to remember. I know *they* say we all look alike, but come on now. A brother has a right to be an individual and not just a slip of the tongue, a legitimate being versus a mere reminder of some man in whom a sister denies having a romantic interest. My name is Christophe Countee McCullen. Awww, yeah.

Yep, Countee. That's my dad's little play on history and our surname. Countee Cullen—McCullen minus the "Mc"—was an African-American poet who grew to fame during the Harlem Renaissance era for his plays and novels, but mainly his poetry. I don't know if Dad in naming me after this extraordinary poet had aspirations for my becoming a literary great myself. But if such was the case, I'm afraid I've sorely disappointed my old man and my namesake. The closest I come to poetry is "Now I lay me down to sleep, I pray the Lord my soul to keep . . ." Amen.

Okay, my prayers have evolved over the years, but I still lay claim to no writing genius whatsoever. Unless you consider the journal I keep on my nightstand something of literary worth.

I picked up the habit of "journaling" back in college. One of my psychology professors—back in the day when I thought I really would become a medical doctor and wanted to be skilled in the psyche as well as the body—assigned us the task of logging our first thoughts upon rising in the morning and our last thoughts before settling to sleep at night. Before painting me any particular shade of angel, do know straight up that I considered it silly female psychobabble stuff at the time. You couldn't pay me to give in to the hype. Okay, so I made a lie of myself and eventually came to appreciate the entire concept. Not only did I receive an A minus in the class, but the habit of tracking my thoughts on paper stayed with me. Over time it developed until my journal entries are no longer limited to just morning and night, nor is my journal chained to my nightstand. I sometimes take it with me to my new office so I can purge myself of toxic thoughts or capture worthwhile musings when my day wears longer than RuPaul's weave.

Oh, snap! Wait a minute. Yes, a brother has his own office now. Yep, I landed the promotion. Can I get a whoop-whoop? Thanks be to God, I am now the new facility coordinator of the Valley Fitness center located in midtown. A brother has the hookup with his own office and parking space and administrative assistant and all the fringe benefits a HNIC deserves. And word has it that Valley Fitness just might be opening another new site. Where? Good ole E.G. Elk Grove, baby. Right in the neck of my very own soon-to-be 'hood. Just as soon as I find a house.

Other than the slight frustration of my housing situation, things have gone very smoothly for me since the promotion. I haven't had any outright instances of mutiny or overt sabotage from employees. In fact, an overwhelming majority have demonstrated genuine support. Except Ethan—our aqua aerobics instructor—who was also a contender for my job. A couple of times I've caught him eyeing me with a strange look on his face. Of course, he slapped a smile on his pink lips as soon as he realized I was watching him as well. But that's all good, too. Knowing I have a disgruntled and potential rival in my ranks helps keep me on my toes.

I look forward to a possible transfer to the new facility; still I'd miss my current stomping ground. Our midtown site is strategically located right in the thick of things—walking distance from the capitol building, the downtown mall, and a vast business district—so we service a diverse clientele who benefit from the varied hours and close proximity of our particular physical-improvement facility. We cater to

white-collar professionals and politicians who come by early mornings or late nights, account executives who bring clients on guest
passes to play a game of racquetball during lunch hour before discussing contracts or closing deals, as well as normal everyday resi-
dents from surrounding neighborhoods.

We were mislabeled the "gym of the slim" by one newspaper colum-
nist who implied that we serve only the elite and the petite. Now, I
admit in times past things might have appeared that way. We were op-
erating from a very Eurocentric paradigm and perspective. Plain
English? Things were a little too white and uptight. You know your
gym is too Mayberry USA when your aerobics instructors think Jane
Fonda is "the bomb." Yes, "the" bomb, not "da" bomb. But I'm here
now, in a position of power, and things are about to change. Of
course, I must be savvy about it and not overturn the system in a day.
I have to ease the resistant ones gradually into my program. You
know, sway them gently, make them think adding a Caribbean dance
class or an African rhythm section to the CD catalog or holistic herbal
supplements at the juice bar or Afrocentric oils in the massage salon
was somehow one of their very progressive ideas.

Even so, I must say Valley Fitness is pretty smooth. Our facilities
have been viewed as elitist, perhaps, because of the services we provide. In addition to your standard free weights, aerobics, sauna/
Jacuzzi, health bar kind of gig, our clientele may also take advantage
of services such as a full-fledged on-site day spa complete with massage therapists, licensed nutritionist, manicurist, and cosmeticians—
thanks, Vanessa; a brother proposed and actually had your idea
implemented, so stay after one of your workouts and get your weave
tightened. We feature aromatherapy and relaxation products including cassettes, CDs, and even videos. And the clincher? We've contracted with a local cleaner who offers dry-cleaning service with a
smile. So as you can see, Valley Fitness isn't your typical sweat tank. It's
on the real and I intend to keep it that way. Especially with my first inspection pending.

The regional executive board is good for popping in unan-
nounced. Their idea of a forewarning is simply a letter stating, "We
are pleased to inform you that we will be visiting your facility soon."
Soon usually means anytime in the next two months. We just won't
know when. Visiting means interrogating. Pleased means their pleasure, my pain.

The board's impromptu visits can consist of a thorough inspection of every room, every piece of equipment, and a mini audit of accounting records. They're even known for walking up to a patron who is on a treadmill or bouncing about in an aerobics class and asking point-blank questions regarding the client's satisfaction with the site and the personnel who serve them. Things had better be on the up-and-up or immediate action is imminent. A couple of years ago a facility coordinator was "dismissed" when someone at the juice bar served a customer a fruit-and-protein smoothie made with fermented juice. In my opinion that action was a bit extreme, but you'd better believe a brother checks the expiration dates on his perishables.

Even with this inspection looming over my head, I have to admit things are still pretty good in my world. Of course, my world would be far better if a moving company were packing my belongings in boxes and preparing to move me into my new house in Elk Grove or Laguna, but such is not the case. My initial offer was not accepted. Apparently someone else outbid me by a measly seven hundred dollars, and that was enough to seal the deal. So I've moved on to potential house number two. In the meantime, I'm still living in a condo that long ago outlived its usefulness.

I am a big man. I need room. I've come to like wide-open spaces that aren't confining, that are large and liberating. This little rinky-dink two-bedroom, one-bathroom, half-a-kitchen, three-quarters-of-a-living-room, hint-of-a-yard dwelling is not for me. When I first bought this condo I figured it to be the perfect bachelor pad. Not too big, not too small, yard maintenance and repairs covered by the fees I pay to the owners' association. Now I've tired of the—as Nana would say—"cute quaintness" of it all. I need to stretch out and try my hand at owning something real.

Don't get me wrong. I'm not ungrateful. I'm just being up-front with myself and recognizing I've reached my limit. I've crossed the barrier to a new milestone, and I'm not afraid to be legit. I need more.

Let me help you know exactly where I'm coming from.

You see, as a child I occasionally endured thinly disguised envy and even contempt as a result of my father's status. Growing up as a PK, a preacher's kid, I was sometimes snubbed by my peers whose parents could not provide them with many of the benefits afforded me by my dad's station in life. Critics can say what they will about the fragmentation of the black community, but I am a living witness that black churchfolk will take care of their own.

Because of the generosity of my father's parishioners, I never went without what I truly needed and always had more than enough. Either pity for my motherless state, appreciation for my father's services, or pure Christian charity led these saints to bring bags filled with school clothes, toys, books, edible goodies, or whatever else they felt I needed to our home. As my father was well able to provide for me himself, the gifts of his congregants often created an abundant overflow. So much so that my father encouraged me to give to those less fortunate versus hoarding up too much for myself.

Of course I did this, grudgingly at first, just to appease Dad. But over time I did it willingly. Usually. I admit it was hard letting go of some of those gifts and goods, but when I did I was rewarded with a sense of my own humanity. That is, when I didn't encounter the proud, resistant, even angry glares of the peers to whom I was "handing out" the wares. They were polite with Dad and their own parents standing by to witness the exchange, but as soon as we were alone again—on the playground or in Sunday school—I heard what some recipients really felt. *Show-off. You think you're better'n us. Don't want yo' leftovers, boy.* So I was left to deal with the social breach our questionable affluence caused.

As a result, I guess I grew up trying to prove I was down, to show myself true to the brotherhood/sisterhood, to minimize the disparities between myself and the poorer community with whom we lived. Perhaps this is why Dad never moved us into the 'burbs even when he could well afford to do so. He didn't want to distance us from the people he served. Instead, we remained in the modest three-bedroom, two-story brick house he purchased as a wedding gift for my mother. Sure, over the years he added to the structure, renovated the interior, and gutted rooms to enlarge them. But even as his congregation grew to include upwardly mobile young professionals, and older executives who were—as Dad says—"doing nicely" themselves and running in droves to purchase homes in trendy and well-to-do neighborhoods, Dad stayed put in the "cute quaintness" of his conjugal abode.

It seems that I've taken my lessons in humility to another level altogether. Whereas Dad wanted to stay close to the church and his community, I wanted to distance myself from false notions of my being an uppity sort. Perhaps that's why I initially fought to attend California

State University with many in my running circle instead of the University of California, where the tuition cost a good arm and two legs. But Dad won out, reminding me it was his hard-earned money being spent on my college tuition at the educational system of his choice. So, to the U.C. I went.

You know, I've never really considered this possibility until now, but maybe all this angst is what prevented me from pursuing a career in medicine. My immaturity and ambivalence may have kept me from seeking a higher call, one that if attained could have very well contributed to the further success and well-being of the people from whom I came. Hindsight is twenty-twenty and anger can be futile. So rather than fume over lost time and wasted talents, I'd rather free myself to be me.

Which is exactly why I drive an expensive car and wear designer clothing. Because I can. I've been given a position of power at my place of employment, and let it be known I am anticipating the option to purchase my very own Valley Fitness in the years to come. But for now, I'll concentrate on finding and buying a house. I am reconciled with the fact that I've been tremendously blessed. I don't apologize for what the Almighty bestows on me. Am I living large and in charge? I guess I am! How you like me now?

The phone rang three times before her answering machine clicked on.

"Hi, I'm not in. Leave a message and I'll get back with you soon. I promise."

I have to give it to her, Reina has one of the silkiest voices I've ever heard. And as luscious as her speaking voice is, her singing is even better. She's doing the world and herself a great disservice in not singing. According to Reina, she's simply taking a sabbatical, trying to refocus and recenter her life and herself. My opinion is truly unsolicited, but I'm thinking she's dealing with a lot of fear and anxiety resulting from her current state of being. Of course I've noticed her weight gain over the past few years. I am a health professional. I take note of these things. Still, I don't consider her weight gain a valid excuse to refrain from her gift and calling. I've offered, in so many subtle ways, to help her overcome the issue. Guess I should just be straightforward and come out with it, letting her know in no uncertain terms that she's killing herself softly, and it's time to return to living.

The answering machine beeps, giving me permission to speak.

"Hey, beautiful. I want to proposition you." I laugh aloud at my own double entendre. "Call me." I'm thinking if the house sale goes through, perhaps Reina would be interested in renting my condo. It could prove a viable solution for us both.

It's practically nine o'clock on a Wednesday night and Reina's not home watching one of her favorite TV programs or surfing on the World Wide Web? There's only one logical explanation. Jamal. Why doesn't she just admit she's doing more than showing the brother around town? I have yet to meet the man, but believe you me, I've heard his virtues sung more times in this past week than I can shake a stick at. What exactly does that mean, shake a stick at? I got that from Nana. Just one of her countless homilies.

Someone's knocking.

"Yes."

My office door opens and a face peeps around the frame.

"Hey, Chris, you forgot to pick up your mail from the front desk."

"Thanks, Jenn." It's the front desk supervisor. She plops uninvited in the chair across from my desk. That's Jenn for you, brazen as all get-out, but one hell of an administrator. "Come in. Have a seat."

She laughed.

Now, I admit I've had no experience dating women of a Caucasian persuasion. My predilections haven't led me to sample the "lighter" fare. Still, I'm a man and I have eyes, and my eyes tell me that Jenn is attractive just the same. And unless my wires are cut, the woman's been tossing vibe at me for a while.

"Hey, Chris, can I put in a request to have next Friday off?"

"I don't see why not. Just make sure there's adequate coverage at the front desk."

"I've already done that."

"Then I guess you've already assumed I'll say yes."

She laughed again.

"Well, it's just that I met someone and he wants to take me up to Tahoe to ski before the spring thaw sets in," she explained, batting her eyelashes coyly at me.

Did I ask for an explanation? We all accrue vacation leave. I don't need to know all the particulars of her life. This is a prime example of what I mean about Jenn throwing shade my way. This woman seems to find it necessary to divulge personal facts that I care nothing about. Is she baiting me, tossing hints, hoping I'll make a move before she's too far gone in a relationship of another direction? Sorry, darling, but I don't play savior.

"Just fill out the request form and slip it to me before you leave tonight. Please."

She actually looked disappointed.

Unbelievable.

Recovering quickly, she bounded from the chair, her tight little Valley Fitness shorts cutting into her overly muscled legs. Now, I like big legs, but I'm not trying to date a woman who could crush my back with one thigh.

"Oh, here's your mail," she stated, handing me a stack of envelopes as if just remembering the mission that brought her into my office in the first place.

"Thanks." I tossed them onto my desk for later.

"Need anything else?" Jenn asked, swinging her too-long, overly frizzy, fried strawberry blond perm over her shoulders as she paused at the door.

"Not a thing," I assured her, shaking my head and hoping the woman would take a hint without me having to bounce vicious and hurt her feelings. Luckily, she smiled and bounced down the hall, leaving me to the privacy of my affairs.

Time to shut my office door. That's one of the privileges of being the big buck in the big house.

I have to get back to the records I was reviewing before Looking for Mr. Lover Man interrupted. If I concentrate hard enough I can be finished by ten, go home, take a shower, grab a bite to eat, and snatch a few good hours of sleep before starting all over again tomorrow. Man, I tell you, I'll be glad when my first inspection is finished and a brother can resume a life that's seminormal.

It was after eleven when I finally turned off my computer and closed up shop for the night. Still, I had to take files home with me, sliding them into my leather bag that was a promotion gift from Dad. When I reached to grab my key ring off the top of my desk, I noticed the mail I earlier tossed on a stack of already opened correspondence. Nothing of interest . . . except a small envelope the size of a party invitation. My eyes were really too bleary to read it, so I decided to take it home with me as I turned off my office lights and headed out, saying good-night to the late crew before exiting the building and walking to my vehicle, where it was parked in the spot marked RESERVED: FACILITY DIRECTOR. Aww, just one of the many perks I'm paying a cost to enjoy.

By midnight I had showered, shaved, and had a bowl of the home-made chicken chowder Nana brought over the other day. It was rather nippy for a March night, so I closed the wide-open bedroom windows before settling back in the warmth of my empty bed. I fully intended to extract those file folders from my bag and review some facts and figures before snatching a little shut eye, but enough is enough. And then I remembered the envelope in my bag. I found it and began to read.

Chris,
Congratulations on your much-deserved promotion. It's going to be great working with you more closely day by day and night by night.
Here's to a more fulfilling association,
An Admirer

What kind of mess is this? Am I supposed to laugh or what? This has to be a joke. A more fulfilling association? For whom? I mean, come on, now! Stop the ambiguous bull and come correct with it. Be woman enough to step to me and make yourself known. Color me stupid, but I am not amused, *Jenn!*

Should I be flattered? Or frightened? I can really do without a fatal attraction right now. I rub my head and read the note again, certain the writing is Jenn's, when a hint of some fragrance clinging to the ecru-colored parchment paper hits me in the nose. Waving the stationery directly beneath my nostrils, I inhale. The paper is scented. It's not frilly or flowery. It's . . . androgynous. Neither feminine nor masculine. And somehow it's oddly familiar and freaky. Now that ought to have been cause enough for concern, but it's late and I'm too exhausted for terror. Even my journal will have to wait. When faced with the light of a new day I'll decide my course of action and what emotion to assign to this possibly bizarre episode. Right now I'm only cognizant of one pressing need and that is sleep. Jenn and her note-writing self can wait until morning.

You know I've heard Nana say that God takes care of babes and fools. I'm not sure which category I fall into, but He certainly took care of me. I thank Him for giving me the foresight to tighten up my ship and get my house in order. Don't you know an hour had barely passed from the time I arrived at my office the following morning until Jenn came barging through the door all animated and stuttering in her excitement that the board had arrived. Our conversation regarding the little note she delivered yesterday would have to wait.

Wouldn't you know it? They would waste no time in coming to check out a newly promoted brother. They can drag their feet for up to two months on a visit to Mr. Charlie's club, but they rush to see what kind of zoo the Affirmative Action animal is keeping. Well, I'm ready. They can take their best shot.

And they did, too. I mean they went over our computerized accounting ledgers, our membership records, and employee files with a superfine-tooth comb. They even randomly selected and phoned a few members on our active rosters just to ensure that they were living, breathing people and not fictitious names invented to inflate our numbers. All four members of the board took turns testing various pieces of our fitness equipment for performance and safety. I thought we might need to dial 911 for one member in particular when he called himself testing the new StairMaster. The only stairs he'd climbed recently were probably a stepladder that elevated his short, stout self so he could reach the soft-baked chocolate-chip macadamia-nut cookies hidden on the top shelf of his kitchen cupboard. I thought only facility owners could be elected to the executive board. You would think the man would utilize his own gym and practice what he preached. I was tempted to offer him a special VIP pass to our facility, but I rather enjoy bringing home a paycheck every week and want to keep it that way.

Three hours after it began, the "visit" was through and so were we. The sigh of relief the staff collectively exhaled when the board finally departed was thick and palpable. All eyes were on me. Their questioning looks were clear. Did we pass?

I stood there at the front desk, stalling, trying my best to look somber and disheartened, but it didn't work. My man Stevie Wonder could see the smile behind my feigned gloom.

"We're home free!" I assured my staff.

They started cheering and slapping high fives and dancing like *Riverdance* on crank. Someone started an Arsenio Hall "woof woof" bark, and soon they were all barking and pumping fists in the air and looking just as goofy as you please.

"All right, all right, folks. Keep it down," I urged, motioning for a lower-decibel noise level with my hands. "We have clients in here trying to enjoy their workouts without sound effects from the zoo."

"Let's celebrate!" someone hollered.

"Yeah," someone else concurred.

"Name your pleasure," I replied.

"Pizza."

"Beer."

"Chocolate raspberry cheesecake."

"Pizza, beer, and chocolate raspberry cheesecake with whipped cream."

I laughed. Funny how even fitness buffs can't seem to think of a better way to celebrate achievements than with food.

"How about bagels?" Ethan the player-hating aqua-aerobics instructor suggested.

"Perfect. It's my treat," I assured everyone. "Any preferred flavors?"

So many options flew at me that I finally gave up, deciding to buy several dozens of mixed varieties.

"I'll go with you, Chris," Jenn graciously offered, smiling wide and batting her baby grays at me. A brother was trapped until Ethan, an unexpected ally, came to his aid.

"Hey, Chris, my cousin owns the bagel shop up the street. If you don't mind my going with you, I can get us a discount or at least a couple of containers of schmear on the house."

Relieved, I gladly accepted Ethan's offer to accompany me to the bagel shop, to Jenn's dismay.

Big mistake.

We were feeling so good and the weather was so nice that we chose to walk rather than drive the few blocks. Ethan talked nonstop all the way there and all the way back, segueing from one seemingly seamless topic to another in an endless stream. The only time he shut his trap was when I placed our order with his cousin. True to Ethan's word, we were given a discount and three complimentary tubs of different flavored cream-cheese spreads. I gave his cousin my thanks and told him to come by and see me for a free two-week pass to our fitness facility in exchange for his generosity. Back on the block, Ethan resumed his chatter, which did not end until we returned to Valley Fitness, laid out the bagels in the employee kitchen area, and I escaped to my office.

I didn't stay there long. I was so pumped about our passing inspection that I decided to move about, check on our clients, and see how they were faring. I stopped by the juice bar and was able to convince one of our testiest but most loyal customers to try the peach mango smoothie with one of the new circulation-improving herbs I had incorporated into our vast stock of traditional supplements. Two successes in one day. A brother was on a roll.

I should have stopped while I was ahead. I sat and chatted with a few customers soaking in the sauna, then headed to the locker room. Now that I was facility director I had my own locker that was practically a closet in my office. I no longer used the assigned employee space I'd maintained before, and needed to remove the few articles of clothing and toiletries I'd left behind. As I was walking down the hallway, just before I rounded a corner, I stepped right into a conversation that was meant to be private.

"I don't think you're the boss's type, Jenn," my aqua aerobics instructor was saying.

"Oh?" was her disbelieving response. "What's wrong with me?"

"Nothing. You're decent. You're just not—"

"Not what?" Jenn demanded, sounding defiant.

"Well," Ethan suggested, "you might want to deepen your tan a bit."

I stepped around the corner and smack into the middle of their secretive laughter. I'd never seen a deeper shade of crimson than that on their faces when they saw me standing there. Looked like they'd been spray-painted at a tagging festival. Poor things. I wanted to laugh, but they were mortified enough as it was. Instead, I nodded and continued walking in the direction of the locker room, a petrified silence at my back.

Jenn could deepen her tan until she was fried to a crackling crisp and still this fish wasn't biting.

I cleaned out my locker and returned to my office. I had to phone one of my boys so we could get a good laugh out of this.

The call never happened. My day took an even more dramatic turn that left me speechless and not knowing exactly who, if anyone, to call or what, if anything, to say.

I stopped by the front desk for something, I can't even recall exactly what now, when the front door opened and in walked Ethan's bagel shop-owning cousin. I waved and shook his hand when he drew near.

"Hey, pretty nice facility you've got here," he remarked, looking about.

"I would have thought you would have been by before, seeing as how you're related to one of our best instructors."

He beamed.

"Yeah, well, the bagel business keeps me busy. But, hey, this free two-week pass was an offer I couldn't refuse. So here I am to collect my reward."

I clapped him on the shoulder and offered him a seat at the front counter while the day-shift receptionist located the secured box in which we kept complimentary passes. We chatted and waited as she logged the certificate number on the pass along with some data on its recipient in the database before handing it to me. I gave it to Ethan's cousin, who was extolling the virtues of an excellent massage therapist who was looking to contract her services with a fitness center.

"Would you mind phoning me with her name and number later?" I asked, thinking it might be a perfect solution, as our full-time massage therapist planned to quit and be a stay-at-home mother when her baby arrived a few months from now.

"I'll do you one better. I'll write it down for you now. She's my sister-in-law, so I know her phone number by heart."

"A little nepotism, huh?" I joked, causing him to chuckle heartily.

I started to offer him pen and paper, but he was already pulling them from the back pocket of his khakis. In big, bold letters, he scrawled the data across a piece of expensive-looking blank card stock. He handed me the card, I thanked him, and was just about to slip the card into my own pocket when I suddenly stopped.

I'd seen this ecru parchment before. Was my nose deceiving me or was I getting a whiff of something familiar? I fanned the card beneath my nostrils just to be sure.

"Nice, huh?"

"Where did you get this?" I asked.

"I'm having new business cards made and thought it would be great to have cards that actually smell like fresh-baked bagels. You know, get the tongue salivating and make folks run to see me. I'm telling you, that Ethan is a genius."

"Ethan?"

"Yeah, it's his creation. He can make stationery with any scent you like." He suddenly clamped his mouth tight, then slowly, cautiously resumed speech. "I hope I'm not getting him into trouble—"

"N-no, I'm aware that he's involved in an entrepreneurial venture. There's no conflict of interest, so it's not a problem."

"Whew! That's good to know. Well, hey, you might want him to design some cards and things for your gym here. Just make sure he doesn't make them smell like old socks and dirty sneakers." He laughed at his own joke. I tried, but sound was caught somewhere between my belly and my mouth. We shook hands again and he headed toward the front door, promising to be back soon to work up a sweat.

I reexamined the card in my hand. The handwriting was much like that on the note still resting in the zipper compartment of my leather bag. Sloping, scrawling. Big and bold. I sniffed the card again. That's it! That androgynous fragrance, neither male nor female, indeterminate and elusive was that of, can you believe it, fresh-baked bagels! Here I was trying to imagine what flower, what oil, what seed could possibly have lent its scent to Jenn's note when it was none of these. Merely bagels . . . and Ethan!

"Hey, Chris, don't forget a sub is filling in for my morning class tomorrow. I'll be back in time for my one o'clock class as long as the dentist doesn't drill a hole in my head." He laughed. I turned.

There he was, fit and jovial, pink lips smiling. Ethan. The mystery writer. Now I understood those piercing looks that I misinterpreted as the stares of a jealous rival. Now I knew why the man babbled nonstop all the way to and from the bagel shop this morning. He was nervous. Now I, unfortunately, know why he tried to dissuade Jenn in the hallway with that need-a-deeper-tan bit. He was trying to disqualify the competition.

Ethan had evidently swallowed one mouthful of chlorine too many in that aqua-aerobics class of his. He might be gay but I was not. Was I? Holdupholdupholdup! *Hold up!* Of course I'm not. But what would lead him to think I would be open to his affections? What did he see in me that I didn't see in myself? Okay, okay. Let's slow this roaring train a minute. I could be wrong. How do I really know it was Ethan who penned the passionate prose?

"Ethan, can I have a moment of your time?" I asked, walking toward my office before he could even think to respond. Once there, I searched my leather bag until I found the sordid little note that started all of this.

Slowly I pulled it from the bag, held it in clear view, and got all the answer I needed.

His embarrassed, hope-filled face told the sad story. Poor Jenn. I had accused her falsely. Not that she wasn't trying to get at a brother, but she was innocent of penning some pathetic little juvenile anonymous love note.

I wanted to punch Ethan in his soft green eyes. I felt like ramming my fist against the side of his finely chiseled jaw.

I had to vomit or drink something that would settle my stomach and that wouldn't make me gag. I needed to pray, scream, cry, and cuss, because a brother was confused as all get-out.

I needed a cigarette and I don't even smoke.

VANESSA

A pril was a mere glimmer in the distance and already things were heating up in the nation's capital. The sun was spiteful, a breeze came to visit only at night, and the air was hot enough to suck a Jheri Curl dry.

Despite the sultry weather of Washington, D.C., Vanessa was enjoying her stay. So much so that she found it hard to leave. She saw black folks in all shapes and shades, professions and play. When, if ever, had she seen brothers riding Jet Skis and other watercraft on the Potomac or any other lakes? Sisters owning and running posh five-star restaurants complete with crews of all-African-American servers decked in crisp white shirts, shin-length aprons, and linen cloths draped over their arms, talking about "Will there be anything else this evening, Miss Taylor?" *Yeah, gimme an all-over body massage and wrap my food to go. I'll have dinner in bed, thank you,* Vanessa wanted to holler. But she didn't. She kept her cool and tipped the brothers real good.

She found a black-owned day spa, a beauty supply store that featured products imported from the Caribbean islands, jazz clubs and dance halls galore. She dined at an Ethiopian restaurant where diners at their individual tables ate from huge communal bowls with their hands. Vanessa had to admit the forkless meal took a bit getting used to. But once she overcame her inhibitions, Vanessa was good to go, throwing back couscous and some savory chicken-and-lamb dish like a pro, not minding the sauce dripping from her fingers and smearing her perfectly manicured nails.

D.C. felt good. The streets were crowded, the people were friendly, and Vanessa felt a strange sense of belonging that fueled her resolve. She was a woman on a mission that would begin and hopefully end in the great district black author and inventor Benjamin Banneker helped design. It could very well be that one of the brownstones she passed daily, when walking or riding in a cab through the tourist district and residential sections or back to the hotel, housed the woman who had given her life. The very territory that gave rise to memorials to Lincoln and Jefferson, the United States Capitol, the White House, the Library of Congress, and the Supreme Court's building, could very well prove the sight of Vanessa's own quiet entry into the world.

The annual convening of the NBBA, the National Black Broadcasters' Association, had concluded days ago. Vanessa had actually enjoyed it this year. In times past, the convention tended to be stuffy, bourgeoisie with all those uptight, I-don't-eat-neckbones-anymore kind of professional black folks who pronounced every syllable and consonant while speaking during sessions, but still ordered a "mamoosoo," instead of a mimosa at the dinner table at night. Vanessa had to laugh. She no longer ate neckbones either, but she did have sense enough to know that mimosas were meant to be savored with brunch, not prime rib and broccoli Florentine.

The executive committee had purposefully attempted to move away from the staid, dry, or emotionally charged topics of the past. No "What's wrong with rap music today" or "Taking back prime time" rhetoric was espoused this year. Instead, there were notable motivational speakers, and recognition and awards for outstanding documentaries, news coverage, and radio shows. There was a much more relaxed and intimate atmosphere. One of the members of the existing executive committee had even intimated that he would recommend Vanessa as his replacement for next year's board. What a definite feather in her cap. That was the highlight of her stay, until now.

Now Vanessa stood clutching a crinkled piece of paper in her hand, gazing up at the building before her. *Walk up the steps and open the door, girl,* she repeatedly told herself. But no matter how fervently she urged her feet to move, Vanessa was frozen on the Washington, D.C., sidewalk staring up at the brownstone building of her birth.

She was born at home, or so all the clues indicated. Either her parents did not have enough money or health insurance to cover the hospital bills her birth would have produced, or they were from the old school and preferred the trustworthiness of a familiar midwife to a physician's lofty book learning. Which was the case? Vanessa was uncertain. She would pose the question and hope to be given an answer. Just as soon as her feet got with the program and moved up those steps that loomed before her like the stairway to heaven.

"Are you lost, lady?"

Vanessa felt a tug and, looking down, found a brown cherub of a girl pulling on her skirt. Vanessa smiled. The child had a head of thick ponytails decorated by countless ribbons and barrettes in every hue of the rainbow. She was at that age where a missing front tooth was her badge of honor, signifying her passing from babyhood into that limbo state where one waited for adolescence to descend with a holler and a shout.

For the first time since arriving at the steps, Vanessa looked around, taking in the scene about her. School had been dismissed for the day. There were children playing stickball on the streets, a group of girls jumping double Dutch on the sidewalk. An ice-cream vendor pushed a cart, ringing a bell and hawking his cool wares. Somewhere someone was playing the local top-forty station, treating the neighborhood to the blaring volume of his or her radio. It was surreal, like something straight out of a Spike Lee joint. Vanessa felt as if she had just walked back in time, back to a place where she belonged, a place she never enjoyed but somehow knew.

"Well, I don't think so," Vanessa finally responded to the child's inquiry.

"Whatcha looking for?"

Vanessa unfolded the crumpled piece of paper that had been folded and refolded countless times. She squatted on her haunches until she was eye level with the child.

"Can you read?"

The girl put her hands on her nonexistent hips.

"Of course I can! I'm seven years old. My gramms taught me to read when I was little."

Vanessa laughed.

"Okay, then read this to me," Vanessa said, holding the paper out to the child.

As if to salvage her injured dignity, the brown cherub read in a loud, clear voice the address written on the paper. Then she pointed at the brownstone that Vanessa had been facing.

"It's that one right there. The same one where my gramms and gramps live. You just don't have no unit number."

One of the children on the block yelled out, waving to the little girl to come and play.

"'Bye, I gotta go," Brown Cherub quickly told Vanessa. "Who you looking for?" she asked, not bothering to await a response as she trotted up the street to join her peers in their games.

"My mother," Vanessa softly confided to the afternoon. Taking a deep, almost painful breath, Vanessa willed herself to move one step at a time. Slowly, her limbs came to life and she took that first step that would lead her to her past and perhaps her future.

Brown Cherub was right. The one piece of information Vanessa's soror had failed to provide was the actual unit number of the home in which her birth mother resided. She nearly panicked. Her soror, the one who worked with a family court judge, had been so generous and helpful. She bent rules, called in favors, did more research and tracking than Vanessa could have ever asked for. Vanessa's birth records had been unsealed, the identity of her biological parents revealed. Now there she stood in the lobby of the brownstone, not knowing which way to go, on which door to knock. So close and yet so far.

Vanessa did her usual. She counted backward from ten, inhaling, exhaling deeply into her lungs in an attempt to calm her jittery nerves. *You've come too far to give up now*, Vanessa told herself, reminding herself that the lack of a unit number was really a minute oversight, indeed. If she had to knock on all four doors in the spacious building, she would. How hard could it be? Then she had a better idea. The mailboxes! Surely the tenants' names would be on the shiny silver mailboxes fitted into the wall of the lobby.

Vanessa hurried forward and began scanning the labels. Nothing. Not even one name remotely similar to Taylor. Vanessa reexamined the piece of paper in her hand. There really was no need to. She had memorized every detail it contained. Still, with growing alarm, she scanned the paper once more just to be sure she had not misread anything. Disheartened, Vanessa concluded she'd made no mistake. There was no evidence of her parents' existence there in the brownstone. And without proof of their living, the mystery involving her own being would remain unsolved.

Vanessa leaned back against the wall. Eyes closed, shoulders slumped, she felt the first wave of sadness swell within her breast. She had such hope, such expectation that today would be the first day of the rest of her life. She would find roots, history, her story. Connections. Answers. What were the circumstances surrounding her birth? How had she come to be a ward of the state? Did she have any other living family members? Who did she look like, her mother or her father? Whose genetic makeup was responsible for her cinnamon brown skin, her topaz eyes, her full lips, her even fuller hips? Were there health issues, a predisposition to certain ailments in her lineage? So many questions. Absolutely no answers.

Somewhere a door opened.

"That gal better not be out there playing in that water," someone fussed with that certain blend of annoyance and concern that only mothers can evoke. Vanessa opened her eyes and watched a wizened little woman shuffle to the main entrance of the brownstone, then throw back the front door with amazing strength to step out on the landing and look up and down the street. Apparently satisfied that whoever she was checking on was not violating her "no water play" policy, the woman stepped back into the lobby and saw Vanessa for the first time.

"Hello," she said, her voice amazingly strong and smooth.

"Good afternoon," Vanessa returned as brightly as she could.

"Why you standing there holding up that wall like that? You sick?"

Vanessa swallowed hard. Yes, she was sick to her heart, and without an apparent cure.

"You got no home training, gal? I asked you a question. You sick or what?" the elder woman repeated, shuffling nearer Vanessa, her eyes squinting as if to readjust themselves to the lighting indoors. She stopped suddenly, pulling away as if Vanessa were an apparition of some sort. Slightly unnerved by the recoiling woman, Vanessa carefully watched as the woman's wrinkled eyelids rapidly, repeatedly danced open and closed over watery eyes of some indiscriminate hue. They were almond-shaped eyes that must have been lovely in the woman's prime. Just then they were windows filled with anguishing stories and forgotten truths.

"Vera?" the old woman whispered, stepping so close that Vanessa smelled the odd fragrance clinging to her clothes: ginger, vanilla, and liniment. "Vera Ann, how many times must I tell you to stop hanging out here with your tail hanging out for all these no-'count boys to see? Get your fast-ass self back in that house."

"I'm sorry, you have—"

"Sass me again and see if I don't whap you one good time. Get!" The woman shooed Vanessa past the mailboxes, around a corner, and through an open door of a rather large, extremely tidy unit on the first floor of the building. The woman slammed the door behind them, ignoring Vanessa's protests that she was mistaking her for someone else. "Go put some clothes on. No, better yet, sit your tail down on that sofa there and don't get up until I finish with you."

Vanessa hurriedly obliged, looking down at the silk, mudcloth patterned sarong skirt set she was wearing. The hemline was just above her knees. The matching tank top was modest, not low cut. She was decent. What was all the fuss about? Vanessa laughed aloud. Here she was worrying about an obviously senile woman's opinion of her clothing, a woman who thought she was someone named Vera . . . Ann.

"You finding humor in the situation, gal?"

"No, ma'am," Vanessa croaked, unnerved, her voice suddenly shaky. Discreetly, she unfolded the paper holding the opening scenes of her life that was still fiercely clutched in her palm as the woman set about "schooling" Vanessa on the virtues of modesty and propriety. On the bottom half of the page was a minuscule photocopy of her birth certificate. Vanessa squinted and read, *Birth Mother's Name: Veran Taylor.* Holding the paper closer to her face, Vanessa scrutinized it further. She held it up to the light streaming through an open window in the apartment. She gasped. She had erred. Someone's handwriting had been too large for the assigned space, their letters flowing beyond the borders and into the adjoining box. Her mother's name was not Veran. It was Vera Ann Taylor.

"Put that down and pay attention," the elder woman snapped.

"Yes, Gramms." She said it without forethought. The words just slipped from her tongue in a most natural fashion. The effect was instantaneous. The old woman grew calm. She sat in the armchair directly across from Vanessa, and stared until huge tears welled up and splashed onto her sunken cinnamon-brown cheeks.

As if awakened from deep slumber, the woman sat up suddenly, her back ramrod straight. "I'm so embarrassed," she stammered. "That's never happened before." She covered her mouth with trembling fingers, shaking her head slowly from side to side. "You're not Vera Ann, are you?" she asked in a voice filled with grief and shame.

"No, ma'am. I'm not," Vanessa answered, her own eyes filling with tears for the woman's pain. "I'm her daughter."

The woman leaned close. She hesitated a moment before reaching out wrinkled little hands to cup Vanessa's face in her palms and run her fingers up and down the sides of her cheeks, her forehead, across her shoulders, down her arms, as if searching for some linkage that would prove Vanessa's claim. Without warning, she crushed Vanessa to her chest, sobbing uncontrollably.

"Thank you, Lord," she cried again and again.

Vanessa was uncomfortable. She was being fiercely clutched by a perfect stranger who might or might not have a firm grip on reality. But then it clicked. This was no perfect stranger. This woman rocking her gently in her arms was her very own grandmother. Willingly, Vanessa relaxed and gave in to an embrace of ages that seemed to last an eternity.

"Spitting image, you are," the woman stated, releasing her at last, her piercing funny-colored eyes scrutinizing every inch of Vanessa's being. She chuckled happily, then suddenly sobered. "You're the baby, aren't you? You're not that first child that was taken from us by your daddy. I told Vera Ann that man meant business. She just wouldn't listen. Kept running around with no-'count boys until Taylor did what he said he would." She sighed as if her heart hurt. "He took that oldest baby and moved clear 'cross country. But not before he put her in a fix again." She paused to pull a handkerchief from the pocket of her housedress and wiped her teary eyes. "She didn't know she was carrying you until after he was gone. But when she found out she went after him. Didn't have no more money than a little bit. I told her not to go, but Vera Ann Smith was always stubborn. Spoiled, really." The woman's laugh was a mixture of pride and pain. "But somehow that hot-tail girl of mine made it."

"Smith?" Vanessa's brows furrowed. "I'm sorry, but wasn't my mother's last name Taylor?"

Her grandmother pursed her lips together and quickly glanced away.

"No, baby, your mama and daddy never married." She looked

Vanessa straight in the eye. "That's why you and that oldest baby were born at home."

Vanessa sat back and ran her fingers over the close-cropped hair at the nape of her neck. That confirmed things. Vanessa's soror had had a terrible time tracking hospital records detailing her birth, leading them both to consider that perhaps hers had been an at-home birth. Furthermore, Vanessa's birth certificate listed her mother as Veran Taylor when in fact she was Vera Ann Smith. Vanessa suddenly had a headache.

"It was different back then," her grandmother explained. "Marriage was a requisite to motherhood, as it should be. Single women didn't have no business spreading they legs and getting themselves in a family way. There was stigma."

"So illegitimate babies were born in secrecy," Vanessa tonelessly stated.

Her grandmother nodded.

"When and if it could be done that way, yes."

Vanessa felt as if she were trapped in some turn-of-the-century Deep South drama where midwives were whisked in and out of one-room shanties in the middle of the night to deliver some poor "scandalous and indecent," knocked-up, silly young thing of her "plight."

"So-o-o, Vera Ann met up with my father again?" Vanessa asked, desperately trying to digest what she had just learned.

Mrs. Smith gave Vanessa an incredulous look, as if she should know that nothing was impossible once Vera Ann Smith set her mind to it.

"Sure did. Found Taylor out there in that crazy California—"

"My mother is in California?" Vanessa asked, sitting forward on the edge of her seat.

"Maybe." It was such an ambiguous response in such a tone of finality that it did not invite further exploration. Vanessa instinctively knew not to push that particular topic any further. She had many questions, burning questions. If they were to be answered, then she must accommodate the moods and methods of those controlling that much-desired information.

Seeing that Vanessa would press no further, Mrs. Smith continued.

"Your mama thought they could rekindle a flame and set up house, but she was too late."

"How so?" Vanessa inquired.

"Taylor found himself another woman. From what I know she was fixing to get divorced and had a child of her own. They was planning on getting married and raising they children together. But Vera Ann stepped in before things could happen." She paused, shaking her head sadly. "Lord, she just didn't handle things the right way."

Vanessa reached for the old lady's hands. She wanted to know exactly how Vera Ann had mishandled the situation. She sensed some dark and brooding truth hanging between them. But she never had the chance to uncover the deed. Just then the front door swung open and in bounced Brown Cherub, smelling of earth and sun and air. Pure and clean.

"Gramms—" She paused when seeing Vanessa. "I know you. You're the lost lady."

Out of the mouths of babes came wisdom and wit. How right she was. Vanessa was more lost now that she had found a link in her parental chain than before. Who was she? Who were these parents of hers who, for reasons unknown, could not stay together, one fleeing to the opposite side of the nation only to be pursued by the one left behind? Why had they never married? And what had Vera Ann done to keep such pain, decades later, deep-rooted in her mother's eyes?

Brown Cherub skipped over to her gramms, leaning against the old lady and wrapping her tender arms around the wrinkled, worn neck.

"Is the gingerbread done?"

That explained the scents that earlier greeted Vanessa outside in the hall.

"You have home training, gal?"

"Yes, ma'am," Brown Cherub meekly replied.

"Then say hello to your second cousin. This here is your great-aunt Vera's daughter, Vanessa Ann."

"Hi, Vanessa," Brown Cherub said, suddenly shy.

"Vanessa?" Gramms repeated. "Since when do you call grown folks by they first names? Put a handle on that. It's Aunt Vanessa or Miss Vanessa, but it ain't just plain Vanessa to you. Understood?"

Brown Cherub nodded.

"Good."

Suddenly tender, Gramms lovingly stroked the little girl's head, playfully pulling one of her ribbon-bedecked ponytails. "This here is my great-grandbaby, Celine. She spends a lot of time with me in the summers."

Vanessa reached out and shook the tiny hand that was offered.

"I'm taking care of Gramms until Gramps comes home," the little girl proudly stated in a most grown-up fashion.

"And where is your gramps?" Vanessa asked, smiling.

"My husband's away on business with my oldest daughter, your mama's sister," Gramms abruptly stated. She cleared her throat loudly. "So how old are you now, Vanessa Ann? Twenty-six, twenty-seven?"

"I'll be thirty on my next birthday."

"Thirty? Ooh, my. How time flies," the elder woman stated, and exhaled, as if mourning stolen moments. "You're a pretty thing, too. Looking just like your mother with those funny-colored eyes I gave her. Inherited them from my mama, myself."

"Gramms!" Celine whined, indifferent to the sharing of intimate knowledge taking place in her midst. "Can I have some gingerbread, *please?*"

"May I, not can I," the elder woman corrected, lightly swatting the little girl on the rear. She eased herself up from the overstuffed armchair and ambled toward the kitchen. "Come on here, you two, and help yourselves. I'm too old to be waiting on young folks."

Celine danced into the kitchen, proudly displaying her knowledge of the layout as she showed Vanessa where to find napkins, a glass for her milk, and two teacups for the grown-ups' brew. Brown Cherub sipped her milk and munched her bread, chattering to her captive audience as Vanessa sat eating warm gingerbread and sipping hot peppermint tea with Gramms. Gramms claimed it was her preferred flavor. Like grandmother, like granddaughter. Vanessa had found a glimmer of herself.

Three hours ago Vanessa Ann Taylor was an orphan. Three hours later Vanessa Ann Taylor had found a living, breathing family who embraced her as their own. She had a grandmother who drank peppermint tea and baked fresh gingerbread and reminisced of days gone by. Some of her memories were amazingly clear; others were cloudy at best. At least Gramms had memories. Which was more than Vanessa could say for herself. Things upon which she would one day reminisce were yet in the making.

She had family. A grandmother, a grandfather, an angel of a little cousin who loved old-fashioned oven-baked treats and spending time with her great-grandparents during the summers. Vera Ann Smith had two older sisters, and they had husbands and children, and children who had children. Vanessa's circle had expanded beyond her wildest hopes. Did she want to meet them? Gramms had inquired. Most of the family lived in D.C. or nearby in Virginia and South Carolina. Gramms had only to make a few phone calls to inform them of Vanessa's resurrection and they would be in D.C. on—as Gramms put it—the first thing smoking.

Vanessa was touched by her generosity, extremely pleased to discover she had such an extensive family. But she needed to digest this overwhelming nugget bit by bit. Perhaps before she left D.C. she could begin to meet her clan. Perhaps, until then, Vanessa could glance through family photo albums to acquaint herself with her people.

Gramms would only offer albums of recent photos featuring her grands and great-grands, Vanessa's cousins. Though Vanessa wanted visual pieces to the puzzle of her parents' sordid love affair, Gramms was either unwilling or unable to comply. It was as if Vanessa—so like her mother, according to Gramms—was all the reminder, all the shock the older woman could take in a day. She would not allow herself to dive any deeper into the pool of their past.

Vanessa masked her disappointment, reminding herself that good fortune had smiled on her. She had made an extraordinary connection in such a short time. She could neither force nor expect her grandmother to readily dredge up too many old recollections so soon. After all, Vanessa was a nearly thirty-year-old blast from a past fraught with riddles and discordant rhymes.

Hours had passed since her return, and still Vanessa sat on the terrace of her hotel room overlooking the large diamond-shaped pool many stories below. The night air bore only a slight resemblance to the warm day that was no more. Cold air ruffled the hem of her gold-and-red Kinte lounging gown, playfully tossing tendrils of hair about her face, kissing the close-cropped strands at her nape and temples. Still she sat, hoping the chilly air would clear her mind of rambling thoughts.

If she focused hard enough, Vanessa could just make out the dome of the Jefferson Memorial in the distance. Had President Jefferson truly believed in the inalienable rights of man? If so, why had he not gone against the grain, risking public outcry and personal ostracism, and abolished slavery a near century before Lincoln? Honest Abe, the Great Emancipator, had ended a war, not liberated a people in whom he detected no degree of humanity. The great one had even supported the Back-to-Africa movement, the colonizing of Sierra Leone with American slaves just to be rid of his dark burden. Perhaps that was what she had been to her parents: a dark burden not worth bearing. Or as Sally Hemings was to Mr. Thom, perhaps Vanessa was something to be kept secret until reluctantly discovered.

Vanessa shook her head as if to rid it of pessimistic notions. She had been given a priceless gift. Why waste the joy of locating family on self-doubt and unbelief? But she found it hard not to dwell on the decision her parents made to give her up for adoption, an adoption that had never taken place. There were so many questions to be answered, so much longing to be fulfilled. Instead, she forced herself to consider the joy of it all. Her life had been altered by a wizened little woman's leaving her apartment to ensure that her great-granddaughter was playing peaceably and as instructed. How different would her life have been had she grown up with Gramms, eating gingerbread and playing in the comfortable neighborhood streets, instead of with overburdened foster families?

Vanessa's mind hurtled back in time and she reluctantly recalled all the homes, all the people, all the places she'd tenuously lived. Musical homes. That was what it was. Just as soon as she gained some semblance of comfort, pop! She was uprooted and sent off to live somewhere else. Why had it been so excruciatingly difficult to place a little orphan child in a place she could call home? *That was then, this is now,* Vanessa told herself, trying not to allow the anguish of her yesteryears to blight the promise of her present. Yet she couldn't help remembering the pain of never putting down roots, the childish games she played that she was on yet another adventure to someplace grand whenever the social worker showed up on the doorstep, that look of pity in her soft blue eyes. Off they would go, Vanessa reminding herself as she sat quietly in the back of the social worker's pristine car not to become attached, not to get comfortable, to always keep a bag packed and be ready to go at a moment's notice.

She frowned as her thoughts spiraled on.

What brand of woman was her mother? By all accounts she was beautiful. An enticement to the opposite sex. Hotheaded. Impulsive and unconventional. Vera Ann had obviously loved Vanessa's father. Why else would she, pregnant and having barely a cent to her name, up and leave the comforts of her parents' home to traipse thousands of miles on a tedious journey just to find Taylor and the child he had taken with him?

For the first time since learning the sketchy details of her mother's past, Vanessa paused to consider another someone who had suddenly surfaced in her life. She had a sibling! Somewhere out there lived someone who shared her parental lineage, her DNA, her story. Vanessa had an older sibling. Did her sibling still live in California with their father, their mother? Where was she/he and what was her/his name?

The thought was thrilling, intoxicating even. To come from nothing and arrive at something all in one day was more than good could ever be. She was the baby. Someone's baby. The last-born of two. Vanessa was no longer seeking a father, a mother. She had to expand her search to include a sibling designed with her own flesh and blood.

Never could she have imagined that her quest would lead her to place flowers at the foot of the Vietnam Memorial. No one told her to expect the death of a parent before barely knowing his life. But there she stood, tracing what was left of her father with a slim, quivering finger. Sgt. Philip Andrew Taylor. Her daddy had loved her enough to give her his name. She was no miscellaneous bastard. Taylor belonged to her and she to it. His name was forever etched in stone and on her heart.

Gramms had, having finally delivered the sad news, offered to come with her for moral support, but Vanessa declined, stating that she wanted to be alone. Tourists and visitors, family members and strangers stood at the wall reading the names of fallen soldiers who had died serving and protecting their country. Even so, Vanessa was alone, wrapped in a poignant grief that only she could bear. It somehow joined her with her slain father, crossed the great divide between life and death, and whisked her to a quiet place where time stood still. She felt his spirit, loving and strong. She felt his bravery and sense of justice. She still had yet to view a picture of his face, but Vanessa knew him, saw him in the light of her soul. He was beautiful. He belonged to her and she to him. She welcomed his aura and felt a piece of her missing self come home.

Home was where she longed to be. Vanessa cherished the days and nights spent with Gramms and Celine. Slowly, as if realizing she could trust her with the truth, Gramms opened the coffers of history and showed Vanessa how she had come to be and of whom she was made—except, of course, for her parents. Vanessa leafed through more photo albums, heard more tales, talked with more relatives than she could count. It was wondrous, enlightening, spectacular, and mind-boggling, indeed. But California was calling her name. The irony was not lost on her. Vanessa's race to the nation's capital had taken a sudden turn. One search had ended. Another was about to begin. Two days after saying hello and good-bye to her father's name on a memorial wall—her emotions mixed, hopes fueled high— Vanessa boarded the plane to retrace her miles back to a starting place called home.

Thunder and hailstorms forced the plane down in Dallas. There would be a slight layover until weather conditions improved and air-traffic controllers gave the green light that the westward travelers might continue. Until then, as inconvenient as it might be, the huge silver bird was an earthbound thing.

Vanessa wanted to spit. This journey home was proving increasingly bothersome. Her departure from Washington, D.C., had been any-thing but easy. Though they had been in her life only a short time, it was difficult saying good-bye to Gramms and Celine. Their somber departure had been eased only by Vanessa's anticipation of what lay ahead. A mother. A sibling. Somewhere in California they lived— Gramms indeed confirmed that fact—not knowing Vanessa was com-ing to find them. What would their reunion be like? Tearful? Joyous? Apprehensive and reserved? Vanessa let her imagination roam to ex-plore the possibilities, construct the scenarios.

She was busy building a happy reunion when the phone rang.

She should have known better than to answer her ringing cell phone, should have allowed the call to roll over to the answering ser-vice while she continued to evoke images of loving embraces and beautiful cinnamon-brown faces. Mere minutes later Vanessa wanted to run through the airport screaming and pulling what little hair she had out by the roots, wishing she could strike every sound, every word she'd heard into oblivion.

Her mother was dead.

Gramms had never said a mumbling word. Why? Why was her mother's oldest sister, the one away on business with Gramps during Vanessa's stay, the one to break the heartbreaking news? Was Gramms evil, demented, did she need to be put away in a home with twenty-four-hour care so she could not hurt herself and others? But she had been so loving, so gentle with both Vanessa and Celine. So what if she had mistaken Vanessa to be Vera Ann when they'd first met? Gramms was not crazy. Was she? And even if she was, not one of the other relatives Vanessa eventually met clued her in to a thing.

No, her aunt concurred, Gramms was neither evil nor senile. Gramms had just now been informed herself. The "business" the aunt had been occupied with during Vanessa's visit had taken place at the bedside of her dying baby sister. Yes, in California. She had assumed responsibility for the return of her sister's remains to Washington, D.C. No, there was no need for Vanessa to abort her flight home. There would be no funeral service, no interment of the body in the family plot alongside kin who had gone before. Vera Ann was to be cremated, per her request. No, thank you, Vanessa would not like any of the ashes as a keepsake. Yes, the aunt knew the cause of death. No, she couldn't rightly call it natural, per se. Only natural in that it was a logical conclusion to a life poorly lived. No, she would rather wait until Vanessa had returned home and was surrounded by the comfort of loving friends before divulging the gruesome details. She was truly sorry.

Vanessa silenced a too-still, too-small voice lost beneath the clamor of her own yearnings and practically begged her aunt not to withhold from her the truth she was due. Reluctantly, painfully her aunt obliged, filling her newfound niece's ears with ponderous reverberations no mother's child should ever bear.

REINA

Reina was growing more nervous by the minute. Where in the heazy was Vanessa? Didn't she know they were waiting for her? If she didn't get home soon, Reina was about ready to toss open the refrigerator and grab that humongous apple-caramel-crunch cheesecake Phyllis had sent and commence to slicing and dicing and serving herself a taste. Just to calm her nerves.

She had wanted everything to be perfect. Your best friend turned thirty only once. Too bad Phyllis had long ago selected this very weekend to surprise her husband with a romantic getaway to the Napa Valley wine country, because Reina could sure use her help in more ways than one. She wanted a listening ear. She needed to talk openly and freely about her growing feelings for Jamal Williams. They were in constant contact with one another and something steady, but difficult to identify, was growing between them. Reina's lack of clarity was frustrating and she felt truly on edge. Vanessa needed to hurry up and bring her butt home so they could carry out this little celebration, then spend the remainder of the evening talking things over and out.

Reina cringed, her thoughts interrupted by the singer the deejay had brought with her to deliver a special rendition of "Happy Birthday." The wanna-be Luther was seriously off pitch.

No, no, like this, Reina silently screamed as she walked along the beautifully set tables ensuring that everything was nice and neat. She'd heard the no-singing crooner rehearse his song long enough to learn the melody. Shoulders back but soft, Reina hummed aloud, the words eventually overtaking her tongue and flowing from her mouth. The key was perfect, allowing her to shimmy down deep into the contralto range of her multioctave voice. A little Anita, a little Oleta, a lot of Reina. Dang, it felt so good to sing. So natural, so necessary. How had she ever allowed herself to quit? Vanity. Pride. Shame. None was excuse enough to force her into a nonmusical exile. What a waste of talent and time.

The applause was startling. Reina opened her eyes to find her small impromptu audience clapping, smiling, save the man whose song she'd just commandeered to perfection. Only he bore a scowl of displeasure. Lips twisted, eyes nearly slits, he hissed at her softly enough for Reina's ears only, "Diva dog!"

Reina laughed nervously, gave a mock bow, and hurried away back into the kitchen. Had she crossed a boundary? Was she on the verge of reentering the world of music, the thing she loved most? Time would tell.

CHRIS

I was glad for something, anything, to do that would keep my mind occupied. I've had enough of this internal dialogue and dilemma that has been incessantly yapping far too long. I think I've successfully managed to "look" normal, undisturbed until now. But I feel as if this ruse is thinly veiled and near exposure.

Reina keeps looking at me, watching me so intently as if trying to knock a hole in my skull so she can reach my thoughts. I keep her at bay with quick humor and a good front. You know how we brothers can mask a mountain, front like everything's everything and pigs' feet taste good. We are master perpetrators. Probably a holdover from all that shucking and shuffling we were once forced to do. You know that, *Yes, suh, boss, ebbythin' be jus fine. Naw, suh, Mr. Charlie, we don' be needin' no new shoes. Dese heah ones you don' gabe us ten years back jus' fine.* Survival. That's what is was all about then, and that's what it's all about now.

I'm pissed. Why should someone else's desires outspeak, outweigh my own? It makes absolutely no sense to me! Let's keep it real. Here I am, a grown man knowing what I'm all about, where I'm going, and how I intend to get there. I have goals, long- and short-term. I have a foolproof plan of action with step-by-step instructions. I am a Renaissance man. A real 100 percent USDA-approved black man.

So why am I tripping? Because that pink-lipped pansy stirred up my

Kool-Aid without a spoon. I never invited his interests or his intentions. I never asked to be the object of his same-sex desires. I never intimated, indicated, suggested, or confessed it. I'm not effeminate. I don't walk with a switch, talk with a lisp, or write with a limp wrist. I've never been tempted to date a white woman. I sho' 'nuff ain't tryna be bothered with a white man. My name is not Mandingo, and I don't do circus tricks.

Okay! Come correct with it, now.

I have to calm myself and continue helping Reina set up this party for a scrimp of a guest of honor who is nearly two hours late.

VANESSA

Vanessa was a mess by the time the aircraft landed at Sacramento Metro. She should have accepted Chris's offer to pick her up. Instead, she had thought a nice ride home in a taxi with no one asking a thousand questions about her trip would be a good thing. Now she needed someone to connect with, someone who loved and cared for her. She felt more alone now than ever before in her life.

Vanessa sat in the backseat of the not-so-clean conveyance and watched the landscape whiz by. The Saturday-evening traffic was light until they reached the downtown area. Nightlife was alive in the river city. From Interstate 5, Vanessa caught a mere glimpse of Old Sacramento, but she didn't need to see the streets to know shops were well lit, sidewalks were crowded with persons strolling and enjoying the sights, parking structures were nearly filled to capacity as the crowds increased this time of year.

As they passed the harbor, Vanessa thought of the Set. She hadn't been back since the last time, the time she saw stank Keith and his equally stank, patchy-headed wife. That seemed so long ago. So much had occurred in her life until Vanessa had completely forgotten the man and her misplaced affection. The pain that had once been raw and overwhelming had fizzled into a tiny ball of nothing.

Unlike her daughter, Vera Ann Smith had not known when to let go. All of Gramms's tutelage and guidance had fallen on deaf ears, and her attempts at intervention had proven futile. Vera Ann Smith lived the way she chose. She had all the answers; she knew more than anyone else's story could ever convey. She was arrogant, conceited, and considered her beautiful body an instrument of trade. In the end, Vera Ann had traded her body, her soul, herself for nothing but death in return.

For the first time in her life, Vanessa truly considered the heavy magnitude of her own wanton ways. She'd gone from one man to the next, seeking, searching for something to fill the gaps in her gouged spirit. She had been intimate with men who meant her no good, cohabited with brothers who failed to come home at night. She screamed, she cried, she bought their lies as they soothed her wounded ego with their lips, the rocking of their hips, the thrusting of themselves deep into her injured core.

Vanessa was so caught up in her ruminations that she did not notice the phalanx of vehicles parked around the corner and up the block from her home. The taxi rolled to a halt. The driver turned off the meter.

"This is it, ma'am," he told his backseat passenger.

"What?" Vanessa was startled. Glancing about her she realized she was home. She closed her eyes and sighed. It felt good to be back. She hoped Pharaoh hadn't given Reina a hard time or traded Vanessa in for a new mommy in her absence. She hoped Reina hadn't stunk up her kitchen with grease or pork, or pork grease and greasy pork. She certainly hoped Reina had not rearranged the cabinets or the furniture in one of her domesticated fits. *And God, please, puhleez*, Vanessa prayed, *don't let me find any more of my underwear soaking in Lysol in the mop bucket.*

"Need help with your bags, miss?"

Vanessa stopped toying with the sash about her trim waist, twirling and rolling her finger in the soft peach-and-navy fabric.

"Well . . . yes. Thanks," Vanessa answered, unbuckling her seat belt and exiting the vehicle. Might as well make the man earn his tip. She stretched, a full-body kind of stretch that snaps, crackles, and pops everything worth adjusting. Her audible sigh floated out into the April air. She wanted a shower, a shampoo, and a shave. Her armpits were itching from a stubble of new growth. Conscientious, she lowered her arms and smoothed her sleeveless silk-and-rayon sheath dress back down over her hips.

"Nice neighborhood," the driver commented as they traversed the steps to the front porch. "Is it always this quiet or does it ever get rowdy around here?" He chuckled.

"Only if my next-door neighbor forgets to recharge the battery in her cordless phone. Never mind," Vanessa said, seeing the quizzical stare the man gave her. "How much do I owe you?" she asked, searching her purse for her keys.

She never got to use them, and the cabbie had no time to answer. The front door swung open and there stood Reina, a thunderous scowl clouding her usually clear copper complexion.

"Where have you been?"

"Hello to you, too," Vanessa retorted, taken aback by her best friend's sudden uncalled-for fury. This was not the welcome she wanted to come home to.

"Shoot, 'Nessa, we've been waiting for hours."

"We who?"

Just then Chris walked into view.

"Welcome home, gorgeous," he said, his voice sounding drained despite the customary lopsided grin playing about his sexy lips, his eyes suddenly sparkling upon sight of her.

"Hey, Boo," Vanessa returned, trying to ease past Reina's bulk to place her bags inside.

"Excuse me, but I did ask a question," Reina blazed, moving aside only slightly. Reina obviously had something she needed to get off her bosomy chest. But it would have to wait until later. Vanessa was not in the mood.

"Dang, girl, what is your problem? Are you hungry or something?"

"You need to check yourself, wench," Reina answered with a flat palm in Vanessa's face.

"Don't wreck yourself, stank," Vanessa returned, ignoring Reina's gesture. "Here, can you help me with my bags?" Vanessa requested, picking up a piece of luggage and pushing it toward Reina.

"What do I look like? A Pullman porter?"

Chris laughed.

"I swear, you two need Jesus. Give me the bags, gorgeous. I'll take them upstairs for you."

"Thanks, Boo." Vanessa turned her attention to Reina as Chris disappeared. "Ree-Ree, are you okay?"

If Vanessa wasn't mistaken, she thought surely she heard tears in Reina's voice when she responded.

"I spent almost two months getting this shindig ready for you. I wanted everything to be perfect, and now it's all jacked up. You're two hours late and folks are tired."

Vanessa was puzzled. She had no earthly idea what Reina was going on and on about, and she really had no desire to get into anything deep with the girl tonight. Vanessa just wanted to take a hot bath and go to bed. But by the look of things that bath wouldn't come anytime soon. Wearily, Vanessa pushed past Reina and into the living room, where she flopped down onto her imported Italian leather sofa. Vanessa laid her head back against the butter-soft cushions and sighed through pursed lips. Lord, was she beat!

"I have no idea what you're talking about or why you're in a such a tizzy but—"

"Oh, so now I'm just going off for no reason!" Reina exclaimed, sounding defensive as she raced into the living room where Vanessa sat.

"Either that or you need some Midol," Vanessa quipped, feeling the beginning of a headache coming on. She closed her eyes and kneaded her brows.

"You know what?" Reina placed her hands on her bountiful hips. "For all I care you can just shove this little gig up your tight-enough-to-bounce-a-quarter behind."

"What's wrong?" Chris asked as he rejoined them.

"Don't ask me," Reina said. "After all, I'm just talking out the side of my neck. Right, 'Nessa?"

Vanessa chuckled mirthlessly.

"Sounds like it to me."

"Why did I even bother?" Reina fumed, feeling suddenly bitter. Her efforts were unappreciated. "You just can't do for some folks. What a waste. And to think I had my mouth hooked up all day for some of that—"

Vanessa tossed her hands in the air.

"Is food the axis of your cosmos, Reina? Can we get a life already?"

Chris whistled softly. Whatever the situation was that he'd stepped into, it was spiraling out of control with a quickness.

"Ouch, Vanessa. Come on now, ladies, let's not do this," Chris mediated.

"No, let's," Reina said, waving away Chris's peaceful plea. "You have something to say to me, Vanessa?"

Yes, as a matter of fact she did. *I'm tired of you staring in my grill all day, every day. I want you out and my house back.* Furthermore, Vanessa wanted to tell Reina she could to go to Hades on a Hot Wheel, but her bulk would probably prove too much to fit through its fiery gates. Vanessa opened her mouth to speak her thoughts, but better sense got the best of her. She simply shook her head, declining to bite Reina's bait.

"I think I just said it, don't you?" Vanessa eased up from the sofa. "I don't have time for this," she announced. "I've had a long day, and I'm going to bed."

"You don't have time?" Reina repeated, moving aside as Vanessa sashayed toward the stairs. "Well, excuse the hell out of me for interrupting your flow—"

Vanessa paused midway up the stairs and whirled around.

"Reina, find a rack of lamb or a smoked turkey or something you can snack on and raise up off of my last good nerve!"

"Oh, no, you didn't!"

Reina started for the stairs. Chris intervened, gently but firmly holding her back.

"Oh, you got all kinds of hunger jokes tonight, don't you, Beastie Butt!" Reina cried.

"Vanessa, keep walking," Chris cautioned, slowly punctuating each word like a hammer on an anvil. But it was too late. Things had already slipped over the edge of reality.

"Yes, I do, Busty Brown," Vanessa shot back, a twisted mask of annoyance on her face as she searched her dress pockets in a deceptively calm fashion. "You're food-deprived, Reina? Fine. Here, fetch, zoo creature!" she yelled, hurling a foil-wrapped package of airline-issued honey-roasted peanuts at Reina's chest. Wildly, Vanessa rifled through her purse. "What else do I have? Here you go, Hungry Heffa." She flung a tin filled with breath mints at her human target. Sugar-free gum, liquid blue breath drops, a stale granola bar, and individually wrapped peppermints flew at Reina with the force of a hurricane.

"Ouch!" Reina yelled as Chris ducked and dodged the edible missiles connecting all over Reina's body with lightning speed.

Reina grabbed the fallen missiles, only to fling them back at the crazy woman on the stairs.

Chris jumped to the side, out of the line of fire, and just stood there, amazed, trying hard not to be amused, wondering who opened the infirmary gates to let the insane loose.

Reina ran into the living room and came back holding a bowl of assorted gourmet nuts.

Pling!

She clocked Vanessa with a shower of cashews, pecans, and macadamia nuts upside the temple.

Out of ammunition, Vanessa rifled through her wallet until she found a handful of change.

Ka-ching!

Coins of all kinds came raining down on Reina's head. She backed up, grabbed Chris, and ducked behind him for protection. Holding on to Chris with one hand, Reina continued her counterattack with the other.

"Here, buy some stock in Frito Lay's or Jen and Berry's, why don't you," Vanessa yelled, letting loose another barrage of quarters, dimes, and nickels.

"That's Ben and Jerry's," Chris corrected.

"Shut up, Chris!" both women yelled, pausing in their mutual combat to catch their breath.

"Why you gotta yell at a brother!" Chris returned, insulted.

"Stop always referring to yourself in the third person. It's so annoying," Vanessa snapped.

Chris shook himself free of Reina's grasp.

" 'Ey, you know what? Vanessa. Reina. This is your mess. Handle it. I'm out!"

Chris turned on his heel, slipping on cellophane-wrapped peppermints as he went.

Crash!

He went down, connecting soundly with the foyer's hardwood floor.

Reina froze.

Vanessa came running down the stairs and was instantly on her knees, at his side.

"Chris! Are you hurt?" she cried, grabbing him gently by the shoulders and rolling him over so that he faced her.

"I'm fine. 'Ey, I said I'm all right, all ready. Okay!" Chris near-about shouted, irritated by Vanessa's sudden show of concern. "Just help me up."

"Help your own self up, punk," Vanessa spat, feeling shunned. She stepped back and crossed her arms.

Chris bit his tongue and pulled himself up slowly, feeling a sudden soreness in his ribs. Looking from Reina to Vanessa and back again, Chris merely shook his head. He would not, no matter how tempting, step into madwomen's conflicts and act the straight-up bodacious fool.

"You two deserve each other," Chris stated, while gently rubbing his now tender midsection.

"Yeah, and you deserve a woman but we know you won't get one anytime soon," Vanessa shot back.

Chris shot Reina a venomous glare, his teeth grinding ever so slightly.

"Don't look at me. I didn't say a word," Reina defended herself.

"Say a word about what?" Vanessa questioned, angry silence her only answer. "Oh, so now you two have secrets. That's perfect."

"No one's keeping secrets," Chris amended grudgingly. "With you in D.C., we didn't have a chance to—"

"Really, I don't care," Vanessa assured, interrupting Chris, waving him aside as she stalked off toward the kitchen, her friends in tow. "All I care about right now is getting some peace and quiet."

"We'd better jump, Chris," Reina spat. "We have our marching orders."

"That's right. Take your little happy, gay selves out of my house," Vanessa suggested, only to grow instantly quiet at the panged expression Chris bore.

He turned on Reina.

"You really can't hold water, can you?"

"Chris, I swear I said nothing," Reina replied in earnest.

"Why don't you just let me handle my business like a man—"

"I would if you were one!" Reina spat.

An unholy hush enveloped the room.

Vanessa looked to Chris. Chris glared bullets at Reina. Reina strutted over and snatched open the refrigerator door. She grabbed a two-liter bottle of frosty cold diet Dr. Pepper, snapped the cap, and took a long, satisfying swig. She plopped the half-empty bottle back into the refrigerator.

Vanessa grimaced.

"Really, Reina, you can't find a glass—"

Reina grabbed the first thing she could find. She spun and aimed. *Swoosh! Whap!*

A huge wad of Phyllis's apple-caramel-crunch cheesecake lay smeared against the side of Vanessa's head. She stood there, mouth agape, disbelief smeared all over her face. Right along with the cheesecake.

Looking defiant and feeling victorious, Reina daintily licked her fingers.

Chris laughed despite his need not to.

As unexpected as snow in July, hot tears fell unhindered down Vanessa's cinnamon-brown cheeks.

"You have to go. Both of you. I want to be *alone!*" Her voice caught. She cleared her throat. "I have enough to deal with having a dead daddy, a sick and messed-up drugged-out, dead convict of a mother—" Her voice broke and Vanessa could not continue.

They stood, the three of them, as if frozen in time, each caught in the sticky mess of the chaos they had created.

Reina was the first to speak.

"Vanessa. I-I didn't know. I'm sorry. Why didn't you tell us earlier?"

Vanessa jerked as if burned when Reina touched her shoulder.

"Where's my freaking dog?" she asked, ignoring Reina's attempt at sympathy.

"On the patio," Chris answered lethargically.

Vanessa left the kitchen and walked down into the den, and with a violent yank of a cord, opened the off-white, floor-to-ceiling, pure cotton blinds that accented the lovely, muted earth-tone decor of the room.

"No, wait!" Reina cried just as the blinds swiveled open. She gasped in horror, remembering she had left the sliding glass door open so that the revelers could hear their cue to yell . . .

"Sur-r-r-prise . . . !"

It was one of the weakest and most pitiful birthday cheers anyone never cared to hear. Even so, Vanessa screamed, startled. They stood there, a crowd of friends and coworkers who had gathered to celebrate her birthday. Someone tried blowing a noisemaker. It sounded like a choked goose. Someone else weakly tossed a handful of festive confetti. Might as well have been spray-painted dandruff. It was no use pretending. Their faces told the story. The entire cast assembled for Vanessa Taylor's thirtieth surprise birthday party had been treated to front-row seats at the battle of the bold and not so beautiful.

Vanessa saw the festive tables, the deejay, the catered affair, the multihued balloons and streamers, the gorgeous two-tiered birthday cake and presents stacked high on a table on the redwood deck. A huge colorful banner swung overhead in the April breeze. HAPPY BIRTHDAY AND WELCOME HOME, VANESSA! it read. The birthday girl stood there, dumbfounded, saying nothing.

"Excuse me, but can I get my fare?"

The profound silence had been so long and so heavy that the sound of his voice triggered a chorus of screams.

There stood the cabdriver at the kitchen entrance, his hat folded in his sturdy hands, wishing he had never turned off the meter. He could have made a killing.

REINA

"What do you think, Suzy, am I nutty in love or just nuts?"

Reina's favorite doll sat on the bed, refusing to give an answer.

Reina grinned and swiveled her legs over the side of the bed.

She did not need Suzy's reply or any of *Abulela*'s stash of herbs, potions, or lotions to know for certain that yes, she, Reina Kingsley, had a thing for the man. More was going on than just the rent. Her nose was wide open and what she smelled was mighty good.

Well, almost.

Reina raised an arm and sniffed her pits and was offended herdang-self. It was time to introduce a little soap to a little water and say *adiós* to day-old stank. Reina padded into the bathroom and turned on the shower full blast.

Thirty seconds later the tiny room was filled with saunalike steam. Just the way Reina liked it. Disrobing, she removed the elastic band from her ponytail, and allowed her heavy hair to fall free. It fell across her shoulders, partially shrouding her nakedness beneath the thick, black waves.

When was the last time she had had a haircut? Reina stepped into the shower, concluding that her hair had not seen a pair of scissors since she had it cut and styled for a cousin's wedding—in which she served as one of thirteen bridesmaids decked in some atrocious dusky rose and black taffeta monstrosity—back in her high school days. Reina shook her head, remembering that disaster of a wedding and the equally farcical marriage it produced. Thirteen had not been her cousin's lucky number after all.

That was more than a decade ago. Reina had not done much to her hair since then. She was an easy-maintenance kind of woman. She could not be bothered with all that primping and prepping and painting of face, nails, or hair. She preferred things au naturel. Simple. Just have *Mamí* or *Abuela* or Nita—before her great prison escapade—trim the ends to keep them neat. Reina could wash it herself. And thank God for those two-in-one shampoo/conditioner products that further cut the hassle in half. With hair as heavy and thick as hers, Reina welcomed any lazy way out.

Briskly, Reina worked the coconut-scented liquid into a foaming lather, massaging her scalp with a firm, gentle motion, working the suds from scalp to ends. Maybe, just maybe, it was time for a change. Cutting her abundant hair would lighten her load. Literally.

But Jamal liked her hair. Said it was lush. Could he touch it? No! Reina always exclaimed. It became a game between them. Jamal would playfully plead over the phone or via e-mail for Reina to just let him wrap a finger in the silk of her mane. She laughed in the steaming shower. The man was crazy. And, oh, so much more.

He was attentive, easy to talk to, and possessed a warm sense of humor. His touch of old-fashioned gentlemanly charm and courtesy didn't hurt matters, either. He was never late for their "meetings," as Reina referred to their time together. He always dropped her off at home at a decent hour and he never made a move on her. Not that she would have protested. Or at least she didn't think she would. Reina couldn't let her mind go there and imagine romantic possibilities. Not yet. Instead, she rubbed and scrubbed the thoughts right out of her head.

Reina allowed the lather to remain in her hair while she rubbed a loofah sponge, smeared with some exotic-smelling shower gel *Abuela* had concocted for her when she moved in, over her body. The fragrant gel held a hint of an undertone that Reina could not identify, but it was lovely nonetheless. Probably just another one of her grandmother's crazy herbs.

Living with her grandmother was actually rather cool. *Abuela* was . . . different. Some said odd. Others said *loco*. Even some of *Abuela*'s great-grandchildren, the youngest ones, were scared to spend the night at the house. But Reina knew there was nothing to fear. Her grandmother was special. Had been as long as Reina could remember. And when *that woman* she once called best friend had unceremoniously evicted her the night of the party disaster, *Abuela* had opened her doors and provided a refuge to her homeless granddaughter.

Trifling as it was, being evicted from *that* house actually worked for her good. Reina was with her grandmother now, and she had no complaints.

It felt good being with her grandmother, knowing that *Abuela* was not alone in the big Victorian monster of a habitat all by herself. Reina felt watchful, protective of her maternal grandmother. *Abuela* would never admit it to anyone, not even God, but she was getting on in years and could use a hand around the house, with chores and shopping and paying bills and the like. Reina's baby brother, Raj, came over on Saturdays to tend the yard and do any heavy lifting or minor repairs. Still, Reina felt better knowing she was there on a daily basis, ensuring her grandmother's well-being.

They were still barely on speaking terms, Reina and her bratty baby brother. Full reconciliation was a long way off, but at least they could be in the same room at the same time without trying to see who would get and who would give a black eye or a split lip first. At least Reina had helped her mother acknowledge her personal point of view, even if she did not agree and thought Reina out of line for telling a parent how to parent. Yes, *Mamí* acquiesced, indeed she had given her son too much freedom, while curtailing her daughters' activities. Yes, she was guilty of playing the double standard, of giving in to and upholding *Papí*'s old-school patriarchy. She honestly thought she was doing what was in the best interest of her children, trying to keep her daughters safe while liberating and launching her son into manhood.

Reina sucked her teeth. The whole lot of them were wackier than a little bit. It might be better for Reina to never have children. If a family's lunacy was a genetic carryover, then Lord bless the child born of her womb.

Hmmm . . . the child of her womb?

They would have beautiful brown bouncing babies, Reina and Jamal. With her copper and his hot-chocolate-with-a-splash-of-cream-colored skin, her deep black and his coffee-brown eyes, his chiseled bone structure, and her international house of heritage descent.

Beautiful brown angels. Their babies would be big. Huge. Reina was five-feet, nine inches tall. Jamal was, what, six-two, six-three? Both tall and sturdy, both over two hundred pounds. She was ready to sign up for a caesarean now, because Reina was not about to lose her mind squeezing out some twelve pound, eleven ounce, twenty-four-inch baby. *Good God!*

Screech! The rusty old pipes groaned in protest as Reina shut off the water, the intrusive sound putting a halt to her wild imaginings.

Reina stepped from the shower and proceeded with her morning regime. Her skin was soft from a generous application of baby oil, silken with a light sprinkle of powder here and there. Her hair was damp, but no longer dripping. Reina tossed her towel in the hamper. As she did so, her eye caught sight of the shiny white contraption on the floor beside the tall wicker bin. A scale! She shivered. *Ewwww!* Sistah-hating contraption. Who invented personalized, for-bathroom-use scales anyhow? The only things that deserved to be weighed were fresh produce and risks in life. Reina stepped onto its flat face, intending to relieve herself of her angst by jumping up and down on the scale until it broke with a loud holler and a cracking of plastic, a shattering of glass. She wanted to see that crazy dial spin itself into utter oblivion.

What was going on? Reina was seeing things. Stupid scale was messing with her, trying to be nice to save its life. She stepped off, allowed the dial to return to zero, then stepped back on again. No, no, and no! It just couldn't be.

Abuela had a digital scale in her bathroom. Why, Reina would never know. The woman had weighed one hundred and twenty-two pounds since Moses parted the Red Sea. Reina could use *Abuela*'s scale just to verify her findings. It had to be accurate, since it was one of those fancy-schmancy, physician-recommended contraptions that cost entirely too much money.

Wrapping her favorite bright blue terry-cloth robe with Daffy Duck embroidered on its breast pocket about her body, Reina opened her bedroom door and poked her head out.

"*Abuela?*"

"*Sí, nieta.*"

Her grandmother's voice floated up the stairs in response to her granddaughter's call. The sound carried as if *Abuela* were somewhere in the sunroom. Probably watering her jungle of plants or something.

"Nothing. Just checking on you," Reina replied before taking advantage of the situation to run down the hallway in her bare feet, her damp hair floating heavily behind her.

In the safety of her grandmother's private bath, Reina locked the door, dropped her robe, and held her breath. Closing her eyes, she stepped onto the scale. *Please, God, be good to me today.* Reina opened her eyes and screamed, covering her mouth to stifle the piercing sound.

This physician-recommended measurer of meat and men could not possibly be wrong. It had the same reading as the one in her own bathroom. Reina stepped off the scale, dazzled and delighted.

Two hundred and thirty-five pounds. She was fifteen pounds lighter than she had been two months ago. Fifteen pounds! When was the last time she lost fifteen pounds? When was the last time she lost fifteen ounces?

What a wonder!

At her former residence, Reina had made it a practice of walking Pharaoh every night with or without *that woman.* She had been walking regularly with Phyllis at work during their breaks. They had even started meeting on Saturday mornings for an hour-long trek, alternating each week and meeting at a park nearest one home or the other. She had been eating better, increasing her fruit and vegetable and whole-grain intake, while steadily reducing the chocolate and fat and snack-food binges that could last for days. Okay, weeks. But fifteen pounds? Reina was truly amazed.

What if she enrolled in that weight-management program offered through her HMO? That was how Phyllis had lost her weight When they first met, Phyllis was a fuller-figured gal. Reina never considered Phyllis fat, just stacked. Now her bodily proportions were noticeably different. Phyllis's waistline was neat, her thighs were slimmer, her face less puffy and her cheekbones more defined, and her gluteus maximus was a tad more minimus. A tad! Sister still had one of those high-and-mighty behinds like . . . well, *that woman* and Reina's former best friend. The nut.

A brilliant smile broke across Reina's face. She could do this. A medically supervised weight-loss program, she admitted, was probably best for someone like her. Reina needed structure. She needed to be accountable to someone. She was not interested in quick-fix gimmicks. Reina had already tried the bulk of them: liquid diets, diet pills, rice diet, cabbage-soup diet, all-meat diet, dog diet. She could afford to give this one more try, one more safe and sane opportunity to restructure her world. She would do this for herself and her future.

"*Abuela?*"

Reina walked through the house calling to her grandmother. There was no response. It was a lovely Saturday. One of those typical California-postcard kind of days. The temperature was in the mid-eighties, the sky was clear, the sun was bright and bold and beaming. Reina felt energized after her walk with Phyllis. She had a reasonable breakfast of pineapple wedges, peach yogurt with granola sprinkled on top, an English muffin with a shot of some fake butter spray, and low-calorie peach fruit spread. And thirty-two ounces of water. Reina found it worked best if she refilled her thirty-two-ounce supermug with water twice a day and downed its contents. She could not be bothered with sipping eight ounces here, eight ounces there, counting and recalling whether or not she had met the daily requirement. A sister had better things to do with her time. Namely, find her missing-in-action grandmother whom she had not seen since breakfast.

"*Abuela!*" she called again, louder.

"*Sí, nieta,*" her grandmother answered her granddaughter. Reina followed the sound of the voice coming from *Abuela*'s sunroom.

The sunroom was a veritable jungle filled with a plethora of plants, domestic and exotic, lush and vibrant and obviously well cared for. The windows faced east, allowing brilliant morning light to flood the room with its pastel yellow walls and hardwood floor. There was minimal furniture. Just an extra-wide, extra-long sofa and a pair of matching chairs covered with a soft yellow fabric—atop of which *Abuela* had placed beautiful floral-print throws and pillows—two small glass tables in the shape of flower petals, and a tall solid-brass lamp. One wall was entirely comprised of built-in shelves on which sat precious photographs and equally treasured crystal hummingbirds, butterflies, frogs, and sundry other creatures of nature. *Abuela* truly was a woman of the earth.

"What are you doing?" Reina asked, entering the room. Her grandmother sat in the middle of the sofa, books spread all about her on the sofa and the floor about her feet. Reina walked over and picked up one of the books. Photograph albums.

Abuela looked up and smiled, and Reina was struck yet again at the physical likeness between her mother and her grandmother. *Abuela*'s hair was silver and *Mami*'s was still black, or so read the label on the Clairol box she bought every other week, but they were so alike in stature and carriage and demeanor. *Mami* tended to be a tad bit excitable and frisky at times, but there were many moments when she possessed a sweet calm accompanied by a knowing look in her eyes that reflected the wisdom of the ancients. Very much like *Abuela*.

Abuela patted the sofa cushion next to her. Reina sat, edging close to her grandmother and looking over the tiny woman's shoulder to stare at the worn album in her aged hands. Together they sat laughing over family pictures—generations portrayed—some in black-and-white, others in color. Some worn and frayed about the edges, others in perfect condition. *Abuela* paused, her eyes suddenly misting with tears, at the sight of her wedding photograph. Reina smiled at the likeness of her grandparents. He was solid, handsome, and bore a look of good-humored mischief. She was so young and frail, and there was a hint of fear at the corners of her eyes.

Abuela laughed.

"I was so afraid to marry your grandfather."

"Why?" Reina asked, shocked at the revelation. All she remembered of her grandparents' marriage was that it had been warm and loving and absolutely enviable.

"I did not love him," *Abuela* stated, laughing at Reina's shocked expression. "I didn't even know him. Ours was an arranged marriage."

"No-o-o!" Reina sang. Her grandmother nodded her head. "I never knew that."

"Aww, keep living and you'll learn something new every day," *Abuela* responded, pinching Reina's cheek and sounding just like *Mami*. Reina smiled, realizing she did miss the daily interactions with her mother. "I remember throwing a tantrum when I learned that I was to be married. I cried and screamed and threatened to run away or starve myself to death."

"What happened?" Reina asked, intrigued by a side of her grandmother that she had never known.

"My mother, your great-grandmother, slapped my face and told me to go wash the dishes." *Abuela* cackled at the memory. "I did but I *accidentally* broke two of her favorite coffee cups in the process."

Reina laughed, imagining the feisty, tempestuous, but lovely girl her grandmother must have been. "So what happened?" she asked.

"The rest is history. I married your grandfather and fell in love, and gave him six sons and two daughters to prove it."

Reina sat quietly for a moment, soaking in the precious sight of her grandparents' wedding photo.

"*Abuela*, when did you know you loved *Abuelo*?"

"On our wedding night when I had my very first orgasm."

"*Abuela!*" Reina screeched, causing her grandmother to laugh hysterically.

"Oh, *nieta*, granddaughter, don't act the prude. Lovemaking is beautiful. And your grandfather"—*Abuela* paused to fan herself with the album pages for emphasis—"he could make love like—"

Reina put a finger in each ear and sang to drown out her grandmother's voice.

"La, la, la, la. I'm trying not to hear you, *Abuela*. Da, da, da, da."

Abuela laughed and wrapped her arms about her granddaughter. Reina leaned against her, placing her head on her grandmother's tiny but firm shoulder. *Abuela* gently stroked her thick hair.

"*Abuela*, how does a woman know when she's in love? I mean . . . how much time should pass in a relationship before you even think about such a thing?"

"I knew I was eternally in love with your grandfather the moment I felt—"

"Uhh, that's okay," Reina interrupted. "I'm not trying to be corrupted here."

Her grandmother chuckled.

"*Mi reina*, you really are a queen. You just don't know it yet."

The comment caught Reina off guard.

"What do you mean?" she asked.

"Just what I said. Your mama didn't give you your name for nothing." *Abuela* sighed. "Listen, child, I won't be here much longer—"

"Don't say that," Reina urged, sitting up and looking at her grandmother with fearful eyes. "*Abuela*, you're not going anywhere anytime—"

"Hush! You know it and I know it. I'm leaving." *Abuela* pushed Reina's head back against her shoulder. "Who's going to make you see the light when I'm gone? Huh? You're blind to your own beauty, *mi reina*. You slouch around scared of yourself, always looking at others, praising their virtues when you don't even peek at your own. Wake up, *nieta,* before it's too late."

"*Qué pasa?*" Raj shouted, interrupting the highly poignant moment by bounding through the front door and into the hallway. "*Abuela,* where are you?"

"In the sunroom."

"Wassup?" Raj chimed, crossing the room to embrace his grand-mother and plant a sloppy kiss on her cheek. "Yo, Reina. Whatcha know good?"

Reina rolled her eyes. "I know you need to put a belt on and pull those pants up from drooping down around your narrow hips."

Raj sucked his teeth in reply.

"You don't feel me, girl. You don't know my game."

"Your game is lame—"

Abuela clapped her hands.

"Not today, you two. I want peace in my house. *Comprende?*"

Of course they did. *Abuela* might be old and she might be small, but they'd both, as misbehaving children, felt the sting of her correc-tive hand on their backsides. *Abuela* did not play. They "yes, ma'amed" her with all due reverence.

"*Abuela,* do you have a box or chest I can use?" Reina asked, stand-ing and easing a sudden crick out of her neck.

"What size?" *Abuela* asked, handing Raj an armful of photo albums. "Here, *nieto,* help your granny put these away."

"Large enough to stuff Raj in," Reina answered.

"*Abuela!*" Raj whined, acting all injured and offended.

Abuela shot Reina a warning glance, but failed to keep the smile from playing about the corners of her mouth.

"I want to pack my winter clothes," Reina offered.

"Check the garage or the shed."

Reina headed toward the garage.

"Look hard enough and you'll find it, *mi reina.*" *Abuela* called out before Reina disappeared from sight. Reina paused, understanding full well *Abuela* made no reference to tangible containers, rather to the core and cradle of her very soul. What she needed was locked somewhere deep within.

* * *

Raj was out in the backyard trimming hedges to the beat of whatever mess that was playing through the earphones of the Walkman attached to the waist of his baggy pants. Reina found nothing suitable for her use in the garage. So she journeyed outdoors to continue her hunt in the back yard shed, suddenly realizing her question remained unanswered.

When would she know if she was in love? Why was she even bothering to question such a thing? Because Chris was right. She was touched by the bug. It could very well be that Jamal had her nose more wide open than she cared to admit. With a toss of her head and a scratch behind the ear, Reina considered the notion.

Reina hummed aloud as she moved about, carefully stepping around gardening tools, fertilizer, and an assortment of other supplies *Abuela* stored in the shed. Reina's mind flashed back to her grandparents' wedding photo and *Abuela's* raucous reference to their loving. Reina chuckled softly. Her grandmother was a mess. But she wasn't senile or stupid. *Abuela* had more sense than a little bit. Reina would be foolish to dismiss her words without a thought.

You're blind to your own beauty, mi reina. *You slouch around scared of yourself, always looking at others, praising their virtues when you don't even peek at your own. Wake up,* nieta, *before it's too late.*

The message echoed throughout the center of her being, this time in Jamal's voice.

He had made similar statements to her on more than one occasion.

Why aren't you as generous and gracious with yourself as you are with others?

Reina did not understand. Jamal was forced to break it down, hurting her feelings in the process. He hated overused, simplified buzzwords, and it was not his intent to reduce or trivialize the matter, but Reina's self-esteem was in need of repair. Why could he, and everyone else who knew and loved her, appreciate her beauty, her warm and carefree spirit, and appreciate her, not in spite of, but all the more for, her frailties? Reina did not put on the same fronts as most people. She was genuine, open to others. She was, sadly enough, closed to herself.

Reina wanted to laugh it off, but that was impossible, Jamal's words hit home. Reina's issues, her esteem, were not solely contingent upon her weight. It took some time, but Reina finally realized that her weight was a product, a manifestation of her inner turmoil. Not the other way around. It was time she was honest with herself, did some soul searching and self-examination of things she refused to acknowledge or admit to anyone, especially herself.

Jamal. He was sometimes brutally honest, but without brutality. He actually cared about her feelings, was sensitive to how his words might affect her. Reina smiled, thanking fortune for bringing such a good friend into her life. She looked forward to their phone conversations, became worried and even irritable if she did not hear from him on a regular basis without explanation. If things continued to proceed in the way in which they were, Reina would find herself smack-dab in—

Pain. "Ouch!" she wailed, grabbing her sneakered toot, trying to ease the throbbing in her big toe. There in the dark recesses at the rear of the shed, Reina, engrossed in searching overhead shelves, had stubbed her toe against the corner of something tall and solid and concealed beneath an old blanket. Holding her foot and ready to curse like a woman in labor, Reina yanked away the blanket. There stood the cedar armoire her grandfather had imported from Puerto Rico as a wedding gift for his bride. It stood six feet tall, and its wood had a lovely sheen despite its age. *Abuela* cherished the piece. Why in the world was it out here in the shed? And why were there extension cords snaking out beneath its double doors?

How odd. Putting as much weight on her hurt foot as she could stand, Reina pulled open the doors and stared. The armoire's shelves had been removed. Instead, within its confines stood a tall metal cabinet just slightly shorter than the armoire itself. Curious, Reina tugged on the door of the metal cabinet. It was locked. Her curiosity suddenly escalated. Reina glanced about the dimly lit shed until her gaze fell upon a tiny key ring dangling from a hook on a nearby wall. Heart pounding, mind racing, Reina tried each and every key, but none fit the lock.

Reina stood there, playing with her still-loose hair, growing increasingly intrigued by the minute. She had a thought. Testing her theory, Reina ran her hands down the sides, over the top of the metal cabinet. Nothing. Ready to kick the cabinet with her good foot, Reina glanced down. There on the bottom, in a corner of the armoire, sat something that sparkled faintly in the dim light of the shed. Triumph spread through her as Reina snatched up the tiny metal key and inserted it into the cabinet's door.

Violà!

There was a click and then the door swung wide.

What Reina found left her even more puzzled.

Tiny lamps hung from the ceiling, casting smooth blue light onto the soil and plants within. Why in the world would anyone plant herbs in a box and keep it indoors with false light and—

Herbs? Reina looked closer, squinting, not believing her eyes or her nose. No, not here in *Abuela*'s shed! She grew livid. Who had lost his or her right mind and dared to plant illegal substance on her grandmother's property? Her head snapped up as the sound of the Weed Eater filled the interior of the shed.

Raj! Reina scowled, watching him prance about the hedges, head bopping, mouth moving in time with the music blaring through his headset. Narcotics! That explained his crude and rude behavior, his staying out late doing only God and the law knew what.

Reina slammed shut the cabinet door and stormed out of the shed and across the backyard.

She snatched off his headset and spun him about.

"Hey! I was listening to—"

Whap! Reina slapped him soundly across the face. Raj was so taken aback that he just stood there, his mouth open, his eyes wide for seconds on end. He stared at his older sister as she lit into him, hollering about his deceitful ways, his pretending to help *Abuela* with the gardening only so he could do a little growing of his own. He was a disgrace. First it was their oldest sister Nita and now him.

By the time his wits returned and Raj was able to react, *Abuela* was already hobbling down the steps from the sunroom out into the yard, trying to determine what the fuss was all about.

Everyone was babbling at once, no one making much sense. Someone had to restore order.

"*Cállate!*" *Abuela* hollered, silencing her warring grandchildren. "Quiet! What is this foolishness?"

"You have to see this," Reina exclaimed, grabbing her grandmother's hand and hurrying her into the shed. "Look at this!" Reina cried, showing *Abuela* the proof of Raj's crime. "That hoodlum is growing marijuana in here," Reina said, pointing at Raj, who stood in the doorway looking confounded and confused. He opened his mouth to protest, but *Abuela* raised her hand, silencing him.

"Those are my plants," *Abuela* stated, looking her granddaughter square in the eye.

Reina could only stare at her grandmother in disbelief. Was she growing senile or was she trying to protect Raj's narrow behind? Just like *Mami.*

"Aww, snap! *Abuela* smokes weed," Raj proclaimed, sounding amazed and impressed as he sauntered over to peek into the open cabinet. He reached out to pluck a leaf, but *Abuela* popped his hand.

"Hush, foolish boy. I don't smoke ganja. I use it with my herbs. For medicinal and . . . other purposes," she stated mysteriously.

"That's what I'm talking 'bout," Raj said. "I'm feeling ill myself. Can I get a little cure?"

Abuela lightly whacked the back of his head. "Don't be flip." Taking the key from Reina's palm, *Abuela* locked the metal cabinet— careful to slip the key down the front of her dress between her breasts—closed the cedar doors of her precious armoire, and covered it once more with the blanket. Without a backward glance, *Abuela* turned and vacated the shed as if nothing out of the ordinary had occurred.

"Wait, *Abuela,*" Reina cried, following her grandmother outdoors. "You can't grow marijuana."

"Who says?"

"The United States government," Reina declared, looking at her grandmother as if she had truly gone out of her mind.

"I'm from Puerto Rico. I have my own rules."

"*Abuela* , but you—"

"Not another word, Reina." *Abuela* warned, turning to look up into her granddaughter's eyes. Reina grew silent. "Learn not to meddle so much, *nieta.* Look to your own business for a change." Seeing the hurt expression in her granddaughter's eyes, *Abuela* softened her tone and ran a hand down her granddaughter's cheek. "Besides, you don't know what seasoning I used in that salad you ate two servings of last night. Do you?" She smiled broadly. "You don't have to keep wondering about the source of that lovely little mysterious undertone in the shower gel I made for you." Then she winked. "And it helped me to keep falling in love with your grandfather until the day he died, if you know what I mean." *Abuela* walked away, laughing wickedly.

Reina just stood and stared until her brother's voice snapped her from stunned disbelief.

"Told you I had nothing to do with that," Raj said. Reina glanced over at her brother, who stood beside her, looking wounded. She had overreacted, hurt him and accused him of something he had not done.

"Raj, I'm sorry," Reina repented, reaching for her baby brother. He pulled away from her, but not too far. Reina grabbed his hand, forcing him to stand still as she moved to stand before him. He looked off into the distance, refusing to meet her gaze. Gently Reina grasped his chin and forced him to face her. Lightly she touched the red splotch on his cheek where she had struck him, unjustly so. She kissed the bruise and opened her arms. Slowly, reluctantly, Raj stepped into her embrace.

"Raj, I-I'm so sorry." She began to sob. "Please forgive me. For everything." She felt his resistance give way to something tender as his shoulders heaved as if in great relief. Reina understood. The burden of contention was lifting from her shoulders as well. It was time for peace. Peace with *Papí*, with Chris and Vanessa, from whom she was estranged, but most important, peace with Reina Kingsley herself.

CHRIS

I could tell the Set was bumping when I pulled into the parking lot. There was a line outside the door. Sisters, brothers, and others were waiting to get inside and get their jazz on. Although the winter crowds were pretty consistent, things didn't usually heat up until this time of year. Judging by the overcrowded parking lot, the Set was hot this May night.

Tiny, the "quality control officer"—fancy title for bouncer—saw me walking across the parking lot and waved. Why do brothers over six-feet-four and upward of three hundred pounds insist on calling them-selves Tiny? Whatever. Anyhow, Mr. Misnomer waved me forward, grasping my hand to give me the black man's secret code handshake. The same handshake I saw two white boyz (one with blond dread-locks) exchange the other day. Can't brothers have nothing?

"Go'n in, bruh. They're in the back room."

"Thanks, Tiny," I humored him, snatching a bit of the conversation between two sisters just behind me near the front of the line.

"Who is he?" one asked, sounding all indignant and disgusted be-cause I had been permitted in before her.

"I don't know, sisterfriend, but I have a sudden craving for a little rump roast."

I glanced over my shoulder and caught a brazen gaze as it traveled up from the region of my rear to my face. She smiled. She had deep

dimples and a small gap between her front teeth. Her modified natural framed her heart-shaped face with wild twists and curls. Cute. I
promised myself I'd find her later and find out if she was made of
something substantive besides a perfect body and a bodacious attitude. Not that I needed or wanted a love connection, mind you. Just a
little stimulating conversation would do me fine. For now.

My NBA fellas were already gathered in the private room located at
the back of the club. We were ready to celebrate one of our boys', the
club owner's brother's, last night as an unwed man. We pooled our
monies and really did it up right. There was champagne, a catered
spread, and we even gave the brother a few gifts. Mostly gag gifts like
aprons, oven mitts, toilet bowl brushes, and pumice stones to get the
crust off his heels.

"Yo, Chris is finally in the house," one of the brothers called out.
"What's up, man? Is your watch broke or something?"

"Or something." I laughed, exchanging back-slapping hugs and
greetings with the crew. Someone handed me a glass of champagne
just as our host for the evening tapped the side of his own glass with a
fork handle. The rowdy revelry died down.

"Aiight, y'all. Let's do this. Our man, here," he said, clapping our
boy on the back, "is about to make that move and do the do."

Cheers and whistles and sounds of fake, exaggerated crying filled
the room.

"That's enough! As I was saying, we have cause to celebrate tonight.
There's one less brother on the singles market. That means more
honeys for us."

Several minutes passed before our juvenile joy ended. Then our
traditional send-off began. We filled a beer stein with the keeping-it-
real customary grape Kool-Aid with a twist of lemon. The saluting
brother started off with a toast, took a drink, and passed the glass to
the brother beside him, who would also do the same, toast and drink.
It wasn't as easy as it sounds. We had to offer our toasts without using
the words *marriage, husband, wife, spouse,* or *sex,* and all of our toasts
had to bear reference to the chosen topic of the night, candy. I know.
It's crazy, but hey, brothers are entitled to some stupid fun, too.

We heard some silly, straight-crazy mess like, "May you and the old
lady live long and get your *Almond Joy* on *Now or Later.*" Or, "Be gentle
with her *Milky Way* when satisfying your *Big Hunk.*" And, my personal
favorite, "Don't let your *Starburst* until she's had her *Good and Plenty.*"

I was weak. Rolling.

It was all good.

We were sitting, eating dinner, having a seriously good time when a little of my good humor took a leave of absence. One of the brothers who owns his own private investigation agency met up with me. After playing catch-up with each other, he told me he had an update.

I hired him to investigate my mother's death. I decided to make the move the night of Vanessa's surprise party. Speaking of which, I know Reina was outdone, having put so much effort into making Vanessa's surprise birthday party a success. She meant well but made a mess. I understand Vanessa is hurting over her parents' deaths. Believe me, I know. Still, she didn't have to go off, cutting up like some juvenile delinquent denied an overdue dose of Prozac. But that night was the night I decided to discover some things. Since truths were being revealed and cryptic secrets unsealed, I figured it was time to get to the bottom of the matter of my mother's demise.

Now, here I was trying to swallow a mouthful of prime rib without choking. My moment of truth had come. I wiped my mouth and excused myself from the table.

"Go ahead and finish eating your dinner, Chris. It can wait," my brotherhood private eye told me. I was immediately suspicious. Most folks can't wait to tell you good news, not that there was anything good about my mother's dying prematurely. But I had an inkling that what I was about to learn was something worse than I was ready to hear.

I was right.

We found a relatively private corner in the back of the room where we could talk. I listened attentively, silent the entire time my private sleuth quietly disclosed the information he had successfully uncovered. He promised to send me a written report first thing Monday morning. He wished me well, and patted my shoulder, trying to ease the weight he'd just placed there. I needlessly reminded him to send me an invoice for payment, and thanked him for his time.

I needed a breath of fresh air badly, so I eased out of the room. I was on my way up the stairs when I crossed paths with Dimples, the woman with the mod afro and booming body.

"Hey, handsome," she said, smiling and showing that cute little gap between her front teeth. "Can I join you?"

I rubbed my brow. Any other time, any other day, and I might have gladly accepted her company. But tonight was not the night.

"Sorry, I have to step out for a while."

"Can I step with you?" she coyly inquired, obviously not feeling my vibe.

"Thanks, but no thanks," I said, taking the stairs two at a time in my hurry to inhale clean night air into my hot, dry lungs.

Tiny, the doorman, eased back and allowed me to slip past the sliver of doorway space not filled by his frame. I was in a hurry, walking fast and seeing nothing until she came into view. I couldn't help myself. I had to slow my roll and appreciate this jewel of perfection striding majestically toward me. Or rather, the Set. But she had to pass me to get to it. So I stood there and drank in the sight, me and several other brothers standing there in the line.

From head to toe, she was truly divine. Where do I begin? I'll work my way up. Shapely legs. Thighs and hips that could bring tears to a brother's eyes. A tiny waist and firm breasts. Full, pouty lips. Cinnamon-brown skin, high cheekbones, golden eyes, and a soft, close-cut hairstyle that accentuated her perfectly beautiful oval face. And she smelled good, too. Like light and warmth and luscious secrets. Dag, I wasn't really ready to admit to anything. But it had been so long since I'd seen her that she took me by force and by surprise and yanked the emotion right out of me. Yep, I think I'm sprung and have been sprung for quite some time.

"Hey, gorgeous." She was so absorbed with extracting something from her beaded evening bag—money for the club cover charge, I presumed—that she nearly bumped into me. I caught her about the waist before she could.

A tender smile stole across her face.

"Chris," she practically moaned, wrapping her arms about my neck and hugging me tight.

I admit I held on to her, too, tighter and longer than I probably should have. Blame my dejected state. I needed to cling to something, someone solid just then. And Vanessa Ann Taylor was more solid than a little bit. She felt good in my arms. So good I found it hard to let her go. Truth be told, she was in no hurry to vacate my embrace, either. We just stood there, reunited, something akin to newfound revelation passing silently, boldly, between our bodies.

She pulled back just enough to look up into my face.

"I've missed you, Boo."

I smiled. She hadn't called me that in a long time. But then again, she hadn't called me. Period.

"I've missed you, too, gorgeous. You look good," I said, glancing down at some little formfitting taupe-colored silk, sleeveless dress thing that stopped midthigh, trying not to drop my eyes to the hint of cleavage that peeked over the low-cut, square neckline.

"You look even better," she purred, disengaging herself from my arms. She stood there, seemingly absorbing every nuance of my being. "What's wrong, Chris? What's happened?" Vanessa asked, amazing me as she always did with her insightful perception. She read a brother too well.

"Feel like going for a ride? I need to talk," I said, making myself vulnerable to her wishes. She had expected to enjoy a night out at the Set, not sit up playing Dr. Laura with me. I have to give her credit. She never missed a beat.

"Follow me home so I can park my car."

I was in the coupe, backing it out of its parking space faster than Tiny could inhale an eight-piece bucket of the Colonel's chicken, extra crispy.

Thirty minutes later, we were westbound on Interstate 80 heading toward the Bay Area with no particular destination in mind. I had the moonroof open, letting the natural night light spill over our bodies as the soft instrumentals playing on the stereo soothed our minds. We hadn't said much since leaving Sacramento, just small talk that was comfortable and safe.

Something shifted between us. It started when I walked out of the Set and saw her coming toward me, unaware of my close inspection of her person. Okay, so the shift occurred that night, but like I said much earlier I've been faking the funk, acting as if I don't need anyone for far too long. This woman has been toying with my vacillating affections for quite some time now without even knowing it. I knew it the night she returned from D.C., ending an absence and filling a want in my life that I had been too reluctant to admit.

Vanessa poses an enigma. How can one woman walk with such sultry confidence and apparent power, her hips swaying gently on the wind, and still have a look of innocence about her eyes? I've wanted to hold her, to soothe her, to scold her on more than one occasion. I long to help her deal with whatever challenges, whatever the pains are that plague her life. Afterward, I want to rest in her arms, to let down my facade and be a man, tears and all.

I am not imagining things. We connected on a different plane tonight, but I'm not one to let the moment rule me. Remember, I'm a man with plans, short-term and long-range. I have to examine this thing from all angles. I can't take advantage of Vanessa's concern for me, or the vulnerability she's feeling as a result of recent occurrences in her own life. This new development and my understanding of it may take some time. And we're both worth every minute. I just pray it doesn't take too long.

"Chris, I'm sorry for everything that happened that night," Vanessa told me, breaking into subjects that we both needed to deal with. I didn't need to ask to which night she referred. I knew. "I was downright ugly."

"Yes, you were. Throwing trinkets and things at folks," I reminded her, making her laugh. "But we were all pretty ugly."

Vanessa nodded.

"Have you talked to Reina lately?"

I confirmed that I had but that everything wasn't exactly right between us yet.

I glanced away from the roadway. Vanessa sat looking out the window at the mountains in the dark distance. Whatever her private thoughts, I was swept up in her silence.

Her voice brushed against my ears, breaking the hush with velvet fingers.

"So what's up with the gay thing you and Reina tried to keep from me?"

I smiled crookedly, briefly, before divulging the details of my recent and unwanted amorous adventure.

"Did you tell Papa McCullen about poor Ethan's misplaced affections?"

"You're kidding, right?" I cast a sidelong glance Vanessa's way. "I'm not trying to have Pops show up at the gym with a bottle of blessed oil sanctifying my office and casting out demons."

Vanessa laughed deeply.

"And what do you mean, 'poor Ethan'? I'm the victim here," I insisted playfully. I think.

"Why, because a gay man was interested in you?"

"Straight skippy, yeah! I'm not trying to go out like that."

"You're homophobic," Vanessa teased.

"I am not, but so what if I were? I have the right to be politically in-correct if it means not having *my* sexual preferences trampled on and discounted."

"True. I guess it just goes to show that the big, bad black male is not invincible."

"Meaning?"

Vanessa reclined her seat slightly and leaned back into the night.

"Black machismo is not an impenetrable shield. You can grab your crotch, drink all the brown bag-wrapped forties you want and still be . . . vulnerable."

"Is that how you see me?" I asked, setting the cruise control and stretching my cramped legs as best I could. "Are you saying I overdo the black-buck thing to look indomitable?"

"No, you're more an Armani-, Mizrahi-wearing, Moët sipping kind of—"

"So now I'm a puff because I enjoy the finer things in life."

Vanessa laughed.

"No, Boo, you're all man," she cooed, "and I like you that way."

Taken aback, I couldn't respond. I just sat and stared ahead at the dark highway winding us farther from home.

There was nothing between us except stars and moon. I felt con-nected to Vanessa in a way I had not before. There was something new, something deep between us that broke all pretense and barriers and left me feeling, as she said, vulnerable. So when she asked what had upset me earlier so that I looked as I had when we met at the Set, I didn't hesitate to convey my news.

"I know how my mother died."

Vanessa reached over to take my right hand, cupping it gently in her soft palm, her attentive silence my encouragement to continue.

I told her all about my private-investigating brother and his find-ings.

My mother, overwhelmed by the demands imposed upon the wife of an up-and-coming young minister, had revolted and bolted out the door. She was through sharing her husband with needy parishioners, tired of prying eyes watching her every move, having to live openly and exposed to and pulled at by everyone. Committees here and there, preparing food for church dinners and banquets, sacrificing her life, her time. She wanted her privacy, her freedom to come and go as she pleased without some motherly figure or waspish sister or saint telling her how to live, how to cook, how to keep the reverend happy. Why wasn't her own happiness considered? She tired of the overwhelming scrutiny. So she left.

With her lover.

My mother met a man with a small child of his own. They wanted to marry and move away to raise their children together in quiet, inconspicuous wedded bliss. There was just one small problem: my father refused to divorce her. Certainly it was no great secret that the young pastor's wife had stepped out on him, but to divorce would be a far worse scandal indeed.

Fine. Not a problem. My mother took matters into her own hands. She still had keys to the house.

One night, long after we had gone to bed, my mother slipped into the house. She meant to abduct me, to take me with her and her lover back to his hometown.

"I was her ransom. Either my father gave her a divorce, or she would take his child."

Funny, I can see this all so clearly now that someone has given me permission to remember.

I was bundled up in my mother's arms, and she would have made it successfully out of the house except for the fact that I started crying for my favorite toy, a plush elephant that held bronze peanuts in its mouth. Anxious to quiet me, my mother hurried back into my bedroom and found the toy. In her haste, she thrust it at me, but I was unable to grip it. It slipped from my hands. The elephant fell, metal peanuts popping loose and crashing loudly onto the hardwood floor. Peanuts rolled underfoot, my mother stepping on them, losing her balance, causing us both to crash to the ground.

Dad came running into the hallway, his pistol in hand. I can see his face, a mixture of panic and hope as he took in the sight. Recovered, my mother stood there with me in her arms. Was she coming back to him or was she leaving him for good? It was the latter, and she was taking her son with her.

Dad placed his pistol in plain view on the built-in wall shelf in the upstairs hallway. Whether as a threat or to show his good intent, I don't know. My father was a gentle man and loved his wife dearly. I don't imagine he would have enacted such violence against her. All I know is that placing that pistol there was a wrong move.

I remember crying as my mother hurled vile vituperations at my father, claiming he adored the church more than she, that he was probably having an affair with the church secretary, that he didn't truly love her. He just wanted an armpiece, a sanctimonious symbol that he could parade in front of his minister friends, flaunt before his board of directors and community leaders. Well, she was no man's token. She had found someone who loved her for who and what she was, who thought her perfect, and was willing to let her live and be free of outrageous expectations and demands no matter how holy or God-ordained they might be.

"Christophe, stop crying, son," I can hear my father saying, reassuring me that everything would be all right. I quieted instantly. That made my mother even angrier, seeing the power of the bond between my father and me, the way he could soothe me where she could not. Mother shook me in her anger, causing me to cry harder still. My father lunged for her, pushing her away from me. She bounced against the wall. He grabbed me and held me protectively to his chest.

My mother went wild. She screamed like a madwoman, viciously striking at my father, who tried to ward off the blows while shielding me.

"Put him down!" she screamed. "Stop babying him. You'll ruin him. He'll turn out to be weak just like you!"

My father placed me on my feet, pushing me behind him, telling me to run into his room and lock the door. I quickly obeyed. The door provided no barrier between me and my mother's ranting, my father's trying to rationalize with a woman who was too far gone. She must have rushed at him, trying to get through him to me. He must have fended her off, forcing her backward. Perhaps they remembered the pistol at the same time, but she reached it first, grabbing it and shooting wildly at the target of her scorn. I heard a thud. Everything went silent.

I hid in a corner, afraid to move.

Apparently the neighbors, having heard the gunshot ring into the night, called my grandparents and the police. Papa was still alive back then. My grandparents rushed over to find me locked in my father's bedroom, my father on the floor in the upstairs hall in a thick pool of his own blood.

"Oh, Chris, I'm so sorry," Vanessa softly commiserated, tears in her voice and on her cheeks.

"I don't know how or why I blocked all of this out," I said, angry with myself for the years of tormented ignorance caused by my own denial.

"Boo, you were just a little boy, a child. You blocked it out until you were ready and able to deal with it." She squeezed my hand. "You did the best you could with what you had."

I ignored the comfort Vanessa offered, and continued with my saga.

Dad had to be rushed to the hospital for emergency surgery. He had been shot, the bullet barely missing his liver. He had a good chance of survival, provided infection did not set in. He would be hospitalized for some time. I stayed with my grandparents, who, whenever I asked for my father, told me he was away on business, which I somehow knew was not true.

As for my mother, she died the night she tried to kill my father. She rushed to her lover's home, frantically urging him that they had to leave right then and there. No, they were not taking her son. They had to go, and now!

They fled in her lover's car. She drove. They were on the highway heading out of town. It started to rain. The red lights atop a police car flashed through the darkened interior. My mother panicked, thinking she was being pursued for her attempt at murder. She forced the car to flee faster. The car was traveling too fast for the wet road conditions. They went around a sharp curve. The brakes failed. The car spun out of control and slammed through the freeway guard, flipping over the concrete barrier and plummeting down onto the embankment below. My mother was killed on impact. Her lover was paralyzed. The only one to walk away from the wreckage was the toddler, her lover's child, who had been sleeping peacefully, buckled snugly in the backseat.

God takes care of the innocent.

By the time I finished emptying my soul, we were near the city of Berkeley. Did Vanessa want to stop here or travel over to Frisco? Frisco was her preference. Then San Francisco it was.

We pulled up to the tollbooth and I gave the attendant the required fare. We pulled forward and then I broke. I had to maneuver the car over to the shoulder area just beyond the toll plaza, turn on the hazard lights, and shift the gear into park. Before I knew what hit me, I was outside doubled over, vomiting my insides out.

Vanessa was there, applying firm pressure from her hand at the small of my back, moving, rubbing tender circles about my shoulders with her fingers. It was so soothing I felt free to eliminate the toxins in my soul. I stayed there, doubled over, releasing a pain far beyond the physical.

"The police . . . only meant . . . to issue a fix-it ticket because of a broken taillight," I choked and sobbed in between retching out the foul irony of it all.

I felt like a seriously overgrown baby when I could finally walk, and Vanessa helped me back to the car and into the passenger seat. I was pitiful. I just sat there and let my goddess get behind the wheel and take us over the bridge and into the city of lights.

VANESSA

Vanessa leaned casually against the side of the car as she waited for Chris to return from the men's room. The night air was delicious. San Francisco felt cool and invigorating. It was nice being able to get away from home, from things, if only for a minute. The closest thing she'd had to a vacation was her recent trip to D.C. And in the very end, that had proven to be far from relaxing.

With a finger, Vanessa twirled the thin gold choker, adorned with tiny seed pearls, that lay delicately against her throat.

Gramms. Celine. They provided fond, soothing images and memories. But Vanessa could never forget the flight home and all the grief it delivered. For thirty years there was no one. Then, suddenly, she had a father, a mother, a sibling, and an extended family. She had actually stood in the home of her birth experiencing indescribable but conflicting emotions resulting from her shrouded entry into the world. Vanessa Taylor had gone from nothing to something all in a day. Now, once again, she was a parentless child left to deal with a consuming loss. Her father was a mere inscription on a war memorial wall. Her mother was dead to the world, finally free of the miserable prison she'd created for herself. Vanessa's sibling? He or she was nothing more than a mere nickname that could not be traced.

How was it that her grandparents and her aunts and uncles had allowed Vanessa and her sibling to be taken away? They should have fought for Vanessa and the other child. The family had rights.

Vanessa shook her head as if to clear her thoughts. It just did not make sense. Vanessa would never allow her child to be taken from her. She would never allow someone else to exert parental authority over her own flesh and blood, to take away what was rightfully hers.

She stopped playing with her necklace.

But then again, she wasn't having children. And she sho' 'nuff had no plans to marry. Vanessa had a career to pursue, dreams to capture. Every now and then, the thought came to tease her. Perhaps she should start her own public relations firm. But Vanessa honestly concluded that she was not ready for the demands such an undertaking would require. Perhaps one day in her future, but now was not the time. Besides, KSAC was good to her, had been good to her since her days as a college intern. Vanessa planned to ride her wave of success until the water ran dry. And when, in the next few years, her director finally retired to Hawaii with her husband and their three pot belly pigs, Vanessa planned to fill the vacancy without hesitation. When that happened Vanessa would be too busy for babies. She had a plan. Marriage and motherhood just did not fit the script.

Vanessa paused, warily considering the idea of holy matrimony. She concluded she did not trust that sacred institution. Why should she? Who had a solid marriage? No one Vanessa knew. Well, maybe. Look at Mr. and Mrs. Kingsley. They were crazy as heck, but they loved each other to life. Her grandparents, though she had not been around to experience the power of their union firsthand, had shared more than fifty years of marriage and were still going strong. Okay, so there were a few good unions left in the world. Still, Vanessa was leery.

And what if she one day woke up, her biological clock screaming louder than Chaka Khan holding a high note, and decided she needed a baby? Would marriage matter? Not according to powerful women from Murphy Brown to Madonna. Not according to power-hungry women like Vera Ann Smith.

Two babies. One daddy. Both out of wedlock. Perhaps her mother had done things backward, Vanessa grudgingly conceded. Maybe if she *had* married Vanessa's father before popping out babies, they would all be together as one happy family today. Instead Vera Ann chose to have children before having a committed relationship. She, the one with the power and the potential to suffer most, had set them up for failure from the beginning. Now where were they? Two were in the grave. One felt as if she were playing about the fringes of neurosis, and the other was nowhere to be found.

Vanessa tried to hold on to hope, but it was slick and elusive. She had known too many setbacks, too many disappointments. She wanted to be optimistic. She could use some of Reina's sunshine wine, or whatever it was the woman downed to keep the pep in her step. Vanessa simply could not stomach another disaster. She did not have the strength to endure an ordeal of searching for her lost sibling, only to receive more devastating news, as she had with the loss of her parents. Rather than set herself up for such a possibility, Vanessa merely resigned herself to pray that her lost sibling was alive and well, healthy, somehow happy and loved.

From her vantage point, Vanessa saw Chris enter the service station rest room with a bag filled with products he'd just purchased in the convenience store meant to settle his stomach. Guess that included ginger ale, a toothbrush, mouthwash, mints, and gum to cleanse his mouth and freshen his breath after his little regurgitation episode on the side of the highway.

Vanessa smiled as, moments later, she watched him exit the rest room. He was too much. Beautiful. Confident. He was an *Ebony Man* cover come to life, swaggering just enough to let you know he felt good about who he was. What a waste and a shame. Vanessa did not date friends, and Chris McCullen had been such a true friend for such a long time that getting with him was out of the question. Too bad. So sad. Her loss. Some lucky sister's gain. Right? Or could it possibly be time to reexamine her platonic policy? Didn't friends make the best lovers?

"Lawd, I must've died and gone to heaven, cuz angels don't live on earth!"

Vanessa's thoughts of Chris were rudely interrupted by a man standing too close to her for comfort, looking like that little crack-head kleptomaniac in that comedy starring Ice Cube and Chris Tucker about one day of the week in a happy 'hood of L.A. Vanessa had been so engrossed with watching her friend that she failed to even see the man approach. Little Man, small enough that Vanessa could see the top of his crusty scalp, was seriously invading her space and needed to back it up a foot or four.

Vanessa chortled. Was he for real? Must have been, because he decided to go for the gold.

"Give me your digits, darling, and let me treat you to some finger-licking loving."

Appalled, Vanessa rolled her eyes and walked away, rounding the car to the passenger side, cautioning herself not to wax wanton on the man. No neck rolling, finger wagging, hand-to-hip, lip smacking for her tonight. She was tired. Besides, the poor thing was obviously lost in space. Where did he get his rap? Some 1972 paperback edition of *Pimpology 101: How to Play Da Hoes like a Game of Dice*, complete with illustrations?

"Mmm, mmm, mmm! It must be jelly cuz jam don't shake like that!"

"How are you, my brother?"

Little Man whirled around and looked up at six-plus-feet of solid muscle with a masked scowl on its face.

"Eh-h-h, fine, my man. Just tryna share a little conversation with the lady here," Little Man said, nodding toward Vanessa.

"I see," Chris calmly stated as he walked around the car to open Vanessa's door. "Ready, baby?"

"Yes, Boo," Vanessa purred, playing her part to perfection.

Little Man threw his hands up in mock surrender as Chris handed Vanessa his package before firmly closing her car door.

" 'Ey, you can't blame a brother for tryna get his swerve on with a woman as fine as yours. No harm intended." Little Man started to walk away, then suddenly stopped. "Say, brutha, can you loan me a couple of dollars? My car ran out of gas and I need to get to the other side of the Bay so I can check on my mama."

"Sorry," Chris stated, unfazed.

"It's cool, it's cool," Little Man stated, and scurried off.

"You need to stop flirting with strangers," Chris scolded as, back in the driver's seat, he turned the key in the ignition and shifted his coupe into gear.

"Uh-huh, Chris, look!" He followed Vanessa's finger pointing toward Little Man, who had hopped on a little red bicycle and was pedaling out of the service station parking lot, bike squeaking and groaning loud as a rickety mattress beneath a five-hundred-pound sumo wrestler lost in the throes of a nightmare.

"Guess his *car* has gas after all." Vanessa laughed.

"Guess I need to beef up my weight lifting if I'm going to be with you."

"Puhleez," Vanessa muttered, feeling a tingle race through her blood. Did Chris mean that? Did he really want to be with her?

"Hey, you never know when I'll be required to flex a muscle and beat somebody off of you. Not that I blame a brother for trying."

They pulled out into traffic and headed for the wharf, Chris grinning, Vanessa left to ponder the weight of his deceptively lighthearted words.

She told him all about her mother as they sat in the cool of the night, perched on the hood of Chris's coupe as they overlooked the San Francisco Bay.

Vera Ann Smith, pregnant with her second child, rode the bus from the nation's capital to Sacramento, California, in hopes of finding her man. He had threatened to leave her many times before. He wanted to be married. She refused his proposals, saying she was too young to settle down.

"She was old enough to make babies but too young to be married," Vanessa said with a sad shake of her head before continuing her tale.

Vera Ann was young. She was young and spoiled and conceited, playing vengeful games with Taylor whenever she could not have her way. Eventually he had tired of her spoiled tantrums, her petty tirades, her turning to other men when he wouldn't conform to her childish demands. Yes, he adored her, but that did not require him to subject himself to the twisted abuse she called love. She had only so much time to straighten up and fly right or he was out the door with *his* child.

Vera Ann dismissed his warnings, knowing she had the goods, relying on feminine wiles that he seemingly could not resist to keep Philip Taylor right where she wanted him. She called his bluff and lost, miserably. He took their firstborn child and left, bound for California and a better life.

Vera Ann was not to be left behind, discarded like so much unwanted refuse.

Scared out of her wits but fueled by despair and a tankful of fury, she made it to California. How she found her man, Vanessa would never know. Whatever her methods, her scouting proved successful.

Only problem was that by the time Vera Ann found Philip, he had found someone else who was ready and willing to embrace Philip Taylor and his child.

The man was in love.

Vera Ann went all the way off, throwing rocks through his apartment windows, relentlessly stalking him and nearly causing him to lose his job with her lunacy. She wanted her baby back. She wanted him. She threatened to abort the child in her womb if he did not come back to her, but being so far advanced in her pregnancy, doing so would have killed her in the process. Vera Ann was too beautiful to die, so she allowed the fetus to come to full term.

Her second child was born, a beautiful baby girl whom she named Vanessa Ann. Certainly that precious baby would be enough to haul her man back to her side. He came, but not for her. He wanted to raise Vanessa along with their oldest child, who was two years old at the time. He wanted Vera Ann to relinquish her parental rights. Vera Ann strung him along, promising to give him Vanessa just as soon as the baby was weaned from her breast milk. That would give her enough time to work up a plan.

"The details get a little sketchy here," Vanessa admitted. "Maybe she planned to burn down his house or tamper with the brakes on his car," Vanessa caustically stated. "Who knows? All I know is that my mother never had a chance to put her plan, whatever it was, into action."

"What happened?" Chris quietly asked.

"My father died in Vietnam."

They sat on the hood of the car watching the rolling waters of the bay.

Vanessa shook her head, baffled by so many things, ravaged by too many emotions.

"It's all still so overwhelming. I feel like I'm searching in the dark."

"Your aunt or grandmother can't help you with understanding everything that happened?" Chris asked, reaching over to gently knead the muscles in her tense neck.

She sighed at the touch of his strong hands.

"I think my aunt is trying to shield me from truths she feels I can't handle, similar to how your family treated you. Know what I mean?"

Chris nodded.

"That I do," he agreed, maintaining a steady, kneading motion against her tense muscles. Slowly her body began to relax under his gentle ministrations. "So, what of the oldest child, your brother or sister?"

Suddenly Vanessa stiffened. A moment later she scampered off the car's hood and hurried away as if to put distance between herself and the ghosts of her parents' past.

It never should have happened. Now Vanessa understood what Gramms meant by saying Vera Ann just didn't handle things properly. She was impulsive, quick-tempered, self-centered, and immature. It was all about her. No one else mattered save how they fit into her plans. And when her pawns failed to be strategically placed as she deemed fit, then Vera Ann went off. Literally.

Philip Taylor's death hurled her over the edge. She was obsessed with him. He belonged to her. Not their children. Not that other woman. Not the U.S. armed forces. He belonged to her, Vera Ann Smith. And when death came a-knockin' and stole him out from under her, she could not handle being defeated by an eternal opponent. Vera Ann went capital C-R-A-Z-Y.

She was institutionalized for decades. When, no thanks to the Reagan-Bush administration, she was released onto the streets of a society that was suddenly foreign to her, she could not cope. Vera Ann committed petty theft, turned tricks, slept in alleyways, and dined from garbage bins. Slowly the nature of her offenses worsened, and it was not long before she was picked up on charges of grand theft auto and attempted robbery. She was sentenced to twenty years in prison.

She served only ten. While incarcerated she got a whiff of drugs and became addicted, selling her body to prison guards to supply her habit. Using dirty needles, passed from de facto pimp to pimp, Vera Ann inevitably contracted HIV and, without proper treatment, eventually died of full-blown AIDS just days before Vanessa's thirtieth birthday.

Vanessa walked down to the ocean's edge. Picking up a stone, she skipped it across the water, causing tiny concentric circles to dance across the waves. She was angry. She was hurt. She was grieving. She felt helpless, useless in the face of great loss.

Vanessa stood there, trying to impart her anger into each and every rock she tossed. She never looked away from the water's hypnotic sheen, but she felt Chris come to stand beside her.

"My mother's last sane deed, if you can call it that, was to place my sibling—who was returned to her when my father died—and me up for adoption after our father's death."

Chris was speechless.

Vanessa's laugh was brittle and without mirth.

"She wanted to hurt my father even in his grave by discarding the very ones who meant the most to him."

Chris reached for her, wanting to wrap Vanessa in the shelter of his arms, but she moved away, avoiding his touch. She did not want to fall. She was balanced, precariously, on the edge of a dangerous precipice. If he touched her she would lose what little grip she had left.

"I have no idea what became of the older child. Maybe he or she was adopted, maybe not. All I know is that"—Vanessa paused, trying to fill her lungs with much-needed air—"I was left to rot as a ward of the state."

"Why didn't your mother's people try to find you?"

Vanessa sighed. Chris had asked the very thing that had plagued and haunted her mind for some time. Finally, she had to admit her family had been in the dark. They had been up against the demons of their demented beloved just as she had been.

"My mother lied through her teeth. She told my grandparents that we were dead, had died in some apartment fire. She even had newspaper clippings to prove it."

"What?" Chris exclaimed incredulously.

Vanessa played with the pearl-and-gold necklace about her throat.

"Random clippings, random story."

"And they bought it?"

"I don't know," Vanessa sharply retorted. She exhaled loudly, her mouth a round *O*. "I guess not," she continued, her tone considerably softer. "My aunt says they tried for years to find us and the truth, but eventually the trail ran cold. We were untraceable."

Vanessa shivered.

"Are you cold?" Chris asked, his voice so solicitous and so gentle Vanessa wanted to scream. She made no attempt to respond. She merely stood there looking out over the water, bitter anger rising in her heart, tears blinding her view. She was breathing hard, set to collapse into some uncontrollable fit from which she might not ever recover. A strangled moan escaped her slightly parted lips. "Vanessa?"

The urgency in his voice snapped the slender cord that kept her hold on reality.

Lord, help me, please, was all she could think before the tumble began.

Vanessa caved in on herself, moaning out a pain of decades. A pain of unrequited love and abandonment. She wildly resisted the arms that sought to grab her, to pull her back from the pit of despair. She wrestled, wanting to be left alone to fall into whatever hell awaited her. But he refused to turn away or let her go there alone. If she was going, he would go with her.

"I'm here, baby," he whispered over and over again. "Hold on to me. I'm here."

Mercifully, he reached her in the knick of time, shooting a glimmer of hope through the opaque mire of her despair. She felt him in the midst of her pain, knew he would not leave her to fight it alone. She would be all right. After a while.

Vanessa gave in. She cried and cried and cried some more until it felt as if her entire being were made of age-old floods. She cried herself tired. She cried until she felt she might one day be strong. Like a libation on the altars of the elders, Vanessa Ann Taylor poured out the broken offering of her lacerated soul against a cleansing backdrop that deeply pulsated *hold on to me, baby, I'm here.*

Little more than an hour had passed since Vanessa's collapse into and eventual rise from despair. Yet it seemed like an eternity had come and gone, skipping and flitting across the pages of her life with fleet feet and gossamer wings. And she was alive to tell the tale. She might have been down, but she was not out. Broken, but not irreparable. Bruised, but able to heal. Contrary to how she had felt mere moments before, Vanessa would live and not die. She had survived and would somehow savor life once more. God had answered her prayer and helped her up from death's doors.

A bright, clear moon decorated the water's waves with diamonds and light. They sat together on the cool sand, sheltered by a sweet cloak of hard-won peace.

Vanessa felt as if she could eat a horse. She was so empty. So very pleasantly empty and clean.

"I'm hungry, Boo," she murmured as she leaned her back against the solid wall of his chest, her bare toes buried beneath the sand. Chris sat behind her, his arms a protective shield about her as Vanessa used a stick to lazily draw indeterminate figures in the sand.

"Vanessa?"

"Hmmm."

"Do you realize that the only time you refer to me as your Boo is when you're single?"

The stick in her hand ceased its drawing motion.

"I'm always single."

Chris laughed.

"You know what I mean. When you're in between men."

"In between men? Make me sound like a straight-up heifer, okay?" Vanessa muttered, turning just enough so that she could look into Chris's eyes. Her brow furrowed, she gazed at him. "Are you trying to say I use you as a surrogate lover?"

"If only." Chris chuckled deeply.

"What does that mean?"

Chris paused a moment, growing thoughtful. "It means I tire of watching you undermine your worth messing with these knucklehead bad-boy types who screw you over and leave you high and dry. Then after they're gone, and only then, you lean on my shoulder and let me hold you." Vanessa could feel the steady hammering of Chris's heart against her back. "I'm not some sort of stand-in to keep you feeling connected to the male species until some other brother comes along to carry you away."

"That's not fair, Chris. I do not treat you that way." Vanessa turned toward the water again, resuming her doodling in the sandy shore, a bit offended. "And wait a cotton-picking minute," she said, whacking him on the knee.

"Dang, girl! You tryna put a brother in traction or something?"

"What about you? 'Gorgeous' this and 'gorgeous' that. I'm only gorgeous when your bed is empty."

"No, baby, you're gorgeous always," Chris answered, knocking the fight out of her fists.

"Don't play sweet with me now," Vanessa cooed, leaning back into Chris's embrace, resting her head on his shoulder as she reached up to stroke his cheek. Suddenly the magnitude of his words hit her. *Then, and only then, you lean on my shoulder and let me hold you.*

"Chris, you said that in my 'downtime' I lean on your shoulder and *let* you hold me as if you've actually *wanted* to hold me. Right or wrong?"

Vanessa had never really known Chris to be at a loss for words, but right then and there he was. Several moments passed before he could respond. He did so by seizing the hand with which she stroked his cheek and brought it to his mouth to gently graze her palm with the silk of his lips.

Vanessa wasn't sure if it was the night air or not, but she shivered.

Chris spoke, tightening his grip about her.

"You'd get no complaints from me if you stayed right where you are right now."

Vanessa was dumbfounded, motionless. What in the world was going on here? They had always enjoyed a close relationship, physically, spatially speaking, even while still respecting one another's space and boundaries. She and Chris had always taunted and teased one another, their jesting often playfully sprinkled with sexual overtones and innuendoes. But never had that teasing become more than that, mere folly and fun. Indeed, something was somehow changing between them. Something was different. And a tad bit frightening. Vanessa's emotions, blissfully cleansed though they might be, were still raw. They had both endured enormous upheaval tonight, Chris and Vanessa. They had shared and exposed something greater than deep, dark family secrets. They had exposed themselves. This gave her pause.

"You know about Daphne and how I burned my love-club card after she jacked me."

Vanessa nodded.

"I guess you kind of issued me a new one."

"Issued you a new one," Vanessa echoed. "Boo, I'm not getting this. Can you just come out and say what you need to say and—"

"A brother's in love with you, gorgeous, okay!"

She had to laugh. Only Chris could put it in such a way and it still be sweet.

"What brother?"

"This brother," he whispered in her ear. "Vanessa, I love you."

Whoa! Chris never called her by her Christian name. The man was serious.

That threw her for a loop.

Vanessa had to back this thing up, slow her roll, and find her footing. Chris ranked somewhere near the top of her what-a-man rating scale. Any single sister in her right or left mind who was looking for a good man to call her own would relish the possibility of Chris McCullen filling the bill. But the thought scared her. She could not afford to confuse issues, to turn to Chris just to find solace in her state of abject loneliness. Besides, as Chris himself indicated, he was not a toy. He was not a prop, a pawn, some freeze-dried-add-water-and-pour-yourself-a-cup-of-hunk. Chris deserved better than that. And, yes, so did she. Vanessa wanted that something special, but she didn't know if she was ready.

"I don't know what to say," she softly replied.

"I didn't ask you to say anything," Chris swiftly interjected. "Just sit with it. Let it marinate for a while, then come back at me with what's in your heart. Okay?"

"Okay," Vanessa agreed.

"Promise?"

"Yes, Chris, I promise."

"Good. Now get off of me; my legs are numb."

Pressing against his thighs for leverage, Vanessa pushed herself up and onto her bare feet. She reached out a hand and stumbled in trying to help the solid mass of chocolate-brown body up off the ground.

"You need to pump some iron, woman. You're getting weak," Chris teased, wiping clinging sand grains from his linen slacks.

"I can outlast your built body in Tae Bo any day of the week," Vanessa challenged, assuming a sparring position.

"Tae Bo? Please! That's for broke-down boxers."

Her laughter felt fresh to her soul. She brushed the seat of her dress and the bottom of her feet free of sand.

"Tae Bo requires endurance and control."

"I prefer to reserve my endurance and control for other indulgences," Chris stated, his old teasing self, lifting an eyebrow for emphasis.

Vanessa sucked her teeth and slipped on her heeled sandals, easing the satin straps about her ankles.

"Your reserve should be overflowing by now, Monks-R-Us," Vanessa cracked, and took off back in the direction of the car.

Chris shook his head, enjoying the motion of her ocean as she sauntered across the sand. He called out, "We could deplete it by morning."

Vanessa spun about.

"No, you didn't! You are so nasty."

It did not take long for Chris to catch up with her, his purposeful stride considerably longer than Vanessa's.

"No, I'm not nasty. Just needing and wanting you."

Vanessa could only stare.

"Girl, come here before you freeze in place," Chris said, draping an arm about her shoulder. They walked in quiet harmony, noticing for the first time other late-night strollers delighting in a serene, panoramic ocean view.

"Question for you, gorgeous."

Vanessa grinned.

"Answer for you, Boo."

"What brought you to the Set earlier tonight?"

Vanessa replied without hesitation.

"I needed to drown my sorrows in a tub of male affection," she readily admitted.

Chris was momentarily taken aback by her prompt and forthright reply.

Vanessa continued.

"I didn't need some gratuitous booty call. I just needed to feel wanted after learning about my mama's drama. I had to remind myself I was beautiful. Desirable and worth loving."

Chris nodded, not appreciating, but nevertheless understanding her sentiments.

He reached for her hand. Vanessa slid her fingers in between his so that their hands intertwined perfectly.

"You are that and more."

The Lexus, parked securely beneath a lamppost, beckoned them near. They were both tired, physically and emotionally, and ready to go home. Unfortunately, they had a ninety-minute ride ahead of them.

"If you'd like some help locating your lost sibling, I can put you in touch with the same brother who did some investigating for me," Chris offered softly as they neared the car. "Okay?"

Vanessa nodded.

Chris stopped, turning her so that they stood facing one another. Her eyes sparkled with the fresh weight of unshed tears. He pulled her into his arms and tenderly kissed the crown of her head.

"Everything is going to work out," Chris assured her, as if possessing special insight or magical powers to ensure his promise.

Vanessa listened to the whisper of his embrace.

Hold on to me, baby. I'm here.

She answered in kind.

I'm holding on, Boo. Truly, I am.

REINA

She was glorious. Alone. Her presence filled the stage, captivating her audience as they sat spellbound, devouring every satin-wrapped lyric that floated out of her mouth. She was radiant. Marvelous. She sang with abandon, as one who was dead but now lived to tell the story to all who would hear. Life after death was on her lips, artfully twisting her precise phrasing, inspiring her improvisation, amplifying her voice and illuminating her once-shadowlike being as it unfurled, spreading, filling the room with dazzling liquid gold.

The final note soared from her softly painted lips to hang suspended in time above their heads. Slowly it dissipated, leaving an aching silence in its wake. Slowly movement and outside sound returned to those who listened, who strained to capture the fading echo of a voice responsible for sending them to rapture and back. So surreal.

The reaction came quickly, loudly as they sprang to their feet to thunderously applaud their thanks, their joy and adoration. It grew louder still. It seemed a never-ending roar sprinkled with whistles and bells of cheer.

Shrill bells. Insistent bells. Chiming bells that interrupted the flow of her dream.

Reina woke with a start.

She had fallen asleep downstairs in front of the television while watching some movie about some sequestered singer who—due to abuse she suffered as a child—never talked, never uttered a sound unless she was locked safely in her room, where she would turn on her stereo and sing until the abuse was a memory suppressed deep beneath the voice of her jubilee.

That must have triggered her dream, sent her onstage to delight her senses with her passion and the power of her own voice. Maybe she would hold on to the dream, to allow it to fuel and feed her resolve to take the stage once again. Or maybe she could grip its encouraging tenor if that gosh-darned phone would stop ringing.

It did just as Reina reached for the cordless telephone on the floor. She was tempted to push *69 for automatic redial, but it was late and she did not feel like talking. Unless, of course, it was Jamal. But it was already after one o'clock on her coast. Surely Jamal was sawing logs, and if God was good, which He was, dreaming sweet dreams filled with her face.

She recalled their most recent phone conversation.

"I believe I'll be able to finalize my decision regarding relocating within the next few weeks or so," Jamal told her, to Reina's instant delight. But then her joy wavered. What if that decision did not include California or Reina Kingsley? Would she be okay with that? "There are just a few more variables I need to consider, but I promise to let you know as soon as I decide."

Reina said she understood and encouraged him to do what seemed best for his business.

"Business isn't the only consideration that matters, Reina."

His voice had been so sweet, so sincere, that her heart ached with something new. Before she could respond another call came through that he had to take, leaving Reina wondering if she was a matter worth considering. Over time, she had been forthright with Jamal about her growing feelings for him, as he had been about his feelings for her. Their affection was mutual. Still, Reina did not feel as if she had the right to sway him one way or the other. If he remained in Atlanta or moved to California, the choice was his to make.

Sighing, Reina retrieved the phone from the floor and returned it to its base on the table next to where she reclined on the sofa. The house was dark, quiet, now that *Abuela* was—

Buzzzzzz!

Someone was laying on the front doorbell like they wanted a taste of buckshot in the kneecaps. Probably Raj trying to camp out here instead of going home at this alley-cat hour and being subject to their parents' wrath, Reina thought. Okay, maybe she was being unfair. Her baby brother, after all, was sincerely trying to mend his ways. *Yeah, right.* There weren't enough needles and thread in the world to handle the task, Reina mused.

Easing her feet into her Tweety slippers, Reina cautiously padded to the front door. She flipped on the porch light and squinted through the peephole. *Aww, suki suki.* What in the world was going on here?

She unlocked the door, barely opening it before it flung inward and she was caught off guard by the arms that encircled her throat, practically choking off her air supply, in an emotion-filled embrace. There she was at dark-thirty in the morning sniffing and choking back tears: Vanessa Taylor. A nasty sight for sleepy eyes.

They had not talked in weeks. Stubborn pride and injured feelings prevented Reina and Vanessa from acting older than their shoe sizes, keeping them at odds one with the other when they both knew better. Just acting out and ugly. Reina refused to bend or give in to the urge to mend her ways with her ex–best friend. If Vanessa wanted to reconcile, she knew where to find her. And so she had.

Took her long enough, Reina brooded, trying but finding it hard to hold on to animosity. Vanessa was squeezing it out of her.

"Okay, already," Reina choked through Vanessa's love-filled stranglehold.

Vanessa stepped back, releasing her hold only slightly.

"We came as soon as we heard," she assured Reina.

"Heard what?" Reina questioned. "And what time is it?"

"Nearly four A.M.," Chris answered, coming through the open door. "Hey, beautiful, how are you holding up? We got here as soon as we could."

Four o'clock? Wow, Reina had slept longer than she thought.

Reina frowned. Why were Vanessa and Chris on her doorstep at oh-four-hundred hours, talking all cryptic and crazy? She was glad they had finally come to their senses and decided to mend their wicked ways. But for real now, they had waited this long. Why couldn't they wait until a decent hour, like, oh, say, anytime after sunrise?

Reina had a flashback. *Don't be hypocritical,* she cautioned herself, remembering a time not long ago when she had stood on Vanessa's doorstep ringing her doorbell for dear life at some unlawful hour, traumatized and needing a place to hide out for a while that turned into months. Life could be ironic at times. Especially early morning before roosters crowed.

She yawned.

"Cover your mouth. I prefer not to see your diaphragm," Vanessa quipped, not really needing to lighten the mood. She was amazed at how serene Reina was. Considering.

The severity of the matter impressed itself yet again on her mind. This was no time for jokes. Draping an arm about Reina's shoulders, Vanessa gently propelled her toward the television room. They sat, Reina flanked on either side by friends she had not seen in too long. She missed them, even if they were no-'count, low-down busters.

"When did it happen?" Vanessa asked, firmly gripping Reina's hands in her own.

"What?" Reina asked.

"*Abuela.* When did she . . . leave?"

"Oh. A few nights back."

"How are you dealing with the loss?" Chris asked.

Reina shrugged.

"When you gotta go, you gotta go," Reina answered.

Chris looked at Vanessa. Vanessa looked at Chris. They both turned to stare in disbelief at Reina.

"What? What's wrong? *Abuela* told me weeks ago that she was ready to leave. It was her choice. So I helped her prepare for her journey."

They were silent, leaving Reina to fill the awkward space.

"In fact, my entire family helped. We threw a party—"

"Huh?" Vanessa's mouth was open. She was stunned. The Kingsley clan was different, but a party? This was not New Orleans. Californians did not march to cemeteries to the tune of trumpets and saxophones, then return home to get their grub on.

"Ye-s-s-s." Reina drew the word out as if talking to someone dim of wit. "A party. What's wrong with that?"

Vanessa was speechless.

"Nothing, I guess," Chris offered, "if that's the way you choose to deal with the death of a loved one then—"

"Wha-huh?" Reina sat back, scratched behind her ear. "I'm lost."

"I know, Ree-Ree," Vanessa empathized. "You and *Abuela* were so close. It's going to take time for the wound to heal."

"What wound?"

"Her death."

"Whose death?"

"Okay, her passing," Vanessa said, as if euphemisms would help Reina cope.

"What passing?" Reina asked, confused as heck.

"Chris." Vanessa looked to him for help. She obviously wasn't getting through.

"No, wait a minute!" Reina insisted. "What is going on here? It's too early in the morning even for the milkman. You're talking all crazy and acting as if I should be mourning over something or someone."

"Reina," Vanessa began as gently as she could, "Chris and I were on the way home from San Francisco when I called and checked my messages. There was one from you stating that *Abuela* was . . . gone . . . and that she left a couple of plants and one of her figurines for me."

Okay. This was getting bizarre. So, yes, *Abuela* did leave a few parting gifts for Vanessa. Did she have to come retrieve them at dark-thirty in the morning?

Realization fully dawned on her. Reina grew chilled at the very thought, but the chill swiftly passed and humor cropped up in its stead. She started laughing and found it hard to stop.

"*Abuela*'s not gone *gone*," Reina finally managed to choke out while gasping for air. "Oh, Lord."

Chris, somehow suddenly realizing the blunder involved, found himself laughing along with her. Only Vanessa sat there looking ready to snatch up the telephone book and find the number for the nearest twenty-four-hour grief therapist.

"But Reina, you were distraught," Vanessa found herself trying to explain.

Reina just shook her head, still laughing and unable to reply.

"You sounded as if you had been crying."

"Allergies," was the one word Reina could manage, wiping her eyes and trying to regain control of herself. "Whew! Okay, I've had my laugh for the millennium," Reina said, standing. "Now, get to steppin' so I can go to bed."

"Wait! What's going on here?" Vanessa wanted to know, agitated and concerned, yanking Reina back down beside her.

"You overreacted, gorgeous," Chris commented, trying to smooth Vanessa's ruffled feathers. "Reina, where's *Abuela*?" Chris yawned, stretching legs cramped from sitting so long. From the beach to the car for the long drive home and now here. He was sleepy and hungry.

"In Puerto Rico. *Abuela* got homesick, so she's gone to stay with her sister until the fall. I hope it's changed so much that *Abuela* doesn't recognize it; otherwise she'll probably stay in Puerto Rico for good."

Vanessa felt like a grade-A fool.

Chris chuckled, grabbed one of the throw pillows from behind Reina's back, and, propping it beneath his head, reclined across the sofa, his long legs stretched out across both of their laps.

"Well, there you have it. Matter resolved. Good night," he said.

"Hey!" Vanessa protested, pushing his legs away. Undaunted, Chris propped them up again, right back where they had been.

"Comfortable, Boo?" Vanessa sarcastically questioned.

"Hand me that afghan on the arm of the couch and I will be."

Vanessa tossed it at his head.

"Love you too, baby," he said, spreading the cover across his long frame and sinking down for a quick nap.

The dynamics of the interaction between them was not lost on Reina. She placed her thoughts in her pocket for later.

An awkward silence ensued until Vanessa broke it with a heavy sigh.

"Guess I made a mess of things," she quietly admitted, staring at the television, not really seeing whatever it was that was playing.

"It was a misunderstanding," Reina soothed, suddenly feeling benevolent. She could afford to be forgiving, seeing as how Vanessa had made the first attempt by reaching out to her. No matter that it took a garbled and misconstrued phone message that *Abuela* made her promise she would deliver to prompt Vanessa's actions. "It's kind of funny when you think about it."

"I'm not just referring to tonight, Reina." Vanessa soothed her temples with her fingertips. For the first time ever, she felt uncomfortable in Reina's presence. She forced herself to make eye contact, to not avoid the weight of her actions. "I'm referring to the party. Our friendship. Everything."

Vanessa launched into a heartfelt apology that served to completely thaw the ice between them.

They sat quietly talking, sharing an understanding, growing in their estimation of each other.

Their differences had formed the basis of their initial attraction. Those differences had been appreciated, respected, until they blurred reality, trying to manipulate one another into forms that best fit their individual needs. And when those forms failed in their compliance, hell broke loose and their friendship fried in the fire.

"Ree-Ree, I'm sorry," Vanessa apologized. "I was caught up in my own world and didn't bother to call home to let anyone know my flight had been delayed in Dallas." She paused, smiling. "I've never had a surprise birthday party before, but believe me, that's one birthday I will never forget."

"Girl, wasn't it scandalous! You acted a natural-born nut, throwing food all over the place—"

"Me? If memory serves me right, I was the one wearing a side order of cheesecake in my hair."

Reina laughed.

Chris snored deeply.

Vanessa rolled her eyes and continued.

"At least I didn't leave the back door open for all of Sacramento to hear our four-one-one."

Reina grimaced.

"That was terrible, wasn't it?"

Vanessa smiled.

"Straight-up outrageous!"

"Well," Reina said, squirming and shifting into a more comfortable position beneath the weight of Chris's legs, "may it never be said that Reina Kingsley doesn't know how to throw down on a party. Want excitement? Dial 1-800-DRAMA."

A peaceful silence descended when, finally, they sobered from laughing.

Suddenly Reina snickered.

"And that poor cabdriver. Did you have to let Pharoah in the house to chase the man around the kitchen and into the broom closet?"

Vanessa tossed her head back and chuckled, a deep-down sound that did her heart good.

"Like I really knew my dog would react that way."

"Who're you kidding? You have a hound from hell," Reina quipped. Reina glanced at her best friend, glad to be sharing the moment with her. A thought struck her. " 'Nessa, do you realize this is the first time you and Chris have been simultaneously single?" Reina pointed out.

Vanessa looked at her sharply before refuting Reina's observation.

"That's not true. We've both been without significant others at the same time in the past."

"But you weren't content to be alone," Reina stated matter-of-factly. "You were always looking and making yourself available. Am I right?" Reina inquired, stifling a yawn with the back of her hand.

Vanessa gave Reina's theory some thought. Okay, so maybe she did have a valid point. In times past, even when Vanessa was without a man she was thinking of how and when the next one would enter her life or how she might help facilitate his arrival. These past few months since her Keith Lymons debacle had provided the first real, as she herself had stated earlier, "downtime" Vanessa had allowed herself. And in the void of a man she had finally started facing facts. Difficult though it was, Vanessa admitted to herself that she was guilty of searching for love in all the truly wrong places, of being self-destructive by leasing her heart to counterfeit lovers who could never satisfy. Until now.

Peering at Chris to make certain he was asleep, Vanessa conveyed what had transpired that evening between the two of them by the shores of the San Francisco Bay, wondering if he was the real thing.

"I knew it!" Reina exclaimed.

"Shhh!" Vanessa cautioned with a finger to her lips. Whispering, she said, "You didn't know anything."

"I did too," Reina continued at a much lower decibel level. "I could tell something was up with you two. Ooo, I have to tell Taz and Suzy C."

"You are so silly."

"Yeah, so, is this a reciprocal kind of thing or what?"

Sighing, Vanessa slipped her barking feet out of the cute little strappy sandals she'd worn far too long that night and tucked her legs beneath her bottom.

"Ummm . . . well. No! Shoot, Ree-Ree, I don't know. I'm confused." Vanessa bit her lip. "I mean, the man is fine and sexy as all get-out. But he's my boy, my friend and—" Vanessa inclined her head as if she realized the vanity of her resistance. Her voice took on a tender note of affection. "Chris is already precious to me. I can imagine us in love."

"Well, what are you going to do?"

Vanessa shrugged.

"Guess I'll do like Chris suggested and let it marinate a spell. I just want to do this love thing right for a change."

"Don't let it marinate too long. The man's been single and celibate for over a year. Your booty may explode when he finally gets to tap it."

"Oh, my gosh. I cannot stand you!" Vanessa screeched, laughing.

"Shhh!" Reina mocked. "No, for real, be wise and take your time. But by that same token, don't let fear make you drag your feet. And trust what he says, 'Nessa. Chris has always been straight-up with you." Reina grew serious. "If he says he loves you then he does. Don't try to read in between the lines and find an out. And don't forget friends sometimes make the best lovers," Reina stated, unaware that she echoed the very thought Vanessa had entertained hours before.

"Who died and crowned you Dr. Ruth?" Vanessa asked, rubbing the balls of her feet.

Reina grinned.

"I've earned my credentials the hard way," she said rather mysteriously.

Vanessa inched closer to Reina and nudged her friend's shoulder with her own.

"Speaking of friends and lovers, how's Mr. Williams?"

Reina blushed just slightly.

"Jamal is fine. Thanks for asking."

"'Jamal is fine. Thanks for asking,'" Vanessa mimicked. "Girl, *puh-leez.* How is the man?"

"Honey, finer than wine and more than divine."

"Otay, gimme some," Vanessa said, holding up her hand so they could exchange a high five. "That's what I'm talking about. So let's get up in your business, Love Doctor. Are you ready for a bicoastal relationship?"

"Nope."

"Okay. So, what are *you* going to do?"

"Help him unpack his boxes," Reina answered.

"What? He's moving here?" Vanessa squealed.

"Be quiet!" Reina held a finger to her lips, nodding toward Chris's slumbering form. "It's a slight possibility. Remember, that's why Jamal was visiting Sacramento in the first place. He was investigating an opportunity to form a partnership with a college classmate of his who's established a real estate development company committed to urban development, and to building up our communities and not just the suburbs and commercial districts."

"That's right! Impressive," Vanessa said, nodding her head. "Okay, so why is his move only a slight possibility at this time?"

Reina shrugged.

"His family, except for Bryce and Phyllis, are all on the East Coast. He'll have to make new contacts and secure new deals if he moves out here. Basically, Jamal would have to reestablish himself professionally and socially."

"So?" Vanessa intoned, as if such things were a given in any such situation, her manner implying that they need not pose barriers to a brighter outcome.

"There's a lot involved," Reina lamely replied, as if defending some implied indecisiveness on Jamal's part.

"Including you?" Vanessa inquired. "Are you a factor in his equation?"

Reina was unsure how to respond. Certainly there was a part of her that wanted to be the prime factor in his equation. But would her affection, her person, prove persuasion enough? What had *Abuela* said? She was a queen without even realizing it? But then, *Abuela* was biased where Reina was concerned.

"Okay, the possibility is great; still it's a big decision to make," Reina offered.

"He's a big boy."

"Mmm, that he is."

They giggled wickedly, muffling their laughter as best they could so as not to awaken Chris's tired self. They need not have bothered. The man was snoring soundly, sawing logs and calling hogs.

"I think you need to know whether or not Jamal's move to the wild, wild west is even remotely contingent upon you," Vanessa matter-of-factly stated, examining the flawlessly manicured fingernails on her left hand as if pearls of wisdom were reflected in the soft, opalescent polish. "And if you ask me, I think it is."

"You haven't even met Jamal. How would you know?" Reina asked, propping her feet up on the solid mahogany coffee table, trying to regain a modicum of comfort beneath the solid oak of Chris's abundantly muscled thighs.

"I have too. I talked to him on the phone a few times when he called you at the house."

"That's not the same," Reina argued.

"Anyhoo," Vanessa sang in dismissal, "tell me something. Have you done anything to sway his opinion?"

"Such as?"

Vanessa rolled her eyes.

"You know."

"No, I don't."

"Reina, quit acting. Has Jamal had a whiff of the yum-yum yet or not?"

"No! You are so nasty!"

"Me? You were the one talking about my booty exploding—"

"That's different. You've known Chris forever. I've known Jamal all of two minutes and here you go—"

"Cap the rage, sisterwoman. I was just checking," Vanessa emphatically stated. Her sudden smile held a glimmer of approval. "That's a good thing."

Reina was shocked, to say the least, and her face told the tale.

"Don't look at me like that. I'm serious. Keep your goods to yourself and don't spread them all around town for any old Tre, Dushawn, or Harry to sample." Vanessa nestled deeper against the couch. "Trust me. I know what I'm talking about. Spreading the yum-yum won't buy you love."

"You have a point there, sisterfriend."

"Can I get a witness?"

"Amen," Reina piously replied.

Vanessa stretched and yawned, her stomach protesting loudly in the process.

"I'm starving."

"Want to go out for breakfast?"

"Who's driving? And who's paying?" Chris asked, eyes still closed, arms still folded atop the afghan coverlet keeping his body warm.

"Uh-huh, look-a this Negro here. Frontin' like he's asleep just so he can eavesdrop on a sisterlicious conversation," Reina accused.

"I was asleep, beautiful, until you two started talking about spreading breakfast to all the Troys and Duvons in town," Chris stated, rolling over onto his side.

"Get the facts straight, Boo. And get your behind out of our faces!" Vanessa cried, pushing Chris's backside for good measure. The man did not budge.

"Like a rock, huh?" He laughed, taking his time getting to an upright position and relieving their laps of the luxury of his legs. "Gorgeous, let's go feed this woman. Looks like she hasn't eaten in weeks."

"She looks like she could use an intravenous feeding," Vanessa quipped, winking at Reina.

"Really?" Reina chimed, delighted that they had taken notice of her weight loss success.

"You look good, beautiful. You really do," Chris assured her.

"Do I?" Reina inquired again in disbelief.

"Stop fishing for compliments, girl. You look good and you know it," Vanessa said, standing, stretching her cramped muscles. "How much weight have you lost?"

"Your age and half of mine," Reina said.

"Thirty plus forty. Seventy pounds? You go, stank!"

"Shut up, wench."

"For real, Ree-Ree, you look fabulous," Vanessa encouraged her friend, hugging her quickly. "Whatever you're doing, keep it up. It's working wonders for you."

Reina aimed the remote control at the television, turning it off. The first rays of a rising sun crept about the closed blinds to whisper a morning greeting to the room and its occupants. Reina felt as bright and promising, as soft and delightful, as the honey-colored velvet caressing the early dawn.

CHRIS

I was not eavesdropping. I was sleeping. For real! I just happened to have been drifting in and out of slumber and my ears snatched a taste here, a touch there of the—to quote Reina—"sisterlicious" conversation between her and Vanessa. So please don't hate a brother for having big ears and excellent hearing.

It's extremely rewarding to know I'm not the only one touched and tempted by the notion of romantic motions. I know I'm not shooting blanks in the dark. Vanessa is feeling the rhythm right along with me.

So we're both proceeding with caution.

You have to appreciate that this is not easy for either one of us. I've always considered Vanessa to be a beautiful, desirable woman. But she was my girl, my confidante. My movie partner, my jogging pal, my multipurpose cohort. Love connections were not in our script, but now the script has been flipped.

I understand Vanessa's wanting to "do this love thing right." I mirror that sentiment. I'm not trying to jump stupid on her and take us places neither one of us wants to go. Believe me, I've been on the ragged edge of romance and it cuts deep. I've been fried, tried, and kicked to the side. I'm not trying to limp that way again. Still, there comes a time in a man's life when he can't run anymore. He has to stand and face the things that have him ducking and dodging, bobbing and weaving. Or so my pops tried to tell me on many an occasion. I guess I finally got the message.

So I'm standing fast even if it hurts. Even when I feel like lacing up my Nikes and jetting the other way. I stand. Even when ugly little reminders of how I got played walking around thinking I was in love and about to be some baby's daddy come to whisper trouble in my mind. Even when I recall that my mother did this love thing so wrong, abdicating her responsibilities to her husband and child so she could go play house with someone else. Even when.

And I know I told Vanessa to take her time and let this thing marinate before making a declaration or breaking a brother's heart. But I'd best 'fess up: caution and all, I'm chilling on pins and needles.

So here's what I propose: a frank and open and honest conversation between the two of us allowing us to examine this thing from all sides and give us a chance. I guess I owe Cupid an apology.

Three days later, our answering machines are playing an endless game of tag. I call Vanessa. She calls me. I page her. She pages me. Cell phones not on simultaneously. Even our e-mail messages are answered days apart. All the advantages of modern technology and we just can't seem to get synchronized. Our worlds are hitting and missing, skipping out of time like a marching band led by a one-legged majorette with a serious facial tic and a poor sense of rhythm.

What's a brother to do?

Hop in his hoopty and take a spin across the city to her place of business, her house, her beauty salon, manicurist, weave worker, ob/gyn.

Just kidding. Vanessa doesn't wear a weave.

But seriously, though! Any other time, for any other reason, we would have connected by now. Certainly we live busy lives. Her plate is full and so is mine. But come on now. If I had tickets to see Chris Rock live or she had tickets to a Kings versus Lakers game, don't you know we would have already burned up the information highway planning and plotting our night on the town. I've come to a conclusion. I'm not going to let passive avoidance have the best of us. If, indeed, that's what all this hit and miss is about. It's time a brother took matters into his own very capable hands and let the chips fall as they may.

*   *   *

In a moment I will be veering off northbound Interstate 5 and taking the ramp leading to westbound Interstate 80, the same ramp where my mother died. Since obtaining the report from my private investigator, I've gathered additional information that further fills the gaps of a mystery that once mocked me. Dad, having been confronted with my enlightenment, finally came forward with further missing pieces of truth. Never would he have said a word in his attempts to protect and spare me, but realizing my ignorance was no longer his bliss he finally laid it all out, letting the chips fall where they may.

Yes, my mother left him for another man. Yes, she wanted a divorce, and no, he would not grant her one. The report was correct. She did plan to run off with her lover and start a new life, taking me with her and changing our names so that our whereabouts could never be traced. He hated admitting it, but he had played the fool. Dad had stood that night in the space of our upstairs hall, looking at his wife, hoping she had finally returned to us, to him. It was not to be. She would punish him for not agreeing to the freedom she craved. She would take what he cherished most—his son.

Dad almost died that night. Not from the gunshot wound to his flesh, but from the crushing of his heart. Just days ago, I sat gripping my father's shoulders as he cried like a motherless child, reluctantly telling me things he never intended for me to know.

Nana had warned her son that his prospective bride was not *the one.* There was something unsettled and wild about her. She was beautiful, enticing. My father ignored her voice, reducing Nana's words to the mere meddling of a too-attached mother. Too soon after my parents married, my grandmother's words proved themselves correct. But by then it was too late. The McCullen family did not believe in divorce. They were law-abiding, Bible-toting, middle-class black folks still haunted by the chilling whispers of families shattered and torn during slavery. The McCullens were intent on staying together. No matter the often high cost togetherness exacted.

Marriage counseling was either out of the question or virtually nonexistent then. There was no one to rely upon except God. But my mother was through with God and any goodness He had to offer. She wanted out, and by any means necessary.

My father realized his mistake too late. Hearing the commotion in the hall that night, he'd grabbed his pistol, running from his room not knowing what to expect, just knowing that his child was in danger. Then he saw her, my mother, his wife. The woman he'd loved and adored. But when I, as a three-year-old child, cried at hearing my mother holler and yell ugly words at my father, resulting in my mother viciously shaking me, Dad says any and every remnant of love he felt for her vanished into a bottomless abyss. He suddenly hated her. He pushed her from me, secured me in his bedroom, and may have hurt her had she not shot him first.

Later, one of my aunts told me something Dad obviously never would. Why my aunt told me, I'm not certain. Perhaps she was so overly relieved that a thirty-year secret was finally revealed that she gushed it without thinking.

My mother shot my father accidentally. Yes, she reached the gun he'd laid on the hallway shelf before he could. No, he was not her target. I was. She wanted to take what my father cherished most, so much so that he was willing to sacrifice himself on my behalf.

Was my auntie being melodramatic? Did she have her facts twisted? I would hope so, but I may never know. Am I haunted by this morbid possibility? No. Even if there exists a glimmer of truth in what I've been told, the ghosts that plagued my mother's soul are not mine to bear. A thirty-year silence has been irrevocably shattered, and I refuse to allow myself to sulk and slip into an emotionally comatose state because of it. It's as if the fear of not knowing was worse than the knowing itself. Knowledge and truth have set me free indeed. As callous as it may sound, I have to live. I choose to live and not die because of sorrows from the past. I choose life, and in that choice there must be forgiveness.

I choose to forgive my mother for leaving my father and me. I elect to forgive her her indiscretion, her dalliance with a man outside of her marriage. While I was home, needing a mother, she was out playing surrogate stand-in to his child. I forgive my mother for being irrational enough to shoot my father, then flee in the middle of the night, killing herself, wounding her lover, and placing his innocent child in jeopardy as well. I choose to let go and to let God have His way in the matter.

I choose to answer this still-ringing phone before it wrecks a nerve. I depress a button on the console and glance in the rearview mirror realizing that the ramp is so far behind me that it can no longer be seen. I choose to press on.

"Hi, Chris."

It's my administrative assistant telling me something about my two-o'clock appointment with the contractor who was to remodel our weight room being canceled. Could we reschedule for Monday morning? I asked her to pull up my schedule on the computer. Am I free? Yes. Then go ahead and reschedule the meeting. Did I sign the payroll reports? Yes, they're on her desk. Oops, there they are. Right there on her desk in the folder marked *Payroll Reports*. Do I need her to do anything before I arrive at the office? Just get off my phone so I can handle my business. Of course I don't say this. I merely decline her offer and promise to see her later in the afternoon.

Enough with the outside interruptions. Am I not on a mission here? Do I not have a woman to find and heartfelt words to speak? I'm trying to concentrate. Give a brother a break. Like Nana says— and this is nowhere in the Bible—God helps those who help themselves. So I turn off the pager clipped to my belt. I disengage the cell phone and allow any further calls to roll over in to voice mail. Chris McCullen is unavailable to distractions. The brother has to handle his stuff.

Stuff is a bust. Why, when a man wants to take control of certain facets of his life, does he need a woman's permission and cooperation to do it?

Sorry, sir, Ms. Taylor is out of the office until Monday. Do I wish to leave a message? the receptionist asks, greedily eyeing the bouquet in my hands. Is there anything she can do for me? I glance around the plush lobby, rather than tell her she can't do a dang thing for me now or later. I leave the flowers hoping the receptionist will deliver them to Vanessa's desk without killing them with her playa-hatin' fumes.

Check this nonsense out. A minute after I disengage my cell phone, Vanessa calls. But of course I don't get her message until after driving all the way to the television station armed with a bouquet of exotic wildflowers, intending to take her out to lunch and give her ten thousand reasons to enter the luxury of my love. But it isn't happening, no how, no way. Guess Nana was wrong. God doesn't need my help after all. I should have left the cell phone on.

"Hi, Boo. I planned to ask you to dinner tonight, but I just found out I have to pay a visit to our sister station in Los Angeles. There's been some sort of fiasco involving the CEO and I have the pleasure of doing damage control and impression management." She sighs. "I should be back Monday or Tuesday at the latest. I was thinking maybe we could we have dinner and talk then. If that's okay with you. Anyhow, have a good weekend."

Maybe this is really a message from God. Maybe He is trying to tell me something. Leave well enough alone, son. Pack up your pride and hobble on back to the way things used to be.

I feel deflated after hearing Vanessa's voice-mail message. I had planned to have what I hoped would be a very good weekend. Not! The woman will be four hundred–plus miles out of arm's reach. What's a brother to do? Go exhaust myself at work, spend an hour doing a little circuit weight lifting, go home, take a shower, fall into bed, and watch some old black-and-white classic film on video until I fall asleep.

Strike that! It's the second Friday of the month. Our youth ministry basketball team has a game tonight. Man, any other time I'd be stoked, ready to play assistant coach to the team, keeping them fired up and focused on the game. But I'm feeling like I could use a little focus myself just now.

But I go, without complaint, stopping by to pick up Dad on the way. He tries to come out and support the team as often as possible. Of course, this means his regular Friday-night frolic with his old cronies gets postponed until the following week, but Dad doesn't mind. He likes being around young people as much as they seem to enjoy being around him.

I admit it. I lose myself in the game. I forget all about having an attitude, or being upset over my and Vanessa's failure to connect. I am hollering and gesturing and getting all excited and animated with the rest of the crowd. Now, I'm the assistant coach. I'm supposed to play it cool, be calm, act collected. But this is it. It's the final game. It is too good for all of that. You see, we have a young lady on our team, and when our opponents got sight of her they—as usual—assumed she was somebody's weak link to pick on. Wrong! Little Bit, as I call her, might weigh all of one hundred and ten pounds soaking wet but the girl is fierce. Little Bit is lanky as all get-out, five feet, seven inches of arms and legs. She has a serious right hook shot, slam-dunks like the best of them, and can play a mean point guard on occasion.

So there we are. Two minutes left in the fourth quarter. We're down by three points. We have no time-outs remaining. The ball is in our court. One of the fellas passes it to Little Bit. She dribbles up the court, bobbing and weaving, tearing things up. The basket is clear. She sets up for it. Wham! An elbow to her ribs sends her sliding across the floor.

Spectators are on their feet, booing and hissing and hollering at the referees to take care of things. A foul is called. We rush over to where Little Bit lies in pain on the court. She's told to lie still while she's examined. Only when we're satisfied that she's absolutely okay do we help her up. Coach wants to pull her out of the game, but of course she's trying not to hear that. She makes her way to the free-throw line and takes her shot. The first one misses. The second one licks net. It's in. It's good! Now we're trailing by only two points. Two, we tie. Three to win.

The last minute of this game stretches an eternity. I'm rubbing my bald head like it was a lucky charm or something, pacing about, running up and down the court with my team. Seconds on the clock. The other team is in possession of the ball. They're determined to hold the lead, trying to hold on to the ball and run out the clock. But then one of their superstars comes into possession of the b-ball and decides he wants to widen the gap, to send us home crying like punks. He shoots. The ball is floating. One of our boys pops up and knocks it off course. Rebound! We're in possession.

The audience is on its feet, stomping, cheering, encouraging our team to "do it, do it!" Our boy is showing off some fancy footwork, sizzling up the court, dodging playa haters. He does a fast rotation, turning around intending to go up for the kill, but the ball is knocked from his hands. It's loose. She's there like a bullet. She reclaims it just outside of the three-point line. She's pressed hard, finding no narrow escape possible. So what does she do? Little Bit takes it to the head. She shoots and time stands momentarily still.

Buzzzzz! Game over. We win! Little Bit's three-pointer is good.

I think our entire team tries to pick that young lady up at the same time. We hug her so hard we probably leave arm prints. When I look up, her father is crying, her mother is slapping high fives with the women around her, and Dad—the pastor of our church, the right Reverend McCullen—is doing the running man and barking like he was part of Snoop's dawg pound. What a sight. What a night.

Dad and I were still debating—okay, arguing—over the finer points and plays of the game while en route home. We took the team out for pizza after the game. As usual, Dad acted up, challenging the kids in video arcade games and giving them a hard time if they lost and he won.

"Hey, son, don't be mad at me because you woke up on the wrong side of an empty bed."

Now, you know he wasn't right. Throwing a brother's solitary confinement up in my face.

"I thought we were talking about the game, not my life," I shot back, chuckling as we turned onto our street. I had not lived at home in years, but I still thought of Dad's house as my house, his street as my own. "At least I got out of my empty bed without the help of a nurse or a walking cane."

"Your mama's so fat she sat on a quarter and squeezed a booger out of Washington's nose."

I pulled into the driveway, shaking my head and laughing.

"No more basketball games for you. You get around young folks and don't know how to act."

Dad unlocked the front door and we walked into a too-warm house.

"Aww, don't hate. Celebrate," Dad replied, opening the living room windows. Dad did not believe in using the air conditioner unless it was absolutely necessary. Seeing as how the temperature of the June night was only in the low nineties, in Dad's opinion, it wasn't necessary.

I followed him into the kitchen.

"See! That's exactly what I'm talking about," I pointed out, taking a stick of butter from the refrigerator and handing it to my father. "Next thing we know you'll be up in the pulpit doing the Bankhead Bounce and sporting Nubian locks or a skullcap."

Dad laughed as he heated peanut oil in a large saucepan. I found the jar of popcorn in the same place it had been for years: in the refrigerator. Dad claimed the cool air kept the kernels fresh. He passed a hand over his hair.

"Don't think I have enough fuzz left on the skull for any of that." Dad poured corn kernels in the hot oil, covering the pan with a lid. "Should I get a hair transplant?"

I laughed so hard the black-cherry seltzer water I was drinking almost flew out of my nose. I choked. Dad slapped me on the back like he used to do when I was a child, trying to ensure that my airways were clear.

"Maybe I could get a toupee. Or a weave."

I was still laughing.

"Hey, what's so funny about that? There are weaves for men, you know," Dad stated, all indignant while shaking the pot over the flame to keep the kernels from scorching.

For the first time I noticed my father's normally thick head of hair truly was a little less bountiful. I noticed the fine lines around his eyes, the almost imperceptible paunch forming around his middle. My father was aging. What a sobering notion.

"Your mother's insurance money paid most of your college tuition," Dad stated without fanfare or introduction into the topic. Since learning that I knew the truth about my mother's passing, Dad would often drop information unceremoniously into my lap. He was free from decades of secrecy and found himself readily divulging tidbits of the past. Initially he had been furious at my having hired a private investigator, but his fury quickly turned into relief, allowing him to openly communicate, finding sharing to be cathartic for us both.

I said nothing. It was Dad's time to talk.

"The insurance company tried to say there was questionable negligence involved, that the car was intentionally driven through that concrete barrier and over onto the embankment, just so they wouldn't have to cash out the claim."

I watched Dad watch the hot pot, expertly monitoring it so that the popcorn cooked up fluffy.

"Whatever became of the child? The one who was in the car accident?"

Dad shook his head sadly.

"I don't rightly know, son. I believe the child was sent back to its mother, or maybe the woman's family. I can't be sure. So that's that."

I knew conversation about my mother had reached an end.

"Sad," I remarked, snatching up two small bowls and a handful of napkins to follow Dad and the scent of popcorn into the living room. Dad dropped onto his favorite leather recliner and placed a bowl of popcorn on his lap. I rifled through his video collection until I found some old black-and-white Hitchcock classic to thrill us both. I popped the movie in the VCR and plopped down onto the couch.

"How's that pretty girl of mine?" Dad asked, not bothering to set the film in motion.

I knew to whom he referred. Still, I raised an eyebrow, my mouth filled with savory corn, feigning ignorance. I hadn't said a word to Pops yet about my slowly evolving relationship with Vanessa. Perhaps it was time.

I swallowed.

"Vanessa's in L.A. until next week."

"Oh. Sounds as if that's a problem," Dad stated, perceptive as always.

I shrugged.

"Sort of."

Dad sucked his teeth.

"Son, explain 'sort of.' Either it is or it isn't."

"It is," I answered.

"And why is that?"

"Because I was hoping Vanessa and I could get together and talk some things over."

"What things?" Pops wanted to know. "You two in love or something?"

I had to laugh.

"Yeah, Pops, we're in love or something," I gladly admitted. "We have feelings for each other that aren't platonic. But we're taking it one day at a time and trying not to rush things."

"Mmm-hmmm," Dad murmured, sucking his teeth again for good measure. "Well, Christophe, I raised you right. You know to respect the young lady. You can't make her want you. That's something she has to do on her own." Dad propped his feet atop his ottoman, knowing only too well of what he spoke. "Well, son, I'll say a little prayer that everything works together for the good."

"Thanks, Dad."

He smiled.

"My pleasure. Hey, now, don't forget the Juneteenth celebration next Sunday," Dad suddenly cautioned.

I assured him I wouldn't.

"That was a good game tonight," Dad said, taking a sip of his flavored seltzer water. Dad was not senile. He was not randomly skipping from subject to subject without cause. He had a point to make and believe me it would be made. "That Little Bit is a good athlete."

I murmured my agreement, just waiting for the punch line to pounce.

"She doesn't ask for special favors. She gives one hundred percent just like the rest of the team." He paused to toss a handful of popcorn in his mouth. I had to wait as he chewed agonizingly slow, savoring the flavor. "She was knocked pretty hard tonight. But she didn't stay down. She got back up and tried again and helped lead her team to victory. That's what life is all about. Success often comes after pain."

He gave me a smile and little nod of his head as if to tell me everything was going to be all right.

Dad aimed the remote control at the VCR and set the movie to rolling. I stretched out on the couch, watching some old-school thriller, giving Dad's analogy some thought. Things had not gone my way lately. I felt pretty well knocked about and just about out. But I knew better than to lie down and play dead. Life and love kept on moving, and if I wanted any part of them I had to be willing to roll on despite the obstacles, the elbows, the fouls thrown my way. I had to press my way through. I told myself I could and would do it. Vanessa waited on the other side.

RESURRECTION

She saw it, she felt it, she knew it to be. Still, it was simply amazing and it took much getting used to. Gingerly, she stroked the feather-light hair at the nape of her neck. The heaviness was no more. She was free, somehow liberated from weighted mass, figuratively and literally.

Reina recalled sitting in the stylist's chair, nervous but resolute. Her look was dated. Her hair provided comfort and obscurity, allowing Reina to hide behind its massive cloak or style it in such a prudish and unadorned fashion that attention was not drawn her way. But, like Miss Patti sang, she had a new attitude and she was no longer afraid to be seen. Reina Kingsley had stepped from the fringes and fully into the circle of life. Her Morticia Adams look had to go.

Reina did not agree with the hairstylist Vanessa had referred her to. She did not want her hair cut an inch at a time to allow herself to get comfortable with the idea. She knew what she was doing. Cut the hair already! It would and could grow back. Right? Goodness gracious.

Reina loved it! Her new look was chic, stylish, and incredibly low-maintenance. No more little-girl ponytail wound up in an old-lady bun anchored at the back of her head. She had style. Pizzazz. Her fingertips covered with some herb-based moisturizer purchased from her new stylist, Reina combed her fingers through the soft, loose curls, making sure to massage her scalp and coat the newly clipped ends to keep them healthy. Reina gently shook her head, allowing the hair to fall into place, soft curls framing her face and fanning her neck.

"Marvelous, dahhhlink," she purred, smiling at her reflection. Her cheekbones smiled back at her.

Wow, she actually had good bone structure. Was her short, chic hairstyle to be credited for accentuating her facial features? Or was it the weight loss that had taken a little puff and a lot of plump from her jaws? Both, Reina concluded, pleased with the image she beheld.

Weight loss had been a painful, uphill battle for Reina for such a long time. It seemed exacerbated by the fact that she was the only one with a weight problem in her family. Well, her cousin—the one with the thirteen bridesmaids and, now, five children—was a touch chunky, and so was her Aunt Estherlene, Uncle Butchie the cross-dresser's wife. But her cousin had *bébés,* plural, and Auntie had a glandular problem, so they were exempt from ridicule. In times past, Reina had excused herself, faulting her heritage for her heaviness. She was not petite like *Mamí* and Nita and *Abuela* and the majority of the women in her mother's family. Reina had inherited *Papí*'s robust genes. She was built like her paternal grandmother, solid, sturdy. But only when Reina took ownership of her deeds and responsibility for her life and living did she admit solid was one thing, excess and obesity were another.

Yo-yo dieting had only added to her weight gain. It kept Reina in a vicious cyclical battle that sapped her inner strength and stole her soul's joy. Reina had often felt hopeless, destined to a life of weight and pain. Until Phyllis and Healthy Habits.

Reina had to credit Vanessa and Chris for their loving attempts to "help" her, to coach and coax her to fitness. But Reina had always felt morbidly obese in the face of their firm fitness. How could Vanessa or Chris understand what she was experiencing? They'd never had a weight problem a day in their lives. So what if Vanessa thought she had a bubble butt, not that the sister was complaining, mind you. Reina preferred a bubble butt to hippo hips any doggone day.

Reina giggled as she lightly stroked cocoa-colored matte eye shadow across her lids with a soft sable brush, just as the beauty consultant at the salon had instructed her to. Using her fingertips, Reina smoothed the shadow, blending a smoky gray at the corners of her lids until the makeup was flawless. Peacefully Reina concluded that she had inherited some serious hips and plenty of breasts and there was nothing she could do about it, save buy industrial-strength girdles and bras galore.

Thank God for Phyllis.

Phyllis had been there. She knew Reina's plight, the only difference being that Phyllis had actually broken the chains of misery and done something to reverse the pain of her weight gain. And so she introduced Reina to Healthy Habits, being careful not to come off condescending or authoritative or sound as if she were playing savior to Reina's sad state. Reina attended Healthy Habits with Phyllis one evening as a guest visitor. Something clicked. Reina instinctively knew she had found what was right for her.

Reina felt good as she prepared for the annual Juneteenth celebration at Papa McCullen's church. And if last year's attendance was replicated this year, the sanctuary would be packed to maximum capacity, leaving standing room only, and Reina was not trying to stand for three hours in the strappy little high-heeled satin numbers she purchased to match her outfit.

Reina could not recall the last time she'd bought high-heeled shoes. Flat shoes were meant for fat feet, as far as Reina was concerned. She'd been amazed to find that her size–nine and a half wides had shrunk to a nine medium over the past months. So, feeling a bit daring, she asked the shoe department saleswoman to ring up the sexy little somethings before she chickened out. Reina critiqued her mirror image and was glad that she had dared to. The hue of the shoes perfectly matched the ankle-length ivory skirt and camisole set made of some incredibly soft, chiffonlike fabric that whispered about her reformed frame. Reina hurriedly secured the crystal earrings on her lobes, fastened the matching crystal bracelet on her wrist, then slipped on the sheer, matching ivory jacket splashed with tiny pink rosebuds made of crystals and silk.

Reina rushed to grab her purse and rummaged for her keys. She found them at the bottom of her silk bag along with an odd-shaped pouch. Brows furrowed, Reina examined the pouch, bringing it to her nose and sniffing. It was one of *Abuela*'s amulets, probably filled with her grandmother's special herbs and only God knew what else. Of what use was it? Reina didn't need it anymore; she no longer remotely believed in its possibilities. It was an inanimate object made by hands. She didn't need idol gods, idol trinkets, and witchery in her life. Reina knew her grandmother meant well in giving her such strange talismans, but Reina had heard Papa McCullen speak of an all-powerful God who could not be contained in parcels and packages. It was that God for whom her heart hungered. Keys in hand, Reina headed out of her bedroom, tossing the homemade pouch in the trash can as she went.

Chris was trying his best to calm his kids. They were excited. The youth group had been practicing for weeks for today's event. The boys were clowning as usual, adding too many extra bounces in the routine, stomping double, triple time when the move called for only a single step. One of the soloists was off in a corner humming, warming up her voice, and trying to remain calm for her part in the soliloquy that would be a blend of song and speech, while someone else was fussing with somebody about getting dirt on her robe. And on and on it went, reminding Chris why he didn't have kids in the first place. He loved working with young people, but he liked sending them home and returning to the solace of his bachelor pad at the end of an evening even more.

Where was the star soloist?

She was thirty minutes late. If she didn't arrive soon things could get messy. Then Chris recalled that Little Bit could serve as an understudy. The girl could cook up a basketball court, but she became suddenly shy when faced with an audience of a nonsports kind. Chris could only hope the soloist would show. If not, Little Bit was on whether she liked it or not.

Chris blew his whistle. He rubbed a hand over his shiny head. He felt an uncustomary migraine coming on.

"All right, already, now! Line up," he ordered. Little feet and big feet hurried to do his bidding. His fellow youth ministry coordinators helped him help the children assume their rightful positions, going down the roll sheet and calling names in the order they should appear. Everyone was there—except the little late soloist. Chris reached for the cell phone in his leather duffel bag, ready to call her house, when she came dashing through the door, apologizing about having had a flat tire and having to wait while her father repaired it. Chris was relieved, assuring her it was okay, to get in line and breathe deep. He felt a smile creep up over his frown.

Everyone assembled, they joined hands, each sharing how they felt or what they hoped for the day.

One raunchy little fifteen-year-old said he hoped the girl he was interested in was in the audience because he had a couple of special moves up his sleeves just for her. The children laughed uproariously. Chris had to blow his whistle to regain order. One of his fellow coordinators threatened the rambunctious adolescent with a good, old-fashioned switch whipping if he dared show his behind. The boy laughed. The coordinator tried hard not to.

Peace restored, the group resumed the quiet articulation of their hopes for the day. When everyone had finished, they prayed, Chris leading them before the throne of grace to find help in a time of need.

". . . And, heavenly Father, we are thankful that You are with us, strengthening us for the cause ahead. May You encourage and uplift hearts as we bless Your holy name. These things we ask in Jesus' name. Amen."

A chorus of reverent *amens* rippled throughout the room. There was a moment's silence; then pandemonium resumed. Chris could only smile and suck his teeth. He remembered his days of boundless energy and motormouth ability. He suddenly felt ancient amid such youthful exuberance. Carefree spontaneity was a thing of his past. Welcome to adulthood, reservation and responsibility, heartbreak and healing, and the need for shoulders wide enough to weather it all.

Chris could hear music drifting angelically toward them. The service was already under way. For the ninth year in a row the church celebrated Juneteenth, a day set aside and observed by many African Americans throughout the country in honor of those slaves in Texas and other parts of the Americas who had not been informed of their freedom until many months after Lincoln's Emancipation Proclamation was ratified. As if four hundred years of bondage were not enough, many white slave masters exacted additional peonage from persons who were no longer legally their slaves. Talk about delayed gratification.

Chris bowed his head, finding a quiet place within himself to say thank-you to the ancestors for their sacrifices, their blood, sweat, and tears. Someone somewhere had died that he might live. His life was more than meat, his body more than clothes, his heart more than mere want and wish. He, too, could—by choice and not force—delay gratification of the things he wanted today until such a time as they should be. The brother welcomed peace.

Vanessa locked the car door, engaged the security system, and dashed up the street. The church parking lot had been filled to capacity, forcing her to find a space on the streets like so many others who had obviously not arrived early enough for a choice spot. Ferragamo calfskin pumps were not exactly made for jogging. Vanessa had to slow her roll and walk at a dignified pace now or suffer the consequences of too-tight toes and blossoming bunions later.

Vanessa waited in the foyer with other late stragglers while white-gloved ushers searched for vacant seats. She hadn't meant to over-sleep, but her flight from Los Angeles had not arrived until one o'clock that morning. By the time Vanessa retrieved her luggage and made it home, it was after 2 A.M.

Her trip to L.A. was a frightmare. Downright ridiculous! The CEO of their sister television station had really gotten herself into a pickle. You name it: embezzlement, drugs, questionable alliances with shady characters known in the Hollywood district for their less-than-legal sexual services. Enough said.

The sister station's own PR team having been dismantled the prior year by the very CEO now under scrutiny, Vanessa played cleanup woman. Her management staff of trained monkeys could handle PR, or so the CEO thought. But when the chips were down and the media's microphones were pushed in her face, she and the monkeys panicked and jumped stupid. Vanessa Taylor to the rescue, no matter that such cleanups were not in her job description or her contract. A sister had to do what a sister had to do. Now, about that raise?

Thank God for Pharaoh. The oversize canine had roused her that morning with his whining and his wet nose. It was past time for his walk. Mommy needed to get up, and now! Vanessa complied, her cheek slippery with doggy-drool kisses. Realizing the time, she rushed through her morning routine in an effort to make it to the church. Still, she was late, missing the opening prayer, the opening song, the reading of the history of Juneteenth. Finally she made it inside, an usher guiding her to a seat just as the sister with the polished, clipped speech concluded the recounting of historical facts. The applause was firm, appreciative.

"Psst! 'Nessa."

Vanessa glanced over her shoulder just as she reached the pew the usher was directing her to.

She squinted. Some woman was waving discreetly, trying to get her attention. Some woman with a seriously whipped 'do, a radiant smile, a soft air of grace all about her.

"Say wha-a-a-t? *Reina?*"

"Shhh!" the usher silenced her. Vanessa apologized, indicating that there was a seat beside her friend. The usher nodded, leaving Vanessa to her own devices. She had to cross over several parishioners to get to where Reina sat toward the opposite end of the long, padded pew.

"Look at your hair," Vanessa assumed she whispered as they embraced. A blue-haired church mother type on the row ahead of them turned to toss them an evil, warning eye. Vanessa lowered her voice, admiring the glow of Reina's person. "Look at you. Girl, you look . . . absolutely beautiful."

Reina hugged Vanessa again.

"I do. Don't I?"

Vanessa sucked her teeth. "Help us, Jesus."

"I'mma help both of you if you don't stop all that talking," Mother Bluehair said, indignant as she wanted to be. They both apologized again, Vanessa retrieving a pen and paper from her purse.

Where's Chris? she wrote.

Haven't seen him yet, Reina wrote back.

Have your friends arrived?

Two sections to the left, 5th row back. Silver and navy suit.

Vanessa followed Reina's directions, counting two sections over and five rows back until spotting a woman sitting beside a tall gentleman. From her vantage point Vanessa could not see their faces, but it was clear from the way his arm draped about her shoulders, the way she leaned into him, that Bryce and Phyllis Williams were tight and seriously in love. Vanessa smiled and turned away, feeling as if she were intruding on something precious and sacred.

She was about to scribble another message to Reina when the rear doors opened and the church's youth group appeared in the vestibule, beautifully arrayed in white robes, their hands clasped before them as if in prayer. Solemnly, reverently, they marched down the center aisle to the tune of Mahalia Jackson singing "Troubles of This World." Like divine beings, they lined up across the front of the church, heads bowed, palms toward heaven.

Then it happened. Kirk Franklin's recorded voice floated across the sound system, warning of a revolution. The youths discarded their heavenly robes, displaying jeans and customized T-shirts beneath. Turquoise letters emblazoned boldly across white backgrounds spelled out their motto, their message: *Kidz 4 Christ.* They hipped and hopped and thrilled the standing-room-only crowd, bringing the audience to their feet in the three-hundred-seat auditorium. Even Mother Bluehair was up, clapping arthritic hands and hollering, "Praise Him, children. Get jiggy with it!"

Kidz 4 Christ had to wait several minutes for the cheering to subside once their praise performance was complete. One by one they came forward, each child delivering his or her part of a soliloquy extolling the virtues of perseverance, citing the Bible and history and how the slaves made it over, were made stronger because of hardships and struggle. Vanessa was particularly moved by the quiet assurance of one young lady. Vanessa remembered seeing her at one of the youth ministry basketball games. She played on the team. Weeping might endure for a night, she said, but joy comes in the morning to those who refused to let go of God's unchanging hand. It was time to rejoice, to embrace the revolution, to change, for the night was over and the morning had come.

Brother Kirk's music started up again, and Kidz 4 Christ bounced out of the sanctuary, leaving a roaring, cheering audience in its wake. Vanessa smiled at the young lady who played on the basketball team as she passed. Something about her reminded Vanessa of her little cousin, Celine. A little something fluttered in the pit of her stomach. Vanessa missed her family. Maybe she could take a vacation before the summer was over to visit them again. She still had yet to meet her grandfather and her eldest aunt. Better yet, maybe she should invite Gramms and Celine and any other relative who wished to come visit her out to California. Now, that was an idea worth exploring.

Pastor McCullen stood at the podium on the raised dais, splendidly decked in an Afrocentric-patterned robe, a gold cross suspended from a gold-link chain about his neck. He was beaming, proud of the young people, asking the congregation to stand and thank the children and the youth leaders who worked so diligently in their labor of love.

Vanessa, with the rest of the church body, turned toward the rear doors. There stood Chris with his partners in the ministry, grinning that lopsided grin of his and waving at the crowd. Something flickered in her heart as Vanessa watched him. What a man, what a mighty good scrum-deli-icious man.

When Vanessa arrived home from the airport earlier that morning a small package lay on her doorstep. Delivered via courier service, the package was from her office and contained documents for Vanessa's immediate review. To Vanessa's surprise, atop the box stood a vase filled with colorful, exotic wildflowers. Her assistant must have cared for them in Vanessa's absence. The bouquet was still beautifully fresh. The attached card was so simply poignant that Vanessa had to wipe a tear from her tired eyes.

Because I care,
Chris

And though it frightened her to admit it, Vanessa cared, too. She cared for Chris McCullen with a sudden, inexplicable rush of tenderness that frightened her more than a little.

Pastor McCullen delivered a Word with power and simplicity, anointing and truth. "Hold on saints, your morning has come. God is not slack concerning His promises, nor is He a man that He should ever lie to you. What He has said He will do. Just hold on. Be strong. Lift up your eyes and behold the salvation of the Lord. Lift up your heads, o ye gates, and the King of Glory shall come in. He shall strengthen your hearts. Hold on, children, your morning is come!"

There was weeping, shouting, thanksgiving, thoughtful pondering and praising in the house. Hearts were encouraged. Feeble knees and hung-down heads were lifted and strengthened. Bruises were healed. A sense of delayed blessings was eradicated and labor-weary warriors knew sweet relief. The service had come to an end, but before they adjourned Pastor McCullen had a special request.

"This young lady is like a daughter to me. She has a special gift from God. And I know this is on the spot but, baby, come sing a song for your Papa McCullen, please. Saints, help me welcome Sister Reina Kingsley."

It took a moment for Reina to fully comprehend the pastor's request. He wanted her to sing? She turned and saw Vanessa's encouraging smile, heard her clapping along with other congregants. He wanted her to sing!

Hail Mary, mother full of grace. Reina felt a momentary panic. She was brought up Catholic. She didn't know many hymns, many songs appropriate for this setting. This was a black church, a church filled with superb vocalists and musicians. She could not come off like some yokel from the sticks singing some onward-Christian-soldier-marching-off-to-war-sounding something. She had to come correct or not at all.

In a flash, her heart grew still. Peaceful. She remembered that God could not be contained in handmade vessels, but preferred to live and reign within the beating hearts of men. How could she deny offering up the gift He had given? Reina's gift was not for herself alone. She was graced by God for a reason. Part of that reason was to share with others, to create music that brought others closer to truth and peace and promise. This was not a diva moment. It was all about humility. Such as she had, so would she give.

Reina took a deep breath, received a quick, reassuring hand squeeze from Vanessa, then stood and walked to the front of the church, not knowing what she would sing, knowing only that she could and she would. Reina accepted the microphone Pastor McCullen handed her as she mounted the stairs to the stage. She felt his loving embrace, heard his "Sing good, baby," looked at the pianist who sat awaiting a cue, closed her eyes, opened her mouth, and felt the opening words of R. Kelly's "I Believe I Can Fly" waft up from her belly and out over her lips. The message was apropos. Right on time. Just what Reina needed to hear and to say.

When she finished there was not a dry eye in the house, including her own. Reina replaced the microphone in its stand, hearing the cries, the reverberating applause so like that in her dream. She stood at the edge of the stage, her own hands lifted high, her own heart flooded with fresh light. When, finally, she returned to her seat, Vanessa and Chris were both there waiting to enfold her in their arms. Reina cried for the wasted years, the days she had sealed her mouth, her voice shut off from herself, the world. She cried her joy that her morning had come, that her heart was indeed uplifted. She cried at the thanks and appreciation flowing about her. But most of all she cried because she had been cleansed; she had been touched by a loving God who knew her best.

Reina eventually sat, moved, humbled by the outpouring of love. She bowed her head and closed her eyes to give her creator thanks, and in so doing she missed the one man who sat motionless at the rear of the church. Where others stood and voiced their praise, he sat, his tears the only expressive articulation available to his exhilarated soul.

Jamal Williams followed the crowd to the hospitality hall at the rear of the church. The expansive room had been transformed into something grand. Linen tablecloths on round tables decked with spotless flatware, crystal glasses, china, and centerpieces made of flowers and candles. Mouthwatering scents of the catered affair permeated the air, teasing tummies and tempting taste buds. But Jamal knew an enticement of a different kind.

From a distance, he watched her move about the room, effortlessly engaging others in conversation, humbly receiving praise for her performance. Reina Kingsley had undergone a marvelous transformation. He had encouraged, prayed, waited for this to occur. And finally she had come into her own. Jamal was hooked. Sprung. Nose wide open. It wasn't about the obviously new attitude, the new adornment of herself, the revamped physique. He was a black man. He knew how to appreciate a woman of substance. Jamal Williams grew up surrounded and loved by female relatives of all shapes and sizes. He could appreciate the fact that love came in packages larger than size-seven jeans and a six shoe. His mother wore a size-sixteen dress and his father had no problem with the plumpness of his queen. In fact, it seemed that all the Williams boys were prone to prefer sisters with a little tender meat on their bones. Surely Reina's weight loss was not the determining factor for his affection.

It was more than the hair, the clothes, the makeup, or the reconfiguration of flesh on her fine frame. It was something internal that could not be touched by mere mortal hands. It was something precious and spirit-deep that could not be bought with common currency. Her soul had been reborn.

Jamal did not believe in love at first sight. However, he did believe that connections could be made, seeds sown, and blossoms grown in a mere instant when the right person with a right spirit was involved. That was what had happened to and for him where Reina was concerned.

He remembered the night they met. It was at his brother's home. Jamal recalled his sister-in-law prepping him on the car phone as they drove from the airport as if he were about to perform surgery, not come to dinner.

"Jamal, Reina is my dear friend. I don't think she's dated in a while. If you hurt her feelings I will lay a hex on you so thick it'll take God ten years to get it off of you."

Jamal softly chuckled at the memory, making his way around tables, trying to get closer to the object of his affection.

He was just coming to visit Sacramento, to check out some real estate possibilities, to see if the city was all that. What did Phyllis think she was doing, playing matchmaker? His beloved sister-in-law was all up in his Kool-Aid without sugar or a spoon. Jamal was not trying to be bothered. But then he met Reina, and just the sultry sound of her voice, the carefree way she laughed, the unpretentious nature of her person, helped change his mind.

Where was Bryce? He and Phyllis were supposed to be there somewhere. Jamal needed to talk to his brother about the things going on inside of him. But until then, he would just have to flow.

He came up behind her, bent slightly at the waist, whispering in her ear, "Promise to sing to me always?"

Reina spun about. Sheer surprise was soon replaced by pure pleasure. She readily stepped into the circle of an embrace so good she wanted to remain there a lifetime.

He kissed her cheek.

She tenderly stroked the softness of his oh, so expertly groomed beard.

"Jamal . . . what are you doing here?"

The pleasure in her tone made his heart swell, but he had no time to answer.

"Jamal?" They both turned to find a woman standing behind them looking incredulous, yet happy. Reina smiled.

"Finally! Jamal, this is Vanessa." Reina took Vanessa's hand, pulling her forward. "Vanessa, meet Jamal."

He extended his hand.

"It's a pleasure to meet you," he said. He frowned slightly. "You remind me of someone."

"Well, I hope it's someone nice. And I'm sorry, but I'm not accepting a handshake," Vanessa teased, pushing aside his hand and reaching out to hug him. "Not after all the wonderful things I've heard about you."

Jamal returned her embrace, grinning at Reina, glad to know he'd been talked about.

"So this is the infamous Vanessa."

"Now why I gotta be infamous?" Vanessa sulked playfully.

"Because you are," Chris answered, walking up to the trio, linking arms with Vanessa while leaning forward to kiss Reina on the cheek. "My girl burned down the house with those golden pipes!"

"That she did," Jamal agreed. "Jamal Williams," he said, extending a hand.

"Hey, it's good to meet you, brother. Chris McCullen."

"Pleasure."

"Let's find a table before they're all taken," Vanessa suggested.

"Good idea," Reina agreed. She lowered her voice as they walked, the men behind them, so that her words were for Vanessa's ears only. "My dogs are barking. I need to soak off these shoes."

Vanessa chuckled.

"That's what you get for trying to be cute, with your cute self. Girl, forget the dogs. What's up with you keeping secrets? You didn't say anything about Jamal being in town."

"I found out a minute before you did," Reina whispered.

"Hmmm."

"And what does that mean?"

"Just hmmm," Vanessa repeated, claiming an empty table for their party. "So, Jamal, how long will we be graced with your presence?" Vanessa asked once they were all seated. Reina pinched Vanessa's thigh.

Vanessa swallowed a yelp of pain, gritting her teeth and looking at Reina with wide, innocent eyes.

Reina narrowed her eyes and cocked her brows, wordlessly warning Vanessa not to go there. She wanted to talk to Jamal in private before his agenda was made public.

Chris sat back, amused, watching the interaction between the two of them, knowing Jamal was in for the interrogation of a lifetime. He felt for the man.

Jamal started to reply, but was somewhat distracted.

"Excuse me," he said, standing and waving to a handsome couple across the hall. They hurried over. Jamal met them halfway.

Jamal planted a warm kiss on the woman's cinnamon-brown cheek before exchanging a bear hug with the man beside her.

"You are too much! I thought you weren't arriving until tomorrow," Phyllis Williams told her brother-in-law.

"I couldn't wait that long to see you," Jamal teased as they returned to the table.

"Wait a minute," Reina interjected. "Phyllis, you knew Jamal was coming to town and you didn't tell me?"

"I threatened to name our firstborn after our father if she did," Bryce Williams offered, holding out the empty chair beside his brother as his wife sat.

"I love my father-in-law to life, but no child of mine is going to suffer with a name like Creflo Lucrestus Williams."

Laughter rang rich about the table as Jamal resumed his seat.

"Besides." He leaned over and practically whispered to Reina. "I wanted to surprise you."

"You succeeded," Reina breathed in return.

"I'm scared of all this," Vanessa intoned, pleasure on her face as she watched her best friend. "Seeing as how those two are caught up, I'll introduce myself. I'm Vanessa."

"Vanessa!" Phyllis reached across the table and grabbed her hand. "Girl, it's about time we finally got our stuff together and met one another."

Reina was right; Phyllis was good people. Vanessa liked the woman instantly.

"I know that's the truth. It's a pleasure," Vanessa returned, scrutinizing Phyllis's oval-shaped face with its high cheekbones and almond-shaped eyes. "You have lovely eyes," Vanessa remarked.

"You're only saying that because they're the same color as yours," Reina said.

"Then let me amend my statement. Your eyes are exquisitely gorgeous," Vanessa pronounced.

Phyllis laughed and accepted the compliment as further introductions were made.

"Real nice work you're doing there with the young folks," Bryce said, directing his comment to Chris.

"I appreciate that," Chris replied. "You know, your name is real familiar. Bryce Williams," Chris repeated, trying to jar a memory. "Are you in finance?"

Bryce nodded affirmatively.

"I think you helped a friend of mine with some investments," Chris said, referring to the owner of the Set, stating his name.

"I did!" Bryce confirmed, grinning. "Wow, small world, brother."

"Man, you hooked him up good. Give a brother your business card or something. I have a few pennies in my pocket that I want to multiply."

Vanessa laughed.

"Believe me, Bryce, a few pennies is about all he has."

"And you have jokes, gorgeous."

"Speaking of gorgeous, Reina, your voice is incredible!" Phyllis stated in awe.

"It is," Bryce concurred. "I didn't know you could sing like that. You've been holding out on us."

Reina laughed.

"My holding-out days are over. I'm back with a vengeance."

Jamal eased his arm across the back of Reina's chair. A deep smile warmed his face.

"Let's talk later," Bryce suggested. "I know a couple of folks in the recording business and I believe they'd be interested in hearing what you have to offer."

Reina nodded, surprised but pleased.

Just then a voice came across the P.A. system. One of the church deacons asked for everyone's attention. It was time to bless the food.

"You think low-fat chitterlings are on the menu, Phyl?" Reina teased when the blessing was complete.

"Girl, I was only kidding about that. I detest chitterlings," Phyllis stated, twisting her face into a grimace.

"Okay! Thank you," Vanessa agreed. "Innards belong in a garbage pail, not on a plate."

"Now, see, you're about to start some trouble up in here," Jamal cut in. "I'm from the South. Nothing wrong with a little pig intestine every now and then."

"With some hot sauce and corn bread on the side," Chris added, patting his flat stomach for emphasis.

"You know this," Jamal sang, as Chris pounded a fist atop his.

"Well, I'm from the East and not the South, and hog parts are not high on my dietary list," Phyllis said.

"Like folks in D.C. don't know what down-home eating is all about," Bryce remarked, laughing at his wife's adamant disdain.

"Are you from D.C.?" Vanessa asked, pleased at another commonality between herself and this woman she had just met.

"Yes, but I grew up here in California."

"Do you still have family in D.C.?" Vanessa questioned.

"I may have a sister there," Phyllis answered, a curious sadness creeping into her tone.

Before anything else could be said, a uniformed usher approached, informing the party that their table could now join the other diners lined up on either side of the buffet tables. Tantalizing aromas claimed the air. They moved forward with eager anticipation.

"If you find any unwanted swine parts on your plate, Pepe, you can pass them over to me," Bryce Williams told his wife. Phyllis laughed and made a reply that Vanessa did not hear. She stopped so suddenly that Chris ran into her from behind. He spoke, but his words fell away.

Pepe was all Vanessa heard.

A mere nickname that could not be traced.

Chris's private-investigating buddy was unable to locate the whereabouts of her lost sibling. He ran into the same complications Vanessa had: inaccurate hospital and birth records, the Smith family's lack of knowledge of the missing child's whereabouts, Vera Ann's relinquishing of her parental rights. The search was further complicated by the fact that Philip Taylor might have changed the child's name upon arriving in California to protect them from the possibility of being tracked by Vera Ann Smith. The P.I. tried locating the child under both surnames, Smith and Taylor. Nothing. Maybe the child had been adopted and the surname legally changed. He was sorry, but the only thing he had was the nickname Gramms had provided. A mere nickname lost somewhere in the great big world.

Pepe.

Vanessa's legs felt like lead. Her voice trembled when her ability to speak returned.

"Phyllis?"

The other woman turned. The look on Vanessa's face gave her pause.

They regarded one another.

Deeply, Vanessa gazed into the same topaz eyes that reflected a world she caught in her very own mirror day after day. She gasped. Vanessa saw her mouth, her nose, her high forehead and cheekbones. Similarities indeed. Was it enough? There was the East Coast connection. The pet name—a minute clue, but the only clue Vanessa seemed to possess. Were they in the midst of a manifested miracle? Or was God playing with her emotions?

How she suddenly longed to stretch a cinnamon-brown finger across the brief distance and stroke the perfectly oval face of the same hue. But Vanessa dreaded touching an apparition that might too soon disappear.

Phyllis Williams stared, drinking in the sight before her with concentrated effort. Slowly, eventually, Phyllis's eyes grew wide with an undeniable realization. Still skeptical, she shook her head as if to deny the very possibility.

"Do you have a middle name?" she managed to choke out while groping for her husband's hand. Bryce was there, holding fast.

Vanessa could only nod and swallow again and again. She simply could not suppress the overwhelming sense of excitement whisking through her.

"Is it Ann?" Phyllis asked.

Again Vanessa nodded.

Phyllis's eyes glistened with sudden tears.

"So is mine, after my birth mother," she slowly, purposefully stated. "Is your last name Smith?"

Vanessa closed her eyes and breathed deeply. Her voice came as if from miles away.

"No, it's Taylor."

"So was my biological father's," Phyllis replied unsteadily as she leaned into her husband for support and let the tears fall as they might.

Vanessa felt, more than saw, Reina and Chris on either side of her. She reached out and placed a hand on their shoulders in an effort to sustain herself and not collapse into her sister, who was once lost, but now found.

SISTERS

The summer sun had begun to fade. Throughout the day its blazing glory had stroked the earth with fiery fingers and tempestuous tongues, causing children to flock to neighborhood swimming pools or front-yard sprinklers in an attempt to escape the heat while keeping adults indoors in the false comfort created by overworked cooling systems. Now the bold warmth of the day was waning, temporarily resting. Bright light yet covered the expansive sky, but a scorching sizzle was no more.

Ahhh, relief. Soft as a whisper. Light as butterfly wings. Palpable. Sweet as the quickly melting frozen juice bars staining their mouths a subtle shade of wild-berry ice.

"Isn't it funny how you can clearly remember things in retrospect?"

Phyllis Ann Williams kicked a pebble across the concrete walkway. It skipped and rolled onto lush grass weaving a verdant quilt about the park. She smiled almost ruefully, wishing she could somehow turn back the hands of time, calmly conceding that the power of providence was not at her beck and call.

Vanessa merely smiled and nodded. That was all she seemed capable of doing lately, smiling. And why shouldn't she? Her flesh and blood had been restored.

"I was probably, oh, five or six," Phyllis estimated, "when I overheard my parents discussing me—us—one night."

"Us?" Vanessa asked, licking her fruit bar while watching her sister.

"You and me," Phyllis confirmed. "I was acting up as usual, trying to stay up later than my bedtime. I was probably about to pester my mother for a glass of water or something. Like I really needed pee-the-bed ammunition."

"Were you a mattress messer, Phyllis?" Vanessa laughed.

"Girl," Phyllis said, laying a gentle hand on her sister's arm, "my parents were so through with all my bed-wetting that they were about ready to hand me a blanket and pillow and make me sleep on the commode."

"Maybe we should call you PeePee instead of Pepe."

"Ha, ha. Very funny." Phyllis chuckled. "As I was saying, Babysis, I got out of bed one night and headed toward my parents' bedroom. When I neared their open door I heard them discussing how they wished they could find the missing child, that having another little girl would be wonderful, and that it was such a shame that we were . . . torn apart." Her voice caught in her throat. It was hard for her to continue. "That stuck with me over the years, but I guess it wasn't until I was grown that the impact truly hit me and I realized I had a sister somewhere . . ."

Phyllis had to stop. She felt, as she had since discovering Vanessa, highly sensitive and overly emotional.

Vanessa understood completely. Her world was dramatically changed. First there were Gramms, Celine, and the rest of her extended family. Now Phyllis. Her very own big sister. Together they created the only living proof that their parents had once lived and loved enough to reproduce treasures after their own kind.

Vanessa placed a gentle, reassuring hand on her sister's shoulder.

"Girl, you know I know. I feel you."

"I know you do," Phyllis assured her. She took a deep breath, finished the last of her juice bar, and looked for a garbage can in which to discard its wrapper. Sufficiently recovered, Phyllis continued. "Again, I didn't know my parents were referring to me, to you. I didn't even know I was adopted then."

"When did you find out?" Vanessa asked as she deposited her own empty wrapper into the mouth of the trash bin that Phyllis held open for her.

"Right before Bryce and I married."

"No-o-o," Vanessa intoned.

"Yep." Phyllis nodded. "Of course we had to take blood tests in order to obtain a marriage license. My mother freaked out. She probably thought I'd somehow discover my blood type was different from hers and Daddy's, and decided it was time I knew."

"Get out the way!" a childish voice hollered.

Vanessa looked up too late. Three little boys were bearing down on them, rollerblading like bats granted a one-day pass out of Hades. Vanessa tried to hop aside but she did not move fast enough. One little urchin rolled right over her big toe.

"Ouch!" Vanessa yelped. The little trio laughed, Toe Smasher turning about to pop his thumbs in his ears and waggle his fingers at Vanessa.

"Na, na, na, na, na-a-a-a," he sang.

"I got your na-na," Vanessa muttered, lifting her left leg to examine her injured toe.

"Child needs some home training," Phyllis commented, shaking her head in disgust. Taunting complete, Toe Smasher pivoted as if to turn back in the direction his comrades traveled. He overrotated, and before anyone could react he was kissing concrete, red faced, trying hard not to cry.

"Humph! God don't like ugly," Phyllis murmured.

"And the devil doesn't play fair," Vanessa added.

They laughed discreetly, watching Toe Smasher scramble up onto his Rollerblades and hobble off after his companions.

"Are you okay, Babysis?" Phyllis asked, pushing her sunglasses up onto her head as she bent over to examine Vanessa's sandaled foot.

Babysis was Phyllis's very own term of affection for her. Vanessa never imagined that at thirty years of age she would derive such gratification from simple endearments. Neither had she anticipated someone with whom she could share such delights. Life could be so incredibly good.

Vanessa applied weight to her foot. Nothing snapped; nothing creaked. She would live.

"Yes. Thank goodness he didn't hit the toe with the toe ring on it. I'd have to take him to small-claims court for breaking it."

"Your toe?"

"*Psssh!* My ring. I paid good money for this sterling silver." Vanessa giggled. "Two-fifty-nine including tax."

"Girl, please. I'll give you five-eighteen and you can buy two more rings if that means you won't go getting up on some televised court-room drama embarrassing me," Phyllis stated, readjusting her sunglasses.

"Uhh, Yo' Honor, see, it's the principality of the matter," Vanessa caricatured in her best ghettoese, adding a little wag of the neck and waving of the hands for good measure. "Kids these days need to know you don't be rolling up on nobody, cracking they toes and breaking they jewelry. Aiight?"

"I'm sorry, Miss Taylor, but the maximum this court can award is two-fifty." Phyllis clapped her hands. "Case dismissed. Now get ta steppin' cuz you're wasting my time. Next!"

They were bowled over, laughing so hard several bypassers caught their contagious mirth and journeyed on, smiling, not exactly sure why.

The park was crowded. Joggers. Bicyclists. Mothers pushing strollers. Fathers tossing balls to squealing children. Lovers walking hand in hand. The hot and thirsty stood impatiently in line at a concession stand waiting to hand over their cash and currency in exchange for something cool and refreshing.

The nearby amusement center was abuzz with the lively sounds of children racing from one ride to another, seeking to outdo the already declining thrill of whatever carnival-like attraction they'd just experienced. A miniature roller coaster, a chugging train, an old carousel, and giant-sized teacups and other conveyors of pleasure stood waiting and ready to deliver as much pleasure as parents could afford to buy.

"Want to take a spin on the roller coaster?"

Phyllis looked at her baby sister as if Vanessa suffered from heat-stroke.

"I don't do amusement parks," Phyllis informed.

"They're just kiddie rides, Pepe," Vanessa said.

"Your point is?" Phyllis snickered.

"You need a thrill."

"That right there is thrill enough for me."

Phyllis pointed to a huge, nearly vacant swing set located beyond the amusement center.

"You're serious?"

"Race you there." Phyllis dropped into a sprinting position. "On your mark, get set—"

Phyllis sprang forward without the "go."

"Hey!" Vanessa protested as her sister ran across the park. She set out after her, catching up and eventually passing Phyllis with ease. Vanessa reached the swing set first, jumping up and down in the surrounding sandlot, doing a little dance of joy. "Okay! And you have on sneakers while I'm wearing sandals. Who's the woman? Huh? Come on, say it with me."

"You are." Phyllis gasped, trying to catch her breath. "But you had the advantage. You run regularly. I'm a walker."

"Well, walk right on over here and push me, Granny," Vanessa sang, plopping down onto the seat of a vacant swing. "You can do better than that," she teased as Phyllis's first push barely put the swing in motion.

"You try pushing a bunch of booty hanging out of some little denim Daisy Dukes and see how good you do," Phyllis retorted.

"These are not Daisy Dukes. And besides, like sister like sister, sweetheart. Rapper wrote a song about us—like to hear it? Here it goes: 'Baby got crack,'" Vanessa sang, her pitch and her voice leaving much to be desired.

Phyllis laughed.

"I don't believe those words are correct."

"How would you know, church lady?"

"I keep my ear to the ground, girl."

Vanessa smiled.

"Stop, already," she huffed, hopping off the barely moving swing. "You're pitiful, Pepe. Let me push you."

Phyllis sat down, readjusting the soft fabric of her white nylon shorts before gripping the thick metal chains holding the swing in place.

"And don't push me too high," she warned.

"I wouldn't dream of it," Vanessa sweetly replied, pulling on the swing and stepping back to anchor her feet solidly in the sand. She suddenly ran forward, propelling Phyllis and the swing high in the air.

Phyllis squealed. Vanessa cracked up, tormenting and taunting her sister as she pushed Phyllis higher and higher.

"Okay, already, big baby," Vanessa teased as she grabbed the swing and helped stop its forward momentum. Vanessa wrapped an arm about her sister's waist and helped her to her feet. Phyllis wobbled, then steadied. Suddenly she turned on Vanessa, putting her in a chokehold. Vanessa screamed as Phyllis dug the fingers of her free hand into her sides, tickling her.

"Cry for mercy!"

Vanessa was breathless.

"Come on, cry for mercy, you little brat," Phyllis commanded.

"M-m-mercy," Vanessa croaked.

Phyllis relinquished her hold and walked away, squaring her shoulders and switching her hips as if she had just proved who was in charge.

"Better be glad I'm scared of your big black husband or else I would have pulled some Tae Bo on you and laid you out flat," Vanessa called out. Glancing back, Phyllis merely rolled her eyes and stuck out her tongue.

Moments later, Vanessa plopped down beside her sister on the park bench where Phyllis relaxed. Stretching her legs and tossing back her head, Vanessa inhaled deeply and gazed up at the evening sky fabulously adorned with shimmering ribbons in orange and rose, lavender and silver-blue. Summer seduction at its best.

"Look, Babysis."

"Hmmm."

"Look at us," Phyllis repeated.

Vanessa inclined her head. Phyllis's shorts-clad legs were stretched next to hers, touching hers just slightly. Same lovely shade of cinnamon brown. Same shapely calves and thick thighs. Vanessa extended her right hand as Phyllis extended her left. Same long fingers, same narrow wrists. They looked at one another and grinned.

"Our parents had some good genes, didn't they?" Vanessa softly stated.

"Mmm-hmmm," Phyllis agreed. "Vanessa? What's your theory on why Vera Ann gave both of us her middle name?"

Vanessa pursed her lips and looked off into space. At last she shrugged.

"Our conceited mother thought she was all that and wanted to make sure we were too?"

Phyllis giggled.

"That's silly."

"You come up with a better theory, then."

"I don't have one," Phyllis admitted. "Well, maybe she was lacking in imagination."

"Ha! Not our mother. Not the woman who sashayed her pregnant self on a bus and traveled across country to find her man."

"True, that." Phyllis sighed, feeling languid. "Whatever her reason, I'm glad she did. It's just one more thing that binds us together."

Vanessa instinctively knew that Phyllis referred to more than a shared name, more than mere phenotypic similarities. They were knit from the same indelible fabric. Thirty years of separation had come to a glorious end.

They still marveled at how instantaneous their bond had been, how they had somehow reached across the great divide of time and distance to recoup a sisterhood that was without severance. Thirty years of separation had failed to unravel the tie. A new day of discovery, rekindling and reknitting of each other's identity had begun.

Vanessa chuckled.

Phyllis smiled at her younger sibling.

"What's funny?"

"Hortense."

Phyllis shuddered.

"Ughh, don't remind me, please. I'm so glad our father decided to change my name when we arrived in California. Hortense Ann Taylor. That is so ugly!"

"Better you than me." Vanessa laughed. "You think he did it in an effort to further conceal your whereabouts?"

"Honey, I don't even care about the rationale. I'm just glad the man had sense enough to deliver me. God bless you, Father," Phyllis told the sky.

"Reina swears she needs glasses," Vanessa stated after a moment's silence.

Phyllis shook her head, smiling wanly while stating, "Poor thing. That must have been strange for her, realizing that she knew both of us without knowing we were related."

Vanessa nodded in agreement.

"She says she should have seen the resemblance between us, but let's be real. She did not know I had a sister. I didn't know I had a sister."

Phyllis's expression became thoughtful, serious.

"Vanessa, just think. If Bryce had gone to law school instead of majoring in finance, or if his initial entrepreneurial endeavor in financial consulting had been successful, then we might never have moved to San Francisco so he could take a job with his current employer. And if that had not occurred, then there would have been no promotion leading us to Sacramento." Phyllis propped her feet on the edge of the bench, hugging her knees to her breasts. "I never would have gone to work for the state and met Reina, and that might have spoiled or delayed my chance at meeting you."

Vanessa felt a chill roll across her bones.

Now that Phyllis was in her life, it was hard for Vanessa to imagine existing without her. Since their fateful encounter at the Juneteenth dinner in honor of those for whom the dream of freedom had been realized without their knowing it, Vanessa and her sister had dedicated themselves to an exploratory journey of their own. They found freedom from hopelessness. Vanessa knew a sweet deliverance from feeling abandoned, discarded, and cast off like some peculiar refuse. She felt restored.

Often throughout the course of her days since finding her sister, Vanessa would think back, remembering the times Reina had invited her to go out to lunch or dinner or shopping with her and Phyllis, only for Vanessa to decline each invitation for one reason or another. Though it was hard not to berate herself for her unwittingly delaying their fortuitous reunion, Vanessa—taking a clue from her sister—resolved that fortune and providence rested in the hands of the Supreme One who was greater than them both. As Papa McCullen had sagely counseled them, to everything there was a season, and the season of their encounter had been divinely timed and orchestrated by an omniscient being. Their lives were in His hands.

Each day held new discoveries. Bryce had shown himself to be incredibly supportive and understanding, sharing his wife with her sister, affording them the invaluable time they needed to be together, learning and laughing, crying and healing. They both were cognizant of not shutting out those whom they loved, making every effort to stay connected with their circle of friends and family while allowing those connections to help reinforce their own new and intimate journey.

While so very amazingly compatible in nature, Phyllis and Vanessa acknowledged their individual distinctions, already discovering they would not always see eye-to-eye on every issue. At times their opinions differed. They had divergent tastes, likes and dislikes. Early on, Phyllis and Vanessa knew they could not make assumptions about each other. Communication proved an utmost necessity and mutual respect was invaluable. They could and would tread their wonderfully reconnected paths as long as they walked in sync and with the understanding that something so new, so overwhelming and awesome, was bound to indeed be challenging at times.

"Wow! God is so great," Vanessa commented.

"God is good," Phyllis replied.

"Let us thank Him for our food," they simultaneously concluded.

"Amen," Vanessa piously intoned.

Their laughter was like a fresh fragrance on a summer's breeze.

"I love your parents, Pepe."

"They are wonderful, aren't they?" Phyllis concurred. She paused, growing thoughtful. "Babysis, does it bother you to hear me talk about my childhood with them . . . considering your own?"

Vanessa sat quietly. When finally she spoke, her voice was coated with a serenity she never would have imagined possible.

"No." She played with the frayed ends of her cutoff denim shorts. "Actually, I derive some vicarious sense of satisfaction knowing you grew up in a loving environment. Of course, I would have preferred to have had the same experience, but . . . you know . . . at least . . ." Vanessa's voice trailed off. She shrugged her shoulders, looking helplessly at her sister. Phyllis touched her hand. She understood what words could not convey. "Pepe, do you remember our parents?"

Phyllis shook her head sadly.

"Not much. I think I have glimpses of a tall, dark man singing to me while holding me in his arms. But other than that, I can't say I recall very much. . . . Well, there is one thing that comes to me in a recurring dream that I have every now and then."

"What?" Vanessa asked, a hopeful expression on her face.

Phyllis shook her head slowly and paused to gather her thoughts.

"I don't know." She hesitated. "Sometimes I have this dream where everything is dark and wet. I can't see anyone, but I hear this woman screaming that nothing can take her flesh and blood from her except fire."

"And that's somehow related to our parents?"

Phyllis nodded.

"At least to our mother . . . I think." Silence grew between them until Phyllis, with a sudden smile on her face, said, "I do, however, re-member having this sweet-smelling little doll dressed in pink and wrapped in a blanket decorated with teddy bears."

"Really?"

"I think that doll was you, Babysis."

"For real? That is so sweet," Vanessa cooed, leaning her head on her sister's shoulder.

"Don't tease me. I'm serious."

"I didn't say you weren't," Vanessa responded, patting her sister on the cheek while still reclined against her shoulder. "I am sweet and I certainly smell good, but I'm no one's doll."

"You've got that right. Now get your big head off of me," Phyllis commanded.

Vanessa laughed, hopping to her feet, stretching her arms wide, and sighing pleasurably.

"Let's get you home before Bryce comes after me with a pitchfork accusing me of keeping his woman hostage."

"Oh, now, he wouldn't do—" Phyllis clutched Vanessa's arm.

"Phyllis?" Vanessa gripped her sister, who stood beside her, swaying slightly on her feet. "Phyllis?"

"I'm . . . okay," Phyllis breathed. "I-I must have stood too quickly and thrown off my equilibrium or something."

"Maybe your stomach is upset from being on that swing," Vanessa offered.

Phyllis inhaled deeply, slowly exhaling through lips pursed in the shape of an *O*.

"Or maybe it's because my period is late. Ooh, it's getting too dark for these," Phyllis observed, pushing her sunglasses up onto her head and fluffing her thick ponytail as she started walking back in the di-rection of the parking lot, where Vanessa's Solara was parked. "Let's go get some frozen yogurt or a slush or—"

"Uh-uh, hold the phone, sisterwoman!" Vanessa charged, coming up alongside her elder sibling. "Are you pregnant?"

"Perhaps."

"What do you mean, perhaps?" Vanessa asked. "How late is your pe-riod?"

"It's been late before."

"Phyllis!"

"Vanessa!"

"Stop playing with me."

Phyllis laughed.

"A few weeks. Okay, okay," Phyllis surrendered when Vanessa stationed herself in her path and refused to move. "Four weeks, five days, ten hours, forty minutes, and"—Phyllis consulted her watch—"sixteen seconds."

"Don't make me leave you in this park by yourself," Vanessa threatened, knowing she had no intention of doing any such thing. Phyllis just laughed and they walked on.

She was suddenly solemn.

"I'm afraid to take a pregnancy test, Vanessa. Bryce and I have tried to get pregnant for years without success. I guess the idea of conception occurring now right after our being reunited seems too good to be true."

Vanessa nodded.

"Pepe, have you had any telltale signs? Morning sickness? Increased appetite? Anything at all?"

Phyllis glanced down at the Sacramento Monarchs T-shirt she wore. Where it had once been oversize and flowing, the fabric fit across her breasts just a tad bit snugly, the purple-and-black emblazoned butterfly stretching wide its graceful wings.

"Oh, your breastesses getting bigger, huh?" Vanessa remarked. "That's why my brother-in-law's walking around grinning like a forgotten fool."

"Just hurry up and unlock the car door already." Phyllis laughed. "I need to get to a bathroom."

"When do you plan on taking a test?" Vanessa inquired.

"I already did."

"And?"

Phyllis's smile relaxed a bit.

"It came back negative."

Vanessa was undaunted.

"How long ago?"

"Several weeks."

"Well, take another one, Pepe," Vanessa urged.

"Mmm-hmmm," Phyllis responded. "I will."

"When?"

"Soon."

Vanessa unlocked her car door, got inside, and started the engine, never bothering to unlock Phyllis's door for her. She put the car in re-verse.

"Vanessa!"

She put on the brakes and let down the electric window on the passenger's side just slightly.

"Oh, hey, girl. I'm sorry. When are you retaking that test again?"

"Okay, already, brat! I'll call my gynecologist tomorrow. Now open this doggone door."

They exited the parking lot, merging onto a road that led out of the park, past the city zoo, to curve and twist about soft, undulating hills capped with lavish homes designed by imaginative architects before cookie-cutter tract houses were all the rave. Windows down, classical music from a local radio station sounding through the stereo speakers, a perfect summer breeze caressing their faces, the Taylor sisters rode in comfortable silence, observing the scenery that floated before their vision.

"Phyllis?"

"Hmmm?"

"It seems as if God works with you through dreams," Vanessa matter-of-factly stated, never once looking away from the roadway.

"Hmmm, I think you're right," Phyllis concurred. "I told you about the one I had two nights before me met?"

Vanessa nodded affirmatively.

"It was so vivid, Vanessa. I stood there in that dream looking at myself in a mirror, only to have the mirror image come to life and step into the room with me." Phyllis smiled deeply despite the fresh tears in her eyes. "She took my hand and told me that she would find me soon." With a quick flick of her hand, Phyllis brushed away the fallen tears.

"And I did, didn't I?" Vanessa needlessly confirmed and sighed her supreme contentment. "Pepe, I'll go to your doctor's appointment with you if you want," Vanessa suddenly offered.

"You're so special," Phyllis replied. "My OB will just examine me or send me to the lab for bloodwork or to tinkle in a cup. I think I'll manage just fine."

"Well, if you need me for moral support I'm as good as there."

"Thanks."

"Wow, just think," Vanessa said, reaching over to rub her sister's flat stomach. "I could be an aunt soon. You know I'm going to spoil this baby rotten. We'll have cookies for breakfast and—"

"Yeah right!" Phyllis interjected. "More like granola bars and chocolate popcorn cakes. You don't even eat cookies."

"I can adjust. Phyllis?"

Phyllis turned to look at her sister.

"Everything's going to be all right. Like you told me some days back, we serve an awesome God."

Phyllis smiled and nodded, leaning her head back against her headrest.

"True, that. Babysis?"

"Hmmm?"

"Can you get the crawl out of your creep and put a little pep in your step? I have to pee."

Vanessa removed her foot from the accelerator, allowing the car to slow to a mere roll.

"Vanessa!"

Vanessa Taylor laughed uproariously as she propelled the car forward, the light of the moon just beginning to spread the faintest of smiles at their backs as the two sisters moved forward into the future.

LOVERS

The Downtown Plaza, normally sedate so late at night, was alive with exuberant concertgoers. It was Friday. The plaza often proved a drawing magnet to those interested in getting a jump-start on the weekend. Even so, most businesses closed shop by ten o'clock. But tonight was special. A sold-out crowd at the Convention Center Auditorium had just dispersed. Certainly this crowd, exhilarated by the music they had enjoyed, would linger about the plaza in search of some tasty morsel, some liquid with which to refresh themselves. Gourmet coffee shops, restaurants, and even an ice-cream parlor were still open for business. All along the plaza, merchants welcomed patrons into their establishments with bright smiles and dollar signs in their eyes.

"Did you enjoy the concert?"

They walked arm in arm, their pace leisurely and relaxed.

Reina looked up at Jamal, night stars dancing in her eyes.

She was radiant.

"Oh, my goodness!" Reina exhaled. "I have just about every one of Gerald Albright's and Will Downing's releases, but I've never seen either one in concert, not to mention the two together! They were so off the hook that I wanted to take my shoe off and throw it at them on more than one occasion."

"I take that to mean you liked it." Jamal grinned.

"Understatement, darling. I absolutely loved it!"

"Are you sure about that?"

"What? The concert?" Reina asked, looking at Jamal as if he were a brother from a another planet.

"No, the 'darling.'"

Reina blushed.

Jamal laughed.

"Don't choke, sweetheart; it's all good."

They walked on arm in arm, enveloped in the dark and lovely grip of a soft night.

"Would you like to stop for something to eat?" Jamal asked, finally breaking the gentle silence.

Back in the day a good—correction, fierce—concert would have had Reina chomping at the bit and the nearest buffet restaurant, stuffing her face and fueling her tank in her excitement. That was then. This was now. While she was inspired, moved by the electrifying performances of two artists whom she utterly enjoyed and respected, Reina was content, allowing herself to bask in the beauty of the music echoing its refrains in the cradle of her mind.

She was already full.

"I'm not hungry, but we can stop somewhere if you are."

"I am," Jamal replied, patting his tight belly. "I only had a snack before the concert. Just a sixteen-ounce T-bone steak, mashed potatoes, green beans and cauliflower, and a couple of biscuits." He grinned at the incredulous expression on Reina's face. "Just kidding. I only ate one biscuit."

Reina laughed, shaking her head.

"You are so silly."

"Only when it comes to you," Jamal replied, stroking her jaw with a strong mocha-brown finger.

By the time they reached the restaurant, Reina was legitimately hungry after all. Lunch had been her one and only meal that day. She was only inclined to crunch a handful of baby carrots before dressing for the surprise Jamal had planned for her that night. According to her Healthy Habits daily food diary, Reina still had nearly eleven hundred calories and over twenty fat grams to consume. Lord, was she ready to put them to good use!

"Have you decided on your orders?" their waitress asked, smiling, and holding her pen ready for rapid-fire writing.

"I'll have the chicken Caesar salad with the dressing on the side, please," Reina answered, dutifully relinquishing delicious fat-laden thoughts.

"Would you like anything else?"

Heck, yeah! Everything on the kiddie menu and the seasoned citizens' menu, too.

"No, thank you."

"Nothing to drink?"

A chocolate shake, an iced mocha, a latte, and the largest diet Dr. Pepper you can give me.

"Raspberry iced tea," Reina casually responded.

"Would you like for me to leave the dessert menu now or should I bring it back later?" the skinny, anemic-looking smiling waitress solicitously inquired.

"That won't be necessary." The peach tart on the dessert tray across the room was already screaming her name.

"And you, sir?" she asked, finally turning her charm on Jamal.

"How's the shrimp scampi?"

"One of our best-selling items."

"Hmmm," Jamal murmured, giving the menu a final perusal. "Fine, I'll have the shrimp scampi, the steak and lobster combo, the fettucine Alfredo, and the chicken cordon bleu. And hand me the dessert menu, please. I think I'll start off with a little chocolate mousse or strawberry torte."

Both Reina and the server were silent, gaping at Jamal.

"I'm sorry. Is there a problem?" he innocently asked. "Just thought I'd oblige the food-selling campaign you were engaged in a moment ago."

The waitress, understanding the meaning of his message, blushed hotly. She stammered and stuttered while trying to explain away her faux pas.

"Shrimp scampi over rice pilaf will be fine, thank you," Jamal concluded, as unaffectedly as he could.

The server fled the table to the comfort of the kitchen.

"I want to speak with the manager."

"Jamal, she was just doing her job."

"How? By insulting her customers?"

"I'm not insulted," Reina tried to reassure him.

"I am. I don't appreciate her selling tactics."

"Jamal, really—"

"Reina, do you not realize the implications of her methods? Is it a standard practice of this restaurant to badger their customers who aren't—"

"What? Fit to suit a fashion-model size?"

Jamal grew quiet.

Reina reached across the table to pat his hand.

"Come on, Mr. Williams, center. Center. Close your eyes and count backward from ten." Reina, eyes closed, sat, elbows bent at her sides, hands raised, thumbs and middle fingers touching lightly, copying a move she'd seen Vanessa make on more than one occasion. She hummed deeply. After a moment she opened one eye and peeked out at Jamal. He sat, one arm across his broad chest, his other hand stroking his mustached mouth, grinning despite himself. "Is it working?" Reina teased. "Are you calm?"

"Come and find out," he dared her, inclining his head to the side, inviting Reina to move closer.

"Meet me halfway," she challenged.

They both scooted toward the center of the U-shaped booth until they sat side by side.

"Jamal, are you bothered by my size?" Reina suddenly asked the question that had plagued her for some time. Common sense told her he obviously was not. But she needed to open this particular door of communication.

"Extremely," he replied, his tone seductively deep as he reached for her hand. Their fingers intertwined, their hands fitting together perfectly.

"What do you mean?"

"What do you think I mean, Reina? Do you think I'm some weak little man scared off by a few inches of extra beauty?"

Reina smiled. The man had a way with words.

"No, I don't. But it's just that you could have—"

"Baby."

She paused, looking intently at him.

"Please don't go to the 'you can have any woman you want' routine. I'm not after women, plural. I'm trying my best to serve God in a decent way. Besides, women aren't commodities to me. I don't just pick and choose and drop females in some shopping cart on my way out of some imaginary flesh market."

"Humph." Reina smiled. "Guess you told me, huh?" She laughed suddenly. "You sound like Bryce with all that commodity-and-market talk."

He winked.

"Big brother's taught me a thing or two."

"Such as?"

"Hang with me, sweetheart, and maybe you'll find out," Jamal whispered wickedly.

Reina smiled, then sobered.

The mention of Bryce stirred up thoughts of Phyllis and Vanessa, and the recent turn of events.

"I still find it so truly unbelievable that Phyllis and Vanessa are sisters." Reina shook her head in disbelief. "There I was, all the time knowing them both and never once making a connection. I really did not notice the resemblance between them, or even imagine the possibility."

"You didn't know Vanessa had a sibling, let alone a sister, until recently," Jamal offered.

"I know, but they could have been together long before now if I had only paid closer attention. Just think of all the times I tried to get Vanessa over to Phyllis's and vice versa."

"Are you personally responsible for everyone's happiness?"

Reina sat back against the soft vinyl cushion of their booth. She tilted her head and looked across the restaurant, focusing on nothing in particular. She quietly pondered Jamal's question, finally concluding that, no, Reina Kingsley was not God's personal assistant or ministering angel. She had limitations. She had needs and wants of her own yet to be fulfilled. Besides, hadn't she heard Papa McCullen say that God's timing was not our timing, His ways not our ways? What else had he said? To everything there was a season. Phyllis and Vanessa had met when it was their season to do so and not before.

"I'll take your silence to mean no."

Reina refocused her gaze on the kindness in Jamal's face. Softly, she smiled. He had a valid point, one that Reina had tried to reinforce in her mind time and again. Growing up with such a large and extended family and being one of the older cousins, Reina had long ago learned to caretake others. She and her sister had been responsible for helping her mother care for her younger brother. As her big sister grew older and found outside interests that did not include combing nappy heads and cooking for greedy kids, more and more of the burden fell on Reina's shoulders. Just when her brother was more than old enough to care for himself, their oldest sister divorced and was subsequently incarcerated for her illegal extracurricular activities, rolling the care of her two small daughters onto her parents and, of necessity, Reina.

Reina had never known autonomous freedom until now. She had, in a huff, stormed from her parents' house to Vanessa's, and from Vanessa's to *Abuela*'s. Now that her grandmother was in Puerto Rico, Reina was alone for the first time in her life. There she was living in that huge Victorian, as solitary and single as could be. And she loved it. Maybe she would consider purchasing *Abuela*'s house, as her grandmother had suggested.

Her grandmother had sworn her to secrecy. She was contemplating remaining in her native land. Puerto Rico was in her blood and her blood in Puerto Rico. Her grandmother was getting no younger. She wanted to spend the remnant of her days surrounded by the sights, sounds, and smells of her birthplace. She wanted to die and be buried in its arms when her soul flew away.

Reina knew the feeling of flight. She had felt it that afternoon while standing on the church stage singing her heart inside out. She had soared to greater heights and descended to deeper depths than ever before. She felt baptized as, quietly, she asked the Lord God, creator of all, to enter her life, the flame of her discontent extinguished in a pool of perfect peace and praise.

True to his word, Bryce Williams put Reina in touch with music-industry movers and shakers. Sure enough, they expressed an interest in hearing what she had to offer. So Reina let go of years of fear and dared to fly again. She practiced in the shower, in the car, any- and everywhere the mood struck her. She rekindled the gift, stirred it up, and set it free. Now there she was—having wowed a producer or two—working on her very own demo CD. The joy was indescribable, and Reina intended to hold on to joy as long as she could. Reina decided possessing joy required letting go of the weights of her past.

Her voice was a hushed, solemn whisper when she continued.

"No, I'm responsible for no one except me," Reina replied, thinking of how she had tried so hard to please her father, her mother, any- and everyone who placed a demand on her dejected shoulders. But that was then. Today was now. She could let go and live.

Jamal stroked her hand, an intent look on his face. It appeared as if he wanted to say something, but just then their server arrived, a tight smile on her still-red face, trying to serve them as quickly and efficiently as she could without incident.

"Would you like ground pepper on your salad, ma'am?" she hesitantly asked, quickly glancing at Jamal as if afraid to offend.

"Yes, I would."

Reina wanted to laugh. Poor thing was scared stiff.

"Sir?" she asked, turning to Jamal.

"No, thank you, Sherri," Jamal replied, glancing at the engraved name tag pinned to her stark white blouse. She urged them to please inform her if there was anything else they needed before scurrying quickly away.

They said grace and began eating.

"Mmm, this scampi is pretty good. Want a bite?"

Uh-oh. Sign number one, per the book of Vanessa, that a brother was sprung: he actually shared his food.

"No. Thank you."

"How about offering me a bite of that salad?"

Reina laughed.

"Like you don't know what a chicken Caesar salad tastes like."

"That's cold," Jamal replied, taking another bite of his own meal.

Reina wagged a finger at him.

"Listen, brother, you got it all wrong. I am on a restricted-calorie eating plan." Reina speared a tender chunk of chicken breast on her fork and waved it beneath Jamal's nose. "I'm not trying to share. I want each and every calorie due me."

Jamal grabbed her fork and popped the chicken into his mouth.

"Hey!"

"Word to the wise: don't play with a man when he wants something."

"Ooo, la la," Reina purred, bringing her face close to his. "Is that a threat?"

"No, a promise of things to come—"

It was Jamal's turn to protest as Reina took advantage of his distraction to reach into his plate and stab a shrimp with her fork. She nibbled it daintily, dabbing her softly painted lips with her linen napkin.

"Am I too much for you?" she teased.

Jamal, his mouth next to her ear, breathed a little distraction of his own.

"Actually, you're just what I prayed for."

"Jamal?"

"Hmmm?"

"Thank you for the concert. That was a very sweet surprise."

"My pleasure," he answered, smiling down at her. "I'm glad you enjoyed it."

Reina squeezed his arm lightly as they strolled down the well-lit river promenade directly across from the city's one and only ziggurat that served as a business office during the day, a majestically illumined pyramid-shaped edifice by night.

The sounds of loud alternative and pop music floated up from the riverfront eateries that were soon to close for the night. Old-fashioned paddle-wheel steamboats, dinner-cruise catamarans, and other water vessels banked the river's edge. The horse drawn carriages that usually clip-clopped down the cobblestone streets of Old Sacramento had retired for the evening. Only the sounds of moving vehicles and people walking and talking remained to clutter the night air with their sounds.

The farther south Jamal and Reina walked, the quieter it became. It was peaceful strolling along the multimillion-dollar river promenade with its old-style lampposts adorned by intricate sconces high above, and wide mission benches dispersed along the walkway. Singing crickets and bellowing bullfrogs orchestrated their journey.

"Sing a bit of that song for me," Jamal spontaneously requested.

Reina looked at him in question.

"You know. The one you just about fell out of your seat on when Brother Will started crooning it at the concert."

Reina laughed.

"I don't know what you're talking about."

"Come on now, sweetheart. I was certain someone would need to pass a bottle of smelling salts around that auditorium tonight with all you swooning women in the place."

"You're exaggerating."

"Ahhh. Oooo. Ohhh, Lawd, help me," Jamal mimicked in a squeaky falsetto, clutching his heart and playing as if he were about to faint.

Reina shook her head, smiling.

"You need to quit."

"Sing the song then, woman. The one about finding an angel."

"I wouldn't know anything about that, seeing as how that's never happened to me," Reina replied, a serious look of dismay on her face. Jamal stood speechless. Suddenly Reina laughed. "I'm only teasing, precious."

"That's cold," Jamal exclaimed, reaching for her. Reina scooted beyond his reach, laughing at the exaggerated expression of pain on his face as she walked on into the sweet, warm night, leaving Jamal in her wake.

He did not mind. He appreciated the view.

Reina was beautiful. Yes, she pulsed with life after losing a considerable amount of weight. Still, Jamal was astute enough to know Reina's transformation involved more than mere pounds that could be calculated on a scale. She had lost her tentative, closed-off, and afraid-of-self look. She had opened her life to the possibilities of promise, and the promise of possibilities. Abundant life was written all over the woman's being.

Jamal watched Reina as she walked, an added confidence, a certain grace in her motions further accentuated by the silk mudcloth dress she wore, the one her *Abuela* had given her years ago as a birthday present that she could never fit into until now. She was not flamboyant or overstated. Reina's was a gentle elegance, the kind that simply grew greater with time. He did not mean to be insensitive, but what was all the fuss about? Jamal Williams had a definite predilection for voluptuous, full-flavored sisters. He supported Reina's weight-management efforts because he cared about her. He wanted her to achieve the goals important to her. He wanted her to be healthy and to live long. He made certain he did not sabotage those goals or impose his wants, no matter that he considered Reina lovely as she was right then and there.

Statuesque.

Perfect description for this woman with whom he was admittedly falling in love.

Lord, give me strength, he silently prayed.

"Are you trying to make me run after you?" Jamal called out as she walked ahead. "Because I have no problem taking these overpriced shoes off and putting a little Mo Green on you."

Reina laughed and paused in her stride and waited for Jamal to catch up.

She watched his long, purposeful stride, his masculine physique and gentle manner. She thought back to the dinner party and the night they met. Reina felt a glimmer of attraction to the man, yet she suppressed it, doubtful that he reciprocated. She convinced herself that whatever interest she thought he conveyed was a mere figment of her imagination. Time and Jamal proved her wrong, and for that she was pleased.

Reina took a long and hard look at the specimen of God's handiwork closing the distance between them. Jamal did something for her. He was something good to her. His attributes ran a mile long. Not that he did not have imperfections and quirks. Lord knew they both did. But Jamal was good to and for her. He was 100 percent genuine. He listened, he cared, he was open to learning when and where he did not understand. A community-minded businessman, he actually wanted to contribute some of what he possessed back to his people, rather than just siphon off the good of others for his own greedy gain. He was . . . six feet, two inches. Hot whipped cocoa. Close fade and professionally groomed beard, goatee, and mustache. Smelling of Jordan and raw strength.

Reina reached for his hand as he neared. She intended to walk on, but Jamal's grip was firm, stopping her in her tracks.

"I want you to be the first to know that it's a done deal." Jamal grinned at Reina's puzzled expression. "In two weeks' time I close escrow on my house. Here in charming little Sacramento, Califor-NI-A."

"You're kidding!" Reina squealed.

Jamal shook his head.

"I'm bewitched, and I don't mean by the city."

Jamal stared deep into her eyes as if he could meld their hearts together and lead Reina to touch the deeper shades of his being. Looping a strong arm about her considerably smaller waist, Jamal pulled Reina close. With his free hand he tilted her chin up toward his lips. He leaned forward, pausing a breath away from her face. They stood suspended, as if posed for the sake of an artist attempting to capture their likeness for posterity's sake.

Reina held her breath. Her heart beat like a talking drum, telling the state of her affairs to this man as he eased beyond the threshold of her mouth to pause at her ear. Jamal's breath felt like precious wings against her neck. Reina was so lost in his luxury that it took a moment for the message to transmit and her brain to respond.

"I feel nothing but love for you, Reina Kingsley."

He lifted his head, met her gaze, and saw that she heard, that she understood he spoke the truth. It was enough for now, Jamal decided. Smiling, he took her hand and headed back in the direction from which they came.

Suddenly Reina stopped, dragging Jamal's steps to a halt as well.

"Hold the phone, sweetness. I heard you correctly, did I not?"

He nodded.

"You did."

Reina ran a hand through her short, stylish hair. She pulled at her ear. Then she smiled.

Reaching up, thanking God she had had the good sense to pop a stick of mint gum into her mouth mere moments before, Reina knew that inhibition was suddenly a nonissue. Clasping her arms about his neck, Reina eased Jamal's head forward until he was positioned for her convenience. Without hesitation, she stepped closer and stretched herself until she made sweet contact.

I'm feeling it, too, Jamal Williams was somewhere on her tongue, but the words never made it out of her mouth. Reina was just a bit lost in his luxury. His mouth was firm velvet against her lips. Reina felt as if she had unearthed some deeply buried longing, only to discover an ocean of desire. She sighed and broke the connection. *Mmm, Lord, help me to hold out!*

Her shaky exhalation was a very audible thing.

"I think I can sing to you now," Reina offered, suddenly needing to occupy her mind and her time with some harmless distraction.

Jamal shook his head.

"In a minute."

He resumed the connection she had broken, gently touching, probing, tasting her lips, her mouth until they both felt weak with a newfound, robust hunger.

They stood wrapped in a mutual embrace, sharing a consensual wonder. Finally Reina pulled away. She had to. She was not trying to prove freakilicious on the promenade. Besides, she had—they both had—made vows to the Lord to keep it holy, to keep it real.

She brought her head to rest against his jaw. Quietly she began to hum. Softly the words wafted from her mouth for his ears only. She fulfilled his earlier request, singing of finding an angel there in her arms, amused that someone had penned words to express their sentiments felt right then, right there. What was she to do about Jamal Williams? Nothing except hang on tight, enjoy the ride, and remind him—remind herself—at every possible opportunity, in so many wondrous ways, that he was her angel. And she was his.

FRIENDS

Things have not worked out as I hoped or imagined they would. Not like they have for Reina and Jamal, who, by the way, I am very glad for. Even if the brother is constantly walking around with a stupid, morning-after look on his—as Reina would say—*foine* face.

Some brothers have everything.

But I'm not hating. I'm celebrating. No matter that Vanessa and I are still in limbo.

We've made some progress but there could be more.

Okay, you can call me greedy, because I am when it comes to Vanessa. I'd sop her up with a biscuit then lick the plate clean if I could. But I can't, so I just wait and keep my shower water on cool.

It ain't easy trying to negotiate this new relationship and its complex dynamics. Here we are entering a zone we've never before encountered together. You have love and all its wonderful emotions and the sentiments that come with it that can keep you starry-eyed and silly for days. You learn to trust and open yourself and become vulnerable without shame. Then there's the physical desire that can make a brother feel as if he's been in a knock-down, drag-out fight in a dark alley with Tyson, Ali, Frazier, *and* Holyfield whipping up on him. And that's just the desire stage. I can't even speak on the actual indulgence, 'cause we haven't been there yet.

Oh, believe me, it's not that Vanessa and I aren't teased by

Temptation. I am. She is. We are. We have crossed the thinly designed, invisible boundary meant to keep carnal considerations at bay. Unfortunately, we stepped over into Never-Ever Land. Or, at least, that's the way I feel, like we'll never ever make the voyage out of limbo and into the final frontier, with our taking-it-slow-and-easy selves.

Who said patience is a virtue?

Oh, yeah, the Bible.

Well, then, I have to be one of the most virtuous brothers walking the face of the earth, involuntarily so. I warned you once before not to paint me any particular shade of saint. Especially not now that I've aroused from celibate slumber.

My timing is whacked! For an entire year I was fine, minding my own business, content with my job and focused on finding a house. No sex. No problem. Still no sex. Now, believe me, it's a problem. Abstinence ain't easy.

How do we deal with it? We try to remain open and communicative. Now, you know I'm an expressive brother. Or at least I have been until now. Now that this new tension exists between us, I am of the opinion that we just take care of business first and talk second. Don't front on me. We all know to which business I refer, Lord, forgive me.

Together we openly speak of the challenges that exist in this new relationship. Vanessa considers it important that we don't "create" uncomfortable situations for ourselves. Lately she and Reina have been visiting our church along with Vanessa's sister and her husband. My baby says she needs to reform and refresh her spiritual self while keeping her physical nature under control.

I have to say I admire her. Here she is, never having really been exposed to church and the rituals of churchisms, but ever since Juneteenth, since finding her sister and seeing the miraculous change Reina has undergone, Vanessa is finding herself drawn more and more to the Way. The woman has started attending Bible studies, as well as Sunday services. She keeps Pops's ears burning with the incessant questions of a hungry soul. She's finding her place, testing out the waters, and daring to launch out into a deep she has never before experienced. And here I am feeling convicted by her godly quest. Me, a preacher's son. I grew up in the church, but seeing Vanessa's blossoming thirst for God makes me stop and wonder, has the church grown up in me?

Some things make you go "hmmm."

Okay, okay, I need to refocus and concentrate on something other than the fact that I am autonomous, single, and as celibate as a Gregorian monk in a mountain-high monastery overlooking the cliffs of Tripoli. Got any good suggestions?

She opened the sliding door and stepped out into the yard. Chris was on his knees pulling at something in the grass, Pharaoh stretched out beside him gnawing on a chew toy. Vanessa walked over to them, Pharaoh's stump of a tail wagging just so.

"Whatcha doing, Boo?"

Chris did not bother to look up. He was intent on working up a root.

"How long ago was your gardener here?"

"Week before last. Why?"

"You need to hire someone else. You have fungus and dandelion roots choking out your plants."

"How do you know?"

Chris held up a dead clump of flowers as proof.

"Oh," Vanessa responded.

"It's like this all over the place," Chris said, pointing to intermittent spots throughout the yard.

"Okay, I'll look into finding a new yard service."

"Be sure you find one that's thorough and not just some hedge-trimming, leaf-blowing outfit that—"

"Okay, already. I'll take care of it, Boo."

Vanessa returned indoors, forgetting why she had even gone outside in the first place. Chris was in a mood, but she was too preoccupied to deal with him or his mood just then. Vanessa had a lot to do in order to make the house ready for her visitors. She was off-the-hook excited. Her family was coming to visit, and Vanessa wanted everything to be perfect. She relished the pending visit, not just for the time she and Phyllis would be blessed to spend with their relatives, but because the preparations had kept her so busy that Vanessa had successfully avoided dwelling on her predicament with Chris. Until now.

Vanessa grabbed a broom and set about sweeping the kitchen floor. She understood Chris's irritability. She had had to knock the itch in the head with a hammer on more than one occasion. Vanessa was doing her best to allow their romance to naturally bloom without convoluting matters between herself and Chris by giving in to her physical hunger for him. She really was trying to keep it clean, to give attention to more important spiritual pursuits and not wax lecherous on the brother. But old habits died hard.

Ever since their night in San Francisco—a night on which they had made themselves most vulnerable to each other, revealing the ugly secrets of their parents' pasts and holding each other through the pain—Vanessa felt herself drawn to Chris in a most profound fashion. It took her by surprise, and she found it difficult to maneuver through this maze of newfound emotions. Vanessa was afraid a rash leap into amorous love would undermine or even undo what they were building. So Vanessa told herself to leave things status quo for now.

Vanessa whisked the broom quickly about the floor, but she was unable to sweep away a nagging thought. There was something else bothering her about her relationship with Chris. Something that placed her in a different quandary: fear and doubt.

Deep inside, Vanessa wanted to trust life, to trust herself and commit wholeheartedly to a healthy, stable relationship that resonated with the love of a lifetime. But the urge to run and hide before Chris discovered she was a counterfeit—a woman bruised and marked by her parents' abandonment, by growing up unloved—was great. Could she really experience a healing, forgiving love within herself, a profound and pure love for this man? Vanessa swallowed hard. Something deep inside of her assured Vanessa that she could. Still, she wondered.

Finished sweeping, Vanessa filled a mop bucket with scalding-hot water and a liberal amount of floor cleanser. She had to keep busy to keep doubt at bay. Vanessa attacked her chore, flinging the mop about, sloshing water on her bare legs, and doing a rather shabby job of cleaning the floor.

"You're making a mess."

Vanessa glanced up to find Chris leaning against the wall. She continued her task.

"You're not doing anything but splashing water around."

Vanessa whistled some off-the-wall, off-tune ditty.

"Hand me the mop, gorgeous."

Vanessa whistled louder, turning her back on him as she mopped her way toward the kitchen sink.

Chris stalked across the room, fussing at her the entire time. When he came within arm's reach, Vanessa turned sharply, the sink's retractable spray nozzle in her hand. She turned on the faucet and sprayed cold water straight into Chris's face.

"*Eeeee-yowwww!*" Chris bellowed, trying to wrestle the nozzle from Vanessa's hands. Vanessa hollered. Pharaoh rushed into the house, adding his frenzied barking to the mayhem. When, finally, Chris wrestled the nozzle from her hands, he was soaking wet. Vanessa laughed uncontrollably as Chris dried his face with a kitchen towel.

Before Vanessa could move Chris grabbed her about the waist, lifting her off her feet.

"Stop playing, Chris! Stop!" Vanessa screamed amid laughter. When he finally released her, Vanessa was almost as drenched as he. "Ewww, you make me sick." She whisked wetness away from her arms and face. "Oh, hush, Pharaoh! You didn't even try to save me."

Chris laughed, patting the dog on the head.

"That's my dawg."

"Well, you and your dawg can take your miserable selves out of my kitchen so I can clean up the mess you made."

"Are we at fault here?"

"Yes, you are," Vanessa emphatically stated, paper towels in hand, wiping water off the countertops. "If you hadn't been acting all hot and evil like you were on your period or something I would have had no need to hose you down."

Chris chuckled.

"On my period?"

"Yes, your period, Chris. You need to chill."

"So you thought you'd help me out," Chris stated, pulling his saturated shirt over his head, ignoring the urge to point out Vanessa's own testiness.

Vanessa stared at his broad, naked chest. Her eyes strolled down to the rippled, washboard stomach and dared not go any lower. She cleared her throat, averting her eyes.

"Chris, do you mind?"

He stood there innocently rubbing dry his muscular frame.

"What?"

"Put some clothes on," Vanessa implored.

"Hey, I had clothes on before you decided I needed a bath."

"Well . . . do something with yourself. Anything."

He smiled wickedly, harassing Vanessa with his bedroom baritone as he sauntered toward her.

"Look who's bothered now."

"Boo."

"Yes, gorgeous?" He flicked water out of her hair and gently wiped a damp spot on her chin.

Vanessa abruptly turned away. Chris backed up a step, momentarily stunned. When, finally, Vanessa faced him again she found an unfamiliar look in his eyes like that of cold steel.

"You can't cope one minute while I'm supposed to ignore you, in"—he paused, angrily waving toward her with the towel in his hands—"some indecent underwear and a bandage you wanna pass off for shorts and a top."

Vanessa glanced down at her attire and opened her mouth to protest. She shut her lips. Chris was right. But so what? Was she required to wear some floor-length *Little House on the Prairie* gingham gown just to make Chris's life lust free? Vanessa felt angry tears in her eyes.

"I'll bring you a dry shirt," she muttered before swiftly vacating the room.

In her bedroom, Vanessa rummaged through the cherry-wood dresser drawers until she found an oversize T-shirt. She placed it atop the dresser while removing her garments to pat dry her skin with a towel from the bathroom before donning a pair of navy sweatpants and a loose gray cotton top that nearly reached her knees. Snatching up the T-shirt she'd set atop the dresser, Vanessa headed out of the bedroom, closing the door behind her as she went.

Back down the stairs Vanessa marched, concluding that things seemed to be getting overly complex and unnecessarily tense between her and Chris. She wondered if they should just give in to the itch. Lord knew their bodies would find relief. Happy relief, sweet relief, sweaty, all-night-and-into-the-morning-and-the-next-day kind of relief . . .

Vanessa gripped the banister and shook her head. She had to look at herself. She'd been down this road before, using the physical to assuage the needs of the whole being. Been there, done that more times than she cared to admit. It was time for change. She was not going backward into chaos when the promise of clarity stood straight ahead.

Chris was stretched full-length on a patio chaise longue, the sun's strong rays licking the moisture from his once-soaked gym pants. Flat on his stomach, he let the sun caress his broad chocolate back, coating his skin with a soft sheen.

Her voice came to him lightly as he lay, lured into a state of semi-slumber by the warmth of the sun.

"Boo?"

Drowsily he raised his head, and saw Vanessa and the shirt she offered.

"Mmm, I was just about out," he admitted, feeling groggy. "Thanks." Chris slipped the shirt over his head, easing it comfortably down about his body. Perfect fit. Vanessa giggled.

"What's wrong?"

"That shirt fits you much better than it does me."

"You're a little thing, whereas a brother's built," Chris stated, flexing his pectorals, causing the muscles to dance in his chest. "What's the deal with that getup you have on? You don't have to sport your grandmother's fishing gear, gorgeous."

Vanessa poked her tongue out at him.

"Whatever," she slurred.

Chris shifted his body, making room for her on the chaise.

Vanessa did not move.

Chris patted the empty space, inviting her to come.

Slowly, almost reluctantly, Vanessa sat facing him. Gently he took her hand.

"I didn't mean to snap at you earlier, gorgeous. Forgive me?"

"It might take me some time, but I'll get over it," Vanessa answered, sniffing, tossing a bit of melodrama into the pot.

He kissed her hand.

"Thank you, sweetheart."

Chris lay back on the chaise with his arms folded behind his head to look up at an electric blue, late-summer sky.

Vanessa was ready. She wanted to confess her fears and her doubts. She needed to be free of their weight.

As if sensing her plight, Chris opened his arms. Vanessa snuggled up in his embrace, resting her head lightly against his chest. There, in the safety of his arms, she could and would speak.

He beat her to it.

"Vanessa?"

Chris almost never called her by her given name. What was wrong now?

"Yes."

"I leave for the Caribbean three days from now."

Vanessa struggled out of his arms to sit up and stare at Chris in disbelief.

"What?"

"Why the surprise? You know I've always promised myself a trip to—"

"But not now, Boo," Vanessa rebutted. "You s-said you were j-just thinking of going this summer," she stammered in her suddenly agitated state. Vanessa took a deep breath to calm herself. Why was she so upset? "I need you," Vanessa cried. "My family is coming," she added lamely.

"The yard looks pretty good to me. I think my work here is finished."

Vanessa clamped her jaw shut. Her words had come out differently than intended. She hugged herself, rubbing her arms as if chilled beneath the bright summer sun.

"That's not what I meant, Boo." Her voice sounded lame in her own ears.

"What did you mean, Vanessa?" Chris asked, sitting up inches away from her face. "What? You need someone to lean on to help you get through the week ahead? You want a nice, upstanding young man you can introduce to your family in your attempts to prove that you're different from your mother?"

He was merciless, so unlike the Chris she knew.

Vanessa stared at him, her mouth agape. Sadly she shook her head, her chin sinking onto her chest.

"That was so unnecessary, Chris."

Unnecessary, but nevertheless on target. Vanessa realized that in her mind she had concluded, "like mother, like daughter," as if she were inherently inclined to repeat her mother's mistakes.

Placing a finger beneath her chin, Chris forced her to look at him. There was something that sounded like deep-rooted pain in his voice when next he spoke. "You keep pushing me back, baby. You say you love me—"

"I do, Chris," Vanessa earnestly assured him.

"Then why do I feel as if you're keeping me at arm's length? And I'm not talking about sex, sweetheart." Chris took her hand in his. "I know it hurts that your mother lived as she did. I know this! Believe me. But you have to come to a place where you fully understand that your mother's sins were hers alone and not yours by osmosis. Her ghosts were her ghosts, baby. Let them rest."

Vanessa felt tears welling in her eyes.

Chris kissed her softly on the cheek; then he stood, his sudden movement knocking the chaise longue slightly off balance. Vanessa righted it quickly, transferring her weight to its center. She sat and watched him walk away. He paused at the door to turn and look at her. Vanessa saw an agony in his eyes that she had never before acknowledged.

"How long will you be gone?" she asked.

He shrugged his shoulders.

"I don't know." Suddenly Chris smiled wryly, allowing a glimpse of the man she loved to shine through. "Don't worry. I intend to come back."

"Alone?" Vanessa's heart hammered in her chest as she watched Chris watch her for what seemed like an eternity. He merely shook his head as if disgusted with the very question itself. Or was he disgusted with her?

" 'Bye, Vanessa." Chris walked away. "I'll launder your T-shirt before I give it back."

Vanessa sat there unable to move. The minutes ticked by. The light of the sun began to change. Still, she sat staring at the place where he had once stood, back to her, his voice resolute and unyielding. She was confused. Chris was gone. Gone to the islands. Alone. Without her. No ceremonious farewell. No discussion. Zilch. He left her with nothing save a mere promise that he would return some stupid T-shirt that she could not care less about.

Vanessa did not want a shirt. Vanessa wanted Chris, the man. All of him, and that without reserve.

Vanessa Ann Taylor had one life to live and, unlike her mother, she had no intentions of destroying that life. She loved Chris. Deeply. Yes, even passionately. Fear couldn't take that from her. Vanessa hopped off the chaise and ran into the house. *Memo to me: go get your man,* she concluded with a certain air of determination. Vanessa raced up the stairs to her bedroom, stripping her oversize cotton gear from her body and tossing it across the back of her Queen Anne chaise. She rummaged through her closet for something alluring, fully admitting that she had found the man with whom she, safe and secure, could—with God's help—finally unpack her bags and stay awhile.

SISTERS, LOVERS, FRIENDS, AND OTHERS

Reina and Jamal lay in bed talking—on the phone, Jamal at his house, Reina at hers. It had become their Saturday-morning ritual, one awaking the other with an early-morning love call. But Jamal jumped ridiculous with his, calling Reina one Saturday morning at 6:20 A.M. talking about rise and shine while on his way out the door to meet with the contractor and architect hired by him and his business partner to renovate a strip mall in south Sacramento. In drowsy Spanish, Reina gave him a piece of her sleepy mind, switching to English long enough to make sure Jamal understood that if he ever called her again before the crack of dawn's behind she would fix him with some of *Abuela*'s roots. She hung up. Jamal called back laughing, not the least bit fazed. And so the game was on.

Reina fixed him good the following weekend, setting her alarm clock for 3 A.M., that delicious time of morning when REM sleep has passed and deep slumber has kicked in real nice. Using the multiline feature on her own phone, a sleepy Reina dialed Jamal's house phone, cellular phone, and pager. Jamal was jarred from sleep, a cacophony of beeps and trills and whistles sounding in his ear. He got the point real quick, conceded defeat, but refused to pay the penalty: washing Reina's car, buck-naked, in the middle of the street while singing Negro spirituals. And so their Saturday morning ritual became something they both looked forward to, after roosters crowed and dawn cracked the sky, of course.

"Everyone make it in safely?" Jamal asked, easing from the comfort of his bed. He padded into the kitchen and tried to find the cast-iron skillet. Reina had helped him unpack and settle into his new house, arranging the kitchen to her liking. Jamal couldn't find a thing.

"The grandparents and a cousin are staying with Vanessa. A couple of aunts and their husbands and a few other cousins are with Phyllis and your brother," Reina answered, languidly lounging across her fully made bed, tracing the outline of a fat orange cartoon cat and his goofy dog friend. Time to transform her room out of its summer decor. The fall and a chubby bear who loved honey were waiting patiently in the closet.

Unlike Jamal, who was still yawning in her ear on occasion, Reina had been up for hours. She had finished her Saturday-morning exercises, and was feeling fit and fine. But suddenly she felt that crawl-back-into-the-bed-and-lay-it-down urge creep up on her. So she complied, telling herself she deserved an extra rest.

Reina had tried something that morning that she had not done in eons, if ever. She ran. And it wasn't after an ice-cream truck. Reina Kingsley actually ran the last lap of her morning walk. She had felt like dying and calling a limousine to take her to heaven, but she made it through. Running was something Reina would definitely need to slowly—a molasses kind of slow—incorporate into her exercise regimen. "I'm not sure if any more of the clan are coming, but if so I have the house ready so they can stay here."

"Can I come too?" Jamal teased.

"Ooh!" she sang. "Don't even think about it."

"Ol' evil 'oman," Jamal stated, perfectly imitating Mr. Kingsley's Jamaican patois.

Reina laughed. Her parents loved Jamal. Well, her mother did, spoiling the man every time he walked through the front door. *Hola, mi hijo! Are you hungry? Is Reina treating you right?* Of course Jamal ate it up, divulging any infraction, real or imaginary, of which Reina was supposedly guilty. Reina would roll her eyes and leave the two to their twisted devices while she went to find her nieces. *Papí* merely decided Jamal was a decent man. He tried to pretend he was unaffected, not charmed, but Reina knew when her father invited Jamal on one of his fishing trips that the man had won *Papí*'s staunch approval. No one, but no one, intruded upon *Papí*'s fishing trips without his express favor and permission.

"How was your workout this morning?"

"It was good," Reina replied excitedly, rolling onto her back, glancing about her colorful room as she did so. Reina liked the vibe her fanciful decor, her multitude of stuffed animals, candles, and other trinkets created. She didn't need designer this, designer that. What she had was just fine by her.

"What? Did you and Phyllis try something new today?"

"Actually, Phyllis couldn't join me. My girl was exhausted after all the hubbub with the family." Reina sat up, propped against the headboard of her four-poster bed. "Guess what, J-baby?"

"What?" Jamal asked, unable to find the cast-iron pan, deciding to use the electric skillet instead, smiling as he always did whenever Reina used the nickname she created especially for him. Jamal set the electric skillet on medium and plopped six slices of thick bacon on its surface. He was hungry.

"I ran the last lap," Reina triumphantly reported.

"Say wha-a-t? Looka here, looka here. My baby's burning up the track." Jamal plopped three slices of bread in the toaster to stay until his meat was nearly cooked.

"What is that?"

"What?"

"That sound," Reina said, swinging her legs over the edge of the bed.

"Sizzling bacon," Jamal answered dramatically, as if doing a paid advertisement for the meat council.

"Turkey or pork?"

"I'll give you a clue. I'm a black man. Now take a wild guess." Jamal chortled.

"Swine."

"Very good."

"How many slices?"

"Six."

Reina rolled her eyes. The man could eat like a horse and not gain an ounce. Here she was walking four to five times a week, being conscientious about her food intake in her efforts to become healthy. All

Jamal did was play hoops with Chris and Bryce and their crew, swim every now and then, or play a little golf or tennis while wooing clients, and the man remained fit and fine. Who could Reina pay to reconstruct her physiological composition? Did God accept credit cards?

She felt like scolding him. All that pork was not good for Jamal's heart or arteries or his cholesterol. He should pass the plate over to her. She wouldn't eat a bite. She just wanted to sniff a whiff.

Reina padded lightly to her bedroom window overlooking *Abuela*'s flower garden. The hedges and the ivy needed trimming. She would have to remind Raj to get to it. In the meantime, a little overgrowth could not interfere with her ability to enjoy the floral fragrances wafting through the open window. Reina inhaled deeply and smiled.

His bacon cooked nice and crisp, just the way he liked it, Jamal removed the hot meat and placed it on a thick wad of paper towels. Pouring just a bit of the meat drippings out of the skillet, Jamal reserved the remainder, cracking three eggs into the hot grease, and pushed the button to lower his toast.

"I'm proud of you."

"Thank you," Reina responded before launching into a diatribe on how many laps she should run, how many minutes and days per week, how many calories she could further cut from her diet, what aerobics class she could join to maximize her weight loss and continue to whittle away the inches.

Jamal felt his body shrinking just listening to it all.

"Hey, baby?" he interjected when Reina finally took a breath.

"Sí, novio."

Jamal grinned. He liked it when Reina purred a little Spanish in his ear, especially when she called him sweetheart.

"You know you have my support, two hundred and ten percent. But don't obsess over this. Make sure you strike a balance, okay?"

"This coming from a man who's weighed fifty pounds since birth," Reina playfully retorted, not the least outdone by Jamal's customary concern.

"Actually, I'm up to seventy pounds now. Seriously, word to the wise, don't overtax yourself in your zeal. I don't want you getting hurt or falling ill. Besides, have you stopped to celebrate the strides you've already made?"

"Anyhow—"

"I'm serious, Reina. Don't start biting off another hunk of something without acknowledging your triumphs already gained."

Reina thought about it. The man was right, but she wasn't about to let on that he was.

"Okay, already—"

"Woman, don't have me come over there and put you over my knee," Jamal threatened, taking his now-ready breakfast and a huge glass of orange juice into the living room and plopping down in front of the television to watch Saturday-morning sports. "Besides, I love you like you are."

Reina had to admit she looked good. At five feet, nine inches tall, one hundred and ninety-five pounds, and having lost more inches than Glodean White's nails were long, sisterwoman was feeling fierce. Still, Reina wanted to tighten things up a bit, take off a few more inches of "extra beauty," as Jamal had once so eloquently phrased it.

"All right, already. Enjoy your breakfast."

"What are you having?" Jamal asked, trying his best not to crunch in her ear.

"I ate an hour ago, sleepyhead. I had a nice big bowl of toasted oats topped with strawberries," Reina announced, sounding about as excited as the meal she described as she glanced at the black-and-purple butterfly clock atop her dresser. "Woo, I need to get off this phone and take care of some things around the house. See you later?"

"'Ey!"

"Hmmm?"

"Can I touch your hair?" Jamal mischievously inquired.

"Slip me a piece of that pork and I may let you touch a lot more."

Jamal choked.

Reina giggled and hung up the phone.

Everyone was aboard the vessel ready and waiting to set sail. Reina and Jamal. Phyllis and Bryce. Phyllis's parents. Mr. and Mrs. Kingsley and their two granddaughters. Papa McCullen and even his mother, Nana. Gramms, Gramps, their two oldest daughters and their spouses, a couple of grandchildren, and one great-granddaughter, Celine. Only one individual was blatantly absent: Christophe Countee McCullen.

Vanessa stood on the deck of the cruiser looking out toward the marina parking lot. He was nowhere in sight. She hadn't seen him since the afternoon he had informed her he was leaving for the Caribbean. Vanessa bit her bottom lip. She missed him.

She remembered every detail of that day, and how she had rushed to his house ready to relinquish her hold on fear and give herself fully to their relationship. Chris wasn't home. He didn't answer his cell phone. Vanessa sat in her car outside of his house, feeling like a stalker, for over an hour. Finally she gave up and returned home, determined not to let the rift widen between them. She sent flowers to his job. He didn't respond. She finally caught up with him via telephone, inviting him out to dinner so they could talk. Chris coolly declined, stating that he had things to take care of in preparation for his vacation. Whatever Vanessa needed to say could be handled over the telephone. Vanessa had hesitated, knowing the matters that needed to be conveyed required eye-to-eye contact, face-to-face expressivity. Could he spare maybe just an hour of his time? He was busy. Frustrated, dejected, and sick and tired of the mess, Vanessa had merely reminded Chris of today's affair and disconnected the call.

She had hoped against hope that Chris would relent, that he would give her credit for making an attempt to iron out the wrinkles between them, that he would show today. But so far, no good.

"Hey, Vanessa, we really can't afford to hold off any longer," the vessel's owner informed her. He was a fellow member of the National Black Broadcasters' Association. During a recent phone conversation, Vanessa had informed him of her family's impending visit, and her wanting to treat them to something enjoyable and out of the ordinary that Labor Day weekend. He had readily suggested his fifty-foot, double-deck cruiser. Phyllis and Bryce had agreed it was a good idea, so they proceeded, hiring a caterer despite Phyllis's and Reina's protests that they could manage the affair. Vanessa and Bryce were adamant: Let someone else do the cooking and the cleaning. They were celebrating.

"Sorry, but we're dealing with maritime law here. I don't control the waters." He chortled.

"Let's get this party started then," Vanessa offered more brightly than she felt.

The engine's hum grew louder. Dockhands released the moorings.

The vessel rocked slightly as it veered away from the dock; then slowly, smoothly it floated away from the marina. The watercraft was sleek, fast-moving. Minutes later the dock was a mere speck in the distance. It was as small as Vanessa's hopes for a reconciliation with the man whom she was grimly determined to shake from her mind.

Indeed, there was cause for celebration. Phyllis and Bryce made their announcement. Their firstborn child was due to arrive seven months from now. Vanessa was about to be some baby's aunt. What a wonderful feeling beyond compare.

Reina confided in Vanessa and Phyllis that her own sister, Nita, was coming home soon. Probably not before Phyllis's baby was born, but not too long after.

It was a pleasurable day, a memorable one.

Vanessa and Phyllis's young cousins kept the music flowing with the CDs they'd brought from home, careful not to play any of that—as Gramps put it—"wretched rap."

Vanessa loved her grandfather. He was a laugh and a half, stretching truths about how he, while stationed in France during World War I, saved his entire platoon by fighting off advancing Germans with six bullets, a hand grenade, and a pack of firecrackers. The man really was a jewel.

Precious, too, were the sights and sounds of Celine running and racing about the deck with the Kingsleys' granddaughters. Their laughter, exuberance, and unending curiosity about the boat's mechanisms were exhausting but priceless.

She was his rare find and he had no intention of letting her go.

"Take a stroll with me, Miss Kingsley?" Jamal requested, extending a hand in Reina's direction, extracting her from her company of friends.

"I have to ask my daddy," Reina teased.

"Believe me, I already have."

Strains of music, laughter, and conversation reached them even at the back of the cruiser, where Jamal steered them in search of peace and quiet. Redwood benches and folding chairs sprinkled the deck. A soft river breeze floated up toward them and the not-quite-night sky. Sounds of gentle water lapping against the sides of the boat heightened the already restful state of Reina's mind. She felt tranquil.

"How's the demo project coming?" Jamal asked.

"We'll wrap up the first song next week; then we can begin the second," Reina answered, wondering why Jamal was asking. He already knew this.

"What about work?"

"What about it?"

"What are your plans if—correction, when—your music hits?" he inquired, the ever-ready businessman wanting to ensure that Reina had a plan of action and a sense of destiny.

"I have to work to pay my bills, J-baby, so I guess that means I'll be keeping the nine-to-five until things are solid."

He stopped abruptly, taking Reina's hands and turning her toward him.

"Reina, what do you want most in life? I know your music is your passion. But what else do you want?"

Reina searched Jamal's face for a clue to his current line of questioning. Had they not discussed these things already? Jamal Williams knew what she wanted. A house. A good life. Yearly vacations, an art collection, extensive travel, domestic and abroad. Friends. Family. Children. To surround herself with music and beauty and lovely things. Just the simple pleasures of life. What? Was there something she had not indicated that he needed to hear? What had she omitted from the equation?

Suddenly she smiled.

"I want you in my life, Mr. Williams," she answered, her sultry voice thrilling and intoxicating him.

Jamal grinned, somehow more pleased with her response than Reina had imagined.

"Hold that thought," he urged her, releasing her hands and walking away. Reina shook her head. Thank goodness the cruiser had turned around and was headed back toward Sacramento. Brother obviously had had too much sea air.

Reina stood at the rail, hands stuffed in the pockets of her capri pants. She closed her eyes and tilted her face toward the night sky, smiling. Who would have imagined a year ago that her life would be what it was today? Make no mistake, she had gone through familial strife, nearly destroyed friendships, her grandmother and anchor moving thousands of miles away. But Reina had survived and lived to tell the story. She had fought the bulge battle and diet demons. She had war scars but they, too, would heal. She had—having grown exasperated by a religion that dictated her life in a Latin language she could not understand—come to know a heavenly Father to whom she could cry day or night, while serving Him with all of her might. And though Reina had never anticipated nor even contemplated the possibility, she was in love with a good man. A strong man. A man she respected. A man so virile and fine she wanted to slap his mama.

"A present for your thoughts," Jamal whispered softly in her ear. He stood behind her, his arms about her waist, a lavishly wrapped gift box in the palms of his hands. "Happy birthday, *mariposa*," Jamal said, practicing the Spanish Reina was teaching him.

She truly was his beautiful butterfly.

Reina took the package, turning and smiling up at him.

"You know my birthday isn't until next month."

"My calendar's a little fast. Just humor me, please."

Reina removed the gold bow and ribbon, then the Afrocentric foil wrapping paper, discarding them onto the seat of a nearby chair. She held an intricately carved wooden box.

She gasped.

"It's beautiful."

"I purchased it while visiting the Ivory Coast a few years back," Jamal explained. "The carvings are symbolic."

"Of what?" Reina asked.

"Open the lid."

Inside was a black velvet box.

Reina's head snapped up. She searched his eyes for meaning.

"You told me you wanted me in your life, Reina. Do you mean that?"

She was frozen.

Jamal took the box from her hands and opened the velvet lid. Inside lay a thick gold band inlaid with sparkling baguette diamonds.

"Reina Kingsley, will you marry me?"

A stampede of questions rushed through Reina's mind. Was it too soon? Had they dated long enough? Would she, if she accepted his proposal, be guilty of a hasty decision? What did she mean, *if?* Color her crazy, but Reina Kingsley had that knowing she had asked her grandmother about. Jamal was the one. She did not need to, like *Abuela*, wait until after the marriage and the . . . well . . . covenantal consummation to know that Jamal Williams was her man. Still, they would need a decent courtship. No rushing and stumbling over lessons they needed to learn, or insight they needed to gain just to jump the broom and bump into bed.

"You have to ask my daddy," Reina answered, finally thawed, her faculties restored.

"I assure you I already have," Jamal replied. Nervously he fumbled with the ring, trying to pull it loose from its case. In her excitement, Reina tried to help. It slipped from their hands. Reina watched, horrified, as with a metallic *ping* her ring hit the deck and rolled, rolled, rolled to the edge of the cruiser, wobbling precariously there before toppling over into the waters below.

It made a pitiful plop of a sorry splash.

She stood immobile, her hands clasped across her open mouth. A strangled little sound escaped her throat. Her eyes were round and wide when Reina finally turned to face Jamal, who sat on a chair, doubled over with pain.

Tears were streaming down his face, he was trying so hard not to laugh.

Reina just stared at him as if he had lost his mind in a whirlwind.

"Jamal! What's wrong with you?" She was near tears her-dang-self. "My . . . ring . . . just . . . fell overboard."

He really lost it then, howling as if privy to the supreme joke of the century. Reina concluded the man was delirious. He must have realized how much he'd paid for diamonds that would never be this sistergirl's best friend.

"Okay, okay," Jamal choked out between laughter and trying to catch his breath. Still chuckling like a madman, he placed the intricately carved wooden box on his chair, and stood to draw Reina into his embrace. "Okay, I'm sorry, baby. I'm sorry," he soothed, kissing her cheek. "It was a fake. Really, it was," he said in response to her disbelieving glare. "I paid a dollar-ninety-nine for it." Jamal laughed. "I know. That was not nice of me." He reached into his denim shirt pocket and extracted an exquisitely cut marquis diamond set on an antique silver setting. As solemnly and soberly as he could, Jamal held her left hand, slid the ring onto her second finger, and asked again for her hand in marriage.

Reina drew a ragged breath.

"I can't."

Jamal was dumbfounded.

"I beg your forgiveness, but I should have told you this long ago. In my culture, with *mi familia,* there is a tradition. The second-born daughter is never to marry." Reina choked and took a moment to recollect herself. "It is the duty of the second daughter to care for her parents always. The only way to escape my obligation is to castrate my brother to, in essence, make him a daughter of duty." Reina stepped away from Jamal's embrace, her shoulders slumped. She sighed heavily. "I'm sorry, Jamal, but"—Reina spun about, a wicked grin on her face—"don't pull jokes on the queen if you can't take one in return."

Jamal just stood there, his heart pounding, staring at this woman who was toying with his emotions.

"See, you're wrong."

"You started it." Reina laughed.

"You're just wrong. Naw, back up off me," he protested as Reina wrapped her arms about his firm waist. "Uh-uh, baby, it's too late. Gimme my dollar-ninety-nine ring so I can return it to Kmart."

"Oh, let me keep it, J-baby," Reina purred. "Please."

"Promise to love, honor, cherish, and obey me?" He kissed her lips softly. "Promise to cook my dinner, clean my house, raise my babies, and rock my world on a daily basis on command?"

"Whatever, nasty thang."

"Good enough for me."

Their kiss lingered on, sealing the covenantal agreement they would soon embark upon, conveying their heartfelt love and affection that would only grow and deepen with time.

Arms draped about Jamal's neck, Reina wiggled her fingers, her diamond catching and reflecting the ascending starlight over his shoulder.

"Hmmm, I think I like the first one better. Can I just toss this one overboard and opt for one of those two-dollar specials you seem to like so much?"

"Only if you want to see a grown man cry."

*   *   *

There was a full moon. It beamed brilliantly, skipping laughing silver jewels across the river's surface. A late-summer breeze played a game of hide-and-seek, wafting warmly one moment only to hide the next. It was a night for family, for friends, for soft music and sweet sensations.

Phyllis, Reina, and Vanessa sat clustered together like a pack of planning and plotting sisterwomen capable of wooing the world to spill pearls at their thrones.

"We could have the baby shower on this boat," Vanessa said, winking at Reina.

"Oh, no, you don't," Phyllis countered, stretching out her legs. "I haven't eaten a thing except bread and butter since we boarded this beast just so I wouldn't vomit all over the place."

"Ewwww," Reina grimaced, pulling away. "Spare us the details, puh-leez."

"Oh, girl, hush." Phyllis reached over to pat Reina's knee. "You'll be in my position sooner than you think."

"And what position is that?"

"Take your pick," Phyllis replied, a wicked gleam in her eyes. "Missionary. Woman on top. Doggy—"

"Ahhh!" Vanessa shrieked, pressing her hands against her ears. "Excuse me, but you need to watch your conversation. There are innocent parties present. I can't believe you sanctified saints sometimes."

"Ol' nasty mama," Reina added.

Their laughter was warm, rich like sable.

"I am not trying to be lewd," Phyllis began, "just realistic—"

"And raunchy," Reina added. "That's why your belly and your breastesses 'bout to get all swollen. No, not swollen. Swole."

"Otay," Vanessa quipped, slapping palms with Reina.

"I don't know about the belly, but my husband likes my breasts that way."

"Okay, already, Phyllis," Vanessa protested, snickering and shaking her head. "You're just all out the closet with yours now."

Phyllis laughed, reaching over to squeeze her sister's cheeks.

"I'm sorry, Babysis," Phyllis cooed. "I forgot you're trying to achieve a secondary virginity with this abstinence quest of yours."

Vanessa put an open palm in her sister's face.

"Whatever, horny toad. Talk to the hand 'cause you obviously don't understand."

Reina joined in Phyllis's laughter.

"Be proud of your secondary virginity, 'Nessa. I'm proud of mine," Reina emphatically stated. "Well, mine is original, not postcoitus or new conscience. What? What's the matter?" Reina asked upon observing Phyllis's wide-eyed stare and open mouth.

"Not a thing. I didn't know that you're a virgin," she explained.

"You mean to tell me Blabber Butt didn't tell you?"

"I resent that," Vanessa replied, crossing her legs, her soft, thigh-length, flower-print summer dress creeping up a bit. Reina stuck out her tongue.

"I think that's a beautiful thing, Reina. I really do," Phyllis said admiringly. "Jamal knows, right?"

"Honey, puhleez. I told my baby he'd better take this whole year to stock up on petroleum jelly. I am not trying to die on my wedding night."

Vanessa sat there amazed. She just watched the two of them cackling uproariously like they were out of their ever-loving minds. She tried not to join in, but crazy women's mirth is an infectious something.

"Whatcha doing?"

The three women looked up to find Celine standing there, an innocent smile on her face.

Phyllis cleared her throat. Reina kept giggling. Vanessa patted her lap. Celine jumped on her, throwing her arms about Vanessa's neck.

"Gramms says I have to ask you, Auntie Vanessa."

"Ask me what?" Vanessa replied, narrowing her eyes, giving Celine a stern look. "What are you trying to charm me out of now?"

The little girl giggled.

"Can I stay the night with the girls? Mrs. Kingsley says it's okay. And I can wear one of Juliana's nightgowns, 'cause we're the same size. I'll mind my manners. Pretty please, can I?" Celine quickly rambled before her request could dare be denied.

"May I," Vanessa corrected. "So you want me to go home and baby-sit Gramms and Gramps by myself?" Vanessa asked.

Celine giggled.

"You can handle them."

"Humph! You can go to your little sleepover for a price." Vanessa tapped her cheek. "Put her there, partner."

Celine planted a sloppy, noisy kiss on Vanessa's face.

"Okay, now get your big self off of me. And make sure you have all your toys picked up. We're almost at the marina."

"Okay," Celine sang, about to run off, then suddenly stopping. " 'Night, Auntie Phyllis. 'Night, Miss Reina." She waved and then was gone.

"My children are going to be sweethearts just like her," Phyllis informed them.

"*Psssh!*" Vanessa dismissed Phyllis with a wave of her hand. "That little crumb snatcher you're about to have is going to come out whipping you and Bryce into shape, trying to run and rule stuff. But if it comes to Aunt Vanessa's house," she said, pointing at her chest, "trying to pull some mess, we'll see who's boss. I'mma be like, 'Say what, you want your diaper changed? You better stop all that crying and ask nicely.' "

"Silly." Reina chuckled.

"I'm just playing, Boo Boo," Vanessa cooed, leaning toward her sister's belly and rubbing it gently. "You won't even have to wear diapers at Auntie's house. You can just poop and pee where you want. We'll just make your mommy clean it up."

"Get away from me." Phyllis giggled. "Looks like we've landed." The cruiser's horn sounded, as if to confirm Phyllis's proclamation. "Thank God, I can finally get off of this moving monster. I'm taking myself and this sweet thing home to bed and lay it all down."

"What are you going to do about day care for the baby?" Reina asked, as Phyllis eased out of her chair.

"Once I go out on maternity leave, that's it. I won't return to my job."

"You're going to do the at-home-mommy thing?" Vanessa asked. "Of course Bryce is in agreement, right?"

Phyllis nodded.

"Of course. It's something we agreed upon long ago. I plan to stay home at least until the baby is old enough to start school." Phyllis stroked her stomach lovingly. "But, then again, with all the violence and the substandard teaching going on in some of our education systems today, I may home-school my child."

"Dang, girl, you're never gonna get out of the house." Reina laughed.

"Hey, I have nothing but love for you, Junetha Cleaver," Vanessa added, making a play on one of television's quintessential mother figures. "Just don't let me come over to find you wearing pearls and pumps with a vacuum in one hand, a mop in the other, roast in the oven, cookies baking, and a baby swinging from your breast."

"Don't worry, I'll hire a housekeeper and a wet nurse," Phyllis replied.

"Gross!" Vanessa and Reina simultaneously cried, causing Phyllis to chuckle heartily.

"Don't trip; the only nipple besides mine that goes into my baby's mouth had better be attached to a bottle."

"Yeah, but what's in the bottle?" Reina murmured slyly. "A little gin and juice?"

"Naw, girl, just a little holy communion wine," Vanessa answered. "This here is a sanctified baby."

"Wel-l-l-l," Reina intoned, sounding like one of those churchified saints on Sunday mornings in response to Pastor McCullen's message. Standing, she stretched her arms far and wide as if to embrace the night. "Lord, I can barely move."

"That rock on your hand's weighing you down," Vanessa said, smiling.

"Ain't it beautiful?" Reina held out her hand, fingers splayed and wiggling in the moonlight.

"That it is," Vanessa concurred, mirroring her best friend's joy. They stood smiling foolishly at one another. "Can I get and give a hug, somebody?"

They held each other, swaying gently in the moonlight.

"I'm so happy for you, Ree-Ree."

"I know you are, 'Nessa."

"My drama queen's gone and found herself a king," Vanessa cried, punctuating her sentiments with an exaggerated sniff. Reina emitted a false wail.

"Can a mama get in on this love?" Phyllis asked, pouting.

"Come on in here, Pepe." Vanessa extended an arm to her sister. "There's enough love to fit around even your big belly."

* * *

The party dispersed into the night, calling out farewells, stating how thoroughly they had enjoyed their waterbound excursion while locating vehicles and bidding God's peace and blessings one to another.

"I had a good time, baby," Nana, Papa McCullen's mother, stated as Vanessa helped her into his waiting vehicle.

"I'm glad you did, Nana."

"And don't you worry none, baby; that boy'll come to his senses and so will you."

Vanessa closed the door and waved as the four-door luxury sedan pulled away.

"All righty then." She laughed, heading toward her silver-blue Solara, wondering who had told Nana what.

Gramps was already in the backseat, practically asleep. Gramms sat in the front, giving Celine last-minute instructions about behaving herself while at the Kingsleys'.

"You understand me?"

"Yes, ma'am," Celine meekly replied.

"Good. Now give me some sugar."

Celine complied, calling out a good-night to her great-grandfather before running to where her new friends waited. Suddenly she stopped and glanced about, as if remembering something. She raced back to where Vanessa stood with Reina, planning when they would get together to start looking at bridal gowns.

"Want to join us, Jamal?" Vanessa teased.

"Ha! Not in this lifetime. Just tell me when and what church to show up at and I'll be there in time to say, 'I think I do.'"

Reina rolled her eyes and took his hand.

" 'Night, 'Nessa," she said, planting a kiss on her best friend's cheek before walking off toward Jamal's car.

Vanessa waved good-bye as Celine rushed up, grabbing her about the waist.

"Auntie Vanessa, I left my box of crayons on the boat," she whined, near tears.

"Oh, Celine—" Vanessa stopped. The child was obviously upset. No sense in exacerbating the situation by scolding. Vanessa stroked the child's thick ponytails. "What does it look like?"

"It's pink and has stickers all over it."

"Stay there at the car with Gramms and I'll go get it. Okay?"

Celine merely nodded, sniffling.

Lights on the watercraft were already being extinguished. Vanessa hurried forward. She ran up the plank, onto the deck, and right into the ship's owner.

"I'm sorry. My cousin left her crayons somewhere."

"That's all right. I'll help you look for them."

It did not take long for the missing box of crayons to be located atop a table where the girls had played earlier.

"Thank you," Vanessa said, accepting the box. "And thank you so much for a wonderful day at sea. We had a blast. Or as my little dee-jaying cousin would say, it was da bomb."

The man chuckled.

"Glad you enjoyed it. Try it again sometime."

"We will," Vanessa said, imagining trying to drag Phyllis up that plank for her baby shower. They would have to drug her first. Vanessa was going to be an aunt. What a wonder.

"Hey, by the way, have you heard anything about plans for next year's NBBA convention?"

"Well, since I've been elected to the executive committee of the National Black Broadcasters' Association I might know a little something," Vanessa teased.

"Go 'head, sister! I knew about your nomination but I didn't know you had been elected. Congratulations."

"Thanks," Vanessa responded. "The official confirmations will be sent out soon. Listen, I have my grandparents waiting on me. Give me a call and we'll talk."

Thank God, some things were looking real good in her life. More lighthearted than she'd been in days, Vanessa practically skipped down the ramp and onto the dock. Suddenly she stopped.

Several yards away he stood, legs crossed at the ankles, arms across his chest, resting leisurely against the passenger side of the coupe as if perfectly positioned for a photographer's delight.

There really should be a law against a man being too scrum-deli-icious.

Vanessa started toward him. Then she hesitated. The party was over. Why in the world would he bother showing up now? Grimly determined not to let Christophe Countee McCullen get the best of her,

Vanessa ventured forward until they stood an arm's span away from each other, each watching and waiting for an encouraging sign from the other.

"Reina's engaged." Vanessa could have kicked herself. It wasn't exactly how she meant to start whatever conversation there might be between them.

"I know. Jamal warned me he was going to do the do," Chris explained.

"Warned you?"

Chris grinned.

"You know how you sisters are. One of you gets engaged and the next thing we know we single brothers are pushed and pressed mercilessly until we surrender."

"Whatever. So—"

"So?"

"How are you?" Vanessa asked, as if suddenly unsure what to say or do next.

"I could be better, but I won't complain."

"Your father and grandmother just left."

"I know."

"Is there anything of which you don't have knowledge?" Vanessa retorted, feeling inexplicably exasperated.

"Just whether or not your future includes me," Chris answered matter-of-factly. Vanessa had a ready retort on her sculpted lips, but she was interrupted by Celine rushing to her.

"Did you find it?"

"Yep. I sure did." Vanessa handed the child the pink plastic box filled with a rainbow of colors.

She took the box, smiling brightly. Then, as if noticing Vanessa's companion for the first time, the little girl eased closer to Vanessa and held her hand.

"Who is this young lady?" Chris asked, smiling brightly at the child.

Vanessa smiled down at her.

"This is Celine. Celine, say hello to Mr. McCullen."

"Hi." She smiled shyly. "I know you."

"Do you now?"

She nodded.

"We had a slumber party at my Auntie Vanessa's. It was me, Auntie

Vanessa, and Auntie Phyllis," Celine explained. "We ate popcorn and red licorice in the bed and I got to stay up way past my bedtime, but I had to promise not to tell my Gramms, 'cause Gramms doesn't like me to stay up too late." Celine took a deep breath. "And Auntie Vanessa was teasing me 'cause I told her I like this boy who lives on the same block as Gramms—"

"Celine, sweetheart, the Kingsleys are waiting for you," Vanessa interrupted, gently nudging Celine in the direction of the waiting mini-van.

Chris placed a firm but tender hand on Vanessa's arm.

"Wait, let the child speak. So what happened then, Celine?" Chris asked, highly amused at Vanessa's extreme discomfort as he leaned back against the car.

"Auntie Vanessa told me I was too young to have a boyfriend and that I had to wait to be old like her."

Chris chuckled.

"Celine, that's enough."

"Come on, gorgeous. Let the baby speak. So does Aunt Vanessa have a boyfriend?"

"Yes." Celine giggled. She pointed at him and said, "You. I got to see Auntie Vanessa's picture albums. She showed me some pictures from when she was in college with Miss Reina, and some of you."

Chris glanced at Vanessa. She was antsy, shifting her weight from foot to foot.

"I told Auntie Vanessa that you were cute and you should be her boyfriend."

"And what did she say?"

"Chris," Vanessa began, only to be silenced gently.

"Come on now, gorgeous. The floor is not yours. Continue, Celine."

The little girl smiled, thoroughly enjoying being the center of attention.

"She said you were her boyfriend but you were acting up and she was gonna have to put her clown suit on and—"

"That's enough, Celine," Vanessa said, unmistakable finality in her tone. Vanessa patted her firmly on the bottom, shooing her in the direction of those awaiting her arrival. She watched Celine climb into the Kingsleys' van. Vanessa would deal with Miss Mouth later for speaking out of turn and landing feet-first in grown folks' affairs.

"Don't be mad at Celine," Chris urged, as if perceiving the vein of her thoughts. "I goaded her on." He grinned that lopsided grin of his that Vanessa had once considered adorable. Just then, she felt like scrubbing it from his face with lye soap and a bucket of sand.

"What are you staring at?" Vanessa demanded, irritated and fit to be tied. His grin was his only response. "If there's something you'd like to say, please say it already."

"Out of the mouths of babes. So, I'm acting up and you need to put your clown suit on and clown me a bit, huh?"

"I don't have time for foolishness, Chris. It's late and I'm tired and—"

"I'm tired, too, Vanessa." The grin sailed away in the night. "Tired of all this stress and game playing. When you're ready to come correct, call me."

Chris stalked around to the opposite side of the car, opened the door, and would have hopped inside and sped away except Vanessa was right on his heels, slamming the door shut just as he opened it.

Tapping Chris's chest in syncopation with her words, Vanessa hurled, "Why am I the one who needs to come correct?" She waved an accusing finger in his face. "You're the one playing games, not showing up today when you know I needed you here."

Rubbing a palm across his head, Chris exhaled an annoyed sigh.

"Oh, so now I'm a mind reader. Did you invite me or just assume I'd be here today, Vanessa? I am not some trained monkey on a stick that you can manipulate."

Vanessa opened her mouth to speak, but an image of a stuffed carnival-like monkey clapping tiny cymbals together as it bounced up and down flashed across her mind. She started laughing despite herself.

"Shall I get the straitjacket now?"

"Okay, I'm sorry," Vanessa said, choking off her laughter. "You're right, Boo. I've been very difficult lately, haven't I?"

"Lately?" Chris grinned.

"Cut me some slack. I'm about to eat crow. And don't lose sight of the fact that you haven't been an angel yourself lately." Vanessa inhaled deeply, slowly expelling air through pursed lips. "I didn't need you here, today, Chris. I wanted you here."

"Therein lies the difference."

"Hush, I'm trying to come correct." Vanessa paused, glancing out to the water's edge as if clarity floated there. "I've—you have—experienced so many new developments recently that my system has been on overload. Does that make sense?" she asked, looking at him.

Chris nodded.

Vanessa continued.

"It's been very difficult trying to process so many changes. It was easy to hide behind fear and just kind of shut down on some level and suspend myself and our relationship in midair." Vanessa rubbed her arms as if suddenly cold. "I have a history of leaping into relationships that are purely founded on the physical—"

"Is that what you think I'm all about? The mere physical?" Chris asked.

Vanessa leaned against the car beside him and stared off into the night.

"No. It's just that . . ." She paused, choosing her words carefully. "Loving the whole man without having ever indulged in his body is uncharted territory for me."

"Do you love me?"

"Of course I do. How could I not? We've been friends for what seems like forever."

"Vanessa."

"Okay, I'm sorry. Yes, Boo, I am wrapped up, tied up, tangled up in love with you. There! I said it. Satisfied?"

"Maybe," Chris said with a shrug of his shoulders. "So are you ready and willing to experience romance and something more enduring, or do you want to stick with settling for raw boot-knocking sex?"

"Must you put it so bluntly?" she asked, shivering despite the warmth of the night. "You make it sound so cheap."

"Well, isn't it? Wouldn't you be selling yourself short of what you want or deserve by settling for the raw and not the real?"

Vanessa contemplated his words without response, allowing Chris to continue.

"Has this angst contributed to all this sexual agony you've put me through? All this I-don't-want-to-complicate-our-relationship song and dance? You were afraid."

"Oh, listen to you sounding all deprived." Vanessa smiled. "And I'm sorry, but I don't recall hiring you as my therapist."

Chris laughed.

"Really, I'm not trying to play that role. I was simply trying to shed light on the issue."

"You have a point. But you didn't hear that from me. Okay?"

"Whatever you say, gorgeous."

Vanessa smiled ruefully.

"Okay, bottom line, I was afraid to step up to the plate because I wasn't sure I was inclined or even able to enjoy a committed relationship founded on more than flesh."

"And now?" Chris asked, watching her closely.

"I'm ready. Like your grandmother said, I've finally come to my senses."

Chris nodded. *Thank you, Lord!*

"Your well runs deeper than you think, Miss Taylor. Give yourself credit for knowing what a healthy relationship is and is not." Chris lifted her chin until she looked directly at him. "Stop tossing your past mishaps in your own face."

Unexpected tears quickly blurred her vision.

"I just didn't want to destroy us."

"I know," Chris softly stated, kissing away a tear.

Vanessa cleared her throat.

"What about you? You've seemed so sure through all of this."

"I had my moments, but for the most part I was certain that even if it meant confusing issues and letting you use my body to work out your problems, then, hey, a brother was willing to sacrifice himself on the altar."

Vanessa sucked her teeth in response.

"So where do we go from here?" she asked.

Chris stepped back and opened the car door.

"I don't know about 'we,' but I'm off to the Caribbean tomorrow."

"You're still going?"

"What? You think now that we're straight I should cancel my trip?" Chris asked.

"Yes." Vanessa pouted. "Or at least take me with you."

"I'm going away to rest, baby, and the only way a brother can do that is if you're not around."

They shared the laughter.

"You want a little souvenir?"

"Hmmm, how about a six-foot-three-inch, two-hundred-plus-pound Rasta-chocolate-drop kind of brother with Nubian locks and a sexy accent?"

"How about I just buy one of those crocheted caps with the fake yarn dreads sewn on and sport it for you when I get home?" Chris leaned over and kissed her cheek. "Will that work?"

"Add one of those leopard-print loincloths, Boo, and you have yourself a delicious deal."

BEYOND THE EDGE

A year later, Jamal Williams was a nervous wreck. His older brothers, his father, Chris, and Pastor McCullen tried to calm his nerves as best they could before he paced a hole in the ground, but it was not working.

"Who has the ring?" he needed to know for the umpteenth time.

"Man, it's right here," Bryce Williams, his best man and brother, assured him, patting the breast pocket of his beige double-breasted tuxedo jacket with the Afrocentric-patterned vest beneath. "Calm down. And sit down before you break something."

They didn't understand. They weren't feeling him. Jamal was about to take the biggest step of his entire life. Marriage was nothing to play with. Was he ready? Was he willing? Was he able to uphold the bonds of a sacred covenant before God and man? Would he honor and cherish, love, respect, and protect his wife for as long as he lived?

He had a sudden case of the chills. Perhaps he was coming down with something. It might be something contagious or life threatening! He might need to be quarantined. They should postpone the ceremony!

Just as Jamal was ready to bolt and call the Centers for Disease Control, there was a knock on the door. His father went to open it. Jamal heard his mother's voice on the other side. He heard the loving interaction between his parents, heard his mother telling his father that his boutonniere, which had been somehow missing when the florist made the initial delivery, had arrived. He cautioned her to be careful and not to stab him with the stickpin while securing it on his jacket lapel. Mrs. Williams shushed her husband, reminding him that she could sew in the dark better than he could drive a car in daylight.

Jamal relaxed. His parents' marriage had survived many a hardship to last forty-plus years. He glanced around the room and, for the first time that day, realized he was in good company. His brothers were all married, all happy and still in love. They had good wives. They were good husbands. Some were fathers, and outstanding ones at that. Why should he be any different?

Because he was the baby boy, baby child. That was why! Weren't the youngest children, the pampered and catered stock in the brood, the screwups? Didn't they usually tend to break their parents' hearts, to make their parents wish they had tied the tubes, clipped the vas deferens before it was too late? Jamal was ready to bolt. Again.

Then he remembered last night's big send-off: his last night as a single man. The bachelor party. He had actually been offended when seeing the giant eight-foot Styrofoam cake in the middle of the room. He didn't want some stank stripper grinding her near-naked, too-often-seen behind all over the place. He was actually relieved, laughing uncontrollably, when an antiquated old woman dressed in a granny gown with pink sponge rollers all over her head jumped— well, hobbled—from the cake's center, not a tooth in her head, talking about "Surprise, big daddy! I was cute before they baked me in that cake sixty years ago."

Jamal knew then that he was ready. Actually, he was absolutely certain of that fact a year ago. But now that he was perched on the great edge of respectability, he was nervous, feeling just a tiny bit unfit to walk fully into this circle of light.

Once again Jamal examined the men in the room and found them to be upstanding, decent black men. Pastor McCullen. Chris. His brothers and father. He came from the same stock, was cut from the same cloth. He was from the old school. He was nobody's player. He had had no courses in Pimpology 101. He was a one-woman brand of brother. And he was about to marry the one woman who set his soul on fire. He was ready. With the Father God's help, he could and would do this, and do it right for life.

"How're you holding up, son?" Pastor McCullen inquired, coming over to place a steady and reassuring hand on the younger man's shoulder, lending strength where he knew it was needed.

Jamal nodded solemnly at the man of God with whom he and his bride-to-be had undergone premarital counseling over the past several months. Reina had been adamant about their ensuring that their marriage was built on a sound, solid foundation. Who better to go to than the one who sanctioned holy unions in the first place, the Creator? The time they spent in premarital counseling with their new pastor was an investment in their future, a further sign of their commitment, an added surety that they could and would succeed in a day when divorces were a nickel a dozen.

Suddenly Jamal smiled. In a mere matter of time, he would be eternally united with a woman whom he would be blessed to call his wife.

Someone knocked on the door. It was the wedding coordinator.

"Gentlemen, it's time," she called through the closed door.

Jamal felt a hyperventilation attack coming on strong.

Reina was too calm. She had to be semicomatose. All about her, females were fluttering and fanning, primping and painting faces, nails, and whatever else required a coat of color.

Reina sat in repose, a cloth draped about her shoulders as the cosmetician expertly applied her "special day" makeup. Her nails were perfect ovals, an opalescent pearl glossing them lightly. Her legs were clad in sheer, silky hosiery with just a touch of sparkle, her feet already encased in satin pumps with crystal-studded straps about the ankles. She would finally slip into her gown and veil—just as soon as this high-paid magician finished fooling with her face.

The wedding coordinator came through the door, clapping her hands, the epitome of efficiency. In her perfectly clipped voice she announced, "Ladies, ten minutes to showtime. The gentlemen are already assembled with the soloist."

Reina rolled her eyes. This was not a Broadway backstage. *Get a clue.*

"Please, Miss Kingsley, you must keep your face perfectly still," the face-painting wonder worker scolded.

"Sorry."

"No, no. Do not even move your mouth. Absolute stillness."

Reina would have sucked her teeth in annoyance but that, too, would have been cause for consternation.

A few more brushstrokes, what felt like a serious coating of face powder, and Reina was pronounced finished, like a turkey at Thanksgiving.

"Would you like to see yourself now?"

Reina nodded, then shook her head no, then nodded again.

"Okay, but just sit still for a moment or two until the makeup sets."

Reina felt like a plaster mold or something. Accepting the large mirror the cosmetician held up for her, Reina stared in disbelief at the woman gazing serenely back at her. The image was breathtaking.

The makeup was flawless, enhancing her features, accentuating the natural beauty she already possessed. Soft, natural hues. Wonderfully blended shades and shapes. Her eyes sparkled. Her cheekbones were high. Her perfect bow-shaped lips were a pale shade of rose with the slightest hint of gold. Some ravishing woman had traded places with her.

Her mother came up behind her to glance over her daughter's shoulders and into the mirror. The lovely image she beheld sent Mrs. Kingsley into a spasm of tears.

"Don't cry, *Mamí*. Please," Nita—Reina's older released and re-formed sister, who as of yesterday lived in *Abuela*'s house with her two daughters—said, trying her best to comfort their mother. *Mamí* had to be led away by Mrs. Williams, Reina's soon-to-be mother-in-law.

The coordinator popped her head back around the doorjamb, announcing seven minutes and counting.

Giving her signal of approval, the makeup artist indicated that Reina could be moved. Her bridal party made quick haste in helping her step into her gown, clipping on her diamond-studded antique silver teardrop earrings, clasping the tiny diamond-studded choker about her neck. Her veil was secured in her upswept hair. She was unquestionably, undeniably lovely.

Phyllis, Vanessa, and Nita stood there admiring the vision Reina created, her perfect size-twelve body gorgeous in the sleek satin gown with the straight skirt, jeweled bodice with just enough décolletage to set Jamal's mouth watering, and off-the-shoulder cap sleeves, the jewel-studded tulle and satin train floating majestically on the ground behind her.

"I am not going to cry today," Phyllis announced, dabbing at her eyes with a tissue.

"Me neither," Nita agreed, pulling a handkerchief from beneath her bra strap.

Vanessa laughed and went to retrieve a medium-sized box wrapped in festive paper.

"Here, sweetie, we saved the best for last."

What in the world could it possibly be? Reina wondered, in light of all the lovely gifts she'd received at her bridal shower the weekend before.

Quickly, her bridesmaids helped Reina unwrap the box, intently watching her face as she opened the lid to find inside a year's supply of petroleum jelly.

"We didn't want you to die on your wedding night," Vanessa said, "or during your two-week honeymoon in Barbados."

Reina was laughing one moment and crying the next.

"No, Ree-Ree, don't cry. Puhleez don't cry, stank!" Vanessa urged, glancing around to make sure the makeup artist was nowhere near.

"Shut up, wench." Reina laughed, just as Vanessa hoped she would.

"Hold your head back," Nita ordered.

"Pinch the bridge of your nose," Phyllis suggested, dabbing lightly at Reina's eyes so as not to disturb her face.

"Two minutes, ladies! Take your places," the Wedding Wonder commanded, clapping her hands soundly.

"Well, here we go," Vanessa nervously breathed. "How are you feeling?"

Reina nodded, biting the inside of her lip.

"In approximately thirty or forty minutes, you will be Mrs. Reina Williams," Phyllis marveled. "That's if our pastor doesn't get his preach on and have us up in here all day."

"I've already warned Papa McCullen that if he gets long-winded we are walking out," Vanessa informed them. "Or at least going to find a seat in the audience so we can rest our feet."

Reina grinned.

"You look beautiful," Reina finally said, finding her voice. "All of you."

And they did, with their ankle-length sleeveless sheath dresses in pale champagne, their sheer ivory scarves with champagne, gold, and plum flowers trimmed in crystal beads draped across their collarbones to float across their shoulders and down their backs.

"Well, here goes everything." Reina smiled nervously. "I love you."

"We love you, too," Nita replied.

Reina exhaled and grinned.

"Okay, we've had our buppie bride moment; now step off, y'all. I'm trying to get to that altar."

"Do you ever feel as if you're teetering on the edge of reality?" Vanessa asked, her arms outstretched. She stood near the patio rail, eyes closed, face to the breeze as if auditioning for a role with an all-black cast of *Titanic.* The wedding was superb, a solemn yet joyous occasion that Vanessa would never forget. Now the reception was well under way. The Laguna Oaks country club was glorious, surrounded by lush rose gardens through which a sparkling brook meandered.

"Yes, whenever I'm forced to eat your cooking."

Turning to face Chris, Vanessa folded her arms beneath her breasts and shot him a warning look.

"I love you, baby, but you can't cook and you know it."

Vanessa cracked a grin.

"Boo, you slay me," she retorted.

"Lay you? What? You want my body? Told you, you can't have none till you marry a brother."

Vanessa laughed.

"Stop clowning. Seriously, do you?"

"Not really," Chris commented. "There was a time in my life when I felt that things were out of control and that I was losing my grip." Stepping near, he wrapped his arms about her, pulling her close. "But I think my grip is pretty good right about now."

"You'd better stop. The Lord's out here and you're daddy's in there," Vanessa said with a nod of her head in the direction of the reception hall.

"I ain't a-scared of my daddy," Chris boasted.

"Hi, Papa McCullen," Vanessa called.

"Yeah, right," Chris smirked.

"Hi, babygirl. Wasn't that a nice wedding?"

Chris laughed, glancing over his shoulder to find his father looking out over the flower gardens as if he hadn't noticed a thing.

"It was absolutely beautiful," Vanessa agreed as Chris turned in his

father's direction and assumed a more appropriate distance in his father's presence, while still maintaining an arm about Vanessa's waist.

"It was nice, but I don't plan on attending another wedding. Not
even my own," Chris joked.

"And, pray tell, when will that be, son?"

"I won't know until I get the invitation in the mail," Chris jested.

"There you are!"

They looked up to find Phyllis, Bryce, Nita, and the rest of the wedding party approaching.

"Where's my Boo Boo Woo Boo?" Vanessa asked.

"Girl, I could barely pry Amira out of Reina's grandmother's arms
long enough to nurse her."

"Give *Abuela* ten more minutes with Amira's squalling booty and
she'll toss her to you."

"Don't talk about my baby like that." Phyllis laughed. "I think the
photographer's ready for us now. Can we get to the gardens from
here?"

"There's a staircase right over there," Chris answered, pointing in
the direction of the winding stone steps.

"Good, 'cause I can't make it back through that hall and out the
front of the building. My feet hurt," Phyllis complained, looking
down at the satin sandals on her feet.

"Why do women torture themselves trying to look good?" Bryce
wanted to know.

"Because that's the only way we can get your attention," Nita
replied.

"Tell him, girl," Phyllis said.

"Darling, you know you're wrong. You have my attention even
when you don't look so hot."

Phyllis punched her husband lightly on the arm.

"I'm just playing, Pepe. My baby looks good always. Even when
she's drooling in her sleep."

"I'll see you young folks later. I'm going back inside where it's safe,"
Pastor McCullen said, taking his leave.

"The bride and groom, the rose gardens, and an overpriced, attitu-
dinal photographer await. Shall we?" Bryce offered his arm to his wife
and made his way down the steps. The rest of the party followed suit.

"So, do *you* ever feel as if you're living on the edge?" Chris asked, walking hand in hand with Vanessa, their heels clicking quietly across the stone walkway.

"Not anymore," she replied. "I'm firm and centered."

"Firm, that you are. Centered is rather questionable."

"Boo?"

"Yes, baby."

"You've got jokes."

"No, actually, I have nothing but love for you, Miss Taylor."

"Hmm, that's good enough for me," Vanessa said, resting her head against his shoulder as they traversed a well-traveled path. "So when do we move into our new house?"

"We?" Chris chuckled. "We?"

"Speaking French these days?" Vanessa quipped.

"I don't know about *we*, but *I'm* moving into *my* new house next Friday. I have to give it to him; Jamal hooked a brother up big-time."

"That he did. The house is gorgeous," Vanessa agreed. "Make sure you have the TV and VCR hooked up before Saturday morning."

"Yes, ma'am, I know. You have a guest spot on the very first episode of *Urban Speak*, your station's new program, dedicated to young Sacramentans as a forum for their lives and their voices," Chris dutifully recited. "And your subject matter is 'minority adoptions: who's raising our children?'"

"Very good!" Vanessa praised. "So." She paused, looking fondly at Chris. "Can I decorate my rooms any way I like?"

Chris frowned.

"Woman, don't mess with me," Chris replied, stopping to face her. "We've already concluded that there will be no shacking, no cohabiting of any kind between us. Right?"

Vanessa nodded.

"And we've decided we would only . . . be together . . . as man and wife. Am I right?"

Again she nodded, a sly smile shining in her bright, topaz eyes.

"Vanessa." His tone held a warning, his voice dropping dangerously low in his chest. "Quit playing."

"Do I look like I'm playing, Boo?" Vanessa asked, tracing the outline of his full lips with a slender finger. "Today's ceremony touched me deeply. I'm backing up from the edge and running full-speed into the center of my living."

Chris smiled warmly at her.

"You really do favor your mother," he commented, visually recalling the photograph Vanessa's grandmother had had restored and beautifully framed for Vanessa's thirty-first birthday. It was a picture of Vanessa's mother in her youth, a year before Philip Taylor, a few years before their babies. She appeared so carefree, so vibrant and beautiful, her cinnamon-brown face and bright smile exuding an amazing confidence for one so young. Even then, there was the slightest hint of brave defiance in her topaz eyes.

Chris sighed.

"Well, gorgeous, run on and don't stop even when you get where you're going."

Vanessa kissed him lightly. "Thank you, sir, I won't. But I want us to take this journey together."

"So are you proposing marriage?"

Unless the sun was playing tricks on his eyes, Chris was sure Vanessa blushed.

"Yes," she whispered.

"You tryna play with a brother's mind?"

"I'd rather play with your body."

"Nasty thing. You know the scripture reads 'It's better to marry than to burn.'"

Vanessa laughed, firmly gripping Chris's hand as they journeyed forward.

"Forget the burning. If I live out another year as a celibate sister you might just find me sitting in the middle of my front yard eating grass with a pot of grits poured over my head."

Chris chuckled deeply.

"So."

"So?" Vanessa intoned.

"You know I'm going back to school. I don't imagine it will be easy being married to a graduate student."

"My sister did it and they survived," Vanessa stated.

"You're serious, aren't you?" Chris watched her intently.

Vanessa nodded.

Chris smiled.

"Are you going to take me out to dinner, get on one knee, and propose to me?" he asked.

"Absolutely! Just don't wait until then to tell me you're pregnant by another woman."

"That's cold." Chris chuckled, pausing to pull Vanessa close. He kissed her forehead. "I wanna sport a band with a phat carat on my finger."

"Not a problem. I can get one at a discount from Reina's cousin, Gino."

"And I can go to jail for receiving hot merchandise from my wife. Can we continue this discussion later, Mrs. McCullen-to-be?"

"By all means, Mr. Taylor," Vanessa teased.

"A brother loves you, gorgeous."

Vanessa kissed his mouth.

"I love you, too, Boo."

Reina relished the grandeur of their hotel suite. It was a veritable house, lavishly equipped with a sitting room, a huge bedroom, a private balcony overlooking the Sacramento River, and not one, but two bathrooms, all posh and plush throughout. What a way to end her day and start their night.

Reina felt so good she could cry.

Her entire family—Lord, thank You, they'd been on their best behavior, and Uncle Butchie had come in pants and not a dress—her friends, coworkers, and even her Healthy Habits classmates had come out to celebrate and share in their wedding ceremony and to wish the Williamses the best in their new start. That wedding wonder of a coordinator had earned her keep ten times over. From the wedding to the reception, everything had gone off splendidly and without a hitch. Not that Reina Williams remembered every nuance or detail, mind you. She had been too wrapped up in the moment, the majesty, and her man to recall it all. Thank goodness the ceremony and the reception had been videotaped. She and her new husband could go back at their leisure and rewind and review the day as often as they pleased.

Her husband. *Mmm, mmm, double mmm-mmm!*

Jesus, help me to make it through the night.

Reina laughed at her mirrored reflection—pausing to dab a touch of fragrant oil behind her ears and a few other key pulse points that just might be sniffed, kissed, or licked before the night was over— while pondering her grandmother's confession regarding her own wedding night and how and when she truly knew she was in love with Reina's grandfather. Reina did not need to wait for that particular moment to know she absolutely, unequivocally, unabashedly loved her husband. But if arriving at that place was enough to convince her all over again, then somebody, somewhere, needed to pray for Jamal. Reina was ready to convince herself all night and throughout the next day and the rest of her life if necessary.

Turning off the bathroom light, Reina opened the door and stepped out into the sitting room. She caught the first strains of music, familiar music, floating from the bedroom. Jamal was playing the ballad from her demo CD that had garnered enough positive reviews to have several record executives interested in developing this truly talented artist. The very song she herself had penned.

For always I have loved you from the start.
Forever I will hold you in my heart.
My arms are open wide, come near and step inside.
Close to me, you'll always be, love of mine.

Reina picked up the tune, singing it as she walked into their bedroom, only to drink in a sight that made her stop in her tracks.

Her husband lay on the bed, clad only in navy blue silk pajama bottoms, surrounded by a multitude of stuffed animals gaily decorated with ribbons and roses.

"Mr. Williams, you are too sweet," Reina crooned, appreciating her husband for appreciating her quirks. Yes, Reina still loved cartoon characters, and toys, and stuffed animals. No, she no longer wore clothes with goofy Looney Tunes emblazoned all over. Well, not on a regular basis. Unless, of course, you considered the silk robe she was wearing right then and there.

"Mrs. Williams, my queen, you are undoubtedly one of a kind." Jamal shook his head affectionately and laughed. "Not too many men can say their wives came to bed on their wedding nights with comical creatures plastered on their nightwear."

"You like?" Reina asked, slowly pivoting to give Jamal the benefit of a full view.

"Maybe." Jamal grinned.

"Is this better?"

Reina disrobed, dropping her colorful garment soundlessly onto the carpet.

"Happy birthday, sweetness."

Jamal whistled long and low, drinking in the luscious, full-flavor vision of his voluptuous bride arrayed in little more than the suit she entered the world in. Little more raiment. Much more body, developed and delicious.

"My birthday isn't until December," he finally managed to croak, pushing bears and bunnies and sundry other plush creatures off of the bed.

"My calendar's running a little fast, J-baby. But if you prefer you can wait for your gift until then."

"I think not," Jamal replied throatily, instantly up and on his feet, taking his wife in his arms, more than ready to share every ounce of bone-deep love he knew for her. He kissed her long and deep, remembering his father's advice: *Son, Rome wasn't built in a day. Take your time and do it right.*

"Whew!" He whistled. "Hold on, baby; I have something for you."

"I know," Reina purred. "I can feel it."

"Stop." Jamal laughed. "Here, hold on. I'll be right back," he promised, rushing out of the room, returning momentarily with a huge gift box.

"What's in here, my real wedding ring?" Reina questioned, remembering the night Jamal had proposed, giving her a fake ring and almost causing her an asthma attack when she accidentally dropped the ring overboard. Reina opened the box and beamed as she extracted a plush, oversize Suzy Carmichael rag doll.

"I had my mother make it for you," Jamal informed her.

"Oh, I love it," Reina crooned, hugging the doll. "You are too cute, Suzy. But you have to go now because Mommy and Daddy have some business to take care of," Reina said, placing the doll on a chair. "Thank you, J-baby." She kissed him her thanks. Pleasure swirled, and they lost themselves in rapture's arms.

Jamal tried hard not to ooze out of his skin and shoot through the window on the wings of the breeze. Reina felt as if she could melt into the night like lovely shadows in a summer's shade.

* * *

Jamal stretched awake the next afternoon like a panther in paradise with a *real* morning-after smile wrapped all over his handsome face while Reina slept on, thanking God for that year's supply of petroleum jelly and unbridled love that allowed her to discover how many ways she loved her man for life. Mmm, mmm, mmm, life sho' 'nuff was scrum-deli-icious. Living beyond the edge was oh, so very good.